Mending Horses

Mending Horses

M. P. BARKER

Holiday House / New York

Library of Congress Cataloging-in-Publication Data

Barker, M. P. (Michele P.), 1960-

Mending horses / by M.P. Barker. – First edition.

pages cm

Summary: Free and on his own, Daniel Linnehan is nearly sixteen in 1839 when he joins Jonathan Stocking and Billy, a girl hiding from her abusive father, in peddling goods in New England.

ISBN 978-0-8234-2948-6 (hardcover)

[1. Peddlars – Fiction. 2. Child abuse – Fiction. 3. Irish Americans – Fiction. 4. Sex role – Fiction. 5. Prejudices – Fiction. 6. Orphans – Fiction. 7. New England – History – 1775-1865 – Fiction.] I. Title.

PZ7.B250525Men 2014

[Fic] – dc23

2013019208

*This book is dedicated to
the memory of my father, Joseph A. Plourde,
who shared his love of books,
Gil Barons, who shared his love of horses,
and Ellen Levine, who shared her wisdom*

Acknowledgments

Mending Horses came into this world with a host of assistants. It was conceived in Julia Starzyk's Oak and Stone writing group (which included, along with Julia, Anna C. Bowling, Melva Michaelian, Beth Clifford, Lise Hicks, Mary Jane Eustace, Maureen Kellman, Bill Lang, Melinda McQuade, Lauretta St. George-Sorel, Beryl Salinger-Schmitt, and Peggy Tudryn). It received prenatal care from the River Valley Writers (Carol Munro, Paula Bernal, Judy Ebeling, Ruth Ehrenberg, Judy Gibson, Carole Guthrie, Barbara Hand, Ruth Kenler, Ronnie Lieb, Mia Nolan, Mickey Shrair, Sydney Torrey, and Lucy Mueller Young). My Wednesday-night support group, Anna C. Bowling, Melva Michaelian, and Carol Munro, midwived the manuscript and kept me going with comments, critiques, and well-timed whip-cracking, while Carol assisted immensely with editing early drafts of the manuscript.

Many, many thanks to the Highlights Whole Novel Workshop for Historical Fiction, taught by Ellen Levine and Liza Ketchum, two fabulous instructors and gracious ladies. Ellen helped me turn the second half of the book from an amorphous pile of random scenes into something coherent, and brainstormed with me to find an ending. Her help and enthusiastic support were invaluable. Thanks, also, to my fellow workshop participants for encouragement and sympathy.

Thanks to Ted and Annie Deppe and Suzanne Strempek Shea, instructors at the Curlew Writing Conference in Howth, Ireland, which took the book through draft three (or was that four?). And thanks, also, to my fellow participants.

More thanks to Suzanne for her Bay Path College writing workshop, which brought me to draft five (or was that six?). And many thanks to the ladies from that workshop who've continued to meet and have helped through final edits: Sarah Chadwick, Kathleen Garvey, Bernadette Duncan Harrison, Beth Kenney, Melva Michaelian, and Marianne Power.

Thanks to my good friend Jessica Holland, who helped me chop a good thirty or so pages from draft seven (or was that eight?).

Thanks to Storrowton Village Director Dennis Picard, historian extraordinaire, who reviewed the manuscript for historical accuracy. Any anachronisms that remain are in spite of him, not because of him.

Thanks to Denise Farmosa, who allowed me to observe her working with a horse she was rehabilitating, and who read through the manuscript for equestrian errors. (Because I wanted the story to take place over the course of three months, the time Daniel takes to retrain the horses had to be somewhat compressed—not too implausibly, I hope!) Again, any mistakes that remain are mine alone.

Thanks to my former agent, William Reiss of John Hawkins and Associates, Inc., who took a chance on Daniel in my first book; may he enjoy a long and happy retirement. And thanks to my new agent, Marie Lamba of the Jennifer DeChiara Literary Agency, for her enthusiastic support. Thanks to my editor, Julie Amper, for loving this story as much as I do, and to Holiday House Editor-in-Chief Mary Cash, for allowing Daniel to embark on another adventure.

A huge thank-you to Terry Ariano, former curator of the Museum of the Early American Circus in Somers, New York, for putting up with my repeated visits and showing me all sorts of nifty circus records and memorabilia. And thanks to Margaret Humberston, Head of the Library and Archives at the Springfield History Museums, for helping me track down local history details.

And last, but not least, thank you to my husband, Joe, for putting up with me and providing me with chocolate.

I finish this thanks with trepidation, hoping I haven't left anybody out. If I have, please accept my abject apologies!

Chapter One

Wednesday, August 28, 1839, Chauncey, Connecticut

"Mark my words, Walter," Jacob Fairley said to his apprentice. "That horse is stole, and some evil done to get her, too."

The blacksmith jutted his chin at the handsome chestnut mare walking toward his shop. She moved so smoothly that a less observant smith might not have noticed the slight hitch in her gait. But Jacob Fairley had an eye for horses—an eye for people, too. A less observant man might have paid little attention to the red-haired boy leading the mare: a scrawny, half-grown fellow with a spotty complexion and enormous ears. But Jacob knew that the boy's bottle-green jacket, black cravat, and boots were much too new and fine for him. Bare feet, tattered broadfalls, and a patched-at-the-elbows shirt would have suited him better. The horse suited him even less than the clothes. Certainly neither horse nor clothes belonged to him.

"Stole?" Walter's swallow bounced his Adam's apple into a fat lump. "What—what do we do?"

Jacob laid a finger alongside his nose. "We wait, boy. We watch and wait."

The strange boy led the mare into the blacksmith's yard. He nodded to Jacob and Walter and lifted his cap. "Good day, sir. May I?" He gestured toward the trough.

Jacob nodded back.

The mare slurped the water, the boy pulling her head away when she drank too greedily. "Slow, lass, slow," he murmured.

"That's a fine horse you got there, boy," Jacob said. "Your father must'a paid a pretty penny for her."

The stranger gave Jacob a narrow look with his gray-green

1

eyes, then shifted his glance away. He fidgeted with a buckle on the bridle. "She's me—my master's."

"He must regard you highly, putting you in charge of a horse like that."

"Oh, well. It's only fer—for an errand. But her shoe's come loose, see?" He lifted the mare's right front hoof. "Can you mend it?"

"If you got cash money to pay. I don't give credit to strangers."

"Aye—yes. I can pay. I don't want her lamed. My master'll thrash me something fierce if I bring her back lame."

Jacob doubted the boy planned to return to his master. A closer look at the boy confirmed his judgment. While the horse was impeccably groomed, the boy's clothes were rumpled, as if he'd slept out of doors. His hands were grimy, and his face was smudged with dirt and the sparse beard of a fair-haired boy who'd only just begun to shave.

The boy tethered the mare to the hitching post and unfastened her tack. Jacob nudged Walter. He tilted his chin toward the bulging valises. "He don't have that load packed for no errand," he whispered. "Help him put them bags someplace where you can have a look inside." Louder, he said, "Give the fella a hand, Walter."

Walter took the saddle from the stranger and hung it over one of the rails of the ox sling. The stranger shrugged out of his coat, folded it carefully, and laid it across the saddle. He did the same with the vest. He then unbuckled one bag and pulled out a brush and a halter, leaving the flap laid back. Walter rummaged through the open bag when the stranger turned his back to trade bridle for halter and brush the saddle marks from the mare's hide. The stranger talked softly to the horse as he worked, grooming her with sure, rhythmic strokes. It was a pity the boy was a thief. For all his mean looks and shifty eyes, he did have a way with a horse.

"I'll just get my tools so's I can fix that shoe," Jacob said. He jerked his chin toward Walter, signaling the apprentice to join him in the shop. "Well, boy, what did you find?"

"Just like you said, Mr. Fairley. New goods. Clothes and things, all like they was just from the tailor or the store. Money, too. I heard it jingle in the bag. Stole, just like you said."

Jacob nodded grimly and selected a hammer.

"And—and another thing," Walter continued. "Did you hear him talking to that horse, sir?" His voice squeaked a little with excitement. "Strange words. Foreign-sounding."

Foreign. That settled it. "Walt, you run and fetch Constable Ainesworth. Tell him we got a thief here. And who knows but he might be a murderer as well."

"What town is this?" Daniel Linnehan asked the blacksmith.

"Chauncey," the man replied. He bent to take a closer look at Ivy's hoof.

"We're here, lass," Daniel murmured to the chestnut mare. After blundering around the hills of northwestern Connecticut for several days, at last he'd reached the town where the peddler Jonathan Stocking had claimed to have kin, a cousin who supplied the little man with the tinware that he carried in his wagon. If the fellow wasn't in town now, he no doubt would be soon, at least if Daniel recalled their last conversation aright. He'd no idea, though, exactly what he'd say to the man, if the fellow even remembered him.

As he'd done a hundred times since leaving Farmington, he felt his pocket in vain for the wooden horse Da had made for him so many years ago. He'd always touched it for luck or turned to it for comfort the way Ma had turned to her rosary. As he'd done a hundred times, he regretted giving it away as a parting gift to his young friend Ethan.

It was foolish to feel so. He'd no need of toy horses and childish superstitions. He was a free man now, a man of property, no longer a bound boy indentured to work off his father's debts to George Lyman. He had a pocketbook full of papers proclaiming his freedom and his right to all the goods in his possession. Including Ivy.

Especially Ivy. He touched his forehead to the mare's and

3

rubbed her cheek as the blacksmith prized out the nails and removed her loose shoe.

He'd never dared hope to own the mare whose ears flicked to catch his every word, whose heart beat with the same pulse as his own. The only thing he'd wanted more than Ivy had been his freedom, which by all rights should have taken him five more years to earn. But now, two months shy of his seventeenth birthday, he had both freedom and Ivy. He should have felt...should have felt...

A crow let out a raucous cry and soared up from the field of Indian corn across the road from the smithy. The bird swooped and dived and rose again, laughing with its harsh voice, cutting through the air as if it owned it. Aye, he should have felt like that: noisy and glorious and exultant. It should have been a grand feeling in his breast, not a lost one.

He'd never imagined freedom would feel this way, that he'd be hesitant to meet a blacksmith's eye, that a simple business transaction would tie a knot in his throat. He'd thought he'd never be afraid again. But he was still the same boy inside, uncertain, wary of the next taunt or blow.

It was a relief to know that he'd soon see a familiar face. Maybe that was what had drawn him to seek the peddler. Even though Daniel had seen him only twice, the little man had known things about Daniel that he hadn't known himself. He'd known how it was with Ivy, and how Ethan would become his friend, even though Daniel hadn't thought he needed one.

The last time he'd seen the peddler, the fellow had a boy with him, a boy who spoke Da's language and sang Ma's songs. Back then, it had hurt to hear those words, those songs coming from that boy's lips. But now he thought it might feel good.

Walter slipped out of the blacksmith shop and cut around to the road. He glanced back. The foreign boy was bent over Mr. Fairley, watching him work. Walter shivered, seeing how easy it would be for the foreigner to take Mr. Fairley unawares, just like he must've taken the real owner of that horse.

But Mr. Fairley wasn't unawares. He'd been clever enough to see through the stranger's lies and was more than a match for the stranger in wits and strength. Hadn't Walter himself felt the weight of Mr. Fairley's striking arm when he'd dawdled about a chore the way he was dawdling now? *"Run and fetch Constable Ainesworth,"* Mr. Fairley had told him, not stand and think. So run he did.

Tilda Fowler took a wet shirt from the laundry basket and shook it out smartly. The sleeves made a sharp snapping noise as they grabbed at the air. She jabbed a clothes-peg in each end of the hem and stooped for another garment.

"Mama, look! There's Walter Sackett running up the road like the devil's chasing him."

"Sally, tend your chores and don't be dithering about the blacksmith's boy," Tilda scolded her daughter. Lately Sally had nothing in her head but boys, boys, boys. Just the same, Tilda tugged the clothesline down below her nose and peeked over the laundry toward the road.

Walter Sackett looked like a plucked chicken when he ran, all flapping elbows and flailing legs and pimply skin. He caught his toe on a rut and sprawled face-first in the dirt. Tilda ducked under the shirts, headed out to the road, and hauled the boy to his feet.

"What's your hurry, boy? You set Mr. Fairley's shop afire?"

"No, ma'am." He bounced on the balls of his feet as though he needed to find an outhouse quick. "It's robbers—a robber, I mean—I got to get Mr. Ainesworth."

"Someone robbed Mr. Fairley?" Tilda asked.

"No, ma'am. Not yet, I mean, that is—"

Tilda grabbed Walter's shoulders and gave him a little shake. "Spit it out, boy. What do you mean?"

The boy stopped bouncing. "There's this fella came to the shop—a foreign fella, all slicked up in new clothes on a fancy horse and valises full of goods"—he bent close to Tilda's ear and lowered his voice—"all stolen. He tried to make out like they was his, but Mr. Fairley, he knew, but he didn't let on, just so's this foreigner wouldn't get suspicious and bolt. He's keeping this fella busy down at the shop while I fetch the constable."

"Who'd he rob?" Sally asked.

"His master," Walter said before Tilda could scold Sally back to her chores. "Robbed him and murdered him, most likely. Prob'ly lying in the woods with his throat slit from ear to ear."

"Oh!" Sally gasped, her eyes saucer-wide, her hands clasped tight at her breast.

Tilda wasn't sure which disturbed her more: the idea of a robber and possibly a murderer at the blacksmith's, or the way Walter Sackett's eyes latched on to Sally's clasped hands. Or rather, what was beneath them.

"Well," Tilda said, rubbing her hands on her apron, "we'd best not keep you. Run along and fetch the constable."

The boy ran down the road as if the dust cloud at his heels pursued him. "Sally, get inside," Tilda said. She turned toward her daughter, but Sally was already gone, not toward the house, but across the east pasture and halfway to the Wolcotts' place.

"...and there was still blood on his hands." Sally gasped, breathless.

Beulah Wolcott squealed with terror. At least Sally guessed it was terror, though in truth, it might have only been envy that Sally had gotten a juicy story before she did.

"...and his horse's feet were red with it," Sally continued. "Trampled him down after he was dead, you see, so nobody would recognize the body."

"What body?" Beulah's papa poked his head out of the barn doorway.

"The dead man's. The one this foreigner killed," Sally said.

"What foreigner?"

"The one down at the blacksmith's."

There was a clatter of tools, and Mr. Wolcott came out of the barn with an ax in his hand. "There's been a killing down to Jake Fairley's?"

6

"Oh, no, sir." But Sally's heart doubled its pace. It would be exciting if there was a killing, something to talk about for weeks and weeks. "But there is a killer. He killed his master and who knows how many others, and Mr. Fairley is keeping him there, waiting for Walter to fetch the constable."

"A foreigner, you say?"

"Oh, yes. Speaks nothing but gibberish. Probably a Papist on top of it."

Mr. Wolcott hefted his ax. "And Jake all alone with him? Good God!"

The excited flutter in Sally's heart landed in her stomach and turned into a lump of granite. Mr. Wolcott was a slight, even-tempered man. Sally couldn't see him standing against a murderer. Another lump of granite lodged in Sally's throat as Mr. Wolcott kissed the top of Beulah's head. "Tell your mother I'm going to Mr. Fairley's. But don't tell her why," he said. His fingers brushed his daughter's cheek, as if he feared he might not see her again.

Beulah's chin quivered as her father walked away. "What do we do?" Beulah's whisper rose to a mousy squeak.

To the west, Sally saw Mr. Gilbert and his sons digging potatoes. To the south, Mr. Finch gathered windfall apples. When Sally turned back to her friend, Beulah met her eyes and nodded. "We have to hurry."

"Killed them all, and they never had a chance, and now Papa's gone to help catch him." Beulah's voice faded into a series of hiccuping sobs.

Seth Gilbert gave the girl his handkerchief. Poor thing, practically in hysterics, and no wonder, too. "There, dear. We'll go, won't we?" He wondered if there was time to go home for his musket. The only weapons he and his sons, Levi and Noah, had to hand were their shovels and pocketknives, but there was safety in numbers, and with Jacob Fairley and Enos Wolcott, they'd be five—no, four. Best to go now and not waste any time. He frowned at Noah, his youngest. "You're not coming," Seth said abruptly.

Noah opened his mouth to protest, but Seth continued. "Find whoever you can and tell them to join us."

"But I want to go, too," Noah said.

Seth grabbed the boy's shoulder and shook him. "This is important, son."

"You can be like William Dawes and Paul Revere," Levi added.

Seth threw Levi a grateful glance. "Yes, just like them."

Noah puffed out his chest and nodded. "Yes, sir," the boy said, and was gone.

Chapter Two

Constable Chester Ainesworth was having a very bad day. A weasel had gotten into the henhouse during the night and ravaged the flock, leaving only a trio of tough, scrawny hens behind. Of the prized chickens Amelia had fattened and primped for next month's agricultural fair, not a one was left. Cleaning up the blood, feathers, and torn bodies with their stench of tainted meat had been a joy compared to facing Amelia's distress over her lost flock.

After a scorched and dismal breakfast, Chester had discovered a leak in the barn roof that had ruined a good quantity of hay. In the process of mending the damage, he'd spilled a box of nails and hammered his thumb.

In the afternoon, he'd found the cattle placidly grazing among his pumpkins, having broken down their pasture fence and forsaken the tough August grass for the cornstalks standing sentry over the pumpkins. It seemed that everything he wanted to keep in was bound and determined to get out, and everything he wanted to keep out was equally set on getting in.

He returned to the house to find a babble of frantic women, excited children, and agitated men blocking his front door, all of them vexed because Chester had been out when they thought he should have been in. He caught snatches of conversation that made him wish he'd stayed out.

"...he killed them in their beds, the whole family," said Caroline Dunbar in her grating squeal of a voice. "Slit their throats one by one and robbed 'em and then set the house on fire..."

Chester circumnavigated the group, hoping to slip into the

kitchen and fortify himself with a glass of rum before facing the horde. Walter Sackett stood on the doorstep talking to Amelia, his hair sweat-plastered to his forehead. The blather of the crowd kept Chester from catching any of his words.

"...ain't nobody safe in their homes anymore," said a man on Chester's left. "He bashed in their brains while they slept, and then made off with a thousand dollars in silver and gold..."

"...assaulted the women and girls, then chopped them to pieces with an ax..."

Chester told himself that his neighbors were probably stirred up over some newspaper story about a faraway crime. Nothing sensational ever happened here. Chauncey was so tiny, it merited only three sentences in the gazetteer.

"...a gruesome sight as you'd ever want to see," someone grumbled in harsh bass tones. "He cut off their heads with a scythe, as easy as mowing hay..."

Or perhaps the tale of the chicken massacre had circulated through town and returned transmogrified into something more ghastly.

"...and when the constable came for him, he shot him dead," said a voice at Chester's elbow.

Then again, perhaps not.

Daniel stood with his cheek pressed to Ivy's, overseeing the blacksmith's ritual of fitting, nailing, and filing. The familiar task was almost a comfort when set against the uncertainty and bewilderment that had been his lot for the past several days.

The more time and distance he put between himself and Farmington and the Lymans, the more he discovered how ill-prepared he'd been for the journey. The number of simple things he didn't know seemed unending. Finding a night's lodging should have been easy enough. At first glance, landladies and tavern-keepers would greet him with fair and smiling faces. But their smiles faded when he opened his mouth and his Irishness showed itself—that Irish turn to his words he'd fought so hard to keep ever since that horrific day six years ago, when fire had taken his parents, his baby brother, and his home. Now he tried to flatten his vowels like a native-born New Englander. Even so, asking for food or lodging, or a barn to stable Ivy for the night, was a challenge. Perhaps it was because he couldn't remember ever asking for anything where the answer hadn't been no.

Finding his way was another problem. A line on a map and a road on the ground were different things entirely. He might blunder about until winter, trying to puzzle out where to go, where to stay, how to speak, and how not to get robbed. Finding the peddler had quickly turned from a whim to a necessity.

"There, that should do it." The blacksmith released Ivy's foot and straightened.

Daniel blinked out of his fog. "Yes, thank you, sir," he said. At least he remembered to say *yes* instead of *aye* and *thank you* instead of *ta*. He stooped to check the smith's work, then glanced up to ask about the peddler.

The blacksmith wasn't looking at Daniel or at Ivy, but at something behind them.

Releasing Ivy's hoof, Daniel rose and turned. A little sandy-haired man stood at the edge of the blacksmith's yard, an ax in his hand. Another next to him held a pitchfork, and another a spade. There were more behind them and coming up the road. Others carried weapons rather than tools: a rusted sword, a twisted bayonet, battered muskets. Daniel wondered if he'd arrived in town on training day. Perhaps the blacksmith was captain of the militia and . . .

But the men weren't looking at the blacksmith. Their dark, cold gazes were fixed on Daniel.

The constable's parlor was jammed with people, some standing on chairs to get a better view, some trying to shove their way in from the hall. Those out in the yard jostled at the open windows, trying to thrust their heads and shoulders into the room.

Daniel felt as if he stood outside himself, seeing himself as one of the spectators might: a stranger with nothing to say in his own defense. The contents of his bags lay in an untidy sprawl across the constable's table. Funny how quickly he'd attached himself to those bits of cloth and leather and metal and paper. It felt as if his guts were laid out there, instead of only his goods.

"What's the charge, Chester?" snapped a sharp-nosed, silver-haired man who sat in an upholstered chair behind the table. He held a candlestick, which he periodically rapped on the table to silence the crowd. From the man's attitude and the deference everyone showed him, Daniel guessed him to be the justice of the peace.

The constable showed none of the older man's poise. Dressed in sweat-dampened work clothes, he slouched in a wooden chair next to the justice. He stared balefully at the goods strewn across his table. He rubbed his eyes and seemed disappointed that neither goods nor crowd had disappeared when he put his hands down. "Damned if I know," he muttered. "So what is it, Jake?" he said, a little louder. "This fella's stolen something from you?"

"Not yet." The blacksmith stepped forward and crossed his burly arms over his chest. "I never gave him the chance." The crowd mumbled its approval.

"Then why in blazes did you haul all these people into my parlor?" the constable demanded.

"He stole these goods from someone, that's why." The smith grabbed a shirt and waved it under Daniel's nose. "Now tell me how a boy like you comes to have goods like this?"

The justice's and the constable's stares felt like an ox yoke across Daniel's shoulders. "Th-they're mine," was all the answer he could blurt out.

The blacksmith picked up the books: the fat little volume of Shakespeare the peddler had given him and Sir Walter Scott's *Ivanhoe*—a parting gift from Lizzie, the Lymans' dairymaid. Daniel cringed at the sooty marks the blacksmith made on *Ivanhoe's* pages as he riffled through them. "I suppose these are his, too?" The blacksmith sniffed. "I doubt the brute can even read."

Daniel choked back a retort. Whether dealing with powerful men like George Lyman, his former master, or schoolyard bullies like Joshua Ward and his mates, it had always been safest to be mute and passive. But now it was time to say something, anything, and he didn't know what to say. "They're m-mine, too," he stammered.

The room burst into contemptuous laughter. "Yours?" the blacksmith said, echoed by half a dozen others. "*Yours?*"

His mind began to retreat into that safe place inside himself that he'd built when he'd learned that the way to end trouble was to submit and endure. The rapping of the justice's candlestick pulled him away from the temptation to withdraw and give up.

He cursed himself for an idiot. His defense was right there in front of him. He'd just been too daft with panic to tell them about the papers Lyman's son Silas had given him. "I got papers." He gestured toward the table. "Bills of sale. References. They're all there in that pocketbook."

The blacksmith grabbed the small leather case. He let the papers spill to the floor and trod on them. "Forged, no doubt."

Daniel felt as if the blacksmith's boot heel had ground into his chest. "And how would I be forging 'em, then, if I can't read?"

A corner of the constable's mouth twitched up before the man hid it behind his hand. The blacksmith's face flushed, and he looked as if he wanted to strike Daniel. "Stolen, then," the blacksmith said. "How do we know you haven't killed this fellow and stole his goods and his papers?"

"Of course I didn't kill him. He's me."

"And what proof do you have?" the justice of the peace demanded, rapping the candlestick against the table. The constable winced as the metal knocked the polished surface.

"Is there anyone who can vouch for you, boy?" The constable's voice was almost gentle. The justice of the peace looked disgruntled that the constable had taken over the hearing—if the hubbub could be called a hearing—but the constable continued, "Anyone at all who knows you?"

Daniel shook his head. Ivy was the only one who knew him. She could show them all she pleased that nobody else had a right to her, but they'd only see her as stolen goods.

The constable massaged his forehead, then his temples. He

looked almost as miserable as Daniel felt. "So you have no proof you're who you say you are. And you, Jacob"—he pointed to the blacksmith—"have no proof he isn't. And I have no grounds for a warrant."

Somebody at the back of the room shouted, "But we know he's a thief!"

Daniel stared at the papers at the blacksmith's feet—the papers Silas had worked so hard to gather. If they wouldn't believe Silas's papers, surely they'd believe the man himself. "Send word to Silas Lyman in Farmington—Farmington, Massachusetts, that is. He'll speak for me. I used to work for his father, George Lyman."

"And how will he do that with his throat cut?" snarled the blacksmith.

"C-Cut?" Daniel clutched at his own neck. It couldn't be true, and yet it made all too much sense. It must have been an unforgivable betrayal for Silas to turn against his father and help Daniel to freedom. It wasn't hard to imagine the elder Lyman slitting Silas's throat in revenge. What better vengeance than to place all the blame on the Irish lad who'd just left town?

"What—what's become of himself, then?" He barely managed to choke out the question.

"Himself?"

"His da. Silas's da, I mean. George Lyman."

The slight man stepped forward, shoving at Daniel's shoulder. "Don't pretend you don't know. You're the one that killed them all."

"All? They're all of 'em dead?" Lyman had seemed subdued and shaken the last time Daniel had seen him, but mad? Insane enough to kill his whole family and himself?

"All—killed in their sleep," called a voice from the crowd.

The accusations grew louder around him. The justice of the peace and constable shouted for order, and the justice rapped the table, but everything melted into a sea of angry faces, a whirlwind of frenzied voices confirming the death of every last Lyman.

Daniel's knees gave way underneath him. His stomach

rolled and pushed up into his throat. He cradled his head in his arms. "Oh, God, oh, God. Jesus, Mary, and Joseph."

A massive hand grabbed his collar and hauled him upright. "There, you see?" The blacksmith's voice boomed in his ear. "There's guilt written all over him."

Chapter Three

"Mr. S.?"

"Mmm-hmm?" Jonathan Stocking peered through his spectacles at the collection of tousled yellow hair, rumpled clothes, and dirty feet and hands perched next to him on the wagon seat. Hadn't he cleaned the child the last time they'd stopped to water Phizzy? How could a body get so disordered just riding in a wagon?

"There's something queer about this town," Billy said.

"Queer?" Jonathan said. "How do you mean?" He was less concerned about the answer than the child's clothes and hair. Blast that hair, couldn't it stay combed for five minutes?

Billy gestured at the house they'd just passed. "There's no one about. All the houses are shut up tight like it was winter."

"Put your shoes and stockings on." Jonathan pulled out his handkerchief, spat into it, and handed it to Billy. "And wipe that smudge off your chin. There's prob'ly just some doin's down to the common. A fair, maybe, or town meeting or training day."

After scrubbing away the smudge, Billy wrestled grubby toes into grayish socks. The shoes went on next, accompanied by a pained grimace.

"Don't you be making faces like that to my cousin Sophie, now," Jonathan warned. "We're depending on her hospitality."

"If there's a fair, can we go see?" Billy's blue eyes sparkled at the prospect.

"We won't be going that way. Where's your hat?" Jonathan yanked the rumpled blue cap out from under Billy's rump. "Why do you always have to be sitting on it?" He whacked the cap on his arm a few times to beat the dust out of it, then settled the cap on Billy's head. He stuffed as much of the unruly blond hair under the hat as he could and tugged the visor straight. "In case you've forgot, Eldad pays our wages. If we make Sophie happy, then we make Eldad happy. So *if* there's a fair, and *if* you make your manners nice to Sophie, then *maybe* you can go." Billy rewarded the peddler with half a smile. "Anyway, here we are," Jonathan added, as the familiar white house and flower-filled dooryard came into view. Phizzy let out a cheerful whicker and stopped at the front gate.

Jonathan climbed stiffly down from the wagon. He brushed the dust from his jacket and trousers, polished his coat buttons with his cuffs, tugged vest and jacket and collar into place. He wasn't much cleaner than Billy, but then again, Sophie wouldn't expect tidiness from him. As for Billy, well, she wasn't expecting Billy at all.

"How's that?" He glanced up at Billy, still perched on the wagon seat.

Billy's nose wrinkled. "Better, I s'pose." Billy jumped down and applied a whisk broom to Jonathan's elbows, lapels, and backside. "There." Billy gave the peddler a satisfied nod.

Jonathan fluffed Billy's cravat into a fat bow. He tugged the blue jacket straight, brushed the road dust from the child's shoulders, and set them square. "Now, you mind your manners in front of Sophie. Just 'cause she's my cousin don't mean she ain't a lady." Jonathan licked the tips of his fingers and plastered an unruly curl down under Billy's cap. "Best foot forward, remember?"

"Yessir." Billy's right foot moved smartly forward.

They looked down at Billy's dusty shoes, then at Jonathan's, which were equally filthy. They shared a shrug and polished the toes of their shoes on the backs of their trouser legs. The result was more smear than shine.

A curtain stirred at one of the windows. He heard a muffled squeal, and the door flew open. "Jonny! Oh, Jonny, we didn't think to see you for weeks yet!" A plump, blue-eyed woman dashed down the path and squeezed Jonathan in a lavender-scented hug.

"Now, Soph, don't go bruising the goods." Jonathan kissed his cousin on the cheek.

"And who's this?" Sophie eyed Billy.

"A—um—a business associate, you might say."

"William James Michael Fogarty at your service, ma'am." Billy bowed. A stray curl escaped the cap and drooped over one blue eye.

A smile washed over Sophie's apple-round face. She reached out one finger, captured the wayward curl, and tucked it back in. "Sophronia Elizabeth Bartholomew Taylor." She bobbed in a little curtsy. "Delighted to make your acquaintance. Although I fancy you'd be more delighted to make the acquaintance of a peach pie and a cup of tea."

Billy searched the peddler's face for a cue. Jonathan nodded. "She's only asking us to tea, son, not the governor's ball."

"I—uh, yes, please, thank you, ma'am," Billy blurted.

Sophie tucked one hand under Billy's arm and the other under Jonathan's, but Billy pulled away, face stricken with a spasm of guilt. "Phizzy!" Billy said, glancing at the floppy-eared gray gelding who nodded sleepily at the gate. "I got to see to Phizzy first. It's me job." Billy's cheeks flushed with shame.

"I'm sure Phizzy will excuse you for a bit," Sophie said.

"I'm sorry, ma'am, but you see Phizzy *needs* me." Billy broke away to rush back to the horse. Jonathan caught bits of murmured Irish apologies as Billy caressed Phizzy's nose.

Jonathan started to apologize for Billy's breach of manners, but Sophie cut him off with a laugh. "Let the boy be. It looks like he loves that old horse as much as you do."

"Where's Eldad?" Jonathan asked.

"There was some hubbub down to Chester Ainesworth's. He went to see what the to-do was all about. He should be back soon." Sophie nudged her cousin's elbow. "Go show your boy where to put Phizzy. I'll have tea ready when you come in."

Jonathan and Billy led Phizzy to the wagon shed and backed the wagon in. They'd just finished unhitching the gelding when a long shadow loomed in the doorway and a gruff voice boomed, "There'd better not be any tin left in that thing."

Jonathan spun around to greet the tall, gray-haired man. "Eldad! Ain't you a sight!" He gave his cousin's husband a strong handshake and a hearty thump on the back. "So what's this Sophie said about you chasing down some hullabaloo in town?"

"Chasing down a lot of gossip, is more like it." Eldad's hooked nose wrinkled with his scowl. "Seems Jacob Fairley caught himself a thief and a murderer."

"A murderer in Chauncey? Now that does beat all." Jonathan returned to Phizzy, looping the gelding's reins through an iron ring while Billy fetched his halter.

Eldad leaned his long frame against the doorjamb and watched the two work. "The story is he came out bold as brass, looking to get his horse shod. But Jake said he could tell it was stolen, just from the looks of this fella. Foreign, I guess, and shifty-eyed."

Jonathan paused in the middle of trading bridle for halter. "The fella or the horse?"

"The fella."

"Oh. You seen him yourself?"

"I couldn't get in. The whole town must have been crammed into Chester's parlor and yard. By the time I got there, a snake couldn't have slipped in the door."

"So where's this foreign murderer from?" Jonathan gathered up bridle and harness, then gave them to Billy to store in the back of the wagon.

"Seems he worked for some fella up in Massachusetts. Killed the whole family—slit their throats while they were in their beds, stole their goods and took off. Some say he—" Eldad cast a glance toward Billy and lowered his voice. "Some say he assaulted the mother and daughters before he—" Eldad ran his thumb across his throat.

"Funny I ain't heard nothing about it. You know how folks love talking murder with a peddler." Jonathan gestured for Billy to take Phizzy out to a little pen next to the barn. The men leaned on the fence and watched the gelding shake himself all over, then crumple into the grass with a contented sigh. In a moment, all four enormous hooves were waving in the air as the horse erased the harness marks and sweat stains in the grass.

Eldad slipped a pair of segars out of his breast pocket and lit one for himself and one for Jonathan. "He had a valise full of banknotes and forged papers, they say."

Jonathan puffed thoughtfully on his segar. "What's to become of him?"

"He's down to Chester Ainesworth's right now, until Chester can sort the truth out. He's locked up for safekeeping in that shed that Chester has tacked onto his barn. Chester and the J.P. said there wasn't anything to base a charge on, but folks were getting so ugly, Chester didn't dare let him go."

Jonathan shook his head. "Chester Ainesworth," he murmured. "Never struck me as sharp enough to make a constable."

"He's not so dull as some think. He sent Jake Fairley's apprentice off to Farmington to get the truth." Eldad chuckled. "On Jake's horse, yet."

"Well, there's a good afternoon's work done, eh, Jacob?" The bench scraped raggedly against the tavern floor as Ezra Stokes sat down across from the blacksmith.

"You call that done?" Jacob drained his glass and banged it on the table. He nodded at the tavern-keeper for a refill.

Abner came around the bar with a fresh bottle of rum. Jacob hoped somebody besides Abner was keeping track of the bottles. He was sure he wasn't drinking nearly as fast as the others hunkered along the two corner tables, and he was damned if he'd see Abner spread the cost evenly all the way 'round.

Come to think of it, somebody should have been treating *him*. Hadn't he been sharp enough to spy out the foreigner for what he really was? Hadn't he sounded the alarm? And hadn't he stayed, alone and unarmed but for his hammer and tongs, keeping the murderer distracted until help arrived? Who knew how many lives he'd saved?

But Chester Ainesworth would bungle it all with his dimwitted caution. "The man's too big a fool to be constable," Jacob said. He wrapped a meaty fist around his glass and took a long swallow, letting the rum's hot spiciness flood his veins and clear his head.

"Ainesworth?" Tom Shelby said. "He's only doing his job, I s'pose." Shelby's eyes looked dull and confused, like an ox who'd been told to gee and haw at the same time.

Strange, Jacob thought, how drink made some men duller and other men more lively. As for himself, a good dose of rum made everything come sharper. "Chester's too busy fussing about warrants and papers to remember that his job is to keep us safe." A dozen men's heads bobbed up and down over their glasses in agreement.

Shelby shrugged. "The fellow's locked up. We should be safe enough."

Jacob hawked and spat on the floor. "Chester's shed wouldn't hold a goose. That killer will be out and slitting our throats while Chester's waiting for his 'inquiry' to come back." What galled even more was Jacob would be without an apprentice or a horse for the better part of the week. Jacob still wasn't sure how the constable had wheedled him into it. Now Walter and Jacob's horse were off on a fool's errand, and not one word said about who was to pay for the use of Jacob's apprentice and gelding. Nor had there been any mention of a reward for the man who'd identified and cornered the murderer.

"We can set a guard on him," Shelby said. The nods followed up and down the bench.

"And who's to guard the guard to keep his throat from being cut?" Jacob loosened his cravat. Suddenly, the blasted thing seemed to be choking him. Damnation, the room was getting hot. Where was that bottle? Empty. He waved Abner over for another.

"What the hell do we need a constable for, if we got to be guarding his prisoners for him?" Ezra responded with a sarcastic sneer.

"Well, boys," Jacob said, "if Chester can't do his job, we'll just have to do it for him."

Chapter Four

"You still have your fiddle, don't you, Jonny?" Sophie asked. All through the afternoon, she'd been looking forward to two things: an evening of Jonny's music, and a chance to interrogate Jonny about the boy he'd brought with him.

"I figured we wouldn't get a meal free and clear out of you." Jonny nudged his companion. "Billy, go fetch—" The boy disappeared before Jonny could finish his sentence.

Sophie hooked her arm around her cousin's elbow and led him into the parlor. "Now, cousin," she began, her voice treacle-sweet. "Who is that boy, and where did you find him?"

"Why, the angels sent him." Jonny patted Sophie's cheek. "A gift from heaven."

Eldad struck a lucifer and lit a candle. "An outcast from the other place is more like it."

"You wouldn't say that if you'd heard him sing," Jonny said as the boy reappeared in the doorway, holding Jonny's fiddle case.

Sophie settled herself on the sofa while Jonny rosined his bow and tuned the fiddle. She always marveled at where, between chin and shoulder, Jonny found a spot to place the instrument. Even as a boy he hadn't had much neck to speak of, and even less chin. The ratio of neck to chin to jowls hadn't improved as he'd reached adulthood. But somehow the fiddle found a place to nestle while Jonny plucked the strings, then gently massaged them with the bow, transforming their discordant squeal to a contented hum. After tuning, he conferred with the boy, who stood to attention just clear of Jonny's elbow. "A song of Ireland," Jonny announced.

Sophie didn't know a soul who could make a fiddle laugh or

sing or weep the way Jonny could. He could make a tune crawl inside her, familiar as her own heartbeat. Tonight Jonny's fiddle whispered like the wind behind a ship's sails. Even though the boy's words were gibberish to Sophie, they painted a picture in her head of a mist-shrouded island full of green meadows, jewel-bright flowers, and golden-fruited trees. She tasted the sweetness of the fruit, smelled the perfumed air, and her heart ached because something in the boy's song told her the place was as lost as Paradise.

Foolish woman, she told herself. *It's only a song.* But she couldn't pull herself away from it. As the last notes faded, she fumbled in her pocket for her handkerchief and dabbed discreetly at her eyes, hoping Eldad wouldn't notice.

Her husband coughed and blew his nose. "A bit smoky in here, isn't it, dear?" he said gently. "Better trim those candles." He rose quickly and turned away from her.

Jonny and the boy struck up a livelier tune next, full of trills and runs. It was the first time Sophie truly understood what it meant to sing like a bird. She'd heard other singers who could embroider a song more elaborately, but this boy sang as if he'd been hatched with the song inside him. If the first song had been shrouded in mist and melancholy, this one was all joy and light, driving the shadows from the darkest corners of the heart.

Daniel opened his eyes. It was no different from having them closed, except that with them shut, the darkness was something he made himself, and naught to be fearing. With his eyes open, the darkness was a separate entity surrounding him, stifling him. He shook himself like a horse shaking off flies.

He wasn't a child anymore, to fear being shut up in the dark. But sure, he'd acted like a child this afternoon, paralyzed and tongue-tied with fear. Like an idiot child, he'd collapsed and let himself be led away and locked up, unable to say a word in his own defense. He'd not even thought of the peddler, the very man he'd come to Chauncey to find. The peddler was surely clever enough to help Daniel prove his innocence, providing the man could be found. The constable had seemed willing to listen, if Daniel had but the wit to speak. In the morning, he'd keep his wits about him. He'd tell the constable his story and ask him about the peddler. Until then, there was naught to do but sleep, or at least try to.

He curled up in a corner of the shed and tried to retreat to the secret place he'd created inside himself, where all was quiet and green and safe. In his secret place, Ma and Da and Michael were alive and waiting for him. There, he could ride Ivy forever. But the secret place was harder to summon when it was close and dark. Instead, all the dark places of his life would spring at him, and Ma and Da and Michael and Ivy were forever gone.

The ship's berth was like the box they'd put Grand-da in when they put him in the ground. Dark and damp, but without the clean smell of earth. The ship's motion set his stomach jumping. He cried because he didn't like being sick to his stomach. Mama was sick, too, retching into a bucket.

It was all wrong. Mama was supposed to take care of him when he was sick. She wasn't meant to be sick herself. Water—she kept asking for water. There was water somewhere on the boat, but where? The old lady in the next berth would know. He crept to the edge of his berth and reached into the next one. The old lady's arm was stiff and cold.

A light began to glow next to him, as if someone had kindled a fire in the old lady's berth. Only the fire was the weird, cold, silvery-blue of moonlight, not the mellow gold of flame. Instead of a narrow box, the old lady's berth went on and on and on. Instead of an old lady, there was a young man with blond hair and staring blue eyes. The wrist under Daniel's hand was no longer bony and fragile, but strong and muscular.

"Silas?" Daniel whispered. But Silas shouldn't have been on the boat. Daniel's younger dream-self hadn't met him yet.

Next to Silas was another man: Lyman. Then a woman, three girls, a baby. Beyond them more girls, boys, men, women, so that the row of bodies stretched into infinity.

Silas sat up, his head wobbling on his neck like a broken doll's. A gash ran across his throat, the blood seeping down his shirt front. One by one, the men, women, and children beyond him began to sit, exposing a row of torn throats and empty, staring eyes. One by one, each figure touched a finger to its bloody throat, then pointed the dripping finger at Daniel.

Daniel tried to release Silas's wrist, but his hand stuck fast.

"I never! I swear, I never!" Daniel gasped. He ran a hand across his own throat. He'd already removed his cravat and unbuttoned his collar, but the choking feeling wouldn't go away. His other hand closed around something smooth and hard. *Idiot.* It was only an ear of maize, probably left behind from last year's grinding. He ran his thumb along the bead-hard kernels and forced the nightmares away to the corners of the shed, where they hovered and waited.

He twisted both hands around the ear of corn and tried to breathe evenly. Hadn't Ma warned him that wishing someone ill would only come back to him? He couldn't deny he'd wished Lyman and his wife dead. No matter how he'd tried to smother his curses, eventually the black moods would win out, and he'd damn Mr. and Mrs. Lyman in his heart, fancy all the ways he wished them hurt, wished them killed. Now he had his wish, and it turned his stomach.

But he'd no quarrel with Silas. Nor with the children. Even without closing his eyes he could see them, throats laid open like hogs at butchering time. No, he'd never wanted that.

He rubbed his face. It was so damned hot in here. God, he was suffocating, as if somebody had put a blanket over his face.

The door rattled. Daniel flung himself toward the back of the shed, heart racing. He couldn't shake his conviction he was to blame for the Lymans' deaths, as sure as if he'd slaughtered them himself. And now the constable had come to make him answer for it.

He shook his head. It was more than likely the constable had come to take him to the privy so he wouldn't foul the shed. He calmed himself by recalling his hopes for the peddler's aid and the constable's fairness. He began to shape the words to tell the constable his story.

The door rattled again, and the bolt clicked free. Daniel turned toward the sound. He saw the lantern for only a moment before they knocked him to the floor.

Chapter Five

"An uneasy mind makes for an uneasy stomach."

Or was that "An uneasy stomach makes for an uneasy mind?"

"Damn it all," Jonathan muttered to himself. He took another puff on his segar and let the smoke out slowly, as though he expected the smoke to shape itself into the proper words, silvery and soft-edged against the black velvet sky.

The air had a bit of a chill to it, making Jonathan walk a little faster along the road. He'd never held with those who believed that inhaling the night air was a sure invitation to a consumptive death. There was nothing like a brisk evening walk to settle the stomach, and nothing like a good segar to clear the head.

But tonight Jonathan had walked a fair piece and found himself no more easy in mind or stomach than when he'd left the house. The uneasy stomach had a ready explanation: too much of Sophie's fine cooking and too much of Eldad's fine wine and brandy. A man could get accustomed to fine things if he wasn't careful, and then where would he be? Unable to fend for himself on the road. Unable to make his way alone in the world.

Alone.

Why did that word all of a sudden send a shiver down his spine? He'd been more than content with his own company—well, his own and Phizzy's—for how many years now?

"Getting soft in your old age, Jonny boy?" he grumbled. "You got what you wanted, ain't you?" The bee that he'd placed in Sophie's bonnet was likely buzzing around in there as she slept. Jonathan had seen the yearning in her eyes the moment Billy had started to sing. As for Billy, well, Billy had liked Sophie's cooking and marveled over her clean white sheets and feather mattress. Liking Sophie would come soon enough. Yes, Sophie would win the child over and then that bee would have a whole hive full of honey for Sophie, Eldad, and Billy.

Damn it all, though, Jonathan would miss the music. He'd never known a body so hungry for song as Billy. The most leaden tune could pour into those ears, and it would come out of that mouth sounding like gold. And there was nothing like a good song to make folks more willing to part with their money and buy a tray or pan or teapot they didn't need. Folks had been happy to pay for the singing and fiddling alone, and never you mind about the tinware. He and Billy had gotten so they just needed to look at each other to start out on the same song. Yes, he'd miss the music, all right.

Still, it'd be better all around if the child stayed with Sophie. Having Billy just made Jonathan lazy. He'd grown too accustomed to having help to set up the wares, to feed and harness Phizzy. And Phizzy was getting too damn used to being spoiled and fussed over.

As he finished his segar, Jonathan noticed a pair of lights bobbing in the distance and picked out a group of men stumbling across a pasture. Drunk, he guessed, and holding each other up as they made their way home. *You get to depending on somebody, Jonny, and you'll be just like that, unable to stand on your own two feet.*

Besides, too much companionship made a man prideful. He was already growing puffed up from having somebody around who listened to his stories and believed more than half of them, somebody who laughed at his jokes, even the stale ones. It was a powerful temptation to vanity when somebody watched everything you did and copied your ways as if there were nothing finer in the world than to be just like you.

He shuddered to think of anybody looking to him as a model. What kind of sorry life could he offer a child? He'd spent most of his life wandering around as aimlessly as...as...well, as that bunch of drunkards. One of them fell, and the others set upon him with kicks and blows.

"There's companionship for you," Jonathan muttered, crushing the stub of his segar under his heel. Give a man enough drink, and he'd turn on the very mother that bore him.

As the fallen man's companions yanked him to his feet, Jonathan noticed that he seemed to have no arms, or at least seemed unable to move them. There was something peculiar about his head, too. It looked more like an understuffed pillow than a proper head. The armless man lurched into step, like an unwilling calf tied by the neck and led to market.

With a knot in the pit of his stomach, he guessed who the armless man was and what was liable to happen to him. He'd been run out of enough towns to feel a kinship for the man, criminal or no. And so he ran. Damn, his old body was slow and heavy.

He was sweating rivers and aching in every joint by the time he staggered into the house. Perspiration fogged his spectacles, and he groped for the rail as he clomped up the stairs. "Eldad!" he tried to holler, but barely had breath to wheeze out something that sounded like "Da-da-da." It felt as though a giant fist squeezed his chest.

Nightshirt flapping, Billy dashed out of the bedroom. "Mr. S.! What is it? Are you sick?"

Jonathan let Billy guide him to a chair and sit him down. Yanking his spectacles off with one hand, he pulled his handkerchief out of his pocket with the other. He wiped the foggy lenses, then rubbed the cloth over his dripping face. The vise around his chest finally let up enough for him to get real words out. "Get Phizzy. Put his bridle and saddle on. Hurry." Billy disappeared, bare feet slapping down the stairs and across the floor.

Jonathan staggered to his feet at the clatter of a door opening. He slipped his spectacles on, bringing the hallway into focus.

"Jonny, what's wrong?" Sophie's candle cast ghoulish shadows on her face and Eldad's.

Jonathan gripped Eldad's shoulder. "Get dressed. Get Ainesworth and as many sober, sensible men as you can find. You'll need horses. Guns, too, if you have 'em."

"My God, what's happened?" Eldad asked.

29

"It's Chester's prisoner."

Eldad and Sophie exchanged glances. "Escaped?" Eldad said.

Jonathan shook his head. "He's out, but it ain't his own doing. If we don't hurry, the poor fool might not live to see his trial."

It wasn't bloody fair, Daniel thought. He hadn't been free long enough to even know how to be free. And now it looked as though he never would.

The sack they'd thrown over his head reeked of musty dank barns and cellars. The smell drove away any hope of retreating to his safe place. It was gone now, and he'd likely not find it again this side of the grave.

They'd stripped him naked. He tried to convince himself that was what made him shiver, rather than stark terror. But the churning in his belly betrayed him for a liar. He clenched his abdomen tight with every scrap of will he had left. He'd be damned if he'd let his bladder and bowels give way in front of this lot. They'd bloody well enjoy that, wouldn't they? No, he wouldn't give them the satisfaction of seeing him soil and piss himself from fear. His stomach rebelled, tried to drive his last meal up into his throat, where it would be stopped by the rag they'd stuffed in his mouth to silence him. He forced himself to push it all back down and keep it there. He'd be damned, too, if he let himself die that way, choking on his own puke.

Though maybe that would be better than whatever they had in store for him. He thought of all the cattle and sheep and swine he and Silas had slaughtered and skinned and butchered, how the beasts had come up quiet and trusting until that last moment. Was this how they'd felt before the butchering?

No. It wouldn't have been like this at all. Silas had always been careful to stun each beast and slit its throat quickly, so it would feel only a moment's pain and fear. Daniel was sure it wouldn't be that way with him. Not with this lot. The butchering would come first, before the killing.

Chapter Six

Jonathan's nostrils twitched at the smell of fire where no fire should have been. He eased Phizzy to a walk, halting in the woods just beyond the reach of fire and torchlight. Not counting the prisoner, there were a dozen men, mostly drunk, he guessed. A keg sat near the fire, and bottles glimmered in some of the men's hands. Some were armed with sticks, lashes, farm tools, but he saw no guns. A kettle hung from a tripod that straddled the fire. Jonathan shivered as he caught the smell of hot tar.

The prisoner was naked except for a sack they'd thrown over his head to blind him to their faces. Or perhaps to blind them to his. It was easier to torment a man when you didn't have to see your own fears in his face.

No. Not a man, but a boy. The prisoner's pale bony frame had the unfinished look of a boy just starting his last growth, all knobby bones and hairless skin. They'd put a rope around the boy's neck and flung the end over a branch to tether him while they tormented him. Their game for the moment was to pelt him with rotten vegetables and fruit, clods of dirt and stones. He staggered in a ragged dance until the rope jerked him upright like a marionette. Jonathan winced as a stone caught the boy in the chest.

"Well, Phizzy," he whispered, "at least we ain't too late." He drew out Eldad's ancient pistols. There'd only been enough powder for one shot, if the damned thing worked at all. One pistol for noise and the other for show, and he prayed nobody called his bluff. He knotted the reins and let them fall on Phizzy's withers. With one pistol in each hand, he gave Phizzy his head and pressed him into a trot, then a canter.

Phizzy scattered the men and whirled to a stop next to the staggering boy. Jonathan fired the first pistol over the men's heads. Phizzy let out a bloodcurdling scream and reared, hooves pawing the air. The fire's glow made the misshapen gelding look like the devil's own horse. Pride warmed Jonathan's heart. Phizzy was old, but he still remembered his playacting days.

"Christ!" one of the men called out.

Jonathan dropped the discharged pistol and leveled the second one at the crowd. "A fine lot of murderers you are to be calling on the Lord." Phizzy pawed the ground with his front hooves as if he couldn't wait to tear into the mob. The men fell back a pace. At Jonathan's signal, Phizzy bared his teeth and snapped them together with a sharp click.

The men retreated farther. Two dozen drink-blurred eyes tried to fathom who the strange rider was. The smith solved the puzzle first. "It's Sophie Taylor's cousin, that peddler fella."

Jonathan focused on the blacksmith, who was no doubt the leader of this pack of idiots. "Who do you think you are, almighty God, to be killing folk outside the law?"

Fairley said, "We're only giving him what he deserves: a little tar, a few feathers..."

"It's better than he gave them folks in—in—" The speaker hesitated. Bleary-eyed, he glanced around for somebody to finish his sentence for him.

"In where?" Jonathan demanded.

More than half a dozen towns were named and quarreled over.

"And what did he do in wherever it was?"

Arguments broke out over the number of folk the boy had slaughtered and how he'd done it.

Jonathan edged Phizzy between the prisoner and the crowd. When the gelding's shoulder brushed the boy's, Jonathan grabbed the trembling boy's arm and pulled him closer. "My, my, such a dangerous boy," Jonathan shouted. "He must'a depopulated half'a New England." The prisoner tensed as Jonathan's fingers groped for the noose and eased it loose. "I'm glad to see he didn't hurt you none. He must weigh all of a hundred pounds."

"A small man can be just as dangerous as a big one," said a brawny ox of a fellow.

"Seems to me there's a good lot of small men here." Jonathan worked the rope free and slipped it from the boy's neck. He reached for the hood, but the boy collapsed to the ground in a shuddering heap.

The prisoner's fall galvanized the mob. With a cry, they surged forward. Jonathan leveled the empty pistol and coaxed Phizzy into another show of snapping teeth and pawing hooves.

The blacksmith was the only who stood his ground. "What's he to you, peddler?"

Jonathan shrugged. "Nothing. Only I hate to see a good man hanged."

"Good?" The men repeated the word almost as one, then burst into angry laughter.

"Good!" Jonathan shouted over the din. "A good man like yourself, Jacob Fairley. Or you, Tom Shelby. Or you, Ezra Stokes...." He named all the men he recognized, watching their eyes go slack and fearful. A few tugged their hat brims down low over their brows and retreated into the shadows.

A breeze swirled a puff of white up from a sack in one man's hand. Feathers drifted about like flies buzzing around a cow's backside. Jonathan pointed his pistol at the feather-bearer. "If I was you, Abner Bacon, I'd rather face hanging than tell my wife what I done with all them feathers she was saving for her pillows and mattresses."

Abner stared sheepishly into the bag, then thrust it behind his back.

Jacob cackled uneasily. "And why would any of us be hanged?" From the way his eyes wouldn't meet Jonathan's, the peddler knew that sense—or fear—had begun to sober him.

"Well, ain't that the penalty for murder these days?" Jonathan asked.

"It's not murder we're doing. It's justice." The smith pointed a sooty finger at the pale figure quivering behind the gelding's shaggy legs.

"Not if you got the wrong fella."

"We got the right one," Jacob said.

"You do?" Jonathan scratched his chin dubiously. "You seen him do all this robbing and killing? You got some newspapers or handbills telling about it? You got a writ on him?" Phizzy's ears twitched, and for a moment Jonathan thought he heard thunder.

The men shuffled their feet and looked away. Jonathan saw a flash of light in the woods behind the men, and he heard the rumble again. Not thunder. Something better.

"Hell, you can't even agree what he's done or where he done it. About the only thing you can agree on is how to kill him." Jonathan tossed the pistol at Fairley. Reflexively, the blacksmith grabbed the gun before it tumbled to the ground. He held it by the barrel and stared at it as if he didn't quite know what it was.

"If it's killing you want, go ahead, kill him. But you better kill me, too. 'Cause I'll stand witness against every damn one of you." Jonathan stood in his stirrups to get a better view of the forest beyond. He pointed over the men's heads. "And you better kill Chester Ainesworth and Eldad Taylor and all the rest of them sober fellas coming up behind you."

A half dozen horsemen burst from the woods. Some of the mob dropped their torches and ran, stumbling over each other in their drunken flight. Abner Bacon flung his sack at the nearest rider. The bag burst open in a spray of feathers. The horsemen had their hands full trying to calm their shying horses, avoid the fallen torches, and prevent the men on the ground from escaping, all the while trying not to drop their own lanterns or fall into the fire in the middle of the clearing. Eldad somehow managed to keep his own mount calm. He drove together several of the men like a flock of sheep.

Chester leaped down from his horse and pulled off his coat, using it to smother the fallen torches and stamping smaller flames out with his boots. The odors of scorched cloth and leather and burning feathers mingled with the tar- and wood-smoke-laden air. By the time Chester had conquered the fires and reclaimed his gelding, the rest of the horses had settled down, and their riders had herded the remnants of the mob together. Only five remained, trapped in the circle of horses while feathers drifted about them like a freakish snowstorm.

Chester stomped over to stand toe-to-toe with the blacksmith. The constable's face was a blend of crimson rage and sooty black splotches. The smoldering coat in his hand wreathed him in a shroud of smoke, so he looked as if he'd just climbed up from the depths of hell.

"What the devil are you playing at, Jacob?" Chester roared. He jabbed his index finger into Fairley's chest hard enough to make him wince. Fairley looked ready to jab back, when the wind lifted a cluster of feathers and blew them into the blacksmith's face, where they stuck to his sweat-dampened cheeks like a ragged beard. Fairley swore and wiped the feathers away. They clung to his fingers and refused to be shaken off. Flicking his wrist in frustrated attempts to shed the feathers, Fairley looked too much of an idiot to lead anyone, and Chester looked too much of a devil to be defied.

Jonathan dismounted and knelt next to the prisoner. At Jonathan's touch, the boy squirmed away, kicking frantically. Jonathan grabbed the boy's shoulders. "It's all right, son. I ain't one of them." The boy settled like a frightened colt, trembling as the peddler untied his hands, then pulled the sack from his head and the gag from his mouth.

The boy scrambled into the shadows to retch until dry heaves racked his body. When Jonathan laid a hand on his shoulder, the boy jerked away from him.

Jonathan took a flask from his coat pocket. "Here now, son. This'll set you straight." He offered the flask, trying to coax the boy into the light in order to see how badly he'd been hurt.

The boy shied again. The breeze cast a drift of feathers over him. He shivered when they settled on his body. "I ain't going to harm you," Jonathan assured him. He put his hand under the boy's chin and pressed the bottle to his lips to get him to drink. Their eyes met for a second, then the boy turned away, coughing up the spirits.

Jonathan's heart rolled over. "Eldad! For Christ's sake, bring me a light!" He pulled the boy around to face him, cupping the boy's cheek in his hand when the lad tried to squirm free.

Eldad's lantern revealed a pale, freckled, sharp-featured face, his pupils so wide that his eyes looked nearly black.

"Dan'l?" Jonathan said. "Dan'l? Son? Do you know me?"

The boy might have been a wild beast or an idiot child for all the response he made.

"You know this fella, Jonny?" Eldad asked.

"I fear I do, Eldad. God help him, I fear I do."

Chapter Seven

"His name's Daniel Linnehan," Jonathan said. He took a hefty swallow of Ainesworth's rum, its warm bite serving as liquid comfort against what he'd seen that night. "He's bound out to some storekeeper up in Massachusetts. Near's I can remember, the boy's got no kin."

"Do you know his master's name?" Chester winced as his wife salved the blisters on his singed hand. Now that the anger had settled out of him, he looked dirty and exhausted and a good decade older than his years. His bloodshot eyes were circled with fatigue and soot and, Jonathan guessed, more than a little guilt over his failure to keep his prisoner safe. Still reeking of smoke, he nursed a mug of rum in one hand while his wife nursed the other.

If Chester looked the worse for wear, his wife looked the worse for worry. Yet even in a shabby work dress, with her dark hair a-frazzle and her mouth tight with concern, she was a handsome woman. Her brown eyes had an intensity and alertness that were a wonder to Jonathan, given the time of night and how much work the men had brought home to her. She'd tended the boy's hurts and her husband's burns while simultaneously conjuring rum and cider and cake for Jonathan and Eldad. But she'd quickly made it clear to the men that the appearance of food and drink didn't grant them leave to lounge about in idleness. There'd been candles to light, water to be fetched, a fire to be tended, shirts and rags to be gathered, a multitude of orders to be obeyed. She was definitely a woman strong enough to keep a man in his place. Every time she looked his way, Jonathan involuntarily straightened in his chair and tidied his clothes.

"Mr. Stocking?" Mrs. Ainesworth said. "Who was the boy bound to?"

Jonathan rubbed his eyes, realizing that his mind had drifted off without answering Chester's question. "His master?" He scratched his head. Something to do with lying. Lyford? Lyons? "Lyman," he said finally. "Yes, Lyman."

"So that much is true, then," Mrs. Ainesworth said, glancing toward the shadowy corner of the kitchen where Daniel lay stretched out on the settle.

Though Jonathan couldn't see the boy's face, he guessed that Daniel still stared at the ceiling with the same vacant gaze he'd worn since his rescue. Moving with no more will than a puppet, he'd let Jonathan and Eldad wrap a coat around him, put him on a horse, and bring him to Ainesworth's house, where he'd sat limp as a rag baby while Mrs. Ainesworth and the men had washed and tended to him and put a clean shirt on him.

The worst of the boy's hurts were old ones: scars from beatings across his back and buttocks and legs, scars from something else along his arms and shoulders. Jonathan suppressed a shudder at the thought of so many scars on such a young body, such a young soul. "That boy's been used hard," he said.

"Hard enough to make him do murder?" Chester asked.

"No," Jonathan said, though what, indeed, did he know of the boy? He'd seen him all of twice. Still, he'd seen enough to convince him that the boy had a sense of honor—honor enough to spare an old horse's legs and an old man's pride by deliberately losing the race Jonathan had challenged him to at their first meeting. But even an honorable man would do murder in his own defense. Or someone else's.

"Would he steal a horse?" Chester asked. His wife finished bandaging his left hand. She tugged his sleeve to make him hold out his right.

Jonathan had forgotten about the stolen horse. "Was it a red mare?"

Chester nodded and took in a quick breath as his wife dabbed ointment on his knuckles. "A good-looking one, so I've heard, though I haven't seen her myself. She's still at the blacksmith's. I was going to fetch her in the morning."

"He ran off, then," Jonathan said softly. "Ran off and took the horse with him."

"Maybe not." Mrs. Ainesworth shot a cryptic glance at her husband.

Stiffly, Chester started to rise, but his wife patted his forearm to make him sit back down. "I'll get it, dear," she said. She ruffled her husband's dark, wavy hair and kissed him gently on the forehead before taking a candle and leaving the room. She returned with a bundle of papers.

As he leafed through the papers, Jonathan let out a low whistle. Whatever had freed Daniel from his indenture must have been one step shy of a miracle. "So he's free, then. And the mare belongs to him."

"If those papers are real." Eldad's tone warned Jonathan not to get too hopeful.

Mrs. Ainesworth clicked her tongue impatiently. "That boy's only what? Fifteen? Sixteen? Would he know enough to write them, never mind forge half a dozen different hands?"

"The fella is who he claims, then," Eldad said.

"And no thief, either," Mrs. Ainesworth added, a smug half-smile playing across her lips. She cut another strip of linen and went back to work on Chester's right hand.

"So it seems. But it doesn't mean he can't be a murderer," Chester said.

"That boy's no more a murderer than I am," Jonathan said. "I have a sense about him."

Chester raised an eyebrow. "So did Jacob Fairley." He drew in a breath as his wife tightened the bandage around his finger a little too fiercely.

"Do you really believe Mr. Fairley's tales?" Mrs. Ainesworth's voice was sharp-edged.

Chester sighed. "It doesn't matter what I believe. What matters is the truth and the law. In a couple of days, we'll know whether there's any truth to all this talk of murder." Chester started to run his left hand through his unruly hair, then grimaced and thought better of it. "Then I'll know what the law requires me to do. In the meantime, he might as well stay here."

"If you lock that boy up in some dark hole, you'll have yourself a corpse or a lunatic come morning," Jonathan said.

Chester shook his head. "I should have been less worried about keeping him locked in and more worried about keeping everyone else locked out," he said. "I'll sit watch on the boy, just in case anyone tries to follow Jacob's example." He tried to lift his mug, but his bandaged fingers were too fat and slippery to hold it. "I only hope," he said, staring glumly into his rum, "that tomorrow morning Jacob Fairley feels as bad as I know I will."

Jonathan yawned so wide his jaw popped. He looked enviously at the bed Mrs. Ainesworth had made up for Daniel, then at his own mattress, a well-worn tick flattened with long use, which Chester had dragged down from the attic and laid on the floor. His aching joints regretted the impulse that had prompted him to sit watch over Daniel.

"You wouldn't happen to mind changing places, would you, Dan'l?" Jonathan asked.

The boy lay rigid on the bed, his eyes staring blindly at the ceiling. He'd barely reacted when Jonathan and Chester had carried him upstairs into the Ainesworths' spare bedroom.

"Dan'l?" Jonathan waved a hand in front of the boy's face. "You wouldn't happen to mind at least not looking quite so cadaveraceous, would you?" No response. The peddler sighed and pulled the blanket up to the boy's chin.

A light footstep shuffled in the hallway, and the door creaked open. A pair of curious blue eyes stared up at him. "Billy! What the devil are you doing here?"

"I heard Mr. Taylor say you was over here sitting watch on the murderer. So I come to see. Mrs. Constable told me you was in here."

"How'd you figure out how to get here?"

"I seen Mr. Taylor coming home, so I just followed that same road he'd been on. When I saw Phizzy in the yard here, I knew it was the right house." The blue eyes narrowed accusingly. "You didn't walk him out proper or nothing."

"Poor Phiz, I have treated him some ungrateful." Phizzy should have had a long cooling-out walk, some hot bran mash with molasses, and an apple. But all there'd been time for was a brief stroll around Chester's yard before letting Phizzy join Chester's horse in the little paddock, with a quick promise for better rewards in the morning.

"Mr. and Mrs. Constable was in the yard rowing about who was to tend the horses," Billy said. "She was fair cross with him. He done something to his hands, and she didn't want him fouling them up, and he didn't want her doing his work, and they were both telling the other to go inside and leave the horses to him... or her...only they all was mostly talking at once and all together. Then I come along and put things right." Billy's chest swelled with pride. "So Mr. Constable let me put Phizzy in his barn and put down some hay for him, too."

Jonathan was sure that Billy hadn't taken over the situation quite that handily, but what the storytelling lacked in veracity and finesse, it made up for with enthusiasm. "It's Mr. and Mrs. Ainesworth. And all three of you should'a been in your beds 'stead of messing around with horses this time of night."

"That's what Mrs. Constable said, but she thanked me nicely for helping and gave me a grand piece of cake. See?" Billy tugged a handkerchief from a jacket pocket. A shower of crumbs dribbled to the floor. "I saved some for later."

"Well, you might as well stay."

Billy stared down into Daniel's face. "He don't look over much like a murderer to me."

"And how the devil would you know what a murderer looks like?" Jonathan asked.

"Well, there was Mr. Brundidge, the foreman at the mill, who hit his wife with a—"

Jonathan raised a hand. "I don't want to know."

"He was big and fierce-looking, not all pale and weakish like that one. He's..." Billy took a closer look at Daniel's face. "Mr. S., I think we seen him before somewhere, haven't we?"

"Last July when we were up in Massachusetts. He's Irish, like you."

"Irish, bah," Billy said. "I remember him now. Couldn't speak Gaelic no better'n a pig. What's wrong with him, anyway? Would he be having some kind of a fit or something?" A grubby finger reached out to poke Daniel's face.

Jonathan lunged forward and grabbed Billy's wrist. "Good God, what do you want to do a damn fool thing like that for?"

"I just wanted to see—"

Jonathan tugged Billy away from the bed. "What *I* want to see is you going to bed." He nodded toward the tick on the floor. "You can have that." Every aching joint cursed him for yielding even that small bit of comfort.

"But where will you be sleeping?"

"I got to sit up and watch. Make sure he don't start any trouble." As if that was a worry. Jonathan pushed two chairs together, sitting in one and propping his feet on the other. He stuffed his coat under his backside for a cushion. "Think he'd care for a lulla—" Jonathan started to joke, then planted his feet back on the floor and snapped his fingers. "You want to make yourself useful, Billy, why don't you sing one of them Irish songs of yours? Something pretty that don't have anything sad in it. Something that'll ease him some."

Billy's song filled the room with strange, half-magical words. For the first time since Jonathan had found him, Daniel moved of his own will. He turned his head toward the song, though his eyes were still wide and blank. After a time, he pressed his eyelids shut and his body softened. As Jonathan blew out the candle, Daniel's cheeks glimmered with moisture.

Daniel was in the secret place he'd created inside himself after the fire had taken his home and family, when waking had meant fierce pain outside and worse pain inside; when fevered nightmares had alternated with the blistering sensation that phantom claws peeled the skin from his arms and shoulders and shredded the muscles beneath. Then he'd drifted in a green mist. The mist had set him down as gently as one might set an egg in a bed of straw, then faded away. He saw grass, hills, trees so green he could taste their cool freshness like spring water on his tongue, could feel the green softness between his bare toes. The green sparkled in golden sunlight, and the fire along his skin was only the wind or the sun, and there was no more pain inside, for Ma and Da and Michael were right there with him.

The first time he'd woken from his green secret place, he'd screamed at Mrs. Nye and Dr. Corey for dragging him back, for though the pain on the outside might leave him, the pain on the inside never would.

As he'd healed, he'd taught himself to summon the place at will, finding with each visit a new facet to explore. Sometimes he'd meet heroes like Cúchulainn and Brian Boru, or faeries and silkies and such, come to life from Da's stories. After Daniel tamed Ivy—or rather, Ivy tamed him—she was there too, always waiting for him, always his.

His mother was singing. Her copper hair cascaded loose about her shoulders, her eyes bright and unshadowed. Da was there, too, whistling the same tune as Ma, though her voice and his whistling had never been so melodious before.

Then Daniel was riding Ivy, and though they galloped far and away across the soft green grass, the song never faded from his ears.

For a long time Daniel drifted between the green place and the black, trying not to get trapped in the tunnel of bright white pain that connected the two. Eventually, the tunnel fell away, resolving into walls and floor.

"Dan'l? Dan'l? Son?" A calloused hand tested his forehead.

Staring back at him was a pair of green eyes, heavy-lidded like a wise old turtle's, in a jowly round face—exactly the face he'd been seeking. He'd found them, then: the peddler and his boy, for wasn't that the yellow-haired lad peering over the peddler's shoulder? But what had come between the seeking and the finding? "Sir?" He rubbed his eyes and started to sit up. "I've had such a dream." A torch-lit clearing, men shouting, horses churning up the ground. His own stomach turning inside out until it could turn no more. And…snow? He ran a hand across his throat, felt the raw skin there, saw the bruises on his wrists. "Oh, God. 'Tweren't a dream, then."

"'Fraid not," the peddler said. Daniel heard the clink and slosh of liquid being poured. Something nudged his elbow. "Here, son, this'll settle you some."

Daniel took a sip. He coughed as the rum burned his throat, and he shivered at the pictures forming in his mind. The same calloused hands offering a flask. The smell of melting tar thick and heavy in the air. Feathers swirling around him like drifting snow. He clutched the glass with white knuckles. "I—I fancy I'm in your debt, sir." Each word felt like a throat full of brambles.

The peddler shook his head. "I've only put your trouble off a while, not sent it packing. Do you understand what all this is about? Who that is?" He nodded over his shoulder at a man with dark hair, weary eyes, and bandaged hands.

Daniel nodded. A great lump gathered in his throat, and a greater one in his chest. He rubbed his eyes with the heels of his hands, sucked in a noisy breath, and sat up straighter, facing the peddler and the constable. A muscle in his cheek twitched with the effort of holding himself together.

"They're dead, aren't they? Dead, and it's me own fault." With bleak eyes, he stared past the two men, as if he might see the Lymans' ghosts staring back at him from the shadows. The peddler's lad gaped in wide-eyed fascination. Mr. Stocking invented an errand and dismissed his lad, but Daniel was sure the boy would be back with his ear pressed to the door.

Daniel reached for the rum to fortify himself for his confession. The constable pulled it away and gave him a glass of water instead. "So," the constable began, "you're saying you actually did kill somebody?"

Daniel gulped down some water, then shook his head. "But I might as well have. It was on me own account that Silas defied his da. That must'a been what sent Lyman on such a tear."

"You've lost us, son." Mr. Stocking rummaged in his pockets, pulled out a grubby little notebook and a stub of a pencil. "Why don't you start at the beginning of this tangle, and I'll clerk for Mr. Ainesworth here."

The beginning. And where exactly would that be? The day he'd fetched young Ethan Root to serve his bond at Lyman's? Or maybe six years earlier, with the fire that killed Da and Ma and Michael and left Daniel bound to George Lyman? Or maybe the day he and Ma had stepped off the boat to join Da in America? No, it had all started before he'd been born: the day Da had kissed Ma good-bye and left to seek his fortunes in a new land. That was when it had begun. But surely they didn't want to hear all that, did they?

Mr. Stocking seemed to sense how Daniel's thoughts whirled, for the peddler gave him an encouraging show of horsey teeth and said, "The most recent beginning. The one that got you here."

He'd never had to string so many words together at one go before. He started with the paper he and Ethan had found in Lyman's desk: the paper that proved Lyman had cheated Daniel out of his father's bit of land and the ashes of his tiny house. He told how Lyman's son Silas had learned of the paper, and how it had turned Silas against his father. He told how Silas and Ethan and Lizzie had uncovered the rest of Lyman's thefts, and how Silas had been torn between wanting to make things right and fearing that exposing his father would turn the rest of the family homeless—not just Silas, but his three little sisters and baby brother.

"So he bought your silence," the constable concluded.

"After a fashion, aye. Silas said he'd pay folk back somehow, but he couldn't send his da off to prison, not with all them little ones to care for. Anyway, I got Ivy, and I got me own bond and Ethan's canceled, and that was fair enough for me. But it gave Lyman a turn, having Silas stand against him like that. That must'a set him off—that, and fearing Silas might change his mind."

"Set him off?" the constable repeated.

"It maybe ate at him so that he went mad with it, and then..." Daniel shuddered. "It must'a broke him, don't you see? That's why he killed them."

"And you—you saw him do it?"

"Sweet Jesus, no. I never heard naught of it 'til the day I come here, when the blacksmith said they was all killed and me to blame for it. It's true, only not the way he meant it."

"So this Mr. Lyman and his family were all alive when you left Farmington?" the constable said slowly, more as a statement than a question.

"I swear on me da's soul they were. I know it's hard to believe, but—"

"No, not really," the constable said. "As a matter of fact, it doesn't surprise me a bit."

Chapter Eight

Walter Sackett wasn't in nearly as much of a hurry to return to Chauncey as he'd been to leave. His sense of duty and hope for reward had kept him urging the beast north, but the appeal of his mission had worn thin as quickly as the flesh on his buttocks had. The fastest gait Mr. Fairley's nag could muster was neither trot nor gallop, but combined the worst elements of both with the speed of neither. It had taken only an hour of his backside slamming against the saddle for Walter to regret volunteering. In between pulping Walter's behind, the horse had tried to toss him head over heels, wrench his arms out of their sockets, knock his head against overhanging branches, and scrape his legs against tree trunks and stone walls. Walter had arrived in Farmington feeling bleak, battered, and bruised.

He'd found George Lyman's house only to learn that every single Lyman was safe inside it, not a one of them with so much as a stubbed toe. The younger Mr. Lyman had chuckled over Constable Ainesworth's letter and called out every member of the household to meet Walter and prove their survival. He'd then taken Walter to Farmington's constable and justice of the peace to have them confirm the family's continued existence and the foreigner's legal right to the red mare and all the goods she carried. The sack of provisions, and even the bottle of excellent cider that the Lymans' plump, pretty dairymaid had given Walter for the journey home, had been poor compensation for his disappointment.

Still, the foreigner could yet have been a murderer. All Walter had discovered in Farmington was that the fellow hadn't murdered any Lymans. But after interrogating just about every shopkeeper, miller, farmer, and dairymaid, and after reading every handbill, broadside, and newspaper he could find from Farmington back to Chauncey, Walter had gleaned no information about recent murders that he could attribute to the red-haired stranger.

On the final morning of his journey, Walter traveled the least-trodden paths of Chauncey to reach the constable's house. He knew he'd become the town's laughingstock, but humiliation was the least of his worries. That foreigner wasn't likely to see much humor in having been detained for the better part of a week. Were Walter in the stranger's place, he'd thrash the cause of his misfortune into a bloody pulp.

It was close on noon when Walter reached the constable's house. He slid from the accursed horse's back and, rehearsing his tale in his head, knocked at the door. But all he'd planned to say dissolved to mush when the door opened and Walter looked into the sitting room. There at the constable's table, with the constable's very own wife serving him a slice of meat pie, was that red-haired, shifty-eyed foreigner.

The dew-soaked grass chilled Daniel's bare feet. Patches of morning mist settled in the hollows, giving the pasture an eerie, dreamlike quality. A pulse moved through the earth and up through his body. It quickened and grew from a vibration to a sound, drumming in his ears. He turned toward it, arms outstretched to greet the mare. She whinnied and reared, inches from running him down, then bounded circles around him, kicking up her heels like an unbroken filly. Daniel lunged toward her, sent her whirling away, then backed off and let her chase after him. He skipped aside and let her pass, retreated and let her lead the game. He spun himself dizzy, feinting one way and another in a wild dance. Her hooves beat the rhythm and birdsongs served as the chorus for the teasing game of catch-me-if-you-can that was their morning ritual.

Closer and closer she circled him, near enough to touch. He caught a handful of coarse mane, and in a moment was on her back, hugging her with legs and arms, laying his face along her neck and breathing in the sweet, dusty smell of her. He settled into her canter, the rhythm of her body easing his soul, reassuring him that she was safely his.

He rode until the sun burned the dew from the grass, and the rumbles in his stomach and Ivy's drove them toward the constable's house for morning chores and breakfast. He walked her to cool her down, heat rising from her body in steamy wisps.

Releasing her into the barnyard, he groaned when the first thing she did was roll in the dust, grunting happily as she ground the dirt into her sweaty hide. "Don't be doing that, love," he said, though he laughed as she rose and shook herself, showering him in dust, sweat, and slobber. Her lips quested against his pockets for a treat. Her breath warmed his fingers, her muzzle velvet soft against his calloused palm. With the other hand he stirred up the dirt that clouded her neck. "You look a fright. We can't be having that." She pressed her nose against his chest and made a rumbling noise that vibrated deep into his heart.

"Hate to misillusion you, son, but her looking a fright is exactly what you want." The peddler was perched on the top fence rail as if he'd conjured himself there.

Daniel's face grew hot. How long had the peddler been watching? The mare twitched her ears forward and greeted the little man with a cheerful whinny.

Mr. Stocking smiled, a peculiar combination of horsey teeth and turtle-like eyes. "Sorry, there, darling, but vanity'll cost you and your Irish prince awful dear in this world."

"Vanity?" Daniel raised an eyebrow. The only reason a lass would look him over more than once would be to find something new to laugh at. "That's one sin I don't fancy I'm likely to fall into." He fetched a coarse brush from the barn and began working the dust out of the mare's coat.

"A man ain't always vain for his own sake."

Daniel's hands followed the slope of muscle down Ivy's neck, tracing the graceful arc that disguised the strength underneath. "Ah, well, any man'd be vain of such a grand lass."

"Maybe any man could afford to be. But not you."

Daniel swirled the brush lightly over the bony points of Ivy's withers. "I'm not such a dab hand at riddling, sir. Why don't you just tell me plain what you're about?"

"I'm about peddling just now. It's a trade that can learn you quite a bit about human nature." The peddler pried a sliver from the fence rail and picked his teeth with it. "You know what makes a good peddler?"

Daniel shrugged. "Sharp talk and fast dealing, I s'pose."

Mr. Stocking shook his head. "You got to anticipate people's expectations. A boy like you, traveling on your own, can't afford to give 'em any surprises."

"Could you p'raps be a bit plainer?"

Mr. Stocking pushed his hat back, the sun winking off his glasses. "It's not me that needs to be plainer, but you." He pointed a stubby finger at Ivy. "And her."

"She'll no more be plain than I'll be an Irish prince."

The peddler shook his head. "Then you'll have trouble wherever you go."

"Trouble," Daniel repeated, the word sitting in his throat like a lump. "I thought I was done being knocked about after I left Lyman's." Mr. Stocking and the blacksmith's lad had cleared his name in Chauncey, but what about the next town and the next after that?

"I'm afraid the likes of you and me ain't never done being knocked about, son."

"Don't we never get to do any of the knocking?"

"Chester tells me he gave you the chance to knock back, but you didn't take it."

The constable had spent the better part of a morning explaining how Daniel could bring charges against the blacksmith and the other men. "Aye, well, I'd have to stay here and see it out, now, wouldn't I? And who knows how long that'd take?" Daniel said. He wasn't sure which weighed on him more: the prospect of trying to convince a justice of the peace or a court to take the side of an Irishman, or the idea that he'd be setting the Aines-worths against their neighbors. The constable and his wife had been more than kind; they'd even offered Daniel a job on their farm, but he couldn't see staying in Chauncey, daily facing the blacksmith and his friends.

The peddler leaned forward, elbows on his knees. "I got some heartless things to learn you, if you want to get by." He nodded toward Ivy. "You got to give up your idea of what she ought to be, just for a bit, anyway. And you got to make yourself what people expect you to be." He chewed the end of his toothpick thoughtfully.

"I tried to look a gentleman, and they thought me a thief, never mind all them papers Silas give me."

Mr. Stocking pointed the sliver at Daniel. "There's your mis-take. You wear your old clothes, let the mare go ragged, ride her bareback with a rope halter, and all folks'll see is a farm boy and his nag. But put on your best duds and slick up your horse, and they'll see a boy with fine things he's got no right to. Once you open your mouth and let some of that Irish talk out—"

"—I'm a thief." Daniel turned away from the peddler and scratched Ivy's ears. He couldn't let her coat go shaggy and her tail and mane full of burrs, let her be less than perfect.

"I'm not saying you should be neglectful, son." The peddler came down from the fence and stood by his side. The little man pulled a scrap of biscuit from his pocket and let Ivy nibble it. "Just put her light under a bushel for a little while." He brushed his hands off on the seat of his trousers. "Anyway, no point gathering troubles. Your name's cleared, you got a fine horse to ride and the world ahead of you."

Daniel pressed his lips together, taking a long time to respond. "Aye, the whole world, and I haven't a clue what to do with it. All me life I've known naught but to obey orders. Now I'm free to be me own man, and I scarce know where to begin, or how."

The peddler smiled and held out his hand. "You can try beginning with us."

Daniel stared down at the offered hand.

"I don't s'pose it was happenstance brought you here, was it, son?"

Daniel squirmed and ducked the peddler's gaze. "I—well, I remembered you telling Ethan you had kin down here. I wanted to ask you about—about heading west."

Mr. Stocking squinted into the sun. He licked his finger and held it up as if to test the wind. "West...hmmm...I think it's... that way." He pointed in a vaguely northeasterly direction.

Daniel bit back a snappish retort when he noticed a corner of the peddler's mouth twitch.

Mr. Stocking clapped Daniel on the shoulder. "No, I didn't s'pose you trailed me all the way down here to ask me what the sun could tell you. Me and Billy still got a fair bit of peddling to do before winter sets in. We'll be leaving next week, after we replenish our stocks and settle accounts with Eldad. You're welcome to come along."

"I don't know naught about peddling," Daniel protested, but he already imagined riding alongside the peddler's cart, and the idea stirred something warm and homey inside him.

"Don't worry, son. We'll make sure you pull your weight."

We. Aye, there was the peddler's lad to consider. The peddler's lad who'd mocked Daniel's Irish. Since waking in the constable's house, Daniel had seen the lad often, but the yellow-haired boy kept his distance, staring at Daniel as if he were an animal in a menagerie. "Your lad'll not be minding, then?"

The peddler chuckled. "Well, it depends on what you mean by minding."

"How *could* you?" Billy's face was crimson. "You didn't even ask me!"

Jonathan bit his lip against a smile and pretended that Phizzy's hooves needed tending. "I seem to recollect that this is my goods, my horse, and my wagon. Seems to me I'm the one gets to say who can ride with me." He peeked discreetly around his shoulder.

With arms crossed, Billy stamped a foot. "He can't come with us. He can't!"

Jonathan moved to Phizzy's hind foot and took his time about studying it. "Seems damned uncharitable of you. The boy could use some company, just like you did once."

"He has a horse. He has his own goods. He don't need us and we don't need him."

"You don't have to fret about Dan'l taking your spot. He can't sing to save his life."

Billy's lower lip jutted out. "He'll ruin everything!" The *everything* was nearly a wail.

Jonathan straightened slowly, feeling his bad knee pop as he eased it into place. "I thought you'd be pleased to have a young fella around to liven things up a bit. Somebody who talks Irish, just like you."

Billy spat out something in that self-same Irish—something Jonathan was pretty sure was a curse. "He talks Irish no better'n a pig. He'll learn you all wrong."

"That ain't why I asked him to come."

Billy hugged Phizzy's muzzle. "We don't need him. Everything's perfect just the way it is." Billy made Phizzy bob his head in agreement.

Perfect. Traipsing around the countryside with a broken-down old fool and a broken-down old horse, not knowing where you'll sleep or eat next? Stay here at Sophie's another week or two, then you'll know what perfect is, friend. Jonathan laid one hand on the gelding's neck and the other on Billy's head, tousling the yellow curls. "No, we don't need him, that's true. But maybe he needs us."

Billy jerked away. "I don't care!"

"What are you afraid of?" Jonathan asked.

"He'll be stupid and rude and nosy. You'll tell him...things."

Jonathan shook his head. "I don't break my promises. He won't be learning your secrets from me."

"Excuse me, ma'am?"

Sophie started, nearly dropping her book. One hand to her breast, she turned to face the boy standing in the parlor doorway. "Goodness, Billy, you made me jump!"

"I'm sorry, ma'am. I only come to ask you a bit of a favor." Billy tugged at his forelock. "I'm needing me hair cut, if you wouldn't be minding." He pulled the curl straight so that it came down past the end of his nose. "Short like this, see?" He combed his fingers through his hair and stopped with his hand barely a quarter inch above his scalp.

"Cut all your lovely—" Sophie bit off her intended lament over the loss of Billy's curls. Cooing over the child's hair would only make him want to be rid of it all the more. "All right."

After she had settled him in a chair with one of her aprons draped about his shoulders, she put her book in his lap. "Here," she said. "You can read to me while I work."

Billy carefully sounded out the title. "*O-liv-er Too-wist. Twist....* But why?"

"Why what?" Sophie combed out a tangle at the nape of Billy's neck.

"Why does he twist?"

"It's his name, you goose. The boy in the book."

Billy opened the book and stared at it for a long time.

"I know it's hard starting in the middle," Sophie said. "I'll tell you the beginning later, if you like."

"I wanted to be looking it over a bit first." Billy glanced over his shoulder at the growing pile of hair. "Are we almost done?" he asked.

"Not even half finished." Sophie planted a hand on top of the boy's head and made him turn back to the book. "You don't have to like it. Just read it."

With a defeated sigh, Billy began, sounding out each word letter by letter. It was excruciating to listen to, like watching a wounded bird flutter and fall back to earth over and over again.

Sophie set down her scissors and comb and knelt on the floor in front of the boy. She tipped Billy's chin so he had to look her in the eye. "How old are you, child?"

"Twelve," he said. "No, thirteen." He pulled himself straighter, but his eyes darted away from Sophie's.

Twelve, most likely, or maybe eleven, if the boy knew at all, Sophie decided. "What schooling have you had?"

"I know I'm a bit slow at the reading, but I'm getting better, really I am. Mr. S. is learning me," Billy said brightly.

"Learning," Sophie repeated. "And what sort of grammar do you have?"

Billy wrinkled his nose. "I never knew me grammar. I s'pose she'd be living in Ireland, if she's still living at all."

"I mean what sort of book is he 'learning' you from?"

"He started with the Bible, but we hadn't got very far into it when he said there's stories in there not fit for young folks' eyes. So he mostly learns me from these." Billy pulled a wad of crumpled papers from his pocket.

Sophie smoothed out the faded advertisements for horses and cookstoves and patent medicines, menageries and traveling acrobats and conjurers. "No books at all?"

"Sometimes. But just as soon as we get to reading one, someone'll be wanting to buy it, so I'm forever missing how the story ends. Mr. S., he's a lovely reader, he is. He can play all the parts while he's reading, just like he was in a show."

Sophie gritted her teeth. "I'm sure he can." She closed her book and laid it on the table. "Never mind. I'll tell you the story. And then tonight we can read some of it together." She went back to work, snipping until there seemed to be enough hair on the floor to stuff a bolster. "There." She handed Billy a mirror. "You look like a proper little man now." The boy winced.

With his hair cut nearly to his scalp, the boy could have passed for thirteen, so long as he didn't stand up and reveal how slight his frame was. Yet at the same time, the exposure of his forehead and ears and cheeks and neck made him seem vulnerable as a newly shorn lamb.

Billy grinned up at her. "Aye, that's grand. Thank you, ma'am."

"Soph, where're you hiding my—" Jonny stopped dead in the kitchen doorway. "For God's sake, woman, what have you done to his hair?"

"I cut it." There was a little more acid in her voice than she'd intended.

"Cut it? Damn it all, you scalped the poor boy!"

"She done a grand job, ain't she, Mr. S?" Billy said. There was a little too much bright innocence in his voice, causing Sophie to wonder if there was more to the haircut than a little boy's wish to look grown up.

"Folks'll think he's got lice. Now, Soph—"

"Now, Jonny," Sophie said, her protest quelling her cousin's. "We need to have a talk about this boy's education." She waved her scissors threateningly under Jonny's nose. "Or, rather, the lack of it."

Jonny deflated like a punctured balloon. "Um," he said. He studied Billy's haircut again. "Very nice. A handsome haircut, very fine indeed."

Chapter Nine

Daniel slapped at a mosquito and wiped the sweat out of his eyes. Whose daft idea had it been to send him and Billy off collecting fox grapes? Ah, yes, the bloody peddler, probably so he and the Taylors and the Ainesworths could have some privacy to decide Daniel's future for him. He stopped short, a bunch of fat grapes warm and heavy in his hand. Mr. Stocking and his friends had proven their good will, and here he was full of ungrateful suspicious thoughts. Maybe the only reason they'd sent him and Billy out was that the ladies really did need to do their jelly making, and perhaps Mr. Stocking only wanted to give the lads a go at learning to be sociable together. But how did one do that?

Billy hacked at the vines as if he hoped to draw blood, and there wasn't much doubt whose blood the lad wanted. Ever since Mr. Stocking had invited Daniel to join them, Billy had done nothing but scowl and cast venomous looks at him.

Daniel took a breath—as much as he could, with the humid air clinging around his face like a steamy damp towel. All they wanted was for him to say a few friendly words and put the lad at ease. It wasn't very much, was it? But he'd no clue how to knit together the little chains of pleasantries that normal folk called conversation, never mind how to spark a friendship. He thought of how young Ethan had befriended him at Lyman's. Ethan had been the one always speaking first, with his endless questions. All right then. He'd start with a question that wouldn't get the lad's back up.

The sweet, sticky aroma of the ripe grapes hung heavy in the air. He could already taste the fruit's promise, and licked his lips in anticipation. So he said, "Won't Mrs. Ainesworth be pleased? She can make barrels of jelly now."

"Barrels?" Billy looked at the wheelbarrow mounded high with bunches of grapes. He wrinkled his nose, as if the fruit wouldn't fill a thimble with jelly. "She'll not be half as pleased to be cooking 'em as we are to be picking 'em."

Daniel wasn't sure whether this was progress or not. It was, at least, more than two words from the other boy's mouth, even if they were hostile words. "Whyever wouldn't she be pleased? She likes to cook, don't she?"

"And I fancy you like doing everything you're s'posed to, now?" It was a good thing the grapes were destined for jelly, for Billy flung them into the wheelbarrow as though trying to pulp the fruit right then and there.

"Work ain't about liking or not liking. It's only about doing," Daniel said. "And anyway, it'd hardly be natural for a lady not to like cooking and such."

Billy grunted. "I'd rather be spending a week picking grapes or cutting hay than an hour tending a mess of kettles in a kitchen."

Daniel couldn't see that tending a pot of jam was any work at all compared to wrestling grapes from a tangle of saplings and vines on a sweltering day that felt more like July than September, all the while watching for poison ivy and plagued by mosquitoes.

Billy stomped off through the underbrush, cursing Daniel for an idiot and a lot of other things that Daniel couldn't catch, except that hearing them reminded him how much his Gaelic was slipping away, no matter how often he practiced it with Ivy.

"Aye, and the same to you, you foul-tempered little wretch," Daniel muttered. He flung himself down on the pond's bank, cooling his feet in the soft mud. Lifting his cap, he raked a hand through his sweaty hair. He picked up a stone and hurled it toward the opposite bank. It fell short and plunked beneath the murky water. "Dammitall," he muttered as he tossed his cap and cravat aside and shrugged off his suspenders.

"What're you doing?" Billy asked. Trousers rolled to his knees, he stood in the shallows a dozen yards away, poking a stick at something in the water.

"I'm having meself a swim." Perhaps it would clear his head. "Come on, if you like." He stepped out of his trousers and kicked them aside.

"I can't—I don't—" Billy backed out of the water.

"I'll teach you." Daniel yanked his shirt over his head. Perhaps a swimming lesson might soften the lad. He waded out, slowing as the water lapped to his knees, then his thighs. He turned to encourage the other boy in, and found Billy staring at him.

Billy's lips clamped shut tight, and his eyes were wide and darting anywhere but at Daniel.

It must have been the scars: the pale stripes and splotches marring his arms and shoulders like spilled paint, standing up in ridges and puckers where the burns had healed badly. He ran his fingers along one long scar. "'T'ain't nothing." He swallowed hard, trying to bring the words without the memories. "Was a fire is all. When I was small—"

Billy glanced up, then just as quickly ducked his head, crimson spreading from his forehead to his collar. He wrapped his arms around himself, clutching at his shirt as if he feared that Daniel would come and snatch it away. Daniel realized it wasn't his arms that the boy was staring at after all. A flash of revelation made him sit down in the pond, his own face burning even though the chilly water reached to his chin.

"Sweet Jesus!" he blurted out as Billy turned and ran away.

Jonathan shoved the map aside. "No, Eldad, I had my fill of peddling down south." He loosened his collar and glanced out the parlor window, which overlooked the surrounding hills, red and yellow just beginning to splash across the green slopes. Although it felt as though summer were back to stay, frost wasn't far off. "I'd rather get my shivers from the cold than from the things I seen down there." He pulled another map from the pile. "What about this Berkshire route? Who's working that one?"

Eldad glanced out the window. "Well, there's—uh, oh." A mischievous grin lit his face. "Send 'em off to pick grapes, that'll make friends of 'em, isn't that what you and Sophie said?"

"Something like that." Jonathan rose from his seat to follow Eldad's gaze.

"Well, only one of 'em's come back, looking kind of soggy and none too friendly." Eldad's blue eyes crinkled with merriment. "Drowned the other one, no doubt."

With a silent curse, Jonathan squinted at the lone figure trudging behind the wheelbarrow. The sour look on Daniel's face made it clear that the afternoon had been a failure. Jonathan had no doubt Billy was to blame. "That little devil," he said as he headed for the door.

As Daniel drew nearer, Jonathan's mind was already whirring with how to smooth things over and try again. "Billy give you a ducking?" he asked.

Daniel dropped the wheelbarrow's handles and thumbed his cap back. "I went for a swim," he said, his voice sharp as broken glass.

An uneasy knot gathered in Jonathan's stomach. "And what about Billy?"

"Run off the minute I dropped me trousers." The boy's eyes were dark with accusation. "Don't s'pose you'd be knowing why, now, would you?"

"Billy ain't too easy around the water." Jonathan cocked his head so the sun was in his eyes. With the light reflecting off his spectacles, maybe the boy wouldn't be able to read his face.

"No, I don't fancy *she* is." Daniel's eyes pinned him hard. "How long have you known?"

"She? Well, uh—" Jonathan began to reach into his bag of peddler's bluff and bluster, then stopped himself. He owed this boy the truth. "Pretty soon after I'd bought off his—her—dammit—*her* daddy. Now look, you've got me thinking about it just when I'd schooled myself to stop."

"Thinking about what?"

"About Billy being a girl."

"How can you not be thinking about it?"

"I can't afford to if I don't want folks catching on. The key to a good performance ain't keeping them convinced." Jonathan gestured at an imaginary audience. "It's keeping yourself convinced." He stabbed a finger at Daniel's chest. "The minute you stop believing you're King Lear and start remembering you're Sam Slick from Podunk, you're doomed."

"This ain't no play."

"No, it ain't. The minute she forgets she's William James Michael Fogarty—the minute I forget it—some constable or overseer of the poor'll be snatching her away."

"At least she'd be brung up like a proper girl."

"She'd be brung up by her father." Jonathan spat a wet, brown stream that splatted hard onto a stone. "Or by nobody, which'd be a damn sight better." He gestured for Daniel to follow him into the cool dimness of the barn. After finding a pair of milking stools, he settled himself into a shadowy corner. "Sit down, son. I got a story to tell you."

Chapter Ten

May 1839, Springfield, Massachusetts

"Hey, Jonny! Somebody's stealing your horse!"

It had to be a joke. What horse thief in his right mind would steal a nag as slack-jointed and swaybacked as Phizzy? Jonathan crossed the smoke-filled taproom and looked out the window. His wagon was there, the shafts empty. He rushed outside. Damn it all, wasn't it that same scrawny boy with the black eye who'd tried to pick his pocket that morning? But the joke was on the boy this time. He'd unfastened the harness and climbed onto Phizzy's back, but that was as far as he'd gotten. He flapped the reins, and his bony heels thumped away at Phizzy's sides with about as much effect as raindrops. The gelding looked over his shoulder at Jonathan with sleepy annoyance, as if asking his master to rid him of a pesky deerfly.

The men who'd spilled out of the tavern guffawed and commenced betting on how the escapade would conclude. The boy tried to jump down and flee, but one of the long reins looped around his ankle and snared him. Jonathan grabbed a handful of the child's trousers and shirt and hauled him upright. "Going somewhere?"

The boy exploded into a wildcat of fists and feet and nails and teeth, spitting out curses in some heathenish language. An elbow sent Jonathan's spectacles flying, and the street blurred into blotches of brown and gray and black. Then the boy was gone, though his curses still rang in the air, and the the crowd's laughter grew louder.

A hand caught Jonathan's sleeve, and someone pressed his spectacles into his hands. He muttered his thanks and set the glasses back on his nose.

A small, wiry man held the boy, cursing him in the same pagan tongue. He slapped the boy so hard that Jonathan expected the child's neck to snap. But the boy gave as good as he got until the man clenched his hands into fists. A blow to the boy's midsection left him doubled up on the ground, the wind knocked out of him. The man threw the boy up against a fence, snatched a stick from the gutter, and began laying it across the boy's shoulders and backside.

Jonathan grabbed the man's wrist before it could land another blow. The boy tumbled limply to the ground. "Is this your boy?" Jonathan asked.

"Me boy?" The man looked confused, glancing from the peddler to the lad. Then he chuckled. "Aye, me boy," he said, an Irish brogue tinting his voice. "Unless his mam was lying to me." He pinned the boy back up against the fence.

"Hold on just a minute, before you beat all the profit out of him."

"Profit, huh? I'll be thanking you not to interfere." The stick cracked down on the boy's back again. The boy's stillness unnerved Jonathan more than his curses had.

"I'll give you fifty dollars for him." Good God, had those words come out of his mouth? Fifty dollars? Nearly a month's profits—a month of dusty travel and sore throats and buggy beds. Two months' pay for a man like the boy's father.

"You think I'd be selling me own flesh and blood like I was selling a dog?"

"Not selling. Hiring him out. He learns a trade, you get some money, I get a helper."

"Mind your own affairs." The boy's father raised the stick again.

"A hundred." The men around fell silent, their wagering momentarily stopped.

The man let the boy fall to the ground. "You'd never."

Jonathan pulled his pocketbook out, fanned his thumb across an assortment of banknotes. "A hundred. I'll give you a hundred for him."

Jonathan could see the calculations working behind the man's eyes. The man rubbed a sleeve across his mouth before he spoke. "Five."

Five hundred? He didn't have that even if he threw in the horse, wagon, and unsold goods. "One twenty-five."

"Four."

"One fifty."

They settled on two hundred. Jonathan cursed himself for a fool as he counted out the coins and banknotes. Four months' profits for something that looked like a pile of filthy rags and greasy hair crumpled in the gutter. "There you go, my friend. Now let's go inside and have a drink while we draw up the papers."

The man stuffed the money into his pockets. "I'm not signing no papers."

"Your word then. Give me your word you got no more claim to him."

A chuckle gurgled in the man's throat. "Aye, you can have him and welcome, for what he's worth." The man thrust out a grimy hand.

It was hard not to wipe his palms on his trousers after shaking the Irishman's hand. Harder still not to slap the barely suppressed grin from the man's face.

What sort of devilish deal had he made? The boy was probably a half-wit. He knelt and turned the boy over. The child was filthy and bloody at nose and mouth. Jonathan pulled out his handkerchief and wiped the boy's face.

"What in blazes are you going to do with him?" Jeremy Warriner, the tavern-keeper, asked.

"I'll figure it out after he's done puking."

"I'm not—" The boy gasped as his breath returned, then he promptly turned his stomach inside out in the gutter.

Jonathan wiped the boy's mouth and helped him to his feet. He felt like being sick himself as he led the boy into the tavern. "You got a private room free, Jerry?"

Jerry nodded and jerked a thumb toward the stairs. "Second right."

"And a tub and some soap and hot water. And something to eat that'll lie easy on his stomach." Private rooms and baths and a nearly empty purse. Oh, yes, Jonathan had no doubt who was the half-wit here.

He half dragged, half carried the boy up the stairs, amazed at how little he weighed and how close to the skin his bones sat. He dropped the boy into a chair, then stood with his back against the door while the boy stared about, wary as a cornered fox. The purple bruise around his left eye gave him a comically fierce look. Jerry dragged a tub into the room. Next came a parade of Jerry's nieces and hired girls with kettles of hot and pitchers of cold water, soap and towels, a plate of bread and jam, and a mug of gingery-smelling tea. The boy's nose twitched, and his eyes followed the plate as the girl placed it on a table near the bed. He rose to follow it, but Jonathan stopped him with a hand on his shoulder.

"Bath first, then eat."

The boy stared at the tub in horror. No doubt it'd be the first bath of his life. He pulled his knees to his chest and shook his head. "I'll not be having no bath."

"Look, son, I'm going to have to share my seat on the wagon with you, share my meals with you, and share my bed with you. I don't want to be sharing your bugs, too."

"I got no bugs." A louse put the lie to that statement by crawling across the boy's cheek. He pinched it dead and wiped it on his trousers.

Jonathan laid his coat and vest on the bed and rolled up his sleeves. "Either take your bath or I'll give it to you. You ain't in much shape to argue the matter."

"I know how to wash."

"Sure couldn't tell from looking at you." Jonathan tossed the cake of soap to the boy. "Why don't you show me, then?"

"What, with you standing there?"

"I may be fool enough to buy you, but I sure ain't fool enough to leave you alone."

Grudgingly, the boy limped toward the tub. He gave the water a baleful look and swirled a hand around in it. He scooped some up and splashed it on his face.

"Bath." Jonathan said. He tucked one sleeve up a little farther and flexed his arm.

"All right, all right." The boy turned away and peeled off his shirt, then wrapped his arms around himself as if he were cold.

Jonathan clenched his teeth to keep from crying out at the sight of the boy's back, so scrawny that his shoulder blades stood out like wings folded along either side of his knobby spine. He'd never seen bruises piled up on bruises that way. "Trousers, too."

The boy winced. "Couldn't you at least be turning your back?"

"Couldn't you at least be not taking me for a fool?" Jonathan mimicked the boy's Irish brogue, hardening his voice to quell the sick feeling in his throat. "You got nothing I ain't already seen. If you're shy about the size of your parts, don't worry. They'll grow."

The boy's neck turned red under the grime.

"You are a wonder, son. Ten minutes ago you were trying to murder me, and now you're acting like you was brung up genteel as a gir—" The word turned into a choking growl as the boy looked over his shoulder, red-cheeked in dismay and horror. Jonathan ran a hand down his face. "No. Please tell me you ain't a girl."

The child stood in silence for a long moment. "Did you really give me da two hundred dollars for me?"

Jonathan nodded.

The girl stooped to fetch her shirt. "S'pose you'll be wanting it back, then."

What in blazes was he supposed to do with a girl? Jonathan wondered, as the child crammed yet another hunk of bread and jam into her mouth. Not that there was much of a girl about her, in spite of her mop of unruly, haphazardly cut curls. She looked as though she'd taken a kitchen knife to her hair. She'd cut it nearly to her scalp in the back, where it was drying into little lamb's wool swirls, while the top was a tangle thick enough to house a colony of squirrels. She'd missed one lock entirely, and it hung down behind her ear, dripping a wet spot on the shirt Jonathan had given her to wear while her newly laundered clothes dried. It was a good thing the shirt covered her nearly to her ankles, for she didn't sit like any proper girl. She slouched in the chair, straddled it, perched on the edge with her feet tucked under her, kicked one leg back and forth, did everything except sit still.

She was rapidly returning her freshly washed face to its former grimy state. A pale smear of butter and bread crumbs decorated one cheek, and her mouth was surrounded with a bright red O of jam that oozed down her chin. She raised her hand to swipe the jam off with her sleeve.

"Oh, no, you don't." Jonathan captured her wrist just in time. "That's my only clean shirt." He snatched a cloth from the tray and dropped it in her lap. "You travel with me, you got to be clean and civilized." God, how would he travel with her? A boy could be a son or nephew or apprentice. But a girl...He couldn't begin to number all the complications that would entail.

She stared at the cloth for a moment. Jonathan drew his eyebrows together in warning. Seeing the wisdom of serviette over sleeve, she wiped her mouth. She frowned at the glob of jam that came away on the cloth, then licked it off.

"You got a name?" he asked.

She drew herself up straight in her chair and recited as if in school: "William James Michael Fogarty."

"William. James. Michael. Fogarty," he repeated slowly. "That's your name, huh?"

"'Tis now." She pulled a mug of ginger tea toward her and spooned sugar into it.

Jonathan put his hand over the sugar bowl after the fourth spoonful. "How 'bout if I just call you Billy?"

Her spoon clackety-clackety-clacked against the mug as she stirred the sugar in. "I s'pose." Leaning close to the table, she slurped her tea noisily without lifting the mug.

"Mister Jonathan Stocking," he said, pointing to himself. "You can call me sir. How old are you?"

"Thirteen." A damn lie if ever there was one.

"Ten," he said, guessing low in the hope that it would shame the truth out of her.

"All right, then. Twelve." She tore off another hunk of bread. "Next month."

Jonathan smiled.

"Why you done it?" she asked around a mouthful of bread and jam, spraying crumbs as she spoke. "Bought me, I mean."

"Damned if I know. Why'd you pick my horse to steal?"

She shrugged. "He has a nice face."

Much as he loved the old boy, Phizzy was flat out the ugliest horse Jonathan had ever seen. But she was right about his face; there'd always been a gentle sweetness in his eyes.

"And—" She fidgeted about, as restless as any boy, and sat back down heavily, nearly upsetting the table with her elbow. "And because he was the only one as would talk to me."

Jonathan pressed his lips together to hold the laughter in. "Yes, well, he's good that way," he began, wanting her to know that he wasn't just humoring her, that he thought it was important, too. "So, um, what... what did he say?"

Her eyes met his, wide and blue and still astonished at whatever had happened between herself and Phizzy, her battered face the most childlike he'd seen it all afternoon. "He said yes."

"Yes," Jonathan repeated softly.

The girl stared defiantly back at him, challenging him to doubt her.

He removed his spectacles, letting the child dissolve into a faceless blur of white shirt and yellow hair. Twenty-five years, he thought. No, more. More than twenty-five years and still that spring morning was sharp and clear in his head. That day he'd stood with his head pressed against Blossom's rump, his arm up to his shoulder in her womb, his nose filled with the stench of manure and blood, and not entirely sure how much of the sweat and fear he smelled was the mare's and how much his own. He remembered groping around in the hot, wet dark of her, trying to turn the colt who wouldn't come. But gradually he'd found nose and legs and shoulder, eased the colt around so slowly it felt as though morning, afternoon, and night passed while he worked.

Then Blossom gave a mighty heave, and Jonathan was flat on his back on the floor, certain that he'd killed mare and colt and himself in the deluge of blood and slime that washed over him, certain that if the hot, reeking fluid didn't smother him, the writhing weight on his chest would crush him to death. He spat and rubbed his sleeve across his face to clear his eyes and nose and mouth. The thing pinning him down looked like a creature dredged up from the depths of the sea, covered in a glistening membrane. Blossom's huge pink tongue descended on the thing, and a bedraggled, damp head emerged. The colt snorted in his face, then blinked sleepily at him. He and the colt stared at each other in breathless wonder. Then the colt touched his forehead with its nose and claimed him for its own. Yes. Jonathan had heard it as clearly as if the colt had spoken. You're the one for me. And Jonathan's heart had answered with the self-same words.

And the damn fool beast had been saying it ever since, more than twenty-five years now. Jonathan smiled and wiped his eyes before putting *his spectacles back on. The girl stared solemnly back at him. Her frown deepened, bracing for his mockery.*

"He said yes, eh? Now ain't that funny?" he said. "First time I met him, he said that exact same thing to me."

"…and it's been me and Billy and Phizzy ever since," Jonathan said. "I know less about being a daddy than Phizzy does, but I'm a better father to her than Hugh Fogarty ever was."

"But it's a son you're making of her, not a daughter." Daniel said. "Don't you even know her true name?"

Jonathan shook his head. "It's Billy she wants to be and Billy she'll stay until it don't suit her no more."

"It just ain't right, her going 'round with a peddler and singing for her supper like a trained canary. What sort'a life is that for a lass?"

A pretty sorry one, Jonathan thought, but that wasn't the point. "It was all right when you thought she was a boy."

"That's different."

"Which would you rather do? Spend your days cooking and cleaning and sewing for a pack of unthankful men, or travel around the wide world with a coupl'a fine horses and a coupl'a fine fellas such as us?" He spread his arms and swelled out his chest.

Daniel squirmed. "That ain't a fair question. I'm not a lass."

"So a girl can't hanker to go adventuring, same as a boy can?"

"But lasses are…well, different. It's unnatural. 'Tisn't the way things're s'posed to be."

Jonathan's voice turned serious. "Son, the way things're s'posed to be is, you're s'posed to spend another five years slaving away for your Mr. Lyman, and maybe another ten slaving away for somebody else before you scrape together enough money for a little shack and an acre or two of rocks and swamp. But here you are with a fine horse, a pack of goods, and a full purse. The way it's s'posed to be is, she keeps house for her daddy and her brothers until they wear her down with work and beatings." Daniel winced and looked down at his feet. Good, Jonathan thought. He was getting through to the boy, making Daniel understand that he and Billy were cut from the same threadbare cloth. "If she's lucky, maybe her father won't kill her, and she can escape to a husband who'll wear her down with work and babies. And if she's very lucky, maybe he won't beat her. As a boy, she's safe."

Daniel chewed his lower lip and scuffed his feet in the dirt. "And what happens when she can't be playing the boy no longer?"

"I've been thinking on that, believe me."

Daniel apparently had been, too. "Your cousin seems a motherly type," he said.

"You think so?" Jonathan asked.

"She could do worse," Daniel suggested.

"Billy or Sophie?"

Daniel peered more closely at Jonathan's face. "You been playing games with me, ain't you? You been planning to leave her here all along." He threw his hands up in disgust. "It's all games with you. Peddler's games and tricks, ain't it? Why ain't you just told 'em straight out?"

"These things take time. Sophie's won Billy's stomach already. Another day or two, she'll have her heart." The peddler took his spectacles off and wiped them on his vest.

Daniel snorted. "If all it took was good eating to win someone's heart, I'd still be back to Lyman's."

"That's why it's lucky you came along. Billy's been spitting nails over my asking you to travel with me. The more she hates me, the more she'll want to stay with Sophie."

"So when exactly do you figure on talking to your cousin?"

Jonathan forced himself to laugh. "I'll burn that bridge when I get to it." But all he could think of right now was how setting off that fire would leave him on the wrong side of a wide, lonely chasm.

Chapter Eleven

Tuesday, September 10, 1839, Cabotville, Massachusetts

"Dead," Liam said, his face gray with sickness and exhaustion. He pulled the blanket over the two lads' faces.

Hugh Fogarty clutched the wall to steady himself. "Both?" He stumbled forward and dropped to his knees by the mattress. The shock of his landing scattered the fuzzy cloud of drunken numbness that had fogged his brain. His hand hovered over the blanket, but he couldn't bring himself to touch it.

Liam rose and stepped aside. "Aye, and where have you been hiding yourself all this time, whilst they were dying, eh?" He swayed over his father, little better than a walking corpse, clothes hanging from his fever-wasted body, eyes bloodshot from wakefulness, sickness, and weeping. Eighteen years old and nearly a man grown, Liam had been broad-shouldered and strong when Hugh had last seen him a few weeks ago. Now it would take but a breath to tumble him.

"You know I've no stomach for illness, Liam," Hugh said. Even now he had to lean away from the stench of sweat, soiled linens, brimming chamber pots. He wanted to take out his pipe to mask the reek of illness and death with the sweet tobacco smoke, but it seemed a sacrilege to do so. God, his lads, his bright-eyed, laughing lads, who'd tumbled about the shanty like a pair of puppies at play, so loud sometimes he couldn't bear their noise and had to strike out against it. Surely, he'd thought, the sickness would go easy with two lads so strong and full of life. How was he to know? How was he to blame? He'd other cares, so many he couldn't number them. "Who'd'a provided for you lads if I'd'a stayed home?"

Liam gestured about the dark, sooty room. "Providing? The

cupboard's bare and the woodbox is empty, and I've not been able to more than crawl. Tell me what the bloody hell you been providing." He slumped against the wall, panting from the effort of his outburst.

Fists doubled, Hugh rose to face his remaining child. The rage ran through him, taking him outside himself, so he felt he was watching another man raise his hand to strike. For once, though, he didn't lash out. He forced his hands back down to his sides. "You don't mean that, son. It's only the sickness talking. If Nuala was here, it would'a been different. She'd'a tended to you lads." He'd not thought he'd miss the lass so much, that day he'd sold her to the peddler. But in no time, the money was gone and the shanty felt as empty as his pockets. And her music, sweet Jesus, how bleak the shanty was without her music. Just like a mockingbird, she'd been, only needing to hear a tune once to learn it, then turn it around and make it hers. So young, and so like her mam with her blue eyes and yellow curls and lovely voice. He'd been an idiot to let her get away.

"If Nuala was here, she'd'a died in a fever, lying in her own filth, just like Jimmy and Mick done," Liam said bitterly. "She was lucky to go like she did. Better for her that way than this one."

Hugh stared blearily at his eldest son, the boy's yellow hair dark with filth, drooping across his sweaty forehead and into eyes blue and cold as steel, a boy's eyes no longer. Liam was like his mam, too, but only the hard bits: the sharp tongue and harsh laugh she'd acquired those last few years. The lad was so young to be so bitter. Margaret had been bitter, too, by the time she'd died. Well, a hard life could do that to folk, and none so hard as Hugh's own. "All gone," he said softly. "All gone and naught I could do." Liam would be next, he thought, already mourning the son who stood trembling against the wall.

Something hit him in the chest, taking the wind out of him. His arms flailed, blindly grabbing the bucket that Liam had thrown at him. Hugh hadn't thought the lad would have the strength to lift so much as a handkerchief, never mind the heavy wooden bucket.

"Here's something you can do," the boy said, pointing to the bucket. "Fetch some water, why don't you? The least you can do is clean 'em up so they can be buried decent." He dropped to his knees and waved the flies away from the blanket, carefully folded it down, every motion an effort for his shaking body. He exposed the lads' ashen faces, then their shoulders, the stench of their sickness, of their emptied bladders and bowels rising as he peeled the blanket back from their grotesquely distended bellies.

Hugh's stomach roiled and he clamped a hand over his nose and mouth to keep the reek out and his dinner in. He tried to turn away, but he couldn't stop himself from staring at the two obscenely inhuman things that used to be his lads. "I can't," he protested, clutching the bucket to his chest as if it could ward off his dead sons' angry spirits, his living son's accusing eyes, his own shame and guilt.

Liam's hands reached out and circled his father's wrists like shackles. The anger and bitterness in his eyes dissolved into exhaustion and tears. "For Christ's sake, Da. Please. I can't be doing this alone. I need you, Da." He gestured toward the lads. "They need you."

Oh, yes, Liam looked like his mam all right. Like Margaret the day she died, her face pale and narrow and full of pain and terror, her grip on his arm suddenly so powerful he'd feel the bruises for days after. Then just as suddenly gone, her hands, face, eyes, empty as his heart without her. Hugh couldn't see his son anymore for his own weeping, weeping all the while he fled the shanty, the empty bucket falling from his arms with a hollow thud.

Chapter Twelve

Tuesday, September 10, 1839, Chauncey, Connecticut

"'Tain't fair, Phizzy." Billy pressed her legs tighter around Phizzy's broad belly, urging him into a canter with calves and thighs and seat the way Mr. S. had taught her.

At first she'd been thrilled when Mr. S. had rescued that gawky lad with the big ears. But now she wished the lad had proved to be a murderer and was locked safely away.

It had been bad enough that Mr. S. had invited that one to travel with them, but now the lad knew her secret. Any day he would tell on her and she'd have to go back to being Nuala, and it would be that new lad traveling with Mr. S. instead of her.

It wasn't right. Wasn't this her true self, this boy she'd invented? Wasn't Mr. S. more her true da than the one she'd been given by mistake?

She leaned forward and wrapped her arms around Phizzy's neck, burying her face in his coarse mane. The moment she'd laid eyes on Phizzy she'd known that she was meant to be with the old horse, though at first she'd not understood that Mr. S. was supposed to be part of her new life as well. Now every day when she was out of doors in the fresh air and sunshine, singing and laughing with Mr. S and tending to Phizzy, her heart told her that this was where she was meant to be, who she was meant to be.

Father Brady had once told her that God never did nothing by mistake, but hadn't God made a horrible mistake taking Mam away? The priest had said it was God's will, that Jesus had needed Mam up in heaven with Him. But Billy had been only six when Mam died, Liam not yet thirteen, and Jimmy and Mick just out of nappies. It was selfish, if not just plain mean for Jesus to be taking folks' mams when He had a perfectly good one of His own up there with Him.

God had made another mistake in trapping Billy in that skin of a girl that weighed upon her like a chain around her soul: an endless chain of soiled and torn clothing and dirty dishes and meals to be cooked. But He'd given Billy the music to show her He was sorry. When the music stirred inside her, it felt like God Himself was calling to her, just like Father Brady said God had called him to become a priest. Surely if God could call a priest to go about in skirts, He could call a lass to go about in trousers.

And then God had sent Phizzy and Mr. S. to finally put things right. It was so right to be free. That girl she'd been four months ago was gone. Dead and gone, and Billy sprung up in her place. And she'd not missed her one single bit.

"Where's Billy?" Daniel asked. He lounged in the Taylors' kitchen doorway like a sprite who'd materialized to remind Jonathan of his sins.

Damn. Had that boy been laying in ambush for him? Why wasn't he at the Ainesworths' helping Chester with his after-breakfast chores?

"Where she always is most mornings lately. Out riding Phizzy," Jonathan said.

"Good. Then now's a proper time to talk to your cousin."

"I'm just waiting for the right moment, son." Jonathan couldn't count how many times he'd opened his mouth to talk to Sophie about Billy, but each time his heart had plummeted into his boots, and he'd never followed through. Why was it so hard to do what was right for the girl?

"We're leaving tomorrow," Daniel persisted.

"I promise you, I'll talk to Sophie in a little while."

"Talk to me about what?" Sophie came into the kitchen from the opposite side of the house, carrying a basket of eggs. Bits of straw clung to her skirt and apron, and a downy copper feather stuck to her cap, bobbing jauntily as she walked.

"Billy," Daniel said before Jonathan had time to invent something else.

"Oh, yes. I've got a thing or two say to you about that boy." She bustled into the kitchen like a mother hen taking over her roost. "What do you mean trotting him all over the countryside and not giving him proper schooling? He can barely write his own name."

"It's not for want of trying." Jonathan bowed his head. It never ceased to amaze him how quickly Sophie could make him feel like a ten-year-old caught with his fingers in the jam jar.

"Well, try harder. I taught you better than that, didn't I? Do you want that boy growing up ignorant?"

"Of course not."

"Then I suggest you start doing something about it." She poured some water into a bowl, then one by one, she put the eggs into the water, checking to see whether they floated or sank.

Jonathan cast a glance toward Daniel. Scowling, the boy made a sharp motion with his chin in Sophie's direction. Jonathan took a deep breath, as if preparing to plunge into an icy pond. "Sophie, you like Billy, don't you?"

"Yes, I do, even if he's a bit prickly. Though I can't say I blame him." One of the eggs bobbed to the surface; she removed it from the water and placed it carefully in the slop bucket, so it wouldn't break and fill the room with a sulfurous stench. "He's had you to himself all spring and summer, and now this stranger comes in and takes all your attention. . . . Sorry, Daniel, nothing against you, but I imagine that's how Billy sees it."

"The little devil barely speaks to me. He's been talking plenty to you, though," Jonathan said. There was nary an evening this past week that Sophie's and Billy's heads hadn't been bowed together over that *Oliver Twist* book, or Sophie hadn't been plying the child with sweets and baked goods. It seemed as though every time Jonathan entered a room, Billy would make a point of complimenting Sophie or asking Eldad a question, and pointedly ignoring Jonathan.

"Only because he wants to make you jealous." Another egg floated and was added to the slop bucket.

"What would you say to him staying here with you?"

Sophie nearly dropped an egg. Her fingers closed around it, and for a moment Jonathan thought she would crush it. But she collected herself and added it to the others. It sank—a good one.

"I know how much you've always hankered after a child," he continued.

Sophie sat down and studied her hands, twisting her wedding ring around and around. "Yes, I did, but it wasn't meant to be. I reconciled myself to that a long time ago."

"Well, here's your chance. If Billy stayed with you and Eldad, I'm sure he'd be brung up right."

Sophie sat in silence for a long time, staring into the bowl of eggs as if it were a magician's crystal ball and she were trying to see her future.

Jonathan crossed the room and put a hand on his cousin's shoulder. "He already likes you."

Sophie patted Jonathan's hand and shook her head. The feather tumbled from her cap into her lap. "He likes my cooking and having a clean bed to sleep in. He doesn't love me."

"Maybe not yet, but he will. Just give him some time."

"It's not fine living that Billy needs." Sophie rose from her chair, her eyes moist. "Oh, Jonny, you're such an old fool." She patted his cheek, her damp hand cool against his face. "Can't you see what's right before your eyes? He worships you."

"Them sour looks he's been giving me seem like worship to you?"

"If he didn't love you, he wouldn't be jealous. He'd like nothing better than to be just like you."

Then God help her, Jonathan thought. "You know I'm not fit to raise a child, Soph."

"You love him, don't you?"

"I couldn't love him better if he was my own son." And that was exactly the problem, wasn't it? Daniel was right; it was a son he'd made of her, not a daughter. "But what sort'a life is it for him to be traipsing around the countryside with a damn fool peddler?"

"It's the sort of life he wants. The same life you've invited Daniel to share."

"Daniel's old enough to choose for himself. Billy doesn't know what's good for him."

"Neither, apparently, do you, Jonny." Sophie straightened Jonathan's collar and brushed off his lapels, the way she'd done when they were growing up together and she was sending him off to school. "There's nothing I'd like better than to have that child stay here, getting proper schooling, apprenticing with Eldad. But he wouldn't be happy. He needs you." Her expression grew stern. "But he also needs an education. Promise me you'll do that for him, and I'll be content." She picked up the slop bucket holding the leavings from breakfast and the rotten eggs. "Now get out of my kitchen." She thrust the bucket into Jonathan's hands. "I have dinner to make."

Jonathan and Daniel walked across the yard to the pigpen, where Jonathan flung the contents of the slop bucket into the trough. The eggs broke, their sulfury odor mingling with the rank stench of pig manure. The hogs trotted up to the trough on their stubby legs and tussled noisily over the scraps.

"Well," Jonathan said, "I tried."

"You didn't try," Daniel said. "You didn't mean to give her up at all. If you'd meant it, you'd'a told Mrs. Taylor she's a girl."

"I promised Billy not to let her secret out. If anybody tells, it's got to be her."

"That ain't a true promise. It's only humoring some childish fancy."

"Someone made you a promise when you were her age, wouldn't you'a held 'em to it?"

Daniel shook his head. "When I was her age, the only promises I got was for thrashings. Can't recall as I'd'a minded were any of 'em to be broken."

Chapter Thirteen

Tuesday, September 10, 1839, Cabotville, Massachusetts

Liam clasped his knees against his chest and rested his forehead on them, but he couldn't contain the shivering. He hardly knew if he was waking or sleeping anymore, things shifted in and out so between the chills and sweats and dry heaves. Christ, he couldn't remember the last time he'd even felt like eating, not that there was anything to eat in the shanty.

Maybe it was all a dream, all that spring and summer since Nuala'd disappeared. Maybe if he'd just lie down for a wee bit, he'd wake up, and there she'd be, fixing dinner and telling him to stop playing sick and get off his sorry backside and fetch in some wood. And there would be Jimmy and Mick teasing and chasing each other about the room and knocking chairs over and Nuala thrashing them with her spoon and scolding and laughing all at the same time. And if it was dreaming he was after, then why not make the dream go back six years and more, and let him wake up a child again and Mam still alive and naught for him to worry about but keeping the woodbox full and keeping out of Da's way when he was in his cups.

I'm sorry, Mam. I'm sorry. She'd left her babies for him to care for, and he'd failed. Failed to keep them from running wild in the streets. Failed to make them go to school. Failed to keep Jimmy and Mick from turning into thieving little fiends, bringing home oranges and sweets and toys. Failed to keep his wages out of Da's hands. Failed to keep the children out of Da's hands, when he was in a temper from the drink. Failed to keep them safe. And in the end, failed to keep them at all. Now they were all three of them gone.

He rocked himself and shivered. *I tried, Mam, I swear I did.* But with Nuala gone, it had been like the house falling down about his ears. He'd not realized how much she'd done while he was off working. There were more mysteries to housekeeping than he'd ever imagined: how to know a good cheese from a bad one, how to take butchers' trimmings and green-grocers' scraps and bakers' days-old leavings and turn them into something edible, how to make it all keep more than a day. He might as well have collected stones and warmed them by the fire; they'd have come out the same as his attempts at breadmaking. He'd even spent hard-won coin on a cookery book by "A Lady," but it could have been a book of magic spells for all he could understand of it. His attempts at laundry and mending had left the clothes looking worse than when he'd begun. And all of it to be done after he'd put in twelve hours and more with shovel and pick and wheelbarrow, digging cellar holes and canals and ditches, and him wanting to do no more than pull a blanket over his head and shut his eyes when he got home.

He'd felt so often like the ant slaving all day while Jimmy and Mick fiddled their time away like grasshoppers. But surely the ant wouldn't have begrudged the grasshopper his fiddling if he'd known how short the grasshopper's season would be. He was sorry now for the times he'd thrashed them and taken away their stolen playthings. Sorry, too, that he'd shouted at them when their laughter and play kept him from sleep. How was he to know how little time they'd have for laughter? How was he to know they'd be crying for help and naught he could do but wet their foreheads while the fever burned them, naught he could do but hold them while they shivered with the chills, naught he could do but watch them while they died?

Now that it was all over, he couldn't even make them decent for the grave. He might as well lie next to them and pull the blanket over his own face and wait for his turn to come.

"No," he said, his voice a croaking whisper. For sure as hell Da wasn't coming back, and if Liam didn't do for them, who would? He dragged himself upright, clutching the wall as the room slipped sideways. He closed his eyes, waiting for the floor to stop pitching. When he opened them, it was like trying to see underwater, everything dim and wavering. Well, he was up; he might as well finish, never mind the clatter in his ears. Just down the alley for a bit of water and back. Five minutes' walking any other day. Five hundred miles today. And back home again with a full bucket... well, that was halfway around the world. No point thinking as far as that until he'd taken those first three steps.

One.... Two... Three.

He gripped the doorjamb and bent to lift the bucket. Christ, you'd think it was full of rocks, so heavy it seemed. Lurching, he made his way outside, where the sunlight assaulted him like a razor blade across his eyes. He'd barely taken a dozen steps when his feet went out from under him. The last thing he heard was the faraway thud of the bucket tumbling down the road.

Chapter Fourteen

Wednesday, September 11, 1839, Chauncey, Connecticut

"Where's Billy? I should make sure this fits him." Sophie pulled a shirt from her basket, then studied it for defects that Jonathan was sure weren't there.

"He's out in the barn, probably brushing Phizzy bald. He's been glued to that horse since I asked Daniel to join us."

"That's one way he can make sure you don't leave him behind."

"You're sure you don't want me to?"

"If you did, he'd be off like a shot, and heaven knows where he'd end up. As long as he's with you, at least there's someone looking out for him."

Jonathan laid a hand on her shoulder. "You'd do it better, Soph. Hell, you near about brung me up."

"Brought," Sophie said, shrugging off his hand.

"Brought," Jonathan repeated. Feeling his throat go tight, he bent to pick up the basket so he could avoid Sophie's eyes. It was unexpectedly heavy. "What you got in here? Bricks?"

"Books."

"Well, that's mighty thoughtful of you." He reached under the clothes and pulled a couple volumes out: grammar, geography, history, arithmetic....

"Those boys need proper lessons."

"I ain't no schoolmaster, cousin." Jonathan emphasized the *ain't*. "I can't even talk—"

"Not *can't*. *Don't*. I know perfectly well what you can and cannot do. You've been a dancing master, a singing master, an actor."

He raised an eyebrow. "So?"

"So, act like a schoolmaster." She folded her arms under her bosom. "Give them proper lessons and set them an example. None of your *ain't*s or *brung*s."

"Maybe I ought'a leave Billy behind after all. The two of you are sure matched for stubbornness."

"Will you be back for Thanksgiving?" she asked.

Jonathan leaned over and gently kissed her cheek. "Cousin, the devil himself couldn't keep me away from one of your Thanksgiving dinners. I can already feel my mouth watering." He stood back, pleased that he'd coaxed a sparkle into her eyes. "Come November, being on the road'll lose its charm," he said. "Once Billy sees a little snow flying, he'll want to settle."

She reached out and straightened his collar. "You never did."

Chapter Fifteen

Wednesday, September 11, 1839, Springfield, Massachusetts

"They're all of 'em dead, Hugh?" Eamon asked.

Hugh started with the weight of his cousin's hand on his shoulder. He nodded, turned mute by a burning feeling in his chest, his ribs like a cage of hot iron bars squeezing ever tighter around his lungs and heart. He couldn't breathe, couldn't think, couldn't close his eyes without seeing Liam's gaunt and wasted face, Death standing at his side as near as Hugh stood to Eamon just now. He blinked, surprised to see Eamon's ruddy, weathered features instead of Liam's, to hear the murmur of the men in the tavern instead of Liam's labored breath. "Christ, me lads," he moaned, scrubbing at his face with clammy palms.

"Here, man, a wee bit of something to settle you, eh?" Eamon pressed a tumbler into Hugh's trembling hand.

The rum went down sharp, a sting at the back of his throat. "Thanks, Eamon. You're a good man," he said, his voice raspy from the weeping he'd done on the long trek from Cabotville. With the second glass, the burning around his heart subsided into a dull ache.

He drew in the good healthy odors of wood smoke and cooking and tobacco, the sweat of working men and the animal smells that lingered on their shoes and clothes. He filled his pipe with trembling hands, hoping the sweet tobacco smoke would purge the stench of vomit and feces, disease and decay from his nostrils.

"'Tis a hard life, that it is," Eamon commiserated, "and naught but suffering for our lot. You shouldn't'a had to bury 'em all on your own."

Hugh's face flushed with shame. No need to tell the man that he'd had no heart to stay for the burying—no heart to stay and see Liam's corpse added to the two lads under the blanket. What good would it have done to watch Liam's life slip away like water through his fingers, just as Margaret's and Jimmy's and Mick's had? His heart was never meant to take such sorrow. So he'd turned his back and put one foot in front of the other, hoping that the farther away he got, the lighter his burden would grow. Only it hadn't worked that way, and he'd found himself at Eamon's door with his insides turned leaden and an invisible chain shackling him to the memory of the room reeking of sickness.

"Another, cousin?" Eamon asked.

"Aye," Hugh said, though he feared there'd not be drink enough in the world to wash his soul clean.

Thursday, September 12, 1839, Cabotville, Massachusetts

How had he managed to stay alive? Liam wondered. Or, rather, who had helped him? Whose hands had laid cool damp cloths across his forehead when he burned and piled blankets on him when he froze and trickled water onto his parched lips? The puzzle wove through his fever-blistered dreams. Sometimes he fancied it was Da, come back to salvage his first and last child. Sometimes it was Nuala. And sometimes it was Mam, and himself but a child and everything the way it had been before it had all gone irretrievably wrong.

He kept his eyes closed, not wanting to let go the feeling that Mam was with him somehow. But eventually the clatter of fireplace tools and pots became too real to shut out. A savory aroma set his stomach yearning. For the first time in he didn't know how many days, he was hungry.

He opened one eye a wee bit. He lay on the floor in the corner of a shanty cobbled together of building scraps, much like his own. But it wasn't his own; from the wooden floor to the whitewashed walls, the battered table and cupboard to the dishes on the shelves, it was all wrong. And there was something very wrong about the woman in the blue dress and brown-checked apron bending over a kettle on the hearth.

It took him a hard minute of thinking to place her, though she lived in the shanty across from his. He'd always turned aside when their paths crossed, avoided meeting her eyes, for who'd be wanting anything to do with such a woman? She lived on her own, earning her livelihood taking in laundry and sewing, though most said she took in more than that. One of the neighbor ladies said she'd go out in the evenings, coming back to her shanty with a different man each time.

She had a weary sort of prettiness about her, grayish smudges of sleeplessness under her eyes, making their color seem brighter and her lashes longer and darker. Most brown-eyed lasses, you'd not notice the color of their eyes from across a room, but this one's were a clear amber, like a pair of ear bobs Mam had once admired in a store. Her brown hair was pulled back in a careless knot, a stray tendril curling limply against her cheek. Some might call that wanton. To him, she just looked careworn, too short of time or money to bother with braids and sidecombs and caps.

He realized that she was saying something. He turned so his good ear was toward her. It hurt to move even that much. Everything ached, like waking up after a thrashing from Da, only the ache went deeper and fiercer than any he'd felt before.

She knelt on the floor next to him. She was younger than he'd expected, perhaps not much over twenty. "Are you awake for real this time?" she asked.

"I—I hardly know," he mumbled. He flinched from her hand on his forehead. "What am I doing here?"

"Not dying, apparently," she said.

"But—but why?" Gingerly, he dragged himself into a sitting position. She helped him shift the bolster and pillow behind his back so he could lean against the wall. He closed his eyes to rest from the exertion.

"Because I'm such a good doctor, I suppose."

He opened one eye. Was she smiling? "Please, miss. Me head's too sore for riddling. Can you just tell me plain what happened? How did I get here?"

"You were lying in my doorway. Can't have young men dying in the street. It's bad for business." She went back to her kettles, poured out a mug of some sort of tea, tasted it, and made a sour face. She chiseled a lump from a sugar loaf and dropped it in the mug. "I tried to have someone carry you home, but when I looked inside—"

"Jesus, me house." He tried to shove the blankets aside and get up, but they tangled like snakes around his legs, and his effort to wrestle them off only made him dizzy. The woman came back and held him still with hardly any effort.

"It's all right, Liam. They're...taken care of. They were all you talked of while you were feverish. So I had them made decent, and your shanty cleaned."

"But you don't even know me."

"I've been here three years. I certainly know my neighbors by now." She got up and went back to her tea. "Even though they wouldn't care to know me."

He looked away and picked at an unraveling thread on the coarse woolen blanket. The only thing he knew about her, besides how she made her living, was that her speech marked her for a Yankee. What other sort of Yankee woman would be reduced to living in the Patch among the Paddies?

She returned to his side, offering him a mug of tea. "For the headache," she said.

It was some sort of concoction of herbs that would have tasted foul even with a gill of sugar dumped into it. He tried to swallow it without grimacing.

"I know," she said. "It tastes horrid. Drink it anyway."

"I'm sorry," he said. "All you done, and I don't even know you." He took another sip of the bitter liquid to show he appreciated her efforts.

He nearly choked on the tea when she replied, "I'm a whore, just as you thought."

"It's not me who ought to be judging folk," he said. "With me da a drunk and me—" A what? *Nothing* was the only word that came into his head. "But even a—someone like yourself has got a name." "Augusta," she said.

"Augusta?" he repeated. "It sounds a bit—" He swallowed back what he'd meant to say, which was that it sounded a bit grand for a whore. Instead he said, "It sounds too harsh to suit you." Neither did she look like a whore—not that he'd be knowing. She looked just a bit on the nicer side of ordinary.

"Augusta," he said, "What if you took sick yourself?"

She shrugged. "It's not as if anyone would miss me. Besides, I thought your father might come back for you." She got up and turned back to the fireplace. "I should have known better."

"What do you mean?"

She took a pair of bowls down from a shelf and began ladling some sort of soup into them. She was careful to put mostly broth into one bowl. "It's hard not to hear your neighbors fighting when the houses are practically on top of each other. It's hard to miss when someone's cursing or quarreling. Or being beaten. At least now you're finally grown enough to fight back."

Finally? Warmth crept up his neck. It rankled him that she'd consider him no more than a boy.

Augusta gave him the bowl of broth and sat on the floor next to him to eat her own soup. He let the first spoonful linger on his tongue before it slid down his throat like a caress. "My God, that's good," he said.

Augusta's mouth pursed as though she were trying not to laugh. "It's only broth."

"Aye, well, you've not had me cooking, have you?" he said. "Thank you. For everything." He nodded toward the door. "And for whatever you done over there."

She looked away uneasily. "It wasn't exactly my doing. I hired somebody."

His own stomach turned at the thought of clearing out the foul mess that illness and death had left behind. "Wouldn't folk be afraid of the fever and all?"

"There's always someone who's willing to do what you won't for the right price."

"I'll pay you back. Whatever it cost you."

She fidgeted with her spoon. "Well, actually, you already have paid."

"With what?" He'd a little money hidden away, but surely not enough.

"For someone with nothing, a pot or a chair is as good as money. Your rooms are clean, but you'll find them emptier than you left them." She got up and set her bowl on the table, then busied herself with tending to the fire. "And they had to burn the bedding."

"I—I hardly know what to say."

"I suppose you're angry."

Maybe he should be. She'd sold his things as if they were her own, and how was he to know whether she hadn't made a tidy profit? But it wasn't her selling his goods that felt odd. It was knowing that she'd seen all the refuse of his life. It was as if she'd stripped all the secret parts of him away while he'd slept, and now she knew everything about him and all he knew of her was her name. "It's not as if I could'a been doing any of it meself," he said slowly. "I'd only'a made a mess of it, just like I done with every-thing else."

"Why wasn't your father tending to you and your brothers?"

"Da can't manage. After me mam died, it tore him apart. Things're difficult for him."

"Difficult." Her voice was sharp as a chisel. "How long ago did your mother die?"

"It'll be six years now."

"Most folks would think six years more than enough time to get over your wife's death, especially when you have children to feed." Her voice grew fiercer as she talked. "If your father can't manage, then who's been doing it all this time?"

"Who else but me? Me and Nuala, I mean. Until she—" Liam shivered. "She's gone, too. They're all gone now."

Chapter Sixteen

Friday, September 13, 1839, Southbury, Connecticut

Daniel eyed the big red farmhouse hopefully. If the sounds of talk and laughter drifting down into the yard were any clue, Mr. Stocking had secured them a fine night's lodging. Maybe a proper room with a bedstead in it, instead of a straw tick laid on an attic floor, or a tavern chamber crammed wall to wall with snoring men.

"You're a good fella, Slingsby," Mr. Stocking said as he came out of the house. He shook the owner's hand with a vigorous pumping motion.

"And yourself, Stocking. A helluva good man. I don't care what anybody says." Mr. Slingsby thumped the peddler on the back.

Mr. Stocking came down the walk, grinning so widely that the sun caught on his gold tooth.

"You're looking fair pleased with yourself, sir," Daniel said. "Did you sell one'a them tin kitchens?" He nodded toward the round-bellied reflector oven that Mr. Stocking displayed as the centerpiece of his wares, the most expensive piece the peddler offered.

"Nearly as good. I got a day's work for you, a night's work for me, free lodgings all 'round, and dinner, tea, and supper, too." The little man puffed out his chest like a banty rooster and cocked his hat aslant to give himself a jaunty air.

"All of that, now?" Daniel said. "You must'a talked a good tale to 'em." Out of the corner of his eye, Daniel saw Billy edge closer, though she pretended not to be listening. She'd said close to naught to either of them for days, though she'd been decent enough to mumble *yessir* and *ma'am* and *please* and *thank you* to the folk they'd lodged with as they traveled. But she'd no words for the peddler or Daniel, except to mutter under her breath about them as didn't know how to take proper care of horses—usually just before she redid whatever care Mr. Stocking or Daniel had given Phizzy. She'd empty his water bucket and refill it, refluff his bedding, unbuckle and rebuckle his tack, until finally they'd left the gelding completely to her care. On the road, she'd sit at the back of the wagon or walk at Phizzy's head, giving the old fellow an earful of her opinions. At night, she'd slouch off to the barn rather than share whatever quarters Mr. Stocking had managed to find. Today, she'd stationed herself at the back of the wagon, plucking a whisk broom bald.

"I got to give some credit to luck and timing," said Mr. Stocking. "Slingsby says there's a fella three houses down busted his foot. He'll pay a dollar for someone to dig his potatoes."

"Aye, there's my work," Daniel said. "And yours?"

"Just so happens Slingsby is having himself a husking bee. I asked him if he could use another fiddler." The peddler tucked an imaginary fiddle under his chin and drew an invisible bow across phantom strings. "More precisely, a fiddler who can call the newest dances, sing the newest songs, and who ain't such a bad hand with the squeezebox, neither." Mr. Stocking cast aside the phantom fiddle for an invisible concertina. "A fiddler who's also a dancing master"—putting one foot forward, he bowed with surprising grace—"to assist the young folks that don't know their heels from their toes, and to educate the old folks in what the fashionable set are dancing in Boston and New York. Who knows but I may even slip in a waltz, after they've drained a keg or two." He took a ghost partner in his arms and bobbed in a little circle in front of the wagon, counting "one-two-three, one-two-three" under his breath.

Daniel raised an eyebrow. "Weren't you telling me just the other day that you'd not been to New York or Boston for three years or more?"

"That's three years sooner than Slingsby has. Anyway,

whether the dances come from New York or out of my own head, they won't be any less new, will they?"

Daniel had a hard time fitting his mind around the idea that folk would pay money to see someone else at play, never mind a whole day's wage for an evening's fun—and bed and board for three persons to boot. It would be like somebody paying him to ride Ivy. "Seems to me there won't be much corn getting husked, what with all that dancing and playing and such."

"Well, that isn't the point, now is it?" Mr. Stocking cast a glance over his shoulder toward Billy, who pretended to be adjusting something at the back of the wagon. "Haven't you never been to a husking bee, son?"

"No. Heard some about 'em. Lyman didn't hold with any such nonsense as huskings and haying matches and frolics. He called 'em sorry excuses for drunken and lascivious behavior."

Mr. Stocking clapped him on the shoulder. "Then you're in for a treat. Never know but you might find a sweetheart there. Find a red ear of corn and you can claim a kiss from the one you love best."

Billy snickered, and Daniel's ears grew hot. "I can't dance or none of that," he said.

"You will," the peddler said emphatically. "Sophie charged me to learn—to *teach* you to be civilized young—uh"—he looked toward Billy, who had now disappeared completely behind the wagon, no doubt doubled over laughing—"civilized young gentlemen." Mr. Stocking lowered an eyebrow as Billy's hat peeked out from around the edge of the wagon. "Those of you that aren't hopeless barbarians, that is." The hat rose high enough so that Billy's eyes were visible, then it ducked down again. "And if dancing isn't a genteel art, I don't know what is."

Daniel's throat was tight, and no amount of coughing seemed to clear it. "I ain't hardly genteel," he finally said.

"Maybe not, but you can dance. I seen you myself, dancing with that horse."

Daniel's face grew even redder at the peddler's mention of his daily game of catch-me-if-you-can with Ivy, a little ashamed that he still fancied such childish frolicking. But there was something that happened between the two of them while they whirled and dodged around a pasture, something different from the riding. There was something they said to each other then, a promise they renewed every day.

Mr. Stocking took Daniel's wrist and placed the boy's hand on Ivy's nose, velvet warmth filling his fingers, her breath softly tickling his palm. The little man placed his own hand on Phizzy's forehead. Billy had crept up from her spot at the back of the wagon, the better to eavesdrop.

"Son," the little man said gently, "don't never be ashamed of what you love." Mr. Stocking took all four of them in with his smile: Daniel, Billy, Phizzy and Ivy. "Or who. Anyways," he added, "I can teach you to dance."

"But it's different, dancing with a lass from, well—" Daniel ruffled Ivy's mane.

"Of course it is, son. A girl don't have two left feet."

Daniel had tied and untied his cravat a dozen times at least. It was no good, he thought, looking at himself in the mirror. No matter how well brushed his coat or how firmly pressed his trousers, it was still just himself, with his spotty face and enormous ears and that horrid orange hair that would not lie proper, not with combing or wetting or bear grease and hair tonic from Mr. Stocking's kit.

He looked out the window into the yard, burnished now by the setting sun. Mr. Slingsby and his sons and hired men had swept and raked the yard smooth for dancing, set chairs and benches and tables of trestles and planking, arranged torches and lanterns to be lit, and piled wood for a bonfire. Mr. Stocking and the other musicians made cat-squawling noises as they tuned their instruments. Instead of yearning toward the smells of meats and pies and cakes cooking, Daniel's stomach recoiled. What place had he among decent folk like that?

The sun was well down by the time he came outside. In the orange blaze of lantern and torchlight, the guests began to gather, lasses in a swirl of skirts and shawls and giggles, gents shaking hands and slapping backs, little ones chasing dogs or chickens or each other 'round the yard. Mr. Slingsby lit the kindling for the bonfire. One of his lads tapped a keg while another set bottles out on a table. Men gathered around and filled their mugs and glasses.

As he skirted the edge of the crowd, the wind shifted, sending a swirl of smoke his way, and his stomach lurched. The clink of bottles and glasses grated on his ears. One of the men made a joke, another shouted a rejoinder, the rest guffawed and cackled. An icy sweat broke over his body. He tugged at his cravat, which had grown mysteriously tight. His tongue felt as though a wad of greasy cotton lay across it, but he couldn't spit the taste away.

He closed his eyes to steady himself, but that made it worse, as though somebody'd thrown a sack over his head. Red flames glowed on the inside of his eyelids, and for a moment he was back on that night, naked and alone and going to be killed. Someone touched his arm, and he shuddered and shied away.

"All right, son?"

He stared at the peddler, the firelight reflecting off his spectacles so that it looked as though he had flames for eyes.

"We're all friends here," Mr. Stocking said. "Nothing to fret over." The little man pressed a mug into his hand, its warmth a comfort against his palm. "Been a long day, huh? Digging all them potatoes."

"Aye." Daniel raised the mug to his lips. The cider was richly scented with cinnamon and nutmeg, a homey sweet fragrance that steadied his galloping pulse. He took a sip. Something in the cider stung the back of his throat and sent warmth down to his belly and through his blood. He let the cider and rum and spices push the bitter memory to a corner of his mind and close the door on it.

"You weren't thinking of going anywhere, were you?" Mr. Stocking asked. "Because we're always short of men for the dancing."

Daniel barely stopped himself from spraying cider all over

the little man's clean white shirt front. "Dancing," he repeated, a different sort of fear curdling his stomach. Thankfully, one of the fiddlers called the peddler aside. Daniel finished his cider, set the mug down on a bench, and turned away. He nearly jumped out of his skin at the figure that appeared next to him: a thin, pale-faced, light-haired girl wearing a white apron over her dress. He backed away and murmured his apologies.

"You're the peddler's boy," she said. "You helped Papa dig his potatoes."

He looked over his shoulder as if there might be somebody standing behind him that she was really talking to. "Uh," he said.

She stepped farther out of the shadows and into the glow of one of the lanterns hung 'round the barnyard. "I'm Sarah." She seemed taller, older than she had earlier. Not pretty by far, but pleasant in spite of her sharp face and shoulders square across as a spade. Eyes and hair of no particular color, her hair done up in an intricate nest of braids, her dress golden as the birch leaves just turning. She touched his wrist, and he nearly bolted.

"Daniel?" she said.

"Um." His collar had shrunk two sizes, and his cravat had turned into a snake, wrapping itself tighter and tighter around his throat. He could feel his eyes bulging at the pressure.

"That's my sister Molly over there. And our cousins..." Apparently unaware of his inability to speak, she pointed out half a dozen young folk settling on benches among the baskets of corn ready for husking. Her hand lightly circled his wrist, her fingers cool against his burning flesh. "Would you like to sit with us?"

"Erf." There was no telling what his inarticulate noise meant, but she smiled brightly and led him away as easily as she might a lamb.

Jonathan chuckled to himself. Who'd've thought that a word and a touch from a skinny little girl would strike Daniel mute and paralyzed? The girl apparently took his reticence for admiration and claimed a seat on the bench next to him. Daniel husked the corn with awkward, mechanical motions, his eyes down, his mouth drawn in a rigid line. Meanwhile, the homely girl chattered away beside him. Daniel latched onto Jonathan with wild eyes, a penned colt seeking rescue. Jonathan responded with a grin. He wasn't helping the boy out of this one.

Daniel let the girl lead him about and bring him a plate piled six inches high. He ate in what looked like numb terror. When it came to dancing, she made sure that Daniel danced nearly every round with her or one of her friends. She even dragged Billy into a cotillion, no doubt thinking that the strange boy loitered at the edge of the party from shyness rather than sullenness.

"I hope the little hellion ain't picking pockets," Jonathan muttered as Billy wove through the dancers. Daniel seemed to let go some of his terror while dancing, perhaps realizing that as long as he danced, he didn't have to talk to anyone. Well, there was nothing like music and dancing to cure whatever ailed a body. Or a soul.

Jonathan loved the way the dancers glowed in the firelight, the shine of the young ladies' tightly coiled and braided hair, the flutter of lace on the older ladies' caps, the flurry of tailcoats and petticoats, the tantalizing glimpses of ankle and calf beneath the swirl of skirts. With red cheeks and flushed faces, drunk with motion, the dancers followed the patterns he created—a long ribbon of brightly colored gowns woven through the warp of the men's dark, sober coats. They whirled through contras and quadrilles, jigs and reels and hornpipes, his bow the magic wand that guided them. He even dared a few intrepid couples into a waltz, once cider and rum had mellowed the old folk, and the dour and disapproving had drifted home to their beds.

A crescent moon smiled over the frolic. Coats and cravats were shed, collars unbuttoned, sleeves rolled. Curls that had been coiled spring-tight at sunset now drooped in limp tendrils, and braids escaped from their pins and ribbons. Crisply starched ruffles and cuffs and bows wilted, and so, at last, did the dancers.

"Finish it out, will you, Jonny?" the flutist said.

"All right, one more then." He flexed his fingers and adjusted his fiddle. When he glanced at the rest of the musicians to see who wanted to choose the tune, the other four sat down as one. They cradled their instruments as if they were children needing to be rocked to sleep, and they nodded for him to begin. Alone.

"Oh, so it's like that, huh, boys? Leaving the old man to finish up?" He couldn't help feeling flattered that they'd left him the stage.

He chose "Oft in the Stilly Night," a sweet and wistful tune that would make the ladies sigh and nestle closer to their beaux and make the old folk shed a tear. It would have been better with Billy to sing it. She could wring the feeling out of it without turning it maudlin. Well, maybe tomorrow she'd forgive him for bringing Daniel along. Or the next day. He lifted his bow, lingering over the opening notes. He played it as a waltz, drawing the melody out with no flourishes or ornaments, letting the tune play the fiddle rather than the other way 'round.

Oft in the stilly night,
Ere slumber's chain has bound me,

Shyly at first, some of the ladies hummed along, putting in a word or two as they remembered. One by one, the voices came together, drew confidence from each other as a glance, a smile, a touch, traveled from friend to friend, girl to boy, husband to wife.

Fond mem'ry brings the light
Of other days around me...

By the chorus, they were singing together, bound by the chain of the song into one hushed voice, a sigh on the night breeze. The first fallen leaves of autumn drifted across the beaten earth of the barnyard, fluttering among the ladies' skirts. The chorus came around again, and a single, sweet, solitary voice rose above the rest, holding the melody as tenderly as a robin's egg.

He lingered on the final note, letting it fade slowly, the ghost of it still on the air after he'd lifted his bow. Then he released his breath and opened his eyes.

Billy stood in front of him, her face solemn under the shadow of her cap. He wanted to ask if it was her voice he'd heard, but it felt like sacrilege to speak just now. Her blue eyes held him, more serious and older than she'd ever looked before. With an abrupt gesture, she snatched away his bow and shoved something into his hand, then disappeared into the shadows. The object was hard and cold and fringed with dead leaves.

"Well, I'll be damned," he said, looking down at the ear of corn, every kernel as red and precious as a ruby.

"I danced last night, Ivy," Daniel whispered as he buckled the mare's bridle. "Me, lass. Imagine that." Clumsily, stupidly, but he had danced. He rubbed the fingers of one hand together, still feeling the shock of touching and being touched, and not a one of the dancers shrinking from him. His arm on a girl's waist, her eyes meeting his, and him not needing to look away. Had it really been him doing all that?

Everything was different today, clearer, sweeter: the slant of sunlight, the breeze on his cheek, even the feel of Ivy beneath him, warm and soft with her winter coat starting to come in. He swore he could count every hair that tickled his bare ankles, every pebble in the road, could even see the ants scurrying away from the mare's hooves.

A little way down the road, a girl ran out of a house and waved them down, pushing her bonnet back to reveal a long, narrow, freckle-spattered face. Somebody who could not have been him slid from Ivy's back and stepped forward to talk to her.

"Sarah," he said, and with the one word the new Daniel slipped away and the old one rushed back into his head, reminding him that he should have tipped his hat and said *Good morning*, should have done anything else than just say her name as though he had a right to.

But she smiled and blushed a little. She'd been making butter; an ivory smear of cream soiled her apron, and two long greasy streaks darkened the cloth where she'd held the churn between her knees. "Did you come to work for Papa again?" she asked.

"N-No. I—we have to move along." He gestured at the peddler's wagon behind him. Billy sat beside the peddler, trying to
fasten a red ear of corn to the wagon.

"Oh. When I saw you coming, I hoped—I mean, I thought—"
She fidgeted with her apron and looked across the road at the
potato field that he'd dug yesterday. "Well." The silence hung for
a moment, then Sarah turned her head as if she'd just remembered something. "Mama needs some milk pans," she called out
to Mr. Stocking. "If you go around to the side—"

While Mr. Stocking drove into the barnyard, Sarah and Daniel stayed at the gate, not quite looking at each other, but not quite
looking away, either.

Sarah spoke first. "It was fun last night, wasn't it?"

"Aye—yes. Grand. Thank you," he said, forcing the *you* to
come out full and round. "It was kind of you to teach me." His
eyes fixed on her hands as something safe to look at: her freckled
fingers, her short, ragged nails, her chapped skin. "Teach me to
dance, I mean."

She picked at a bit of dried food stuck to her apron. "I had a
lovely time," she said. Her feet were bare, like his, her toes curling
in the dust on the other side of the cart track from his. "Is this
your horse?" she asked.

He nodded. It was easier to look at the lass's face while she was
studying Ivy. The straw-colored hair that had been so elaborately
arranged last night was now a single braid coiled at the nape of
her neck. Wispy strands escaped and trapped the light in a haze
of gold at her neck and temples, softening her angular face. She
was all sharp except for her eyes, gold-flecked ginger and cinnamon, crinkling with delight under pale lashes and brows.

"She's lovely," the girl said. "May I?" She reached a tentative
hand toward Ivy's nose.

"Here. She likes this." Not knowing what possessed him, he
took her hand and put it on the mare's ear, showing her where
Ivy liked to be scratched. The lass stood between them, her hair
so close to his face that he felt it like a sunbeam on his cheek. Ivy
leaned into their touch and let out a blissful grunt. When Sarah

laughed, Daniel felt like one of Mr. Stocking's fiddle-strings, plucked and quivering with music.

"You're so lucky," Sarah said. "I wish we had a horse."

"Sarah!" a shrill voice called. "That butter isn't going to churn itself!"

Just like that, the musical feeling was gone. Sarah drifted away from him, lingered in the grass beside the road. "I have to go."

As the peddler's wagon rumbled out of the yard, Sarah disappeared into the house. With a sigh, Daniel collected Ivy's reins. Already the feel of Sarah's hand in his seemed like something he'd imagined.

"Daniel!"

He turned to see Sarah running back out of the house.

"Here." She thrust a little paper-wrapped bundle into his hand. "Some gingerbread for your breakfast." The musty, sour scent of cattle and milk tickled his nose as she came closer, her breath moist against his cheek. And then she was away before he realized that he'd been kissed.

They were barely out of sight of the lass's house before Billy began taunting, "Daniel has a swee-eet-heart! Daniel has a swee-eet-heart!"

Did he now? Surely one kiss and a bit of gingerbread didn't make a sweetheart, especially when he'd likely never see her again. But the thought that he could have a sweetheart, maybe not this lass, but some girl, well, that was something. Billy's taunts wrapped around him like a blanket, making him feel oddly warm and content.

Chapter Seventeen

Liam's shanty was clean and freshly whitewashed, with herbs strewn across the floor and table, the smells of new paint and crushed tansy and mint and lavender overlying the odors of sickness and decay. The two boxes on the floor looked too small to contain the lads whose laughter and foolishness had once filled the room to bursting. Liam knelt next to the rough wooden boxes and set his fingertips along the edge of one lid to open it.

Augusta gripped his shoulder. "Don't. You don't want to remember them like that." Her eyes glittered with moisture. Who had she lost, that she was remembering now?

Somebody—who could it have been but her?—had found the lads' playthings and laid them on the coffins among the herbs: the crudely carved wooden animals he'd made for them, pocketknives, toy soldiers, a Jacob's ladder—the last few stolen. He picked up the Jacob's ladder and let its wooden panels click-clatter down, a harsh echo in the silent room.

"Thieving as magpies they were," he said. "You s'pose it'll be counted against them?"

"I'm a whore, Liam," she said harshly. "What would I know about such things?"

He flinched at her tone and looked up to see her staring out the window, not really looking outside at all, but seeing something deep within. She collected herself with a little shiver and turned to give him a weary smile. "If it were up to me, there'd be no children in hell," she added softly.

He bowed his head and tried to pray for the lads and for Nuala, but he hardly knew what point there was in praying when all the fevered prayers he'd made during the lads' sickness had been rejected, when what he really wanted to pray for was the impossible. He'd thought he'd cried himself dry when he'd been begging for their lives. But he had barely started. He felt as though he'd kneel there trembling and weeping until his own heart stopped.

Gradually, he became aware that someone was stroking his hair. He let himself collapse into Augusta's arms, let her rock him like a child. Then he realized that she, too, was crying. Although he was sure she wept for some hidden loss of her own, somehow it was a comfort to know that there were the two of them grieving together.

Chapter Eighteen

Tuesday, September 17, 1839, Bethel Village, Connecticut

Daniel caught himself whistling as he rode Ivy toward the tavern. He'd been worried at first that he'd be a burden on the peddler, but with the harvest season someone always needed help to bring in potatoes or corn or apples. There'd been barely a day that he hadn't earned his own board and lodging and some besides.

This traveling life was grand, indeed. True, Billy still refused to be civil to him, but it was enough for now that the cloud between her and the peddler had passed. She and Mr. Stocking made a fine pair with their jokes and stories, even if most of the stories were probably lies. Then there was their music; it had been worth throwing his lot in with them if only for the chance to hear them.

Sometimes he felt as though he were perched at the top of a tall tree. He was eager and dizzy and fearful all at once, knowing that a mere gust of wind could send him tumbling back down.

Aye, it was grand to be a free man with cash money in his pocket, knowing that all he needed was his work to prove himself—as long as he kept his mouth shut. The thought toppled him out of his imaginary tree with a very real shudder from his tailbone to his skull. He still had to guard his words to keep the Irish out of his voice. Folk liked the Irish well enough when it was a pretty child like Billy singing a pretty song, but a laborer was another matter entirely. How free would he be now, if not for Mr. Stocking? He didn't feel like whistling anymore by the time he saw the peddler and Billy sitting on a bench outside the tavern, their heads bent over Billy's primer.

"Profitable day, Dan'l?" Mr. Stocking asked, glancing up from the book.

"A dollar." He slid from Ivy's back and reached in his pocket. "And you?" He counted out his share of the room and board.

"Sold two tin kitchens," Billy declared with a grin. "Did it me very own self."

Daniel raised a skeptical eyebrow. She must have been proud to be talking civil to him. "Did you now?"

The peddler nodded. "That's right. He came up with a comical verse about 'em. Put it to the tune of 'Yankee Doodle.' Amazing the things he found to rhyme with 'kitchen.'" *He*, Mr. Stocking had said, referring to Billy, not *she*. It reminded Daniel that folk were in earshot. "I'll have him sing it to you after supper."

Daniel couldn't help smiling. "I've heard of things bought for a song, but never any sold for one before."

Mr. Stocking chuckled. "That's a good one. I'll have to save it to use later." He nudged the lass to make room for Daniel on the bench. "We're just working on our grammar. Care to join us?"

"Grammar?" Daniel glanced over the peddler's shoulder at the book.

"Aye. So I don't talk ignorant," Billy said. "Like you." She let out a little *oof* as the peddler elbowed her in the ribs.

Daniel bristled, but she was right, now, wasn't she? All his *ain't*s and *brung*s had become as much a part of his speech as the Irish lilt that he struggled to disguise. The Irish, well, there was no question of what prompted that. Remembering Ma's Gaelic words and Da's voice kept them with him, even if the only one to hear was a horse. But the "talking ignorant" had come not from sentiment or stupidity, but from spite, a way to irk the Lymans. Mr. Lyman had missed the defiance that lay behind the *ain't*s, attributing them to stupidity rather than obstinance, and had decided that it would be a waste of time to try to beat them out of the boy. Now that the *ain't*s no longer served him, Daniel found them as hard to shed as the upward slant that his sentences took when he spoke.

"Ignorant, aye," he said. He settled next to Mr. Stocking on the bench and looked over the grammar book on the peddler's knee. "But what I really need you to learn me—*teach* me, sir—is how to talk proper, like the rest of 'em." At Mr. Stocking's puzzled frown, he gestured toward the tavern door, where talk and laughter tumbled out in flat, angular tones. "Yankees. Americans. So I don't hang meself every time I open me mouth." It felt like asking for a knife to cut the slender thread that still linked him to Ma and Da.

Mr. Stocking closed the grammar book and leaned back against the tavern wall. His glance drifted across the yard to where Ivy stood tethered, then to Billy on his left side and back to Daniel on his right. There was such a devilish spark in his green eyes that Daniel thought he'd put off the request with one of his tall tales.

"Talking proper, well, I could show you that, I guess," the little man said. "But how about I teach the two of you to act? Then you can talk anyways you want, whenever you want."

"To act?" Billy's face shone with the prospect. She hopped up from the bench as if she were ready to start learning right that moment.

The peddler grabbed her elbow and pinned her with a solemn gaze. "But you got to pay for the lessons."

"How?" she asked. "Sell more of them tin kitchens?"

He shook his head. "I want you to work with Daniel on that Gaelic of yours. So you don't forget who you are."

Wednesday, September 18, 1839, Danbury, Connecticut

Billy was dying of consumption, and all Jonathan could do was sit by and watch. Rain hammered the tavern roof, the wind rattling the windows and moaning as if it were trying to get in and claim her soul. The girl curled listlessly on the settle, wheezing so hard that her eyes watered. She hid her agony in a handkerchief as a gurgling noise crept up her throat.

Daniel snatched the handkerchief away. "Don't be spitting in it! It's me only clean one!"

Billy snagged one corner of the cloth. It stretched between them, threatening to rip. "Give us something red, Mr. S. To make it look like blood."

"He'll do no such thing." Daniel tried to peel her fingers from the handkerchief.

"You want it to look real, don't you?" she pleaded, slapping at Daniel's arm.

He finally rescued his handkerchief and returned it to the safety of his pocket. "You want it to look real, you ought to be down in the cold, dark cellar, not up here cozy by the fire with a cup of tea to hand."

Cozy wasn't the first word Jonathan would have used to describe the dank little room he'd rented just in time to escape the storm. They'd moved the bed and settle twice to get them away from the dribbles now pattering into two buckets and a tin pan. The green firewood sputtered and squealed while gusts of wind sent the smoke down instead of up. The tea and sugar were from Jonathan's own goods, the landlord providing only vinegary ale for drink. But at least they had the room to themselves and were away from the dismal mess outside.

Jonathan cleared his throat noisily. "Let's get to where the ghost of the prisoner's mother appears to see if he's learned the error of his ways."

Billy stood on the settle and emitted a spectral moan, raising her arms to loom over the now invisible prisoner.

"You can't be playing the mother's ghost and the prisoner, too," Daniel protested.

"All right, then you be the prisoner," Billy suggested tartly.

"No. That's fine," Daniel replied. "Seems to me that part was made special for you."

They were acting out an insipid moral tale from Billy's primer about a deceitful boy whose lies had caused his sainted mother's death and led him down a path of wantonness and degradation that finally brought him to gasp out the last days of his wretched life in prison.

"I think you're missing the point of the story, fellas," Jonathan interjected.

Billy shook her head, staring daggers at Daniel. "I see the point just fine."

"And that would be…" Daniel crossed his arms over his chest and tried to look fierce, but Jonathan noticed a twitch at one corner of his mouth.

"Don't get caught," Billy said smugly.

The twitch turned into a smirk that dissolved into a snicker as Daniel swatted at Billy's ear. "Ee-jit."

"Lout." Billy aimed a kick at Daniel's shins. Like Daniel's swat, it never landed.

Jonathan smothered his chuckles with difficulty. "Maybe it's time for geography." He pulled two books from his bag. "Here, Dan'l, you be Europe, and Billy, you be Asia. And why don't you sit on opposite sides of the world while you're at it?" He pointed at either end of the settle, which wasn't long enough by half.

Jonathan's idea about acting lessons had been pure genius, if he did say so himself. Not only had it made Billy's lessons more palatable, but it had cracked the barriers between her and Daniel. Where formerly they'd gotten along like cats and dogs, now they were more like two not unfriendly mongrels. The Irish lessons, on the other hand, were a disaster, with Billy tormenting Daniel over his rusty Gaelic.

"Dan'l's Irish is better than your reading," Jonathan had snapped. As the words left his mouth, the answer had flown into his head. He'd handed Billy her primer and shoved her toward Daniel. "Here. I want you and him to turn this into Gaelic. Together." Now each of them knew something the other needed. But what they really needed wasn't either Gaelic or reading.

Chapter Nineteen

Thursday, September 19, 1839, Cabotville, Massachusetts

"And who are you?"

"Fogarty, sir. Remember? I've been working for you these past two years now, sir." Liam doffed his cap so Mr. Briggs could see his face, but the man never looked up from his ledger, his lips moving as if he didn't want to lose his place in his calculations.

At last Mr. Briggs spared Liam an upward roll of his eyes, then turned back to the record book and papers spread out on the table in his tiny closet of an office. "Fogarty..." He thumbed through the ledger to find the list of workers. "Last you worked was more'n two weeks ago."

"I know, sir. I took sick with the fever. But I'm ready to go back to work now."

Mr. Briggs looked Liam up and down through narrowed eyes. "Fever, indeed." He clapped the ledger shut. "Fever for a bottle, no doubt."

Liam bit down on the anger that singed his face. "I'm telling you no tales, sir. I've been ailing these two weeks and more. Me two brothers died of it, with only me to care for 'em."

"Boy, do you know how many Paddies come crying to me about missing work for your poor brother's or granny's funeral? You seem to have more grannies than a duck's got feathers."

Liam wrung his cap into a sweaty twist, fighting the urge to grab Mr. Briggs by the collar and throttle him on the spot. "It's true," he said between clenched teeth.

"Fine. Show me the death notice in the paper." Briggs opened his ledger again.

"You think there'd be any newspaper taking notice of whether we Paddies live or die? What does it matter, anyway? I'm here to work. Me family isn't none of your business." Liam stepped closer to the table, standing over the builder with clenched fists.

Mr. Briggs rose to meet Liam's glare. "I won't hire anyone who can't hold his liquor well enough to do a day's work." He jabbed a forefinger at Liam's chest. "And I won't hire a liar."

The fever had never burned Liam as hot as his anger did now. It was all he could do not to upend Mr. Briggs's table and throw it in his face.

"I'll speak for him, sir." Ed Callahan stood in the doorway, all six feet tall and broad of him. Liam wondered how much Callahan had heard and how much he'd merely guessed.

Callahan laid a beefy hand on Liam's shoulder. "It's no tale he's telling you, Mr. Briggs. Didn't I see with me own eyes the two lads buried, and Liam here barely able to stand by the grave?" Although Callahan's tone was deferential, Mr. Briggs's power seemed to fade in the big man's presence. Callahan did not remove his hat.

"Did you?" said Mr. Briggs.

"That I did. Wasn't it meself helping to dig the grave with these two hands of mine?"

In truth, Liam had been aware of naught but the two boxes sliding into the earth and the dirt piled over them. There must have been someone stronger than Augusta holding him up through it all, but he'd no recollection of who'd been there.

"He's a good man, is Liam, sir, and not a bit of a drunk or layabout," Callahan concluded.

Mr. Briggs scowled at Liam. "All right. Fifty cents a day. If he can do the work." He jerked his head toward the window facing the partly dug canal, where the work crew was assembling.

"Fifty cents?" Liam protested. "But it was seventy-five before. That's two bits' difference."

"Fifty cents. Prove to me you can do a man's work for two weeks and we'll see about bringing it up by one bit." Mr. Briggs cast an uneasy look at Callahan before settling back in his chair and returning to his ledger.

One bit. Twelve and a half cents, still short of what he'd made before. "And what about me back wages? 'Twas nigh on three weeks' pay you were owing me before I took ill."

Mr. Briggs snapped his book shut. "Give me two weeks' work and then we'll see."

Callahan's grip kept Liam from lunging at Briggs. "Swallow it, lad," Callahan said softly. "Swallow your anger for now. Use it to give you the strength to do your work, aye?" He put a firm arm around Liam's shoulders and guided him out the door and toward the work site.

Slowly, the heat washed out of Liam's face and his fists loosened. When he could finally manage to speak, he thanked Callahan for vouching for him. "I'm grateful, too, for what you done for the lads. I should'a been thanking you then, but—"

"Don't fret on it, lad. Anyone with eyes could see what a state you were in. It's sorry I am we didn't know of your troubles sooner." Callahan's blue eyes went soft for a moment, and he patted Liam's shoulder awkwardly. "All right, then, Liam, let's to work, eh?"

Liam felt as if he'd left work at eighteen and come back at eighty. Lads his own age looked like children. The craggy veterans with work- and drink- and loss-ravaged faces, scarred bodies and souls, the ones who kept to themselves and hacked at the rocky soil and heaved out boulders as if the earth itself were their enemy, no longer puzzled him. He wondered if his eyes had already turned glassy and hard like theirs.

"Well, lads, here's Liam back again," Callahan said.

The Yankees paid him no mind, or at most offered him a curt nod. The other Paddies seemed at first to do the same, but as he made his way over to pick up his tools, each one brushed by him, put a hand on his shoulder, a few words in his ear: "Sorry for your loss." "Lord rest their souls." "Missed you, lad." It was a strange sort of benediction they gave him: a welcome to a company he'd rather not have joined.

Chapter Twenty

Thursday, September 19, 1839, Patterson, New York

"Well, strike me blind if it ain't Fred!" Mr. Stocking exclaimed.

Daniel and Billy exchanged glances. "Fred?" they asked simultaneously.

"Fred Chamberlain." Mr. Stocking poked a stubby finger at the handbill tacked up on the tavern wall. "I haven't seen Fred in a dog's age and then some."

Daniel peered over the peddler's shoulder. "**Prince Otoo Baswamati's Peripatetic Museum and Exhibition of Cultural Artistry and Athleticism**," the bold letters proclaimed. Underneath, a sinister-looking figure in a turban and flowing robes was labeled "Prince Baswamati, The East Indian Mystic and Conjurer." The museum promised a "splendid Attraction of Equestrian and Gymnastic Exercises with a beautiful collection of Living Wild Animals," complete with camelopard; athletes; Madame Staccato, "the Italian Songbird"; Professor Romanov and his six dancing ponies; and Francesca de V., the "Fascinating *Danseuse*," who would perform "wonderful Suspensions and Tourbillions on the *Corde Volante*." All, according to the poster, would be "classic, chaste, morally entertaining, and of the highest order of art such as would command the admiration of the scholar, poet, painter, and sculptor."

Daniel fancied it could take him half the evening to puzzle out all the grand words. Billy slowly sounded out the text, but couldn't get any further than *Peripatetic*.

"It's all just a fanciful name for a circus, isn't it?" Daniel asked.

"More or less," Mr. Stocking said. "Only a museum's more, well, erudite. Morally uplifting," the peddler elaborated when

Daniel raised a skeptical eyebrow. "Hence less likely to attract unwanted attention from the humorless, the sanctimonious, the hypocritical, the—"

"The preachers and constables, you mean?" Daniel said.

"Well, them, too," Mr. Stocking said.

"You ever seen one of these camelwhatsises, Mr. S.?" Billy asked.

"Only seen pictures. It's like God took a goat and a camel and put 'em in a bag and shook it up, then covered it with a leopard skin. It looked so awful, He figured the only thing to do was hang it and try again. But instead of killing it, the hanging only stretched its neck 'til it was that tall." Mr. Stocking pointed to the flagpole in front of the meetinghouse.

"What's this friend of yours do?" Daniel asked. "Muck out after the camelopard and the ponies? I'm not seeing his name in here anywhere."

"He uses his professional name—his nom de plumage, as it were. Fred is none other than Prince Baswamati himself."

"What's a conjurer?" Billy asked.

"Someone who takes your money to make a fool of you," Daniel said.

"Son, I've seen Fred conjure birds out of thin air, make a horse disappear, turn—"

Daniel interrupted Mr. Stocking midsentence. "Turn your pockets empty, is what he's best at, I'm guessing."

"A man's got to make a living somehow, don't he?" Mr. Stocking said. "But what Fred's best at ain't in the appearing and disappearing line. What he's best at is using The Sight: reading minds, telling fortunes, communicating with the spirit world."

Daniel snorted. "Lies and tricks." Still, a shiver trickled down his spine. He remembered Ma's little vial of holy water that she'd touch to ward off evil or to bring good luck. Daniel didn't believe in anything that he couldn't see and touch, though now and again he would involuntarily cross himself or find Ma's prayers springing to his mind when he was troubled or afraid, as if whatever had failed to protect Ma and Da would spare a thought for him.

Mr. Stocking shook his head. "Maybe so, if good observation is lies and tricks. You watch someone close enough, you get to know what he's thinking. And Fred's got a way of saying things so you'd think they was meant for you, even if he said the exact same things to the fella ahead of you."

"Can we see the show? Can we, please?" Billy said.

"Show won't be in town 'til tomorrow. We'd have to stay another night," Mr. Stocking said with apparent reluctance. He peered at Daniel, a mischievous glint in his turtle-like stare. "Got to think about business, not this fol-der-rol-ity."

"Please, Mr. S.," Billy begged, about to explode with eagerness.

"I s'pose you could be selling an awful lot of tin to them folk what's come to see the show," Daniel suggested casually.

"That's right," Billy said. "I'll sell more tin than you could imagine. I promise. I'll pay me own ticket and yours, too."

"But it's *my* tin, *my* horse, *my* wagon," Mr. Stocking said. "That means anything you sell is *my* money, don't it? I think you got to do more than sell a little tin to earn your way into a show." He gestured toward the poster. "'Specially one as good as all that."

Billy tugged at Mr. Stocking's coattail like a desperate five-year-old. "Please, Mr. S. I'll be ever so good, and I won't fight with Daniel even once."

Daniel grinned. "That'd be worth staying for the show just to see." He didn't care about seeing the show himself; it was naught but folk spending money to be fooled and lied to. Although it would be a curiosity to see if them ponies really could dance.

"Whyever are you so mad for washing up?" Billy asked. "I never seen a lad as particular for being clean as you."

Daniel gave her one of his sharp looks. "It's 'cause I don't care for going hungry."

"What's being clean got to do with being hungry?" She perched on the end of the bed and wrapped her arms around her legs.

He leaned closer to the mirror and rubbed a hand across his jaw. "Where I was bound out, you'd come to dinner clean or you'd not get dinner at all. You'd maybe get a thrashing instead." He apparently found a phantom whisker or two and began to lather his cheeks and chin.

"But nobody cares now," Billy protested. Granted, today was special, with them going to Mr. Chamberlain's museum, but surely a quick rinse of hands and face would do. No, he had to scrub himself pink, an entire waste of soap, water, and time. No amount of washing would ever improve his looks. She eyed the bony ridge of his spine. He oughtn't to leave his braces hanging down while he shaved. He was so spindly that one tug on his broadfalls would send them down about his ankles. She measured the distance between bed and door, wondering how fast she'd be able to get out of his reach if she tried it.

"Well, maybe I'm the one caring now," Daniel said. "Maybe I'm not liking folk thinking the way they do about us." He must have read her mind, for he shrugged one strap of his braces over his scarred shoulder.

"Us?"

"Us Irish. They think we're all drunken thieves. I'm not having them thinking that of me."

"You sound like Liam," she said.

Daniel raised an eyebrow. "Liam?"

"Me brother. He's grown," she said. "He shaves for real," she added, as Daniel's razor reached the curve of his chin where he tended to cut himself. "He's got hair on his chest, too."

Daniel squinted one eye sidelong at her and disappointed her by rounding his chin without drawing so much as a dot of blood. "That all you got?" he asked. "Just the one brother?"

"There's Jimmy and Mick, too. They're little." She'd tried not to think much about them since Mr. S. had bought her. Now they seemed like people in one of Mr. S.'s books, far away, with naught to do with her.

"Liam, Jimmy, and Mick," Daniel said. "William James Michael. So that's where you took your name from, eh?"

"I got to be calling meself something, don't I now?" she said.

"Liam was always after us about being decent, but I was hardly seeing the point. Me da *is* a drunk. And everyone's a thief."

"Everyone?"

"Don't tell me you never stole nothing," she said.

He gave a weary sigh. Pulling his upper lip stiff, he worked at it for much longer than even Mr. S. with his dark, heavy beard would have needed.

"That's what I thought," she said.

"Aye, so I have," he finally said. "But them days are over. Anyway, I'm hardly decent people, now, am I?"

"Decent people," she repeated with a snort. "They steal worst of all, don't they?"

"Well, there are them as thinks they're decent and them as really are," Daniel said. "What about Mr. Stocking?"

Mr. S. was far and away the decentest person she'd ever known, never mind what folk thought of peddlers. But to admit that would be to let Daniel be right. "What is it but thieving when you pay ten cents for a thing and turn about and sell it for twenty?" There, she had him. She could tell from the way his mouth did that little fishy gaping thing.

"Business," he finally said, snapping his jaw shut.

"Businessmen is nothing but thieves, they are."

"Fine. Have it your way." He picked up the towel from the washstand and snapped it open to dry his face. Throwing the towel at her in disgust, he turned to snatch up his shirt. "Next you'll be saying that God and all His saints are a pack of thieves, won't you?"

She kicked the towel onto the floor and jumped from the bed. "God's the worst of 'em all. Didn't He steal me mam away? And yours, too?"

He crumpled the shirt between his fingers. "Aye," he said softly. "And me da and brother as well." Turning his back on her, he pulled on his shirt. He took a long time about tucking it in and pulling his braces over his shoulders. Then he stood by the window, looking out at nothing.

Sighing, he rubbed his face and turned around to finish dressing. She couldn't look at him for the longest time, but listened as he moved about the room, putting on his vest and searching for his cravat. The bed ropes creaked as he sat to put on his shoes and stockings. He nudged her elbow. "Put your shoes on, lass," he said softly. "You can't be going to the show barefoot."

For once, she didn't bristle when he called her *lass*. "I'd'a not minded so much had He taken me da and left me mam," she said, picking up her shoes.

He moved over on the bed to make room for her.

"Do you never stop missing 'em?" she asked.

He shook his head. "Ask me again in twenty years." He took her shoes and polished them up against his trousers. "You got your brothers, though. Don't it trouble you to have left 'em?"

"It never troubled them to leave me. Jimmy and Mick'd run about the streets playing all day while I was trapped inside. I could'a been a kettle or a stick of wood or a bucket, for all they'd'a noticed. As long as they can have their fun, they'll not miss me a bit."

"Ah, sure they would."

"Maybe at mealtimes or when their trousers need mending," she said. She tried to push them back into the dark corner of her heart where she'd kept them all the spring and summer, but their laughing, grimy faces wouldn't be shut out. When Mr. S. had bought her, all she'd thought of was how grand it would be never to see Da again. She'd not thought about being apart from Jimmy and Mick forever. And Liam.

"Liam might miss me," she said. Jimmy and Mick would make fun of her singing, but Liam seemed truly glad of it. At night, when he'd come home weary and filthy and blistered and barely able to stay awake through his meal, he'd ask her for a song to help him to sleep. She liked to believe that her music had helped ease Liam's spirit. For what did Liam have but the few minutes of singing she'd given him at the end of his weary day?

"Liam's maybe the only one I know who'd not be a thief," she said. Liam had wanted so hard to be like decent folk. And where did it get him? Jimmy and Mick were thieves and their lives were full of fun and laughter. Billy herself was a thief, stealing Liam's cast-off clothes and abandoning her chores to wander the streets, singing and picking pockets. On a good day, she might bring home as much in a few hours' singing and thievery as Liam did after fourteen hours' work with pick and shovel.

And all the while, when he'd sooner cut his own throat than steal from anybody, everybody stole from Liam. Da, who took Liam's wages when he could, and thrashed him when he couldn't. Jimmy and Mick, who left the kindling for Liam to chop and the water for him to fetch. The merchants who bought things for ten cents and sold them for twenty, and Liam with only nine cents in his pocket. And the men that Liam worked for worst of all, stealing away his time and strength and not paying him enough for his work. And now she'd gone and stolen the music away from his evenings.

"Aye," she said. "Liam might miss me."

Chapter Twenty-One

Thursday, September 19, 1839, Cabotville, Massachusetts

Liam paced the shanty aimlessly. It felt like a huge empty box, with what little remained reminding him that he was the only one left. One chair. One plate. One mug. Da's bed. One of everything, including himself. He closed his eyes and tried to summon up Jimmy and Mick's laughter, Nuala's singing. They were all with Mam now. He felt a sting of envy for their peace.

He buttoned his threadbare jacket, put on his cap, and went out into the muddy alley that passed for a street. Something stopped him before he'd gone three steps.

The last link is broken that bound me to thee...

In among the sounds of wailing babies, cackling chickens, and rooting pigs that usually filled the Patch, he heard somebody singing. "Nuala?" he whispered, turning his good ear in the direction of the song.

The words thou hast spoken have rendered me free...

Damned if that voice wasn't real, and the song one that Nuala herself had sung for him the day before she'd disappeared. He shook his head. Nuala's own song, but not her own voice. This singer's voice was pleasant, but thin and hesitant on the high notes. And she was no ghost.

He crossed the road and rapped on Augusta's door. She opened it, a pair of broadfalls in her hand. At the sight of the trousers, he reddened and almost turned away. Then he noticed the pincushion fastened to Augusta's wrist and the patch half sewn on one knee of the trousers. His neck grew hot at the churlish conclusion he'd made about what sort of work she might be about.

"Liam? I thought you were going back to work today."

"I did." He twisted his cap in his hands.

"It didn't go well," she guessed.

He shook his head. "I couldn't—" He opened his hand, exposing fresh blisters. "It was like I'd never done a day's work in me life before."

Her hand closed over his, cool against his broken skin. "It's all right. You'll get your strength back. There'll be other jobs."

"Aye. But not today." Looking over her shoulder into the shanty, he saw a basket of clothes on the floor and garments spread across the table, from a laborer's coarse frock to a little girl's gown. "It's sorry I am for disturbing you at your work. I'll be on me way—"

She put a hand on his wrist. "Why don't you come in for a bit? Have a cup of tea and visit while I sew."

"It's only—it's a bit empty—" He gestured toward his own shanty. "And I heard you singing one of Nuala's songs and I thought—"

She smiled and nodded as she set about making tea. "Nuala. Yes, the little girl with the big voice."

"You—you knew her? I mean—not just to see on the street?"

"Everybody knew her. Where do you think she learned all her songs? Or how to cook and sew and knit?"

"I never—never really thought—"

Augusta laughed softly. "You men. You think women are born knowing how to keep house, don't you?"

"I—ah—well—"

Augusta set a cup of tea in front of him. "Your sister was a bold little thing. If she heard a song she liked or smelled some fine cooking or needed to learn a stitch, she'd just knock on doors until someone would teach her."

"She did?" Liam felt dizzy, discovering that Nuala had a life he'd been too selfish and stupid and work-weary to be curious about.

Augusta nodded. She sat and took up her mending again. It was fine work she was doing, for all that it was only patching a pair of trousers. She joined the pieces so precisely that the rend almost disappeared under her needle. Why would she need to do aught else to make her living? Another thought, even more unsettling than the first, flashed through his head. "She came here?"

"Now and again. Oh, don't look so shocked. I only taught her a few songs, a receipt or two. I imagine the other ladies here taught her more than I ever did."

"I'm not meaning to be passing judgments, but she knew what you did, uh, do?"

"She knew about the sewing and laundry. The rest?" She shook her head. "It's not as if it ever came up when we talked. She is only a child."

"Was," Liam said, dropping the word between them like a stone.

"I'm sorry, Liam. I liked her. She was an odd little girl. Not afraid of anything. Not, well, not particularly girlish."

"Aye. I remember this one time, I was maybe fourteen. I come home from work and Da'd found out I been keeping back some of me wages. The black mood was on him, and he had me by the hair, and certain I was that he'd flay the very skin off me. Nuala, she'd been making our dinner. It was a meat pie, and little enough meat we ever got. Quick as you please, she snatched the pie up from the bake kettle, wrapped it in her apron, and held it out the window. Somebody's pig was rooting around there behind the house; we could hear it grunting. She told Da if he didn't let me go, she'd toss the pie out to that pig. So he had to be letting me go to save his supper, didn't he, now? But quicker 'n you could sneeze, Nuala took herself and that pie both out the window and into the alley. Then while Da was trying to catch her, me and Jimmy and Mick took ourselves out the door. We all four of us hid and had that pie to ourselves." It felt strange to be wearing a smile, stranger still to hear his own laughter. "It was damn good pie, too," he added, wiping his eyes.

Augusta's mouth curled uncertainly, as if she wasn't sure whether it was all right for her to smile, too.

He took a sip of tea, scalding and bitter. "You taught her that song, then?" he asked. "The one you were singing just now?"

She nodded, her head bowed once more over her sewing as she put in the last few stitches and snapped the end of the thread.

"That was what brought me over." He fidgeted with his cup, stared at the murky clump of leaves at the bottom. "Christ, I must be mad." He pushed the cup away and reached for his hat, but couldn't make himself put it on and get out of the chair, couldn't make himself go back to the empty shanty. "You'll think me mad, you will."

"Whatever for?"

"I was wondering if maybe, just for a minute or two, if you'd mind if I sat here for a wee bit and just listened to you sing."

Chapter Twenty-Two

Friday, September 20, 1839, Patterson, New York

Billy felt as though her eyes had been starving, and she'd never known it until today. The museum was like one of the feasts that a king might have in one of Mr. S.'s stories, with each new course more scrumptious than the one before it. First, there'd been the grand cavalcade parading through town: a dozen or more brightly painted wagons trimmed in gold, with the performers sitting on top, dressed as splendidly as lords and ladies. She and Daniel and Mr. S. had followed the cavalcade to a broad meadow just south of town. She'd gasped at the show pavilion, big and white as a meetinghouse, with smaller tents clustered around it. Spreading out from the tents was just about every sort of traveling crafter and hawker setting up wares and workbenches. There were minor showmen as well: a man with a genuine Egyptian mummy, another with a quartet of dancing dogs, and a third with a panorama of the Great Fire of London. Mr. S. said they were hangers-on hoping to ride the museum's coattails to profit.

"Pit or box?" the ticket seller asked at the entrance to the great pavilion. She was relieved when Mr. S. said, "Box," for a pit sounded like a foul place to watch a show from. She was a trifle disappointed to enter the pavilion and see there was no real pit, but just a place marked off where folk who had bought the cheaper tickets had to stand to watch the show. The box seats weren't real boxes, either, but an eight-tiered structure with planks for seats and nowhere to rest your back but against the shins of the person behind you. The heads of those in the top tier brushed the pavilion's canvas roof.

Mr. S. hustled them into second-row seats. She was glad he

hadn't gotten tickets for the pit. The men and lads were crammed in so tight there, nobody short of a giant would see anything. Folk occupying the box seats looked more genteel, but they pushed and shoved just as hard as the men in the pit to get the best places. The air grew thick with the smells of sweat, tobacco, and livestock mingled with toilet water and hair oil. She'd never heard such a hubbub of talking and shouting and laughing. She'd have found the noise and the smells and the closeness of the packed pavilion unbearable, were it not for the tension of expectation that thrummed through the crowd.

A sharp hissing noise broke through the din. Folk shushed each other and focused their attention on the southern end of the pavilion. A trumpet blew a fanfare, and in came the grand cavalcade. Billy leaned forward, and Daniel did the same.

The museum was such a wonder that Billy could hardly say which act she liked best. The jugglers tossing knives and torches back and forth like they were no more than apples—they were the best until a man came out and wrestled and danced with an enormous bear. He was the best until the rope dancer who tiptoed across a line hung slack between two posts. After that, she twirled and leaped and danced in the air, with only a loop of rope for a swing. She was the best until the dancing ponies, all tricked out in gold-trimmed blankets and red-and-black plumes on their foreheads, their black hooves as shiny as one of Mr. S.'s japanned teapots. They lifted their feet high in elegant prancing steps, as if afraid to get their hooves dirty. They leaped and kicked and trotted in circles while Professor Romanov cracked his whip in time to the music. Then the Professor collected the ponies together, and they solemnly bowed down on their knees like they were praying. And last and best of all, they stood up on their back legs just like people.

She elbowed Daniel. "Aren't they ever so grand?" she whispered.

He scowled and muttered with Mr. S. over Billy's head. Jealous, no doubt, that his precious Ivy couldn't do none of them fine tricks.

After the applause faded and a funny little man had cleaned up after the ponies, a fat lady walked out. She wore a gown of iridescent silk, with jewels glittering at her neck and ears and wrists, but she herself was a bit cow-faced. Like the dancing ponies, she had feathers in her hair, but the ponies were prettier. Billy squirmed with impatience. Then the lady began to sing.

Billy's body broke out all over in gooseflesh. The words were neither English nor Irish nor the Latin that Father Brady chanted at the Mass. The lady's voice wrapped around Billy and lifted her up like she was flying. She closed her eyes and concentrated so intently that her heartbeat matched the pulse of the song. When she opened her eyes, the music shone from the fat lady's face and sparkled all about her. She reminded Billy of a story Father Brady had told about the Holy Spirit coming down on the apostles in tongues of fire, giving them the power to speak languages they never could before. Surely naught but the Holy Spirit could make somebody sing so grand.

When the music stopped, the fat lady shimmered in the applause, bowed with surprising grace, and glided away into the shadows.

Billy tugged at Mr. S.'s sleeve. "Did you ever hear the like? Wasn't she lovely?"

Mr. S. nodded. "Heard something like her once in New York. She certainly is something."

"Could you teach me to sing like that?" Billy asked.

"Whyever would you want to be spoiling your voice? It's fine just like it is," Daniel said.

Billy had just summoned up a retort when she realized that Daniel had actually paid her a compliment. She cast a baffled glance at Mr. S., but he only adjusted his spectacles and shushed the both of them. The crowd quieted down again as a tall, thin man walked out.

He wore a long robe with wide, bell-like sleeves and swirls of rich colors shot through with golden thread. In between the colors were silver moons and stars, mysterious symbols, and tiny bits of glass sewn into his costume. Wrapped around his head was a crimson turban with an enormous black jewel over his forehead. He was tall and gaunt, with deep hollows under his cheekbones and a long hooked nose over a black mustache that drooped down on either side of his mouth. His skin was almost as dark as a Negro's, making him look as though he'd been carved out of wood. Slowly he turned, peering out from under heavy black eyebrows as if memorizing each face in the audience. Everyone fell quiet. His eyes rested on Mr. S. One eyebrow angled up, then the other, and the ends of his mustache quivered ever so slightly.

Mr. S. met the tall, thin man's gaze full on. It was hard to tell, what with Mr. S.'s spectacles and all, but Billy was almost sure that he winked. Then she felt a shiver at the base of her skull, and she turned to see the man staring at her.

Her instinctive reaction was to drop her eyes as everyone else did, but she forced herself to stare back. After all, he was neither East Indian nor mystical, but only Fred Chamberlain, a play-actor from Baltimore. She clenched her jaw and stared back as hard as she could. It was worse than trying to stare down Mr. S. when he'd caught her out in a lie. The man's eyes were as black and shiny as the jewel in his turban. But she refused to blink or turn away.

Slowly Mr. Chamberlain's mustache unveiled a brilliant white smile against the darkness of his face. He nodded once, then spun away toward the center of the ring.

"Secrets!" he said, his voice a shocking boom. Hundreds of backsides shifted uneasily, hundreds of breaths drew in at once. He flung his arms wide, his sleeves unfurling like wings. A pair of ravens appeared and flew above the crowd, shattering the stillness with their harsh cries.

"Secrets," he repeated, this time just above a whisper. "The air is heavy with secrets. They are a burden on our minds. Our hearts. Our souls." His words were elegantly chiseled, the *r*'s rolling from his tongue, the *s*'s lingering ominously. He favored one person with his gaze, then another.

"There are the secrets we keep from others. The secrets others keep from us. The secrets we keep from ourselves." He balled his hands into fists and thrust them down by his sides. Twin plumes of black smoke rose on either side of him. "There are secrets of the earth." He raised his hands, sending white smoke skyward. "The heavens." He whirled, and the gold thread and bits of glass on his robe twinkled like stars. "The seas." Blue scarves flew from his sleeves. He caught them, and they disappeared as quickly as they'd appeared.

"Secrets of the gods." One eyebrow rose, and he smiled with only half his mouth. "Ah, I beg your pardon. In my land we have many gods. Here you have one god, but I think many more secrets, yes?" Somebody giggled uneasily. He brought his hands close to his chest and flung them wide. A woman shrieked as jets of flame shot from his hands. "And secrets of the devil.

"Today, you will see many secrets revealed." As he raised his left hand, one of the ravens returned and landed on his wrist. He fixed Billy once again with his dark stare. "Secrets of the living." He raised his right hand, and the other raven perched. "And secrets of the dead.

"If you fear these secrets, you should leave now." He scanned the crowd for a long moment, as if he really did expect somebody to leave. "You choose to stay? You are very brave. Braver than my last audience." He released the birds with a wave of his hands. "Where shall we begin?" The ravens swooped over the crowd, dipping low enough to make men and women duck and cower.

Billy grinned and poked Daniel. Now here was some fun. A lot of silly folk afraid of a couple of pet birds. No doubt Mr. S.'s actor-friend had a companion in the crowd who would pretend the birds had chosen him and then would feign a trance to make folk think he'd been charmed. Well, there was no point in letting Mr. S's friend have all the fun. Billy stood and put out her arm to make a perch like Mr. Chamberlain had. Before Mr. S. or Daniel could sit her down, one of the ravens landed on her arm. It was heavier than she'd expected, but also more beautiful, its feathers gleaming blue-black, its eyes bright and curious. She reached out a finger to stroke its breast. Its caw stung her eardrums, and it flapped its wings and made as if to peck at her. She hummed a little to settle the bird. It seemed to work: the raven smoothed its feathers and rested more lightly on her arm. When she tried to stroke it again, it let her.

"Very good," Mr. Chamberlain said. "You have discovered his secret."

She looked up sharply. "Me?"

The tall man's smile spread across his entire face. "He likes music."

"That's no secret," Billy said. "Everyone likes music."

"Not everyone." The conjurer pointed to the second raven, which had settled in the rigging near the top of the tent. "Kali has a tin ear. But Shiva—well, perhaps it is not that you have discovered his secret, but that he has discovered yours. Would you care to share it with us?"

"Sh-share?" Billy felt suddenly timid.

The conjurer opened a gate in the fence surrounding the ring. "Come and sing for us."

Billy picked her way across the tier of seats and came into the ring, the raven still perched on her arm. With a clicking noise and a whistle, the conjurer called the bird. To the crowd's amusement, the bird fluffed his wings and settled more securely on Billy's arm.

"Ah, well. Have it your way, Shiva." The conjurer sighed, then turned back to Billy. "Now...what would you like me to call you?"

A little of her earlier sauciness returned. "You're the one s'posed to be knowing all the secrets. You ought to be able to guess what me name is, oughtn't you?"

The audience's laughter warmed her like a stolen sip of Mr. S.'s rum. The conjurer chuckled, too. "I do not guess. I know," he said. "But I didn't ask what your name is. Nor did I ask who you are. I asked what you want to be called. That is quite a different thing."

Billy glanced from the conjurer to Mr. S, sure they'd never had the chance to talk. How could Mr. S.'s friend know? But he looked at her like he could read her thoughts as easy as Mr. S. could read one of his books.

The conjurer tugged at his mustache and shrugged, turning

toward the audience. "Ah, well, it is no concern of mine. Ladies and gentlemen, let me introduce—"

"Buh-Buh-Billy," she said as fast and as loud as she could. "Billy Fogarty."

He gave her an ominous half smile. "So you choose to keep your secret, then?" The conjurer came so close she could see that his colorful robe was fraying at the cuffs, and she caught a glimpse of pouches sewn inside the bell-like sleeves. His mustache moved oddly, and she realized that it was pasted on and starting to come loose. One long finger tipped her chin up. She tried to close her eyes against his stare, but couldn't.

Don't tell, don't tell, don't tell, she prayed.

And then he winked at her. His finger brushed the raven's breast feathers, and his hand settled on Billy's head. "Ladies and gentlemen, there are some secrets that are too dangerous to be revealed. Some secrets that even I must keep. Yes, even a child"— he'd said *child*, not *boy*. But not *girl*, either, Billy thought with relief—"even a child can have such secrets."

The audience, which had been whispering and giggling at the exchange between Billy and the conjurer, fell silent. With one hand still on Billy's head, the conjurer closed his eyes and placed the fingertips of the other hand against the black jewel on his turban. "I sense that this child has secrets and powers beyond your imagining. Why else would this child have been chosen? And so, Billy," he said, opening his eyes, "I offer you an exchange. A song for a secret."

"A—a—s-s-song?"

"Sing to these good people and I will keep your secret safe." He stroked the bird again. "Because Shiva seems to like you." He made a soft chirrupy noise, and the raven nudged Billy's ear gently with his beak.

A song. It couldn't be a common melody like "Touch Not the Cup" or "The False Knight"; it had to be something special, something magical sounding. Irish would sound more magical than English, and she could sing about cows and sheep and pigs and they'd never know. Still, she'd never sung for so many people before. Sweat trickled down her spine, and her throat closed tight. Then she remembered something Mr. S. had said: "*If you think about singing to all them people, you're sunk. Pick one person and sing for him. Or close your eyes and sing for yourself.*"

She coughed the tightness out of her throat and cupped her hand around the raven's breast, feeling the tiny heart beating fast against her fingers. The bird had chosen her; she would sing for him. She chose a song that Mam had taught her about the goddess Morrigan, who took the form of a raven and taunted the hero Cúchulainn as he was dying. Never before had the song felt so true and so sad. Never before had the song made her cry as she sang it. When she finished, the crowd was so silent that she feared she'd made a mess of it.

The conjurer shook his head, blinking several times, as if he'd just awoken. "My God in heaven," he whispered so softly that she could barely hear him. "Where in hell did Jonny find you?"

The applause broke over them so suddenly that it startled the raven from his perch. The bird circled Billy and the conjurer, cawing loudly, before settling back down, this time on Billy's shoulder, where he tugged at her hair as if he wanted a yellow tuft to add to his nest.

The conjurer placed his hand on Billy's head again, raising the other to signal for silence. "As I said, ladies and gentlemen, this child has powers beyond your imagining." He ruffled her hair and added softly, "And mine."

Chapter Twenty-Three

"The Prince will not see anyone." A fortress of a man stood in front of the tent, legs braced wide, arms crossed over his chest.

"Oh, I think Fred'll want to see me," Jonathan said.

"Fred?" The guard blinked. "How do you—I mean, there's nobody by that name here."

"Don't worry, I'm not here to arrest the old reprobate. Just wanting to pay a call on a friend." Jonathan raised a hand at the guard's scowl. "I know it defies credibility that Fred would have any friends, but there's one or two of us that haven't given up on him entirely."

Long brown fingers streaked with white drew aside the tent flap. Fred had discarded his turban; a white band across his forehead showed where Prince Otoo Baswamati's skin ended and Fred Chamberlain's began. Instead of the prince's multicolored robe, he wore a threadbare, stained dressing gown with a large towel tucked into his collar like a ruff. "I swear! Jonathan Quincy Stocking, you old scoundrel!" he cried, grabbing Jonathan by the lapels and dragging him into the tent, waving to Daniel and Billy to follow.

"You ain't gone and made yourself a family man, have you, Jonny?" Fred asked. He'd shed the Indian conjurer's turban and mannerisms, but his deep-set eyes were no less dark and probing. When his gaze targeted Billy, one dark eyebrow arched slowly.

"Traveling companions," Jonathan explained, drawing Fred's glance away from the girl. "A coupl'a boys seeking freedom and adventure and good company. Dan'l—Billy—" He gestured for them to come forward. "Meet Fred Chamberlain. Prince

Baswamati, the Indian mystic and conjurer, formerly Chief Talks With Fire, the Cherokee shaman, formerly Sir Evelyn Higginbottom, spiritualist and prestidigitator extraordinaire, formerly—"

"Now, now, Jonny, no need. Any friends of Jonny's—well, as they say…" Fred offered his hand to Daniel. "Mr.—"

"Linnehan," Jonathan replied.

Fred kept Daniel's hand a fraction longer than courtesy required, a test of some kind in both handshake and gaze.

"And?" Fred turned to Billy.

"Mr. Fogarty," Jonathan said. "Mr. William James Michael Fogarty."

"Mister," Fred repeated, enveloping the girl's hand in his. Her cheeks reddened.

"Mister," Jonathan said emphatically. He clapped Fred on the back, breaking his grip on Billy's hand. "Why don't you boys run along? See the menagerie tent and the mummy and all that. Fred and me got a lot'a years to catch up on."

"Good idea." Fred rummaged among the jars and bottles, rags and brushes scattered across his dressing table and drew out a penny. "Here." He held the coin out to Billy. "Buy yourself a treat."

Billy took the penny mechanically, apparently transfixed by Fred's transformation from Indian mystic and conjurer to plain old Fred.

Daniel nudged her. "C'mon. I want to take a closer look at them dancing ponies."

As the pair disappeared, Fred stared after them like a cat studying a cageful of canaries. Then he shook himself and slapped Jonathan on the back. "Well, Jonny, it's been a few years. Seven? Eight, maybe?" He reached into one of his pockets, pulled out a segar, and gave it to Jonathan. "You're looking well." He snapped his fingers, and a flame appeared in his hand.

Even though Jonathan knew how the trick was done, he still couldn't see where the lucifer had come from or how Fred had struck it. "Still quick as ever, aren't you?" he said.

"No." Fred gingerly peeled the mustache from his upper lip.

"Quicker." He sat on a stool by his dressing table and smeared his face with grease. "How d'you like the act?"

"It's a pip. Best you've come up with yet," Jonathan said, savoring the segar. Fred's taste was still as good as ever. Except for the cot, the tent looked like a gentleman's bedchamber. A painted canvas covered the ground, and furniture and trunks crowded the space: a chest of drawers, a washstand, two chairs and a small table set with a cloth, a bottle, a glass, and a covered basket. All were a bit worn, but they'd been good quality when new. If Fred hadn't come up in the world, he at least was trying to look the part. Jonathan blew a smoke ring that drifted toward the tent's peak. "The birds—that's a brilliant touch."

"I should hope so." Fred's voice was muffled by the rag he used to rub off Prince Otoo Baswamati's dusky complexion. "Cost a pretty penny. They talk, too." He looked up over the edge of the towel, one bushy eyebrow dangling into his eye like a fat fuzzy caterpillar. With a grimace, he yanked it off. He squeezed his eyes shut before he peeled the other one off with a noise like tearing paper. He tossed the eyebrows onto the dressing table next to the mustache. "Trouble with the birds is," he said, scrubbing at his real eyebrows, "you got to remember not to feed 'em until after the show. Out in Ashfield, some idiot gave 'em blackberries a little while before I went on. Must'a ruined a hundred dollars of bonnets and gowns when they flew over the audience. We couldn't get out of that town fast enough."

Jonathan hooted with laughter.

"Where'd you pick them two up? One of your ladies pin a coupl'a bastards on you?" Fred asked.

Jonathan puffed a cloud of smoke between himself and Fred. "They're mine, I guess. But not by blood."

"Got yourself a pair of foundlings, then, huh?"

"We-l-l-l, I'm not exactly sure who found who. They just sort'a happened along, and we kind'a stuck. I got to admit, having a coupl'a young fellas along makes for good company."

Fred leaned over the mirror and tilted his head to see if he'd gotten all the makeup off. "Where'd you find the girl?" He scowled and deepened his voice. "You cannot keep the truth from Prince Baswamati." He rubbed his hands over each other as if casting a spell. "She's good," he said, returning to his normal voice. "Almost fooled me. So, are them two brother and sister?"

Jonathan shook his head. "They only quarrel like they was."

"Females are always trouble." Fred suddenly seemed engrossed in using a tiny pair of scissors to scrape away the traces of makeup clinging to his cuticles. Without looking up, he said, "I'd be happy to take her off your hands."

"Wouldn't you just?" Jonathan narrowed his eyes.

"Anyone else, I'd try to fox 'em into giving her away. But you, friend, name your price and you can have it."

"She's not mine to sell."

"You got a bond on her? Seems a peculiarish sort of indenture, giving a girl to a—what line of work are you in these days, anyway?" Fred unpinned the towel and tossed it aside, then shrugged out of his dressing gown. While seven years had softened Jonathan's middle and grayed his hair, Fred's body was still lean and well-muscled.

"I'm in the peddling trade now," Jonathan said. "I got Billy from a father who's even more of a reprobate than you are."

"So she belongs to him, then?" Fred poured water into a basin and soaped his hands to remove the last of his makeup.

"She belongs to herself. You want to bargain, you'll have to talk to her direct." As a flicker of anticipation crept across Fred's face, Jonathan added, "Of course, I'll advise her, what with my many years of professional expertise and my intimate knowledge of your character."

"All right, Jonny. You got me." Fred shook his head in temporary defeat. "I'll wager you make a tidy profit out'a that girl and her voice."

"I don't keep her for the profit."

Fred raised a skeptical eyebrow. "Aren't you the one who taught me there's no profit in sentiment?" He bent over the basin and scrubbed his face. "What about the boy?" he asked. "He got any particular qualities other than big ears and bad looks?"

"He's mad for horses. Good with 'em, too. And no, he ain't for sale, neither."

"What do you take me for?" Fred raised his head, bearded in white lather.

"A cheat and a rapscallion and a scoundrel. Damned if I know how I ever come to call you a friend."

"Because underneath it all I have a good heart." Fred laid a dripping hand on his chest.

"Underneath it all you're still a cheat and a rapscallion and a scoundrel. But I'm more fool than not, and there ain't no accounting for taste."

"Don't s'pose there is," Fred said, bending back down to rinse his face. "Which is why I'm tempted to make you an offer in spite of your pigheadedness." He groped for a towel. Jonathan put it in his hand. "You still got your fiddle?"

Jonathan nodded.

"Travel with us for a bit. You can peddle whatever it is that you peddle. If you or your...traveling companions feel minded to tread the boards, you can name your terms. It'll be like the old times again."

"The old times wasn't always so good, as I remember." Jonathan settled into one of the chairs and uncorked the bottle.

"Well, the new times ain't, either. It's a poor show that's got only one horse act in it."

"Looks like you've done pretty well for yourself here." Jonathan poured a glass of amber liquid and raised it to his lips. It wasn't the rum or cider he'd expected, but brandy. "Smells like it, too," he said before taking a sip. Brandy, all right, and damn good brandy, at that. "You've even got real talent working for you. Your Italian songbird sounds like the genuine article."

"Actually, she's Quebecois. But who'd pay to hear a Canadian songbird? No, they all got to come from across the ocean." Fred rummaged through the chest of drawers and pulled out a clean shirt.

"Canadian or Italian or Hottentot, you can't hear much better in Boston or New York."

"If only you knew. You try running this show with an Italian songbird who's broody."

"Flatter her. Humor her. Buy her a bauble, and she'll get over being broody."

"It ain't that sort of broody," Fred said as he pulled his shirt on over his head.

Jonathan's first "Oh" was accompanied by a puzzled frown. The conjurer gave him a meaningful glower while pulling the front of his shirt out away from his body. Jonathan's mouth dropped open in comprehension.

"But surely with her—it won't—I mean, she's so—" Jonathan's hands drew an outline in the air about the size of Madame Staccato. "Well, it won't show for quite a bit.... Will it?"

"Showing ain't the problem. We can hide the showing. But she's so worn out she can't get up the wind for the high notes any more. And that's on top of puking her throat raw."

"She was in splendid voice this afternoon."

Turning one of the chairs backward, Fred straddled it and leaned his forearms across its back. "You caught her on a good day," he said, topping off Jonathan's glass. "She can't get closer to high C than A flat, and she's going down steady. In a month, my Italian songbird'll be singing bass."

"It is a dilemma, friend. A dilemma indeed. Is there, um, a Monsieur Staccato?"

"That's the worst of it." Fred pulled the cloth from the basket and tucked it into his collar napkinwise. "If only Neezer could marry her."

"Neezer?"

"Professor Romanov. He was just Ebenezer Pruitt and two stumbling ponies before I made him into something. And he does this to me." Fred took an apple from the basket. "It's a blow to my heart, Jonny," he said, thumping his chest with the apple. "A blow to my heart."

"Why not make the most of it? Professor Romanov woos the Italian songbird. The culmination of true romance on stage before your very eyes. You could get 'em married in half a dozen towns before word got around."

"Neezer can't marry her." Fred bit into his apple with a vicious crunch.

"There's a Mrs. Pruitt?"

Fred nodded dismally. "I'm bound to lose one or the other of 'em before the month is out. And then what do I do with all them damn ponies?"

"The ponies aren't his?" Jonathan asked, taking a pie from the bottom of the basket.

"They were. But the damn fool don't know any better than to play dice with a mystic and conjurer....And then there's the camelopard."

"I wanted to ask you about that."

"Dead. The morbid sore throat. What would you expect with a critter that's all neck? My guess is he was already sick when I got him; I thought the bargaining went too easy." Fred opened one of the drawers in the dressing table and extracted a pair of plates, a serviette, and silverware that appeared to be actual silver. He gestured for Jonathan to serve out the pie. "You know how big a hole you got to dig to bury a thing like that? We'd still be digging yet."

"You'd still be—uh—So, um, what did you do with him?"

"You seen that wagon 'round back? The green one?"

Jonathan nodded. "I figured it was for your costumes and gear and all that." He scooped a bit of pie up with his knife and lifted it to his mouth.

"Well, it was."

Jonathan stopped midbite.

"Now don't look at me like that, Jonny. It's only the skin and bones. He's cleaned up proper, doesn't smell a bit. First I thought I'd get him stuffed somewhere. But that'd be a hell of a thing to be dragging along, 'specially once the weather turns. So now I'm thinking to sell him to one of those zoological societies, maybe in New York. Let *them* stuff him, huh?"

Jonathan nodded, unsure whether to laugh or sympathize. Then a thought occurred to him. "Fred—"

"Mmm-hmm?"

"You said you kept the skin and bones. But what happened to—um—the rest of him?" The pie in Jonathan's plate didn't seem quite so appetizing anymore.

Fred straightened up and grinned. He put his pinky to his mouth as if he were picking his teeth with his fingernail. Then he rubbed his stomach.

"You didn't!"

"I had to get back some of my investment. Fed the carnivores and the whole company nearly a week and sold the rest. He was a little bit chewy, but not bad eating for all that."

Chapter Twenty-Four

Daft, Billy thought. *The lad's daft.* "Whyever don't you just take 'em?" she whispered.

Daniel gave her a sharp look. He paid the vendor, cradled the six apples inside his cap, and tucked the lot under his arm. As they turned away from the stall, he stumbled against Billy. When he recovered himself, he somehow had another apple in his hand.

"Begging your pardon, sir," he said to the vendor in the flat broad Yankee tones he'd learned from Mr. S. "I miscounted. That's seven all together." He paid for the last apple and walked away, whistling between his teeth and tossing the seventh apple in his hand as he went.

Billy followed, wondering what sort of game he was up to. She thrust her hands into her pockets as she walked, then stopped short.

"Hey!" she said, then "Hey!" again, louder, when Daniel didn't stop.

He faced her, walking backward, still tossing the apple. "Missin' something?" he asked.

"That's mine!" she said. Part of her wanted to give him a kick in the shins, but part of her admired the way he'd captured her money along with the apple, all without her ever feeling his hand in her pocket.

"Oh, aye? Seems to me I'm the one as did the paying for it, eh?"

"You got me money, too, you bastard! Give it back! I'll call you out for a thief, I will!"

"Go right ahead, you wee ee-jit. Mr. Stocking'll know who to believe, won't he now?"

Her face grew hot, not with anger, but with the truth of it.

Daniel stooped to face her nose to nose. "What's the matter with you? Mr. Stocking takes us to a grand show, his friend gives you money, and the first thing you think to do is shame 'em both, and me, too, by stealing."

"I—I—I didn't think," she said, heat washing all the way to her belly now.

Daniel knocked her hat askew. "That's your trouble. You don't never think, do you?"

"I do too. I think about Phizzy," she said. "And Mr. S."

Daniel straightened her cap, then yanked the visor down over her eyes. "Well, then, maybe you're not entirely hopeless."

Fumbling with her hat, she stepped forward blindly and walked into an enormous purple cushion. *"Zut, alors! Qu'est-ce que c'est?"* The cushion seized her by the shoulders and shook her. *"Petit cochon!"* the cushion exclaimed, then continued with a string of words so fast and strange that they seemed all one great, long word.

She looked up in horror and awe to see that the cushion wore the face of "M-M-M-adame St-St-St—" Billy couldn't get her mortified tongue past the *St—*.

"Madame Staccato." Daniel grabbed Billy away from the mountainous singer. He made his best bow, his face blushing nearly as red as his hair. "Begging your pardon, ma'am." He snatched off Billy's hat and poked her to make her bow, too. "So sorry, ma'am. My friend doesn't always look where he's going. I hope he hasn't mussed your gown."

Billy wasn't sure whether she'd rather throw herself at the singer's feet and beg forgiveness or simply fall down and die of shame. "I'm sorry, really I am, ma'am."

"And so should you be, you nasty leetle boy," Madame Staccato huffed.

Billy's cheeks grew so hot she felt she might melt into a steaming puddle. Daniel was right; she didn't think, and now her thoughtlessness had ruined everything.

"And who has permit these wicked boys to come, heh?"

Madame said. "I shall call someone to throw you away, *non?*" She rapped Billy smartly under the chin with her fan. *"Regarde-moi, petit vaurien! Regarde-moi quand je te parle!"* Her voice wasn't light and sweet, as Billy had expected, but thick and raspy. *"Mon Dieu!"* Madame clutched Billy's chin hard.

Billy braced herself for the slap that was sure to come.

Instead, the singer patted Billy's cheek and began to laugh. *"C'est le petit oiseau, n'est-ce pas?"* she said. "The little boy with the voice"—she gathered her fingertips, put them to her lips and made a loud kissing noise—*"magnifique!"* She gave Billy a little curtsy.

Billy's jaw dropped. She looked to Daniel for help. "I fancy that means you're forgiven, lad," he said, putting a mocking emphasis on the *lad.*

"You have the gift," the singer said. "There is not so many *comme ça.* Like us, *ben?*"

"M-Me?" Billy's voice squeaked.

"Oui, mon petit. The most of them who sing—feh—" She dismissed them with a flick of her fan. "They sing here." Her fan tapped Billy's lips. "Or here." Madame's plump fingers touched Billy's throat. "But we—you and Madame—we sing here." She put one hand on Billy's chest and another on her own ample bosom. *"C'est vrai, non?"*

"Yes, ma'am," Billy said, though she had no idea what *say-vray* meant. "But your singing, ma'am," she said. "It was like—like magic. I could never sing like that."

Daniel's fingers dug hard into Billy's shoulder, and he made a cautionary hissing noise through his teeth. Billy realized that there could be drawbacks to playing a lad's part. As a boy, how could she ask Madame Staccato to teach her to sing?

The singer laughed again, giving Billy and Daniel an appraising glance. *"Ah, mon petit,* you should hope not, heh, Monsieur—Monsieur—You have a name, but I forget it."

"Billy. William," she said. "And—and Daniel," she added, pointing to her companion.

"Monsieur Guillaume, there are in some places the men who

sing like Madame, but you would not like what they do to make you so." She cast an enigmatic look at Billy's trousers, then a longer one at Daniel's. Billy didn't understand, but from the way the singer's eyes traveled up to Daniel's face, and the way he reddened at her wink, she guessed that Daniel knew.

"*N'est-ce pas, Monsieur Daniel?*" Madame Staccato added before bursting into laughter.

"But could you teach a lad like me to sing…better?"

"Aye," Daniel said. "Mr. Stocking says Billy might make a fair tenor someday."

"Tenor, bass, baritone, you will not know until you are grown." Madame Staccato sighed. "But this—" Her fingers on Billy's cheek were soft as butterfly wings. "It will be lost. *Perdu. Quel dommage! Chante doucement* while you can, *mon petit oiseau.* You perhaps become *grenouille*—frog—when you grow, like this one, *ben?*" She jutted her chin in Daniel's direction. "And now, *mes amis*, it is time for Madame to take her rest." The singer grasped Daniel by the shoulders, squishing Billy between them, so that her face was pressed into Madame's bosom. "*Au revoir, Monsieur le Grenouille.*" Billy heard the distinct smacking noise of two kisses being planted on Daniel's face. Then Madame's face was suddenly inches away from her own, and the singer's plump fingers squeezed Billy's shoulders. "*Au revoir, mon petit oiseau,*" she said, kissing Billy first on one cheek, then on the other. "Perhaps I see you again soon, heh?"

Billy stared after Madame's round purple shape as she bustled away.

Daniel's fingertips nudged Billy's jaw closed. "You'll be catching flies if you stand about like that, *lad*," he said with a smirk. He took one of the seven apples from his cap and bit it, crunching loudly as he walked away. "C'mon, we still ain't seen them ponies yet."

Billy raced to catch him up. "She was grand, wasn't she?"

"Aye. First person I seen who you hadn't none of your smart answers for. I'd take me hat off to her, if I was wearing it."

"That name she kept calling me—*puh-tee wah-zoh*—what d'you s'pose it means?"

Daniel took another bite of his apple and chewed it slowly, savoring it with little *mmmm* noises so Billy's mouth watered, imagining how crisp and juicy and sweet it was. With a grin, he threw the apple to her so quickly that she almost missed it. "It means 'you wee ee-jit,' of course."

The lass had a gift, Daniel thought. So Madame Staccato had said of Billy. Everyone else seemed to agree. It was beneath him to envy a child, and a lass at that, but he couldn't help wishing that he had some sort of gift, too. The jugglers, the acrobats, the rope dancer all had their own particular gifts—gifts that he'd never imagined a week ago. Then there was Mr. Chamberlain, whose gift was to play a part so well that even when you knew it was trickery, you couldn't help being pulled into it. And Mr. Stocking, with his music and his horsemanship and his storytelling and banter, there was a fellow with enough gifts for half a dozen men.

Why did some folk have such gifts and others not? Not that he was ungrateful, he thought, for fear of cursing what he did have, which was more than he'd ever expected. Friends, for one. He'd found and left one friend behind in young Ethan and had discovered another in Mr. Stocking. He glanced sidelong at Billy, contentedly nibbling her apple down to the core. And maybe half a friend when the wee demon was in a fair mood. He had his freedom, and most important of all, he had Ivy. That was more than any man had a right to ask, wasn't it?

The trouble was, his gifts had come from outside himself and could be lost any time. He traced a cross over his heart. God forbid the day Ivy would be gone. What would he have when it was just himself left, but a strong back and strong hands, like any other man? Was it selfish to want a wee bit of that spark that gave Billy her voice or Mr. Stocking his stories?

A nudge at his elbow broke into his musing.

"Get out of that!" He slapped Billy's hand away from the cap full of apples he held in the crook of his arm. "You've had yours."

"Couldn't I be carrying some of 'em? Only three, that's all.

I want to see can I juggle 'em like them fellas in the show." Billy tossed her apple core from hand to hand to demonstrate.

"Oh, aye, and they'd all be ending up in the dust bruised and battered."

"Please? Just to try. You're not going to be eating all of 'em, are you?"

"They're not for me."

"You'll make Ivy sick with all them apples. Give me three for Phizzy."

"They're not for Ivy. Not this time."

Billy's eyes widened. "It's them six ponies, isn't it? Whatever are you going to be doing?"

"I'm not exactly certain just yet. But I aim to have a good look at them somehow."

"Why?"

"There's something queer about 'em."

The dancing ponies didn't look like much without their trappings. The golden blankets had hidden bony ribs and patchy coats. Where the shiny black polish had flaked off, their hooves were cracked and brittle. Still, they picked up their feet with sprightly delicate motions as they milled around the pen.

Daniel took one of the apples from his cap and handed the rest to Billy. "You wait here," he told her before he scrambled over the fence. The ponies scattered, then regrouped in a corner, huddled like sheep waiting to be shorn. He slipped out his knife and cut one of his apples in half, muttering softly about how crisp and juicy it was, just the thing for a good little pony. "Wouldn't it be a shame if I had to be eating it all meself, eh, lads?"

The first pony to come forward was a black-and-white piebald gelding whose shaggy forelock drooped into his eyes. He snorted and shook his head so that the hair swished out of his eyes, then fell back again like a curtain.

"Ain't you the brave lad, eh?" Daniel took a step forward, offering the apple to the little piebald. "Sure and wouldn't you be liking a treat 'long about now?"

The pony stretched his neck out as far as he could, trying to reach the apple without separating from his fellows. Daniel held the apple close enough to tempt him, but far enough away that the pony couldn't get it without taking a step.

The pony came forward.

Daniel stepped back, closed his fist over the apple and brought his hand in toward his chest. The pony followed. It wasn't until the gelding's head was nearly touching Daniel that he yielded the prize. The pony's lips quivered over his palm and made the apple disappear. Daniel stuck the rest of the apple into his pocket as the pony butted him for more. "Oh, no. That's for later. You stand still a bit first, eh?"

Billy started to climb the fence. "Wait," he said, without turning to face her. "I don't think he's ready for two of us yet." Billy sat on the top rail and watched while Daniel ran a hand lightly over the pony, working his way from nose to rump, noting what touch made the beast's skin quiver and what sent the quiver away, what made him cock his leg for a kick and how much to back off before the pony put the foot back down. He circled the pony several times that way, until the animal's wariness faded into resignation, then tolerance, then boredom.

"Let's have a look at them feet, now, eh, lad?" He slid his hand down the pony's front leg. The piebald trembled but didn't bolt. The muscles tensed as Daniel's fingers neared the fetlock covered with matted hair. He leaned against the pony's shoulder so it had no choice but to raise its hoof, let him cup its shaggy foot in his hand.

"Daniel!" Billy said in a loud whisper.

"A minute," he replied, not looking up.

"Daniel!" Billy repeated.

"Hey, you there! What're you doing, fooling around with my horses?"

Daniel's skin quivered the way the pony's had at his first touch. Would every sharp voice set him twitching as if someone had set a constable on him? He focused on the warm slope of the pony's shoulder against his, the coarse dusty hair and bony ankle in his palm, the rough edge of chipped polish under his thumb. He settled his features before looking up. "He seemed lame. I was only wanting to see had he picked up a stone." He kept the hoof in his hand, probing gently along the pastern. The twitchy feeling inside him came back, but for a different reason.

The barrel-chested, dark-eyed man glowering over the fence might have been Professor Romanov's twin, except without the mustache and beard. "And you, are you with him, boy?" he said to Billy, giving her the same wary look he gave Daniel.

"Yessir. We only wanted to help your pony because we didn't see anyone else about." She spoke with the flat Yankee tones Mr. Stocking had been teaching them.

The man's angular jaw glowed pink. "And what did you find?"

Daniel let the pony's foot drop. "Just a bit of a stone caught in his frog. I've prized it out." Following Billy's cue, he drained as much Irish from his voice as he could.

The man cocked his head with a sideways look in his eye, as if he were trying to catch Daniel out in a lie. "Did you find anything else?"

"No, sir, just a stone." Daniel rubbed his palm hard against his thigh, but couldn't erase the feel of what he had found: a rough circle of scarred skin broken and healed and broken again under the shaggy mat of hair around the pony's ankle.

"You think you know something about horses, do you, boy?" As the man came closer, his coat opened a bit. What looked like a small furry animal peeked out of a vest pocket. Daniel realized that the animal was, in fact, Professor Romanov's beard.

"You're the Perfesser," Billy said, her voice treacly with feigned awe. "We seen your show. It's a marvel what you can get them ponies to do."

Professor Romanov puffed out his chest and grasped his lapels. "Ah, well, you have to have the knack for it, boy. Ain't too many that does."

"Our master says ponies are the devil to work with," Billy

continued brightly. "You must have—what, three or four lads helping you with 'em?"

"No, my boy, they are all trained by my hand and mine alone."

"You never! They're lovely, they are, every last one. What are their names?"

"Red, Gray, Black, Brown, Socks, and..." The Professor pointed out each pony, whose color matched its name. "Oh, and Teeth." The last was the spotted pony who'd taken Daniel's apple.

Billy pursed her lips thoughtfully. "Begging your pardon, sir, but those don't sound quite proper names for horses. I mean, it's just their colors."

"Hmph. What's your name, boy?"

"Billy."

"And what's there about you that looks like a Billy?" Professor Romanov stared down his nose at the lass. "Can't answer that one, can you? What good's a name that don't mean anything, huh? Can't answer that one, neither. I say Red or Socks, you know just which pony I want. Got no time to be messing with a lot of fool names like Billy or Harry or Daisy."

"Oh..." Billy gnawed her lower lip for a bit. "But, sir, 'Teeth'?"

"You stay around that pony long enough, you'll see why."

"D'you think you'd be minding if we gave your ponies some apples? Seeing as they were so grand and all, we thought they might've earned a treat."

"Hmmph," the Professor said. "Seems to me it's the one who's trained 'em that deserves the treat." He took a flask from his pocket and pulled the cork with his teeth.

"Can't you have any sort of treat any time you like?" Billy asked, wide-eyed as if she didn't know what was in the Professor's flask. "It's your show, isn't it? You got the best act in it."

Laying it on a bit thick, she is, Daniel thought. He rubbed his hand across his face and pretended to cough to hide his chuckle.

The Professor's suspicious expression melted. "If only the

world worked that way, boy," he said, shaking his head. He tossed back a swallow of whatever was in the flask. "All right. You can give them damned ponies as many apples as you please."

Daniel rubbed his eyes against the haze of segar and pipe smoke that fogged the inn's taproom. Billy tugged his sleeve and pointed out the familiar round shape and faded spencer of the peddler sitting in a corner with a pipe in his hand and a mug and a bowl before him. "Hope we're not too late for supper," she said as they wove their way between the tables.

Mr. Stocking slid down the bench to make room for them. "Where you fellas been?" He waved to the tavern-keeper, held up two fingers, and pointed first to the empty bowl in front of him, and then to his companions. Their host filled two bowls with some sort of stew and set them in front of Daniel and Billy, along with two lumps of grayish brown bread and two mugs of ale.

"Thought I'd have a closer look at them ponies," Daniel said, sniffing at his dish. It had been stewing so long that the vegetables had dissolved into mush, and the meat had shredded into stringy bits. Still, it smelled good, the savory herbs promising to ease some of the bitter taste of his encounter with Professor Romanov. Billy tucked into her meal as if she'd not eaten for weeks, alternately slurping down her stew and gnawing ferociously at her bread.

"They step about pretty sharp, don't they?" the peddler said, though there was no admiration in his voice.

Daniel rubbed his hand on his trousers, as if that could erase the feel of the pony's scarred fetlock. "I'd prance pretty sharp, too, if me feet hurt."

Mr. Stocking nodded. "I thought as much. That gait doesn't come natural to many horses, and it can be a devil of a time teaching it. That Perfesser didn't look like he had much patience for teaching."

"What d'you mean?" Billy asked, a dribble of brown gravy slopping down her chin. Mr. Stocking winced as she wiped it with her shirt cuff.

Daniel set his fist knuckles-down on the table, pretending it was the pony's hoof. "Old scars right along here." He ran a finger along his wrist. "I wager I'd'a found other marks on him, had I time to look for 'em. What d'you fancy done it?" He tore a bit from the center of his bread and worked it into a doughy lump between his fingers.

"Lots'a tricks I've seen fellas use," Mr. Stocking said. "Mustard plasters so they pick up their feet to get away from the sting of it. Chains so the rattling gives 'em a start. It doesn't mean that the Perfesser done it. Could be the fella who owned 'em before he did."

"They didn't look over fond of him when he come over to run us off." Daniel shook his head. "None so pretty now, eh?" he said, with a pointed look at Billy.

She pushed her bowl away with a grimace. "You'll have to tell Mr. Chamberlain before they leave tomorrow," she told Mr. Stocking. "He'll have to stop it."

"And then what?" Daniel pressed. "What's to keep the Perfesser from leaving, ponies and all?"

Mr. Stocking's face brightened a little. "As a matter of fact, those ponies don't belong to Neezer."

"Neezer?" Daniel and Billy repeated simultaneously.

"Perfesser Romanov. Those ponies are rightly Fred's."

"That's settled, then, isn't it?" Billy said. "He'll dismiss that nasty old Perfesser, and then—"

Mr. Stocking took a long swallow of ale. "Yes, it's the *and then* that's the sticking point, isn't it, fellas? Who's to say the next perfesser won't be just as bad as this one? Most men aren't as soft about horses as the three of us."

"Including your Mr. Chamberlain?" Daniel asked.

The peddler hesitated. "That I couldn't say. I never seen him misuse an animal, but I never seen him stop it being done, neither."

"He'll do something if you tell him to," Billy said. "You being such great friends and all."

Mr. Stocking rasped a calloused finger across the stubble on his jaw. "Yes, well, there's friends and there's friends." The peddler stirred uneasily on the bench, then took a decisive breath and continued. "See, it's like this. Fred, he's not the type of fella to let friendship stand in the way of profit."

Chapter Twenty-Five

Daniel shuddered at the screams and grunts from the menagerie tent. He'd no idea whether the beasts were fixing to break loose or were merely impatient for their breakfast. The noises left Mr. Stocking unperturbed, which settled Daniel's nerves some as he and Billy followed the peddler among the cream-colored pavilions, mist swirling at their feet. Silhouetted figures moved about, tugging on ropes and adjusting stakes, securing the pavilions for another day's performance.

A roar of a different kind came from Mr. Chamberlain's tent. "Damn 'em both to hellfire and eternal perdition!" the conjurer bellowed. "And damn you, too, while you're at it."

"Me?" a reedy voice squeaked. "I never saw 'em go!"

The tent flap flew back, and Mr. Chamberlain charged out in dressing gown and slippers. Humbert Lamb, the menagerie keeper, trailed behind. A tall, thin man with wispy yellow hair, Mr. Lamb looked more a scholar than an animal trainer. But yesterday Daniel had seen him waltz with a bear, wear a snake about his neck like a shawl, and wrestle two panthers as easily as a child playing with a litter of puppies. Now, though, Mr. Lamb looked more afraid of Mr. Chamberlain than of his wild beasts.

"What's the trouble?" Mr. Stocking asked.

"They're gone, damn 'em. Neezer and Heloise have run off."

"Professor Romanov and Madame Staccato," Mr. Stocking explained in response to Daniel's and Billy's blank stares.

"I'll bet Howes snapped 'em up," Mr. Chamberlain continued. "I thought I saw one of his people skulking about last night. He's been waiting to snatch some of my talent."

"It's not so bad as all that," Mr. Lamb said timidly. "He did leave the ponies."

"He damn well better have. They're mine. Though how I'm going to—" The conjurer peered narrowly at Daniel. "Jonny tells me you're good with a horse." Daniel had no chance to respond before Mr. Chamberlain turned on Billy. "And I've heard you sing."

"Umm—" Billy threw an anxious glance at Mr. Stocking, then at Daniel.

"Fine. It's settled then." Mr. Chamberlain spun on his heel and stalked away, his dressing gown flapping like wings in his wake.

"What's settled?" Daniel asked as soon as he'd recovered his breath.

"I think it means you're hired," Mr. Stocking said.

"I do believe so," Mr. Lamb agreed. He looked toward his menagerie tent, then in the direction that Mr. Chamberlain had gone. A roar from the menagerie decided him. "Excuse me," he said. "Griselda wants feeding." Looking almost relieved, he dashed away toward his charges.

Daniel shook his head. "What is it exactly that we're hired to do?"

Mr. Stocking chuckled as he dug in his pocket for his tobacco pouch. "That's up to you...Perfesser." He cut off a chew and popped it into his mouth.

"Per—" Daniel backed away. "Oh, no. I can't."

"You wanted to see them ponies taken care of, didn't you?"

"Aye, but not—I mean—I can't—I don't know naught about horses."

Mr. Stocking nearly choked on his chew. He spluttered and recovered. "Son, if you don't know horses, I'm the queen of England." He turned toward Billy. "As for you—"

Billy pressed her lips into a tight line. "I told you he knew. It was that look he gave me yesterday, like he could see right through me." She shuddered.

"When you been playacting as long as Fred, you seen enough

boys playing Juliet and girls playing pages and squires that it's second nature to spot 'em out."

"At least now you don't got to pretend to be someone you're not," said Daniel.

"No!" Billy shoved Daniel away and ran.

Daniel felt thrown off balance more by the horror in Billy's face than the push she'd given him. He cast a perplexed glance at Mr. Stocking.

The peddler shrugged. "Better go after her. You'll catch her quicker'n I will."

Daniel found her in the paddock behind the tavern, where she stood nose to nose with Phizzy, grumbling a string of Gaelic curses into his floppy gray ears. Phizzy nodded sympathetically, his sleepy eyes deep and sad, as if he were pondering how to advise her. Billy cast a withering scowl at Daniel and ducked behind Phizzy's neck. "Go away."

"You can't be always running away from who you are," Daniel said.

Billy stepped out from behind Phizzy, her fists doubled. "This is who I am."

"No. No it ain't, lass."

"Don't call me that!" She flung herself at Daniel, hammering the wind out of him. He sat down hard in the dirt, the shock going from his tailbone to his skull. Billy leaped on him with punches and kicks as hard as he'd ever gotten from a lad, confounding him with how to evade her blows without hitting back. Then she was gone.

Mr. Stocking held Billy around the waist, pinning her arms to her sides. His feet did a little jig as he tried to avoid her kicks. "Damned if she don't fight like a boy," he said.

Daniel staggered to his feet. He stood with his hands on his knees, waiting for his breath to settle. "You—you—" He waved a shaky hand at the peddler. "You're not helping any, leaving her call herself Billy and calling her *son*. You don't even know her real name." He picked up his cap and slapped the dust off against his thigh.

"It doesn't seem to me like you got much call to be telling people what names they can use." The peddler's turtle-like eyes pinned him hard. Mr. Stocking released Billy and cupped a hand under her chin. "As for you...You have a gift, and you ought'a be using it for something better than hawking tinware and patent elixirs."

Billy slapped his hand away. "He'll be making a girl of me."

"And why would that be such a terrible thing?" Daniel ran an exasperated hand through his hair.

"I couldn't be free—not ever again."

Daniel rolled his eyes. "Whatever does being a lass or a lad have to do with being free?"

"If you was a lass, you'd know."

Only a lass could be such a bloody puzzle of unreasonable reasons. He looked to Mr. Stocking for support, only to see the peddler nod sagely as if he understood every word.

"Billy, have I ever made you do anything you didn't want to?" Mr. Stocking asked.

"Besides reading, mathematics, geography, and history?" Billy snapped back.

"And washing up," Daniel added.

Mr. Stocking rubbed his jaw. "Well, that was for your own good. Look, son—" He winced away from Daniel's glare. "What makes you think I'd make you sing for Fred?"

"You want to stay with him, don't you?" Billy asked accusingly.

"Can't say as I'm not tempted. I'd sell a prodigious pile of tinware," Mr. Stocking said. "But it'd hardly be fair if you didn't get a say." He crossed his arms and looked Daniel square in the eye. "Dan'l, d'you want to see those ponies taken care of proper?"

"Aye, but that don't—" he began, but Mr. Stocking had already turned to Billy.

"Billy, do you want to sing for all those people like you did yesterday?"

"I don't want to be a girl."

"Seems to me there's more to be gained by you being a boy.

Everyone expects a girl to have a pretty voice. But a boy...well, that's something different."

"Billy Fogarty, the Irish Songbird." The conjurer puffed on his segar and sent a smoke ring into the air.

"Billy Fogarty, the Boy with the Voice of an Angel." Mr. Stocking blew his own smoke ring, which floated over the ruins of their breakfast and merged with Mr. Chamberlain's.

It was all Daniel could do not to snicker. He took another slice of apple pie, still a bit amazed at the way the morning's events had turned. Once Mr. Stocking had chased down the conjurer and settled his temper, Mr. Chamberlain had summoned two lads who'd transformed his tent from bedchamber to dining room and laid out a breakfast of bacon and fried potatoes, bread and jam, and cold apple pie as magically as Mr. Chamberlain summoned up silk scarves and colored flames. If show folk all ate as grandly as Mr. Chamberlain, then perhaps it wasn't such a disreputable life after all.

"The Boy with the Voice of an Angel," Mr. Chamberlain repeated. "Could be." He swept Billy with a glance. "But that name's got to go. Fogarty." He scowled. "Damn ugly. Needs to be something...I don't know. Maybe something with a bird in it. Bunting? Starling? Thrush?"

"Definitely not Thrush. Sounds like he's got a foot disease," Mr. Stocking said.

"Billy Magpie," Daniel suggested. "For isn't he forever getting into mischief?"

"Raven." Billy pointed at Shiva and Kali, whose beady black eyes stared hungrily at the breakfast table. She took a crust of bread and poked it between the bars of their cage.

Mr. Chamberlain's brows knit solemnly. "Needs something with a *Mc* or an *O* in it, maybe. But I still like that bird idea... Billy O'Bird...Billy McBird....No, that's not it, either."

"Can't say I've ever met any Irishmen named McBird," Mr. Stocking said. "But I've met a few McBrides in my travels."

Mr. Chamberlain snapped his fingers. "That's it! Billy McBride, the Irish Songbird, the Boy with the Voice of an Angel."

"Aye," Daniel said, slapping Billy's hand as she tried to swipe the last bit of piecrust from his plate. "The voice of an angel, and the temperament of the devil himself."

Chapter Twenty-Six

Daniel rested his forearms on the top rail of the fence and stared at the ponies. He thought about the feel of the splintery wood against his skin, the morning sun on his neck, the smell of dung in the yard. He thought about everything except how to train the ponies, because when he did, his mouth went dry, his stomach tightened like a fist, and all he could think of was how impossible it was to take those ruined beasts and have them dancing in a week's time.

"Well, Dan'l?" Mr. Stocking said.

"I don't hardly know where to begin, sir. I'm no horse trainer."

"I'll set you right if you need it, but I got to see what's in you first."

"What's in me," Daniel repeated softly. When he looked inside himself, he saw naught but doubt and fear and an almost-belief that everything he'd ever been told was true: that he was a stupid, clumsy oaf who'd never amount to naught. "What's in me?"

"That's what I aim to find out." Mr. Stocking cocked his head so the light reflected off his spectacles. Daniel was sure the little man did that on purpose, so that the thick glasses became more like a mirror than a window, so's a body couldn't guess what he might be thinking.

"I know naught about teaching ponies tricks," Daniel said.

Mr. Stocking rolled his chew to one side and spat. "Any fool can teach 'em tricks. Teaching 'em trust, now, that's the hard part." Mr. Stocking's finger thumped Daniel on the forehead before he could respond. "Think, son," he said. "Everything you need is in here." He prodded Daniel's chest just over his heart. "And in here. Just think on how you trained Ivy."

Daniel laughed. "I never. She's the one trained me."

"There you have it." Mr. Stocking clapped Daniel on the back and spun him to face the ponies. "I'll check up on you 'round dinnertime," the peddler called out as he walked away.

Daniel walked over to where Ivy stood tethered to the fence. "Maybe you ought to be taming them ponies, eh, lass?" He pressed his forehead against hers, closed his eyes, and tried to remember how it had been, those first few months before he'd won Ivy over.

When Ivy had come to Lyman's, she'd been trained to saddle and harness, and minded well enough in either. But once out to pasture, she'd no use for a scrawny stick of a lad whose only knowledge of horses was how to clean up the messes they left behind. She'd let him get within a whisker of her, then she'd kick up her heels and canter off, spurning him with a toss of her head. An afternoon of it had brought him nearer to tears than Lyman's thrashings.

So what had he done about it? Oh, aye, he remembered now: he'd sulked.

He sat in the grass hugging his knees to his chest, sunk so deep into his black mood that he lost all sense of time and place until something ruffled the hair at the crown of his head. Without looking up, he tried to brush it away, and his hand found something both whiskery-prickly and velvety soft. A spluttery snort showered him with wet, and Ivy pranced away, the bloody witch. Well, he was done with that game. Just to show her how little he cared, he pulled out the apple he'd planned to give her and began to eat it himself.

Her hooves swooshed in the long grass behind him, her questing nose snuffled at his ear. He hunched over his apple, keeping his back to her. He ate the apple down to a knob of seeds and pith and stem, then sucked the last of the juice from it with loud slurps to show her what a treat she'd missed. "So there," he said, showing her the meager remains.

Her breath tickled his wrist as she studied the remnant of apple, its ivory flesh already starting to yellow. Her lips moved across his palm with as little weight as a caterpillar wriggling in his hand. The core disappeared down her throat with one hollow crunch. She whuffed a soft breath in his ear before she walked away.

By summer's end, he could barely remember when she'd not been a part of him.

"Is that the way of it, lass?" he asked, stirring from the memory. "Turn me back on 'em?" She butted his chest with her nose. "All right, then," he said. "We'd best get started."

For the rest of the morning, Daniel sat on a milking stool in the middle of the paddock, studying the ponies while pretending to have no interest in them. He observed the minute changes in the angle of an ear, the flare of a nostril, the rhythm of each pony's breath. He watched how each muscle and tendon flexed and contracted beneath the ponies' dusty hides, the impact of each hoof in the dirt and whether it landed true or crooked. He noticed how the ponies looked to the little gray mare for their cues, and how they stood guard on her, not because she was weak, but because they seemed to depend on her.

At the end of the morning, he rose with stiff legs and a numb backside but a confident heart. After dinner, he returned to test what he'd learned. He studied how they responded to an outstretched arm, an open hand or a closed one, an upright stance or a slouch. How he angled his head, the carriage of his body, and where he directed his eyes could turn them wary or calm. He put Ivy in among them. She stirred them up, then with a nip and a flick of her heels displaced the gray mare as their leader. When Ivy came to him, he watched the ponies watching him, their reluctant interest reminding him of the audience observing Mr. Chamberlain's conjuring act with suspicion and fascination.

Shadows stretched across the pen, and a cool breeze told him the afternoon had waned. The wind stirred the ponies' manes and tails, chilling the sweat on Daniel's body. The outside world came back into focus: the house and barn and sheds of the farmer who'd rented his field to Mr. Chamberlain; the pavilions and the wagons and people milling around them; the noises from the menagerie tent.

He blinked and rubbed his eyes. A strange fluttering around his heart warmed him from inside, even though the late September wind stung his ears.

"Not a bad day's work, eh, son?" Mr. Stocking leaned on the top fence rail, hands together, elbows out, his chin resting on his threaded fingers, his right foot propped up on the bottom rail. Billy stood next to him in an identical pose, except that her head rested one rail lower than Mr. Stocking's.

"How long you been watching?" Daniel asked.

"Long enough," Mr. Stocking said. "Tired?"

Daniel shook his head as he walked toward them. "Nah. I could do this all day." He ran a hand along his jaw. "Funny thing, though. Me face feels a bit queer—sort'a achy."

Mr. Stocking laughed so hard he nearly choked on his tobacco. "Never smiled so much in your life, huh, Dan'l?" he finally said, gasping.

"Grinning like a monkey, you was—*were*—this past hour 'r more," Billy said.

"I think maybe he's grown an inch or two as well, don't you, son?" Mr. Stocking said, giving Billy a nudge and a wink.

Although he knew the peddler was only twitting him, Daniel did indeed feel taller. Older and surer, too, as if he'd started working the ponies as one person but finished as another.

"Congratulations, Dan'l." Mr. Stocking reached over the fence to shake his hand. "You've found your place." The peddler's green eyes held him fast, as warm as the handshake.

The warmth inside Daniel quickly faded, though, as a lanky figure strode over to the fence. "You put them ponies through their paces, boy?" Mr. Chamberlain said, rubbing his hands together briskly.

"I—uh—not exactly, sir." Daniel instinctively stepped back, suddenly glad of the fence between them.

"What've you been doing all day? I got to get them back into the show soon's I can."

"I need to sort 'em out first. Learn their ways and let 'em learn mine." Daniel's throat tightened, making his voice timid and squeaky. His mind became a slate suddenly wiped clean. He looked to the peddler for support, but Mr. Stocking had turned away, one arm draped over Billy's shoulder in private conversation.

"What's to learn?" Mr. Chamberlain pinned Daniel with a glare as sharp as his ravens' beaks. "You think I don't know everything that goes on around here, boy? I told you to run those ponies through their paces, not sit on your backside all morning or stand around and wave your arms at 'em all afternoon."

The ache in Daniel's jaw was no longer from smiling, but from clenching his teeth. The green, secret place inside of him tugged at the edge of his mind. He pushed back against it, forced himself to reply. "I'll start schooling 'em in earnest tomorrow, I promise you, sir."

"They're schooled plenty already. All you got to do is step in where Neezer left off." The hard line of Mr. Chamberlain's mouth softened. "Look, boy, I know you never worked any trick ponies before. But it's not that much different from getting 'em to plow or draw or run. All you got to do is take a switch to 'em, and they'll be prancing up a storm in no time. Just—"

"No. No switches. No chains or mustard plasters or whatever your Perfesser used to torment 'em—"

"I'll have none of your sass, boy!" Mr. Chamberlain loomed over Daniel, glaring like a snake eyeing a mouse. Daniel braced himself not to stagger from the long, bony finger that Mr. Chamberlain stabbed against his breastbone to drive his words home. "Neezer broke them ponies just fine, and he—"

Daniel dug his nails into the fence's gray, weathered wood. He fought the urge to snap the showman's poking finger in half. "Aye, he broke 'em, all right. Your bloody Neezer broke 'em into a million pieces." He spat into the dirt at Mr. Chamberlain's feet. "Well, sir, it ain't breaking that them ponies are needing. It's mending. And that's what I'm bloody well doing." He shoved himself back from the fence and spun away from the conjurer to return to the ponies that he had already begun to think of as his own.

"You testing him out, Fred, or are you just an ass?" Jonathan asked, admiring the obstinate set to Daniel's shoulders as the boy stalked away.

Jonathan nudged Billy. "Go help Dan'l get those horses fed and watered." The girl's glance darted from the Irish boy to Jonathan to Fred, betraying her dilemma: to work with the ponies she'd been yearning after all day, or to stay and eavesdrop on what promised to be an entertaining quarrel between the peddler and the showman. Jonathan lowered his head and peered sternly over his spectacles at her. "Go."

Billy rolled her eyes as she squeezed between the fence rails, but the eager trot that took her to the ponies revealed where her true preference lay.

"You hear the way he answered me back?" Fred went on. "You let your boy talk that way to you?"

"I hope he would, if I was ever being an ass. Anyway, he's not my boy."

"I give him a job, a God-almighty opportunity any boy would give his eyeteeth for, and what does he do? He spends the day playing and making pets of my ponies."

Jonathan spat out his chew and ground it into the dirt.

"Damn it, they're mine, not *his*." Fred waved toward Daniel with a contemptuous motion that stopped mid-gesture as Ivy whirled toward the boy, drawing ponies in her wake.

"Not yet. Give him a few more days with 'em, and they'll think they are." Jonathan watched Daniel teach Billy how to use posture and eyes and hand motions to draw the ponies in or send them away. Already he was experimenting with using one gesture to summon the ponies individually, and another to bring them together as a group. Billy mimicked him gleefully.

"I don't care what they think—it's what they do that concerns me," Fred said. "Every day those ponies aren't working is money out of my pocket."

"You'll have your show, Fred. Or, should I say, your 'cultural and educational exhibition of equitational achievement'?"

Fred darted Jonathan a quick sideways glance, his cheek growing taut as if he had to bite it to keep his expression stern.

"I'll vouch for Dan'l," Jonathan continued, "and you know *I* was never one to let *you* down. I'm still sharp as ever when it comes to judging folks."

"Are you?" Fred asked, his eyes returning to Daniel and Billy and the ponies. "Seems to me you've got a little soft around the edges in your old age."

"Not the edges, just the middle." Jonathan patted his belly. "I still know a promising boy when I see one. Dan'l will get a better show out'a those ponies than your Neezer ever could."

"Spoiling 'em, that's what he's doing." Fred rested one elegantly booted foot on the bottom rail and settled his elbows along the top of the fence. "Mending horses, indeed." He reached into his vest pocket and pulled out two segars, trimmed their ends, and handed one to Jonathan. With his eyes still on the ponies, Fred flicked a lucifer against the fence post, lit his own segar, and held out the match for Jonathan to do the same. It wasn't until he'd blown the first puff of smoke out that he turned back to the peddler. By this time, Daniel and Billy were in the far corner of the pen, the ponies gathered around them expectantly, like children waiting for a treat. "I got to say, though, that's the first time I ever saw those beasts standing on the same side of the ring as their trainer without being forced into it."

Jonathan chuckled. "Well, Fred, maybe you're not quite such an ass after all."

Chapter Twenty-Seven

"Don't worry, Daniel. Mr. Chamberlain won't take the ponies away," Billy said, putting into words the cloud that had hung over Daniel since yesterday's confrontation with the conjurer.

Daniel lifted an eyebrow. Now this was something new. Could the wee fiend be turning human after all? "Huh. I crossed him pretty bad." But Daniel didn't feel a bit regretful. He had decided to pretend he was still in charge of the ponies. First thing after giving Ivy and Phizzy their breakfasts, he'd taken Billy to the showgrounds to tend the ponies. Fed and watered, Gray and Teeth now stood tethered to the fence, warily eyeing Daniel and Billy.

He took a brush and hoof pick from his bag. "Let's see if we can make them ponies shine all on their own, without all them feathers and coverlets and bootblack that Perfesser used on 'em. Too lazy to keep 'em cleaned up proper, he was."

"That's all? Just clean 'em?"

"It's teaching 'em, too," Daniel said. "Teaching 'em we can touch 'em without meaning 'em harm. Showing 'em it can maybe even feel good. Go slow and mind what they like and what they don't, all right?" He tossed her a brush. "A wee bit of a tune mightn't come amiss, neither."

Daniel shook his head over Gray's ragged coat and tangled mane. As he smoothed the mare's coat, first with his hand, then with a gentle but firm stroke of the brush, Billy copied him. He was pleased to notice that Billy's eyes flicked from Teeth's ears to his tail to his feet, watching for signs of fear or temper, that she backed off and started again with a gentler touch if the pony grew uneasy. Slowly, the pony responded, his ears relaxing, his neck softening.

"You didn't like that Perfesser, did you?" Billy asked Teeth, as she rubbed the spotted gelding's whiskery nose. "You'll be liking us much better."

Soothing Gray with his voice and hands, Daniel gently explored her legs for scars, hot spots, traces of old injuries or new. "Oh, and you think the ponies will be getting a vote about who tends 'em?" he asked.

"Mr. S. won't let him take the ponies away. And they're great friends, Mr. S. and Mr. C."

"Oh, it's Mr. C. now, is it?" Daniel said. He fetched the bottle of Sullivan's Liniment he'd taken from Mr. Stocking's kit. "I s'pose next you'll be calling him Fred and taking tea with him and his birds." Daniel shook his head. "They're friends, aye, but this is business."

"Who else has he got?" Billy said. "Even if he does say you're not to train 'em, he'll just put Mr. S. in charge of 'em, and Mr. S will ask you to help, won't he?"

"Perhaps." Daniel poured some of the liniment into his hands, then ran them down the mare's leg in firm but gentle strokes. He'd found no evidence of true soreness, only fear that anyone handling her legs aimed to do her harm. He hoped the soothing liniment and the touch of a hand in kindness would reassure her.

"Besides, if he takes the ponies away from you, I won't sing for him. He won't have much of a show without me and Mr. S. playing and singing, will he now?"

"And whyever would you be doing me such a grand favor?" Daniel peered under the mare's belly at the lass. "You despising me and all."

Billy untangled the knots in Teeth's tail, grasping the hair in small sections and brushing carefully so Teeth wouldn't feel the pull of the brush. "You're not so bad as all that. 'Specially seeing as how you're going to need me help with these ponies."

"So there's the truth of it," Daniel said as he lifted Gray's hoof. "You'll be civil to me only so's I'll let you help with the ponies, eh?"

Something soft hit him on the arse. Slowly and deliberately he set Gray's hoof down, straightened, and turned. A clod of horse manure lay at his feet. Billy stood a little ways off, a devilish grin on her face.

Daniel picked up the turd and flung it back. She laughed as it shattered against her shoulder. In spite of everything, Daniel couldn't help laughing, too. "Enough, lad," he said. "You'll be spooking the horses." He reached for his brush and hoof pick.

"Lad?" Billy repeated. "Did you say *lad*?"

"Surely not." Daniel grinned to himself, wondering if this was the first time he and Billy had ever been truly glad of each other's company.

The thin sunlight did little to burn away the morning chill, but Daniel's work quickly warmed him as he and Billy helped the ponies shed their summer coats in flurries of hair and dirt. They smoothed the soft new hair growing in to meet the coming winter, untangled manes and tails, massaged scarred legs, greased dry and brittle hooves. They'd finished four of them by the time a low whistle broke through Daniel's musings. He looked over the red pony's back at Mr. Stocking.

"You swap those ponies when I wasn't looking, boys? 'Cause these surely aren't the same pitiful creatures that were here yesterday."

"Pretty slick, aren't they?" Billy said. "That one's almost white, now she's cleaned up." She pointed at Gray, who stood with Teeth, Black, and Brown. Compared to Socks and Red, the four clean ponies seemed to glow.

"That's more'n I can say for you two," said Mr. Stocking.

A gritty layer of dirt and horsehair covered Daniel's clothes. He made a futile attempt to dust himself off and assessed his charges. "They'd look a mite finer, had they some meat on their bones. Didn't that bloody Perfesser ever feed 'em?" He traced the ribs that stared out along Red's side.

"They're just about as bony as you," the peddler agreed. "Here, I'll put down some hay for 'em while you get cleaned up for breakfast. You can finish up these last two afterwards."

"We should give 'em new names," Billy said, spewing bits of fried potato as she talked.

"How many times do I have to caution you about talking with your mouth full? Takes a man's appetite away. I despair of ever civilizing you, son," Mr. Stocking said. The man next to him passed a platter of codfish cakes across the table. The peddler grabbed one with his fingers and dropped the hot morsel onto his plate. He shook his scorched fingers and blew on them.

Daniel used his serviette to hide his grin over Mr. Stocking teaching Billy manners. The lesson was further undermined by a teamster on Daniel's left, who hawked and spat on the floor. On the other side of the table, a skinny young tinker broke wind with a noise and smell that did more to ruin Daniel's appetite than Billy's undisciplined chewing.

He pushed his plate aside and leaned over his tea, hoping the aroma would distract his stomach from the odors in the taproom. He'd never been finicky, but after so many years at the Lymans' table, he'd gotten used to eating tasty food among mannerly folk.

"I said, we should give the ponies new names," Billy repeated. "I mean, Teeth, what sort of a name is that?"

"So long as they're treated kindly, they'll not be knowing or caring whether they got good names or not," Daniel said.

"But we'll know, won't we?" Billy said.

The lass was right. After all, he'd known the difference between *Paddy* and *Daniel*. Known and cared. "D'you think your friend'll be minding should we change his ponies' names?" he asked Mr. Stocking. "That is, if he's not given me the sack yet."

The peddler shook his head. "He decided to give you a chance, once I showed him how I could buy us some time." He swabbed a bit of bread around his plate to soak up the drippings and popped the greasy morsel into his mouth.

"Time, aye." Daniel said. "We could use a bit of that." If he pushed the ponies too quickly, he risked losing the sliver of trust they'd begun to show him.

"Fred wants a horse act in his show, and a week isn't nearly enough for those ponies. But we can still give him his horses." Mr. Stocking waved his knife in Daniel's direction.

"We can?" Daniel said.

Mr. Stocking nodded. "While you were delousing the ponies, I was putting old Phizzy through his paces. He can still do the learned horse routine pretty well."

"What's a learned horse do?" asked Billy.

"Counting, telling time, picking pockets, and generally making me look an idiot."

"I wouldn't mind seeing that," Daniel said. "But you said 'horses.'"

"I'm not the only one with a learned horse." Mr. Stocking rummaged in his pockets, pulling out and putting back a shabby little notebook, his pocket watch, and a Jew's harp before extracting his pipe with a satisfied little "ah."

Daniel shook his head. "Ivy's clever, aye, but I never taught her no circus tricks."

"But we're not a circus, are we?" Mr. Stocking said with a wink. "We're here for education and erudition, not entertainment, or so the posters say."

"I know even less of erudition than I do of circus tricks," Daniel said.

"How about that little game you play with Ivy in the mornings?" asked the peddler.

Daniel's face warmed. *Ee-jit* probably didn't begin to describe how he looked when he was blundering about the pasture with Ivy. He scrubbed a hand along his jaw. "You think folk'd be interested in such foolishness?"

"Put that to music and you got yourself a show." Mr. Stocking tucked an invisible fiddle under his chin and used his pipe to mime bowing a lively tune.

"Daniel knows less about music than the man in the moon," Billy said with a scornful laugh.

"It doesn't matter. I'll make the music follow whatever dance Dan'l and Ivy come up with." The peddler laid his pipe on the table and foraged through his pockets for his tobacco pouch. "Now," he said, "about those ponies. I reckon you're not planning on using the Perfesser's old routine."

Daniel shook his head. "All that shouting and whip-cracking and such. If that's what pleases folk, I'm wanting no part of it."

"What pleases folks...Well, I could write a whole library on that." Mr. Stocking lit his pipe. "It mostly comes down to two things: Show 'em something they never seen before, and don't show 'em how you do it." He gestured toward Daniel with the pipe stem. "And if they think you're likely to get hurt or killed in the process, they'll like it that much better."

"Like them rope dancers and jugglers and such?" Daniel said.

Mr. Stocking nodded. "Don't take any more talent to juggle knives than kindling wood, but you can bet your last penny they'll cheer louder for the knife juggler."

Chapter Twenty-Eight

With a sense of guilty fascination, Daniel watched "Francesca de V., the Fascinating Danseuse," practicing on the cloud swing. It seemed impossible that this being of grace and light could be a mere human. So-called decent folk would have called her sinful and heathenish for displaying her body so, and worse, for practicing such gyrations on the Sabbath. But to Daniel, there seemed no more wickedness in her performance than in a bird's flight. If there was any sin, it was not in Francesca's doings, but in his watching them. He couldn't take his eyes from the sweet soft curves of calves and ankles exposed by her short skirt and tights, even though it made him uneasy. Proper ladies were always concealed beneath a fortress of skirts and bodices and mysterious undergarments.

"Who let you boys in? You want to see a show, come back tomorrow and buy a ticket."

Daniel's gaze returned to earth, where the tumblers and jugglers practiced their tosses and falls in the show ring. Two men—one black and one white—juggled knives back and forth. Mr. Sharp and Mr. Dale, Daniel recalled, but he couldn't remember which was which. Four acrobats leaped from a springboard onto each other's shoulders, while a fifth monitored the rope dancer's practice. Blocking Daniel and Billy's way was a bulky man in a patched jacket. He'd not looked quite so threatening on Friday, when he'd worn a top hat and tailcoat and announced the museum's "exhibitions" in eloquent, genteel tones.

The jugglers ceased their practice. "What is it, Mr. Varley?" the white one asked.

"These bumpkins're trying to catch a free show," Mr. Varley said, raising a fist. "I'll give 'em something to look at." A spiderweb of purply red veins stood out on his cheeks and nose.

The acrobats and jugglers lined up behind Mr. Varley—all except the black man, who stood aside with arms folded across his broad chest and an inscrutable expression on his face. The performers formed a solid row of well-muscled young men, the five dark-haired, dark-eyed acrobats ranged like stair steps from the shortest, who looked a little younger than Daniel, to the tallest, who seemed to be in his twenties. They'd been advertised as the Ruggles Brothers, and seeing them up close, Daniel believed that the relationship hadn't been invented. The only one in the row who looked out of place was the knife juggler, a blue-eyed man with ashy brown hair lightly sprinkled with gray. Thinner than the rest, but no less muscular, he sent his blade spinning end-over-end and caught it, grinning as if he were eager to use it.

"No, wait." Daniel put his hands out in a placating gesture.

The girl on the cloud swing shouted the same thing. "No, wait! I'm coming down." The swing was set lower for her practice than it had been for the performance, so she could easily leap to the ground unassisted. Still, the acrobats sprang immediately into action to break her fall if she should miss her landing. She didn't need their help, however, alighting as nimbly as a cat. Daniel noticed that she shared the same dark eyes and wavy black hair as the Ruggles brothers.

"Isn't he that horse boy Mr. Chamberlain hired to take Mr. Pruitt's place?" Francesca said with a sniff. There was something catlike about her face as well as her movements. With feline haughtiness, she looked Daniel up and down so thoroughly that he wished he'd done a better job of washing up after breakfast.

"Come to gawk, have you, boy?" the white juggler said, testing the edge of his knife against his thumb. Up close, Daniel saw that the blade's edge was thick and dull. Still, even if it was a poor knife, it'd make a fine club.

Billy poked Daniel in the ribs to prompt him to speak.

"N-n-no. I n-need—I need—," Daniel stammered.

"Needs a thrashing, I say," said the white juggler. Behind him, his partner smirked.

"Careful, Mr. Dale," said Francesca. "I heard that raggedy peddler he came with is great friends with Mr. Chamberlain."

"Mr. S. isn't raggedy!" Billy burst out. Daniel grabbed her to keep her from lunging at the performers. She jerked out of his grip. "Let's go, Daniel. Who needs their help anyway?"

Francesca raised an elegant eyebrow. "What sort of help?" Although she kept her head tilted at the same haughty angle, her eyes became less narrow.

"Naught," Billy said. "Come on, Daniel." She tugged his sleeve.

"I wanted to ask if you could help us learn a bit of tumbling. Something we could do with the horses." Remembering how Billy had flattered Professor Romanov helped Daniel find his voice. "As you say, we're only the horse boys. We've got no particular talents. Not like you." He squeezed Billy's elbow hard, hoping she'd get the message to follow his lead. "Not that we'd ever have such a gift for acrobatics as yourselves, but maybe if there was something easy you could teach us…"

"Mr. Pruitt never wanted any help," Francesca said dubiously. One of her brothers snickered; the others' sour faces showed their opinion of the departed Professor.

"He never let anybody else near those ponies," said the youngest Ruggles, his scowl deepening.

"Be thankful he didn't take you on, Philo," said the oldest brother. "He'd probably have thrashed you as badly as he did those animals."

Daniel and Billy exchanged glances. Daniel wondered how he could turn Philo's interest in the ponies to his advantage.

"I wouldn't treat a rat the way he treated those ponies," Francesca said.

One of the middling brothers cleared his throat and spat into the grass. "What's worse is how high and mighty he always was, as if folks came only to see him and his mangy beasts. As if nobody but him knew anything about trick horses."

"Good riddance to him," said another middle brother. "He

wasn't ever pleasant to anyone but Madame, and what she saw in him is more'n I'll ever know."

"I can't help feeling sorry for the ponies," Francesca said. "They always look so sad."

"Well, I want to do things different from the Perfesser," said Daniel. "I've a lot to learn, but I'm none too proud to ask for help from them that's smarter than me."

"Flattery, horse boy? To what end?" Francesca's laughter seemed to relax her brothers.

"Just to learn some tumbling, like I said. Something we can do with the ponies."

They all laughed now, including Mr. Varley and the white juggler. A brief smile even flashed across the black juggler's face. Mr. Varley's face grew redder in laughter than it had been in anger. For a few uneasy moments, Daniel feared that one of the purplish veins in the man's cheeks might burst. But finally Mr. Varley collected himself and wiped his eyes with a large pink handkerchief. "You know what they say about pride going before a fall," the red-faced man said.

"Well, sir, I've naught to be prideful about, and I'm no stranger to falling," Daniel said.

"Well said, boy, well said." Mr. Varley clapped a hand on Daniel's shoulder. He put his free arm around Francesca. "Well, my dear?" He nodded toward the oldest brother. "Harry? What do you say?"

The tumblers slowly walked around Daniel and Billy, looking them up and down with the same sort of intensity with which Daniel had studied the ponies. He half-expected them to examine his teeth and check his feet.

"How old are you?" Harry asked.

"Sixteen," Daniel said.

"Twelve," Billy replied.

"Hopeless," Harry said. "Maybe the little one, but the big one…"

"He's positively ancient," said another brother.

"Oh, let him try, Teddy," protested Philo.

"He'll break his head," said a fourth brother. "But it might be fun to watch."

"Will you let us ride the ponies?" Francesca asked. "And let us do some tumbling with them in the ring?"

Teddy's eyes lit up. "We could do Billy Button's Ride to Brentford."

"Dick Turpin!" said Philo.

"The Drunken Cossack!" said another.

Daniel blinked groggily. "Who? What?"

"Riding tricks, boy," explained Mr. Varley. "New and different ways for fools like you to break their necks."

Daniel shook his head dizzily. "I only meant for you to show us some things, not—" The brothers' faces began to harden again, and Daniel quickly changed to a more conciliatory tone. "I mean, I don't even know if they're saddle-trained," he protested. "I don't know yet what they can do, other than what I saw in the show yesterday."

Her dark eyes glowing, Francesca took his arm. "Well, there's only one way to find out, isn't there?"

"Billy Button," Mr. Lamb, the menagerie keeper, said over dinner. "It's a comic piece. You pretend you need to be somewhere in a hurry, but your horse won't stand still for you to mount him. When you finally get on, you're turned around backward, or you get on one side and fall off the other. Then the horse runs off without you, and you chase him around for a while until he ends up chasing you. That spotted pony was doing that routine when Neezer bought him. Only when Neezer tried it, the damned fool just got himself bit."

"So that's how he come to be called Teeth," Daniel said between mouthfuls of chicken fricassee. He'd spent the remainder of the morning bruising just about every limb trying to learn what Harry Ruggles called "a few simple falls." It had been worth the pain for the reward of dining with the performers at their hotel. The food was much better than the fare at the tavern on the other side of town. And there was the added benefit of sitting directly across from Fanny Ruggles, a.k.a. Francesca de V., the Fascinating Danseuse. At least Daniel had thought it would be a benefit, but he found himself so intimidated that he couldn't look at her straight on.

"Neezer was pretty heavy in the saddle," Mr. Lamb said with a chuckle. "He was better working his horses from the ground."

"Someone your size, though, boy, or any of us could do it." Harry Ruggles gestured at his brothers with his spoon. They were lean and light on their feet, no burden at all for the ponies. "I've been known to do a comic turn as fine as any Joe Pentland can come up with."

"What other tricks do you know?" Billy asked, her eyes shining. She'd taken to the tumbling like a duck to water and was eager for more. Daniel, on the other hand, had earned the Ruggles boys' grudging respect not for any native skill, but because of his pigheaded persistence and his ability to endure failures and falls without complaint.

"Harry used to be a wonder at the Drunken Cossack," Philo said.

"Speaking of drunks…," Harry said. "There's this one I've seen where a fellow blunders into the show as if he were staggering drunk. The horse seems about to pitch him off. Then the drunk starts sobering up, so it seems, and he throws off his coat and starts doing handstands or jumping through hoops, all the time taking off another costume, then another, 'til underneath it all, you see it's one of the trick riders in his tights."

"Or *her* tights," Francesca put in. "In some versions, the drunkard turns out to be a lady."

"Sometimes," Teddy stage-whispered behind his hand, "it's really a boy in a skirt and a wig." At least Daniel thought it was Teddy. He still couldn't keep any of the brothers straight except for Philo and Harry. The three middle brothers—Teddy, Moze, and Charlie—didn't stay in one place long enough for him to remember which was which.

"It's much better when a woman does it," Francesca insisted.

"I—I—um, I'm sure it is, m-miss." Daniel wondered if he'd ever be able to look at her without blushing.

"I still think you should put some juggling in," said Mr. Dale as he sent three rusks whirling from one hand to the other.

Daniel grew dizzy at the flurry of ideas the performers tossed at him, stunts enough for ten shows and sixty ponies. He wished he had pencil and paper to write them all down.

"Enough," Mr. Stocking said, banging the table with his knife to quiet them. "You've got the poor fella cross-eyed."

"No, no. I want to hear more!" Billy said.

"I'd like to try riding a Roman team. See, you stand with one foot on each horse..." Teddy put one foot on his bench, kicked a gap between the show's teamsters sitting at the next table, and put his other foot on their bench. He then crouched as if he were straddling two moving steeds. "Sometimes with a third horse in the middle."

Harry crawled between Teddy's legs to mime the third horse, then climbed onto a protesting teamster's shoulders and flipped himself over Teddy's back. "Or they jump from the horse's back over a ribbon or through a flaming hoop," he said when he landed in a crouch.

"Somersaulting on the horse's rump," Philo said, leapfrogging over Harry.

"Or maybe we could do a human pyramid," Charlie Ruggles said, "straddling two horses at a full gallop..." Plates and cutlery went flying and chairs scattered as Philo and Harry went down on all fours and Teddy and Charlie climbed onto their backs. Some of the diners cheered them on and came closer to watch, while others grabbed their plates and retreated to a safe corner or out of the dining room entirely.

"Out!" the landlord's wife shrieked, scattering the Ruggles brothers with her broom. "Out, all of you heathens! Such carryings on, and on the Sabbath, too! If you can't take your meals like human beings, you can eat in the barnyard."

The brothers somersaulted outside. Billy grabbed Daniel's

arm and dragged him out to watch their antics. They shouted more ideas at him, one brother or another miming a horse while the other boys leaped over and around each other. Francesca danced impatiently from one foot to the other, as if she longed to shed her gown and petticoats and join them.

"Come on, Billy!" Harry swooped up the lass pickaback, then tossed her to Teddy.

"It's entirely mad, they are," Daniel said, shaking his head.

"Not entirely," Mr. Stocking said. He gestured with a chicken leg at the crowd collecting in the hotel's dooryard, then at Mr. Lamb and Mr. Varley, who were passing out handbills and urging the bystanders to see the real show tomorrow, only four bits a ticket.

"And I'm to be part of this madness," Daniel said in wonder and trepidation.

"Don't worry, son." Mr. Stocking offered Daniel the remainder of his chicken leg. "You teamed up with me, which means you're already halfway there." He nodded toward the tumblers sporting about the yard. "So, they give you any ideas?"

"A bit of a daft one," Daniel said. "I been thinking it's an amazement to see a horse do clever tricks and such, but for him to stand quiet while there's noises and flags waving and folk leaping about and all sorts of commotion... well, that's something of a trick, too, isn't it?"

"The Incombustible Horse," Mr. Stocking said, with a snap of his fingers. "You bring a horse into the ring, and you set your tumblers tumbling around him, jump another horse over him, get your brass band playing, wave flags, shoot off pistols, light fireworks, and he stands still as a statue—except maybe to yawn to show how bored he is with the whole hullaballoo. It's one of Phizzy's specialties."

"I dare say." Daniel had never met a horse as unflappable as Phizzy. "And once you've made 'em incom—incombustible... well, I fancy that all the other tricks'd come easy as child's play, wouldn't they?"

"That they would. Comes in handy other times, too. Nothing

better than having an incombustible horse when you need to get out of town in a hurry or hide from the sheriff. Takes a lot of patience and time to teach 'em, though."

"I imagine so, 'specially after what that Perfesser put 'em through," Daniel said. He knew he had the patience, if only Mr. Chamberlain would give him the time.

"It sounds a lot simpler than it is. But if you can make 'em truly incombustible, it's pretty impressive."

"Impressive. Aye. And it'd show folk that you can gentle a horse without hurting him," Daniel said. "So maybe there'd be no more Perfesser Romanovs."

"No more Professor Romanovs," Francesca said. "I doubt you'll ever see that day."

For the first time he found his voice with her. "You think me a fool for even trying, then?" he asked.

She surveyed him with that same lingering head-to-toe stare that she'd given him when they'd met. His cheeks burned, but he couldn't look away from her dark cat's eyes. "I think you'd be worse than a fool if you didn't," she said. Something that was almost a smile flickered across her lips before she turned away and went inside.

Chapter Twenty-Nine

Monday, September 23, 1839, Pawling, New York

Daniel started with things the ponies knew already: the plumes and blankets and harnesses that Professor Romanov had used. When he and Billy laid the objects on the ground, the ponies milled away, showing the whites of their eyes as they retreated to a corner of the corral next to the pen where Daniel planned to do their training.

He brought Ivy into the pen while Billy sat on the fence and watched. Another set of watchers collected on the opposite side: a quartet of teamsters who drove the museum's wagons. They passed around a chaw of tobacco and settled in much like the men who stood in the pit and leaned over the low wall around the show ring. The hair on the back of Daniel's neck prickled. He put his cheek against Ivy's and murmured, "We'll show 'em, won't we, now, lass?"

He led Ivy up to the row of objects and let her examine them. As she studied each item and touched it with her nose, he rubbed her forehead and said, "There's a brave lass." He picked up a blanket and rubbed it firmly against her neck, her chest, her back and sides, up and down each leg. She flicked her ears and whuffed curiously at him, bemused by this new game.

Billy took the blanket and waved it about—slowly at first, then with sharp flicks and snaps. If Ivy startled, Billy stopped and waited until the mare calmed. Then Daniel scratched and rubbed and spoke to her, rewarding the calmness and ignoring the starts until she grew bored with Billy's antics and gave the flailing blanket no more than a twitch of an ear.

He repeated the process with each object, hoping that

watching Ivy would show the ponies there was naught to fear. Then he put Ivy aside and led Gray from the corral into the pen. She put back her ears and snorted at the blanket. He let her take her time to look the things over.

"Hey, boys!" the tallest of the four teamsters shouted. "You work them ponies that way and you'll be there 'til doomsday!"

"Quit all that fooling around and just take a switch to 'em," called out a second man whose florid features had earned him the nickname Red.

"Looks like Mr. Chamberlain's leaving his prancing ponies to a coupl'a children," said the nasal voice of the third teamster.

They continued a running criticism of Daniel's training techniques. Although the back of his neck and his ears burned, Daniel tried to make himself deaf to their taunts.

It was another matter for Billy. "Shut up, you bloody bastards!" she shouted.

Daniel clamped a hand over her mouth. "Quiet, you." He took her by the shoulders and shook her, his legs spread wide to keep her from kicking him in the shins. "Quit it, I said." Then he dragged her to the far side of the pen, away from the laughing teamsters. "You can't pay them any mind." His voice was low and jagged.

Billy tried to slap his hands away. "I'll say what I bloody well please."

Daniel released her with a shove that sent her staggering against the fence. "Fine. Then you won't be training these ponies with me." He wagged a finger under her nose, though what he wanted to do was slap her rebellious face as hard as he could, lass or no. "You think it'll be all cheers and smiles when we're working them ponies in the ring for real?"

"I—I never thought—"

"Never thinking, aye, that's always the way with you. How about thinking how long we'll be in this show if you curse out every fool who heckles you from the pit?"

"Hey, Paddy!" shouted Red.

The slur hit Daniel as hard as the slap he'd wanted to give Billy. He dug his fingernails into his palms.

"Hey, Paddy! Maybe you ought'a take that switch to your little brother!"

He was no longer Paddy, Daniel reminded himself. But damn it all, why was it that every time he finally felt himself out of that life, it would come back at him in some other way? "We got to be as incombustible as them horses," Daniel said, as much to himself as to Billy.

"It might not be enough," said a calm voice nearer to hand.

"What?" Daniel's head jerked toward the unfamiliar voice.

The black juggler, Mr. Sharp, faced him over the fence, on the opposite side of the pen from the teamsters. As soon as Daniel met the man's eyes, Mr. Sharp looked down, seemingly intent on the three knives in his hand. "Being incombustible. It's a start, but it may not be enough. Not to them, anyway." He tossed one of the knives and caught it, then flicked the blade in the direction of the pavilion.

"I don't understand," Daniel said. In the show ring, Mr. Sharp spoke with a slow drawl, his sentences full of *ain't*s. But now the man's words came out as clearly enunciated and grammatically correct as if he'd studied one of Mr. Stocking's books.

"Nigger. Coon. Darkie. Paddy. Bogtrotter. Boy." The juggler lifted his head to meet Daniel's eyes. "It's all the same, isn't it? What they call you. To make you less than they are."

"Less?" Daniel repeated, confused. A black man no less than a white one? How could that be true? He remembered his school geography book telling about the four races of man, from the most superior white race to the Asians, down to the savages like the Indians, and lowest of all, the Negro, a degraded race of brutes fit only to serve, so the book said. *Fit only to serve* . . . Indeed, wasn't that what Lyman had said of Daniel once? But there was nothing brutish or stupid in the dark eyes staring back at him, as intense as Mr. Stocking's when the peddler had a hard lesson to teach.

The juggler tossed the knives in a low arc. "Being incombustible, that's good. It'll be enough for them." He made a tiny motion of his chin toward the teamsters, who had lost interest now that

Daniel and Billy had stopped working with Gray. "They don't mean anything." He caught one knife but continued to juggle the other two with one hand. "But some folks won't stop until they get past your...incombustibility."

"And then?" Daniel asked.

The juggler shrugged. "What do you do with a fire you don't want?"

"Put it out?" Billy suggested.

The juggler grinned, a slow bloom of white cutting across his dark features. "Now there's a clever boy," he said, gesturing toward her with one of the knives.

"Like what you done with that rude fella the other day?" Daniel said.

A pair of rowdies had mocked the two jugglers, but particularly Mr. Sharp. "Any monkey can do that," one had taunted. "I could do it easy."

Mr. Sharp had responded, "Yes, boss, you surely can," then handed the tough the three torches he'd been about to ignite and gestured for him to come into the ring. "I'd 'preciate it if you'd show me how it's done, sir," he'd said, opening the gate. The man's friends had laughed and shoved him forward. Mr. Dale, the white juggler, had lit one of his own torches with a great whoosh and come toward the suddenly sober rowdy, who had turned the sickly yellowish white of parchment.

"Now you go easy on Mr. Dale, boss," Mr. Sharp had cautioned the rowdy. "He might not be able to keep up with you." The rowdy had cast a suspicious glare at Mr. Sharp to see whether he was being mocked. But the juggler's face had been creased with concern that looked so genuine it had almost fooled Daniel.

Mr. Dale had tossed his torch into the air, staggered as if he were going to miss it, and caught it barely in time to keep it from scorching the trampled grass. The rowdy dropped his unlit torches and backed away, shaking his head frantically.

"You'd best thank the man, Caesar," Mr. Dale had said sternly, jutting his chin toward Mr. Sharp. "It's very kind of him not to outdo you in front of all these good folks."

From the looks on the jugglers' faces, it had seemed as though Mr. Sharp was the one who'd been put in his place, not the heckler. Amid gales of laughter, the rowdy had headed back to safety behind the low wall surrounding the ring. He'd strutted before his friends as though he truly believed he'd bested Mr. Sharp and Mr. Dale. But he'd kept quiet for the rest of the performance.

"That was a fair bit of acting. I'm none so clever as all that," Daniel said.

"I'd'a set him afire," Billy said. "Well, thrashed him, anyway."

Mr. Sharp nodded. "You could do that. More likely his friends would outnumber you and you'd be the one thrashed. Or you could be smarter than him. Better than him."

"And how do you do that?" Billy asked.

Mr. Sharp smiled. "My father was a preacher. It was something he said all the time."

"Me mam said something a bit like it. She told me not to wish anyone ill, because it'll always come back at you," Daniel said.

"Being a preacher, of course, Papa never held with fighting," Mr. Sharp continued. "And being a black man, well...in most places if I ever laid hands on a white man, I might as well write my own death warrant. Some places it'd be death for me even to look a white man in the eye."

"So you got to be always turning the other cheek, no matter what?" Billy said.

"So I thought at first, and did it ever gall me." Mr. Sharp's fingers tightened around his knives. "But then I saw that being better doesn't mean giving up. It means finding some way other than fighting to win. Like you've been doing with your ponies."

"Me?" Daniel said.

"Ebenezer Pruitt was afraid of being bitten or kicked, so he struck out at them before they could strike out at him. Not too many men are brave enough to win without cruelty. Or smart enough, either."

Could Mr. Sharp be right? Or were these only stories a man invented to make himself feel less beaten down? Yet the juggler didn't seem at all beaten down or defeated.

"Where the other fellow's weak, that's where you've got to be strong," Mr. Sharp continued. "You've got to be quick where he's slow, brave where he's cowardly, clever where he's stupid."

"All of that? It seems a lot to learn," Daniel said.

"You never stop learning. And even then, sometimes you still have no choice but to fight."

At his worst, Lyman had never worked Daniel at as furious a pace as he worked himself to prepare for the show. For an hour each morning, he and Billy worked with Francesca and her brothers, learning falls and handsprings and cartwheels and somersaults and vaults—more falls than anything else, at first. They started practicing on the ground, then on a barrel set up on sawhorses, then on Phizzy at a standstill, a walk, and finally an easy canter, the placid old gelding unruffled by their antics. Then Daniel practiced with Ivy and Mr. Stocking, learning how to swoop up an object from the ground at a canter or how to coax Ivy to cross her front legs daintily as she walked and to prance with light dancing steps that seemed to float.

After his lessons with the tumblers and with Mr. Stocking, he worked with the ponies, teaching them to stand calmly no matter what he touched them with or how he moved about them, showing them not to fear new things, and that the old ones that had once hurt them would do no harm in his hands. He replaced their harsh bits with snaffles and removed the straps on their bridles that had bound their heads unnaturally high. Although Daniel at first objected, Mr. Stocking showed him how to use the longeing whip, not as a means of punishment, but as an extension of his arm, guiding the ponies with a feather-light tickle. Mr. Stocking helped him figure out what commands and tricks the ponies knew, and take note of what they didn't. He showed him how to coax them through simple maneuvers and patterns.

In between it all, Daniel kept the ponies and Ivy fed and groomed and helped the teamsters and Mr. Lamb and his assistants with their beasts whenever an extra hand was needed. He helped set up the museum and menagerie pavilions and Mr.

Chamberlain's dressing tent, the tiered benches for the audience, the low wall that bounded the ring. He helped Mr. Lamb set up the dens for the menagerie stock, and helped Mr. Stocking ready his wagon to peddle his tin after the show. He shined up the ponies' green-and-gold wagon for the Grand Cavalcade Entrée that paraded through town and opened the show.

His week's grace seemed too long and too short all at the same time.

Chapter Thirty

Thursday, September 26, 1839, Sheffield, Massachusetts

"You. Come here." Mr. Chamberlain stood in the entrance to his pavilion, his long arms crossed over his chest, one bony finger beckoning to Daniel. The conjurer slipped back into his tent, and Daniel followed, wondering what sort of trouble he was in now.

"You're not ready for tomorrow afternoon, boy," Mr. Chamberlain said.

"I am, sir, I swear it," Daniel replied. "Ivy and I practiced just this morning. Ask Mr. Stocking—" He realized that there was a whole crowd of people in the tent watching him.

Francesca, Mr. Varley, and Mr. Stocking stood near Mrs. Varley, the wardrobe mistress. Spread across a nearby table were a pile of clothing and what appeared to be small dead animals.

"Yes, yes, I've seen you practice, so I know you can perform, but who are you supposed to be?" Mr. Chamberlain gave Daniel a glower that would have made him squirm had it not been for the bone-deep relief of hearing that the man believed him ready to perform.

"I—er—nobody," Daniel said. "Nobody but meself, I mean."

"That won't do at all," the wardrobe mistress tut-tutted. She sorted through the items on the table. Daniel realized that what appeared to be animals was actually an assortment of wigs.

"Fred wants to make you a red Indian," Mr. Stocking said.

"Whoever heard of a red-haired Indian?" Mrs. Varley said with a sniff. She swept a set of fringed leather leggings from the table in a swirl of powdery reddish dust.

"He could be a gypsy," suggested Mr. Varley.

"Lord, no, he's pale as a fish-belly," his wife protested.

"What about a Cossack?" Francesca said. "A Cossack might have red hair and freckles."

"Who says he's got to have red hair?" Mr. Chamberlain picked up a dark, curly wig and shook the dust from it. Something crawled out and ran up his shirt cuff. He dropped the wig as if it had scalded him. "Hell, Jerusha, don't you ever clean them things?"

"I'll not be wearing someone else's bugs." Daniel poked a cautious toe at the wig, which looked ready to crawl out of the tent on its own. "Why can't I just wear me own things?"

All of them went silent and gave him withering glares.

"A Cossack, definitely." Francesca started up the discussion again as if Daniel hadn't spoken. "He could pass for Russian, don't you think?"

"I don't speak any Russian," Daniel pointed out.

"Varley's going to do the talking," Mr. Stocking reminded him. "If you got to say something, just do it in Irish. Most folks won't know whether you're talking Gaelic or Russian or Hottentot, just so long as it sounds foreign."

"Sit, boy," Mr. Chamberlain commanded, pulling out a stool and shoving Daniel down onto it. "And let's see what we can make of you." He planted a hand firmly on Daniel's head to hold him still, then reached for one of his makeup pots.

Friday, September 27, 1839, on the road from Sheffield to Great Barrington, Massachusetts

A little boy on the side of the road clapped his hands over his ears, and a brace of babies wailed at the boom and clatter of the drums. The trumpet and the French horn blared in a fanfare of noise as glorious and brassy as the golden autumn morning. Stately elm trees shaded the road like a triumphal arch. Daniel urged Ivy to the head of the procession, then halted her at the side of the road so he could take in the spectacle before assuming his own place in the cavalcade.

Waves of people lined the road from Sheffield into Great Barrington. The most aggressive boys shoved their way to the front, while smaller ones sat on their fathers' or brothers' or friends' shoulders. Other children, and a good many adults, stood atop fences and stone walls.

The bandwagon led the caravan, followed by Mr. Chamberlain's red-and-gold wagon. The conjurer sat on top, dressed in his mirrored robes and turban. He let fly a flash of sparks and a puff of colored smoke with a bang that startled the boys who'd gotten too close and sent them fleeing with squeals of laughter. Next came the acrobats' wagon, with Mr. Sharp and Mr. Dale sitting sideways on the two gray horses that pulled it. They juggled half a dozen apples between them, every now and again taking a bite from an apple without losing either balance or rhythm. When one apple was done, the jugglers would let the core fall to the ground, and Mr. or Mrs. Varley would toss in a new apple from a basket sitting between them on the wagon seat. Every now and again, Mr. Sharp or Mr. Dale or Mr. Varley would cry, "Catch!" and fling an apple into a knot of boys, who would wrestle for it as if the jugglers had thrown a silver dollar.

In the road on either side of the wagon, the Ruggles Brothers performed their leaps and somersaults and catches. Francesca, meanwhile, stood on the wagon behind the Varleys, wrapped in a bejeweled, red, ermine-trimmed cape. The cape was merely an old blanket onto which Mrs. Varley had glued bits of glass and edged with moth-eaten white fur that the wardrobe mistress claimed was rabbit, though Daniel had his doubts. Still, Francesca looked regal as a princess. She waved and curtsied to the crowd, somehow keeping her balance in spite of the potholes and ruts that shook the wagon.

Behind Francesca's wagon came Mr. Lamb's menagerie, the bear and the panthers staring nonchalantly at the waving and cheering crowd. Next was the enclosed wagon carrying the snakes and the props. The crowd oohed over the pictures on the wagon's sides, which depicted a viper swallowing a sow and eight piglets.

After the snakes came the antelopes and then the emus. Napping in their cage, the great birds looked like a pile of feathers waiting to be made into pillows. But two men swore they'd seen fangs and claws under those feathers.

Three camels, tethered end to end behind the emus' wagon, brought up the rear of the menagerie. Their jaws moved rhythmically side to side as they chewed their cud, looking not altogether different from the tobacco-chewing men watching from the roadside. One man spat a thick brown stream toward the camels. Lorenzo, the largest camel, belched and directed a splatter of regurgitated hay and grain onto the man's shoes. The human spitter cursed and stepped back while his companions roared with laughter.

Billy came next, driving the six ponies and their wagon. Mrs. Varley had decked the lass out in a green velvet suit and a wool cape that fanned out around Billy's shoulders to hide the back of her tailcoat, which was miles too big. Having no time to alter the jacket, Mrs. Varley had used clothes-pegs and straight pins to gather the slack in back, then concealed the lot beneath the cape. Billy grinned broadly, and Daniel let Ivy fall into step alongside her.

"'Tis grand, isn't it?" she said. "I wish we could parade about all the day."

"Aye," Daniel said with a chuckle. "If you could parade about all day, you could avoid all the work that's waiting for you at the pavilion."

"And you'd not have to think about dancing Ivy before all them folk," Billy said.

"I'd mind what I was saying if I was you," Daniel teased back, poking her shoulder. "It'd take no more'n a tap to send all them pins into you."

"I'd like to see you try." Billy stuck her tongue out.

Daniel drummed his fingers on Billy's top hat, pushing it down on her brow. "It being such a lovely day, I'd hate to be spoiling it by rowing," he said.

Billy shoved her hat back up and gave Daniel her sourest

glare. "That, and you don't want to be sleeping with your eyes open all week, wondering how I'd be taking me vengeance."

Daniel let her have the last word. Some time ago, their bickering had progressed from combat to sport, with him not quite knowing when or how it had happened, the way a touch of frost could mellow an apple from tart to sweet, with no sign on the outside to show the change.

"Well, son, what do you think?" Mr. Stocking asked as Phizzy pulled up alongside Ivy.

Daniel looked back at the wagons that held the tents and ring fence and other gear, the green wagon that held the camelopard's remains. Behind them came a train of curiosity showers, peddlers, tinkers, knife grinders, patent medicine salesmen, and itinerant craftsmen riding the show's coattails into town.

Daniel caught his breath. "'Tis a bit like a dream."

"Enjoy it now, son," Mr. Stocking said with a grin. "Next town, they're as likely to be greeting us with stones and rotten cabbages. And who knows but they might warn us out of this one, if they don't get the show they expect."

"But for now it feels...well, I don't fancy I've felt so grand in me life."

"I know." Mr. Stocking winked. "Kind'a like being an Irish prince, ain't it, son?"

"You look splendid, Daniel," Billy said, fingering the spangles on his multicolored vest.

Between the two of them, Mr. Stocking and Mr. Chamberlain had invented a tribe of red-haired gypsy nomads from the steppes of Pomerania, the location chosen with a hatpin and a map from Billy's geography book. Never mind that Daniel hadn't a clue whether Pomerania had any steppes, or that the only steppes he knew of had to do with dancing and staircases. Mrs. Varley had cobbled together a costume that was part Gypsy, part Cossack, and part Turk, but thankfully included neither wig nor tights. The outfit reeked of tansy, old sweat, and stale tobacco, and had put Ivy off nearly as much as Daniel. She'd snorted and pulled her upper lip back when he'd first approached, and even now cast a dubious eye at him as they waited with Mr. Stocking and Phizzy just outside the show pavilion.

Daniel ran a finger under his collar, wondering how many creatures besides himself resided in the costume. He resolved to boil it the first chance he could get. "I stink," he said.

"That's all right, son," Mr. Stocking assured him. "Just as long as your performance doesn't." He tugged his lapels. "I'm a little rank myself. Maybe I should give Mrs. Varley some Parisian toilet water for her wardrobe trunks." He cocked an ear to the applause that told them that Mr. Sharp and Mr. Dale had just completed their juggling act. "Our turn next, boys," he said, leading Phizzy into the pavilion.

Daniel and Billy followed with Ivy, stopping just behind the tiered benches to watch.

All it took to make the audience giggle was seeing Mr. Stocking and Phizzy walk into the ring. Mrs. Varley had fitted the peddler out with a mustard yellow tailcoat patched at the elbows and splitting along the back seam, which was mended in huge, sloppy stitches. His coattails sported two enormous pockets. From one pocket dangled an oversized watch chain; from the other, a bit of red calico. He tipped his shabby straw hat, then strode toward the middle of the ring as if he were marching in the militia day parade.

Just behind him came Phizzy, a similarly battered hat tied to his head, contrasting with the huge pink bow adorning his tail. The old horse held his head high, mimicking his master's posture and gait. When the peddler took his place in the center of the ring, Phizzy stood a little behind him. Pretending not to notice the horse, Mr. Stocking bowed. Phizzy did the same, extending one foreleg in imitation of his master. The audience snickered and giggled.

"Ladies and gentlemen," Mr. Stocking said. Phizzy pulled his lips back from his teeth as if he, too, were making an announcement. The crowd chortled its appreciation.

"Look behind you, old man!" shouted one of the show's teamsters, who'd been planted in the audience to give Mr. Stocking his cues.

Mr. Stocking looked over his right shoulder. Phizzy sidestepped to the left. Mr. Stocking pretended not to see him. The peddler looked over his left shoulder, and the gelding stepped to the right. They repeated the charade twice more, the crowd's laughter growing as Mr. Stocking mimed confusion. Finally, Mr. Stocking turned to the right and Phizzy stepped in the same direction. The two collided and Mr. Stocking fell on his backside.

Even though he'd seen them rehearsing, Daniel couldn't help laughing. The little man and his horse drew an energy from the crowd that made everything seem funnier than it had in practice. Daniel stroked Ivy's neck, wondering if she, too, would shine more brightly with all them folk watching her. He plucked at the front of his shirt, already soggy with sweat.

The audience tittered as Phizzy snatched Mr. Stocking's straw hat and commenced to eat it. The peddler wrestled it away, crammed the mangled hat back on his head, and turned his back on the horse. Phizzy grabbed the corner of red cloth hanging from the little man's coat pocket. Mr. Stocking stalked off in a huff toward one end of the ring while Phizzy headed to the other, the cloth clutched firmly in his teeth. A series of knotted handkerchiefs streamed from Mr. Stocking's pocket: red, blue, green, yellow, purple...until the last one brought him up short like a dog coming to the end of his chain. He turned, then hand over hand used the handkerchiefs to draw Phizzy in as if he were reeling in a fish. Mr. Stocking crossed his arms and faced down the horse. "I s'pose you think you're clever, do you?" he challenged.

Phizzy nodded vigorously, and the crowd shouted its agreement.

"We'll see about that." Mr. Stocking reached for the chain dangling from his other pocket and yanked out a watch so large it could be seen several rows back. He displayed it to the ladies in the front row of box seats, then held it to Phizzy's nose. "If you're so smart, what time is it?" he asked. The gelding studied the watch for a long moment.

"Humph," Mr. Stocking said, clapping the watch closed. "Not so smart after all."

Just as a titter began to spread through the audience, Phizzy pawed the ground with his left front foot, once, twice, three times. Then he scraped the ground with his right foot once, twice, and continued as the audience counted, "...*eight, nine, ten.*"

"What was that?" Mr. Stocking asked.

Phizzy did it again: three with his left foot, ten with his right. *Three-ten.* The ladies in the front row gasped. What they didn't see was the faint twitching of Mr. Stocking's thumb counting out the hours, then his index finger counting out the minutes.

Phizzy's learned performance continued as Mr. Stocking tested his mathematical skills, then sent him to select the lady with the prettiest hat, the gentleman with the ugliest vest, the child with the curliest hair. Subtle movements of the peddler's fingers told Phizzy when to stop and point his nose toward the chosen person.

"One final question," Mr. Stocking said. "Can you show me the biggest fool here?"

Phizzy paced the ring, his droopy mouth seeming to curl in a whimsical smile. Daniel watched both hecklers and dignified gentlemen wince as Phizzy's sleepy-eyed gaze probed them. The horse paused thoughtfully before each potential candidate, then, with a toss of his head, moved to another as if to say, "Yup, that one's a fool, but there's a bigger one here somewhere."

As the audience both squirmed and hooted, Phizzy worked his way to the end of the ring, where Mr. Chamberlain stood on the sidelines in his Indian mystic costume, arms crossed over his breast. Mr. Chamberlain lowered his chin and scowled his sternest as the horse swept him with his indolent glance. The two faced each other down as the laughter crescendoed, then Phizzy raised his nose toward the conjurer's turban, as if to nibble the black gemstone from it.

"No! No!" Mr. Stocking shouted over the crowd's shrieks. "I

didn't say, 'Show me the biggest jewel.' I said, 'Show me the biggest fool.'"

Phizzy let out a snort that showered the conjurer with slobber, and amiably trotted straight for Mr. Stocking, nominating him the biggest fool with an affectionate nuzzle.

"They're grand, aren't they, them two?" Billy nudged Daniel's elbow. "I fancy half that lot has wet 'emselves from laughing so hard."

"I only hope they don't wet 'emselves laughing at me," Daniel said. He rubbed his shirt cuff along his dripping forehead.

"Never mind that," Billy said. "Just keep your own trousers dry." She stepped forward to take Phizzy's halter and hand Mr. Stocking his fiddle and bow.

Mr. Chamberlain performed some sleight-of-hand tricks while Billy led Phizzy away, and Mr. Stocking rosined his bow and softly plucked the fiddle strings to check their tuning.

"Ready, son?" the peddler asked. Mr. Chamberlain finished his magic tricks and Mr. Varley began his patter about Dmitri, the celebrated Pomeranian horse trainer, who "would present an educational display of equitation, riding an untrained beast in a rude state of nature, without saddle or bridle, and only his hands to tame her."

"Hardly." Daniel's hands were so slick with sweat that he could barely loosen Ivy's halter.

Mr. Stocking tucked his fiddle and bow under one arm, then pulled Ivy's halter over her ears and dropped it on the ground. With a slap on Ivy's rump, he sent her cantering into the ring. The crowd spooked her, and she skittered nervously, lashing her tail and snorting. A murmur rose from the audience, as some in the pit eyed her flashing hooves warily. Daniel stood in frozen admiration, his mind totally empty of what he was supposed to do.

Mr. Stocking poked him with his bow. "Better get out there, son, before somebody remembers they saw you riding her in the entrée."

Daniel stumbled into the ring, his heart pounding so hard

that Mr. Stocking's fiddling seemed an insect-like whine in the background, his mouth so dry that he couldn't muster up the whistle that was Ivy's cue to turn and charge.

Somebody did the whistling for him, and Ivy whirled and dashed at him. He could do nothing but stand and watch the sheer beauty of her legs gathering and extending as she ran. She was almost on top of him, galloping full tilt. A lady shrieked, perhaps fearing Ivy'd run him down. He stood like a block of wood and let her come. Ivy pounded by close enough that he could have plucked a hair from her mane as she passed, and still he stood rooted to the ground.

"Did you see that?" somebody exclaimed. "What's he doing?" asked someone else.

He braced himself for the audience's jeers and boos. But instead, somebody clapped, and the crowd took up the applause. The folk in the pit cringed as Ivy reared before them, and he realized that they hadn't thought him stupid, but brave. They didn't know Ivy'd never harm him.

The mare wheeled and returned to him, skidding to a stop on her haunches. She bounced on her forelegs, inviting him to play. He shut out the crowd and imagined that there was naught in the entire world but himself and Ivy in the sunny shelter of his secret green place. Raising his arms, he set himself free to whirl and run and leap and dance with her. They circled each other, Daniel matching Ivy's steps with his own, summoning her close, then sending her away with a wave of his hand, dodging and feinting around her, then inviting her to do the same with him. He stumbled, and the crowd's anxious "Ooooh!" broke through his awareness, then their cheers resounded as he grasped Ivy's mane and swept himself up onto her back.

She reared and kicked and plunged as if she wanted to hurl him to the ground, but he held on easily. It was all part of the game; she no more wanted to shed him than he wanted to fall. He let her play the wild horse for a bit, then eased her down to a rhythmic canter that was so smooth it could have rocked him to sleep. With a triumphant grin, he raised his arms, and the crowd cheered, believing that he'd bested an untamed beast.

He forgot half the tricks he'd practiced with Mr. Stocking and the Ruggles boys, and the ones he remembered he did badly, but he didn't care, and neither, apparently, did the audience.

Chapter Thirty-One

Friday, September 27, 1839, Cabotville, Massachusetts

"Augusta, I know it's none of me business, but—" Liam pushed the potatoes about on his plate. "I mean, forgive me rudeness, but—Oh, bloody hell!" He tossed his serviette onto the table. He'd been working up the courage to ask for days, and still he couldn't get it out. Maybe he didn't really want to know. But for sure and certain they couldn't continue as they had been.

It had started the morning after he'd been sacked. He'd gone to the well, and she'd come from her shanty on the same errand. He'd nodded good morning, filled her bucket, and carried it back to her shanty—a paltry thanks for all she'd done for him. When she thanked him, he had shrugged. "It's naught." He'd turned to go, but she put a hand on his arm.

"What'll you do now?" she asked.

"Look for work. Hope nobody's been spreading tales about me being a shiftless drunk."

She looked down at the hem of her skirt, none so bold as he'd seen her before. "Why don't you come in for a few minutes and have a cup of tea before you go?"

He shook his head, then realized she might mistake his refusal. "It's naught to do with what you do—I mean—" Was there no way he could say a thing without insulting her? "You're a kind lass, Augusta. But you've troubles enough of your own without hearing mine as well."

She'd smiled at him, that sweet tiny curve of her lips that turned her from common to pretty. "It's no trouble. I'd be glad to have someone to sit and talk to for a little while."

That had been the start of it. By the end of the week, they'd formed a habit of breakfasting together, sometimes in her shanty, sometimes in his, and be damned to what the neighbors might say. How strange it was, that breakfasting with a prostitute now seemed almost normal, that friendship had grown between them so easily. And now he was spoiling it with his fool questions. But he had to know. So he blurted out, "Why, lass? Why do you do it?"

She raised an eyebrow. "I assume you don't mean this." She swept a hand through the air over the remnants of their breakfast.

Liam shook his head. "No. I mean that." He gestured toward the bed in the corner. "You needn't answer if you're not wanting to. But you're such a, well, a decent lass, I couldn't help wondering—" He pressed his lips together. "Ah, I'm blathering on like an *ee-jit*."

Augusta took the serviette from her lap and laid it on the table. "All right, then. I came to work in the mills. I met a young man. I was an *ee-jit*."

"I'm fancying he was the *ee-jit*," Liam said.

"We both were. But he didn't have to worry about it showing." One hand rested on her belly. "He disappeared. I lost my job, my lodgings. I was afraid to return to my family, afraid of everything. This woman, Mrs. Pratchett, took me in. She ran a disorderly house."

Liam's hands clenched into fists. "She took advantage of your situation."

Augusta shook her head. "I had to earn my keep, didn't I? After the baby came, I mean."

"Aye, 'twas mighty kind of her, not sending you out to—to"—Liam gestured toward the bed—"*that* while you were with child."

"She had to be hard to survive, but she loved Grace. My baby." She blinked hard, but couldn't hold back the tears that dropped onto her folded hands. "She loved Grace, and she cared for me... after her fashion. I didn't lack for anything I needed, even when I couldn't work. She taught me how to take care of the baby, to take care of myself, and—"

Liam held up a hand. "I'm not wanting to know what else she taught you."

Augusta raised her head, the tilt of her chin almost haughty. "I couldn't expect you to understand. There's plenty of ways a man can make his way in the world, but damned few for a woman when her sins are out there for all to see." She shoved her chair back and began gathering the breakfast dishes. "Mrs. Pratchett might have been Grace's grandmother, the way she doted on her. It was the death of her in the end."

"Death?" Liam asked.

"That last winter, Grace and I took sick." She dabbed at her eyes with her apron. "I recovered. Grace and Mrs. Pratchett didn't. The rest of the girls scattered, and I ended up here." She piled plates and silverware at one corner of the table. Then she bustled around the fire, stoking the coals beneath the water kettle.

"I'm hardly knowing what to say," Liam said, his mind a tangle. To avoid her eyes, he glanced around her shanty—a hovel not too different from his own and yet not like his at all. When Nuala and the lads had been there, Liam's shanty had been a jumble of wrestling boys, laundry strung before the fire, bed ticks on the floor, dirty dishes on the table, and always the sense of a storm about to break when Da came home. With Nuala and the lads gone, so were the clutter and the jumble, leaving only a houseful of empty in their place.

But across the mucky road, in the same sort of ramshackle house, Augusta had created something that made Liam feel that he could sit for a moment and just breathe. At first he'd thought that it was because the space wasn't crowded with other people's beds and belongings and bodies. But no, it was a feeling that someone paid attention—put a bit of cloth over the window, painted the battered table, arranged the dishes in a tidy row on the shelf. The chairs and table and cupboard were no newer or finer than Liam's, but they looked cared for. One shelf had actual books on it—books that he'd seen her reading as though she enjoyed them. Surely someone clever enough to make more of such a place as this could make more of herself as well.

"What?" Augusta asked. The tip of her nose was pink, and her eyes moist, but she'd collected herself again. She stood with a dipper of steaming water poised in one hand. "You've a peculiar look on your face. What were you thinking?" She emptied the dipper into the wooden wash tub on the table.

"It's your house. Underneath it's as mean as mine, but somehow you've made it pleasant," he said. "Better than you'd expect from, well, I mean—" He scrubbed a hand through his hair as he tried to find the proper words. "Have you never thought of doing anything different?"

Augusta shrugged as she shaved some soap into the hot water and whisked it into a lather. "There never seemed much point."

"You mean—do you like doing—well—"

"Do you like digging canals and cellar holes?" She rolled up her sleeves and submerged a pile of dishes in the soapy water.

"It's money in me pocket, food on me table. I don't think about more than doing me job and collecting me wages."

"Well, then," she said, "It's the same for me: do my work, collect my wages."

"It's never the same at all. What I'm doing—there's nothing—nothing personal about it."

"And you think there is for me?" she asked. "What else is there for me to do when I can't bring in enough with sewing and laundry?"

"Something—anything," Liam said. "You're clever. I see you reading books that I couldn't hardly make heads nor tails of. Clever with your hands, too—Christ." He paced the room. "I mean at the needlework and such, not—not—" He closed his eyes and shook his head in his frustration at always putting everything exactly the wrong way. When he dared to look at her, her cheeks were pink, her lower lip twitching. It took him a moment to realize she was trying hard not to laugh at him. "All right, lass. I'm an *ee-jit*. Shall I be going now?"

"What do you want to do?"

Want? God, there were so many things he wanted. Wanted Nuala and Jimmy and Mick back, first of all. Wanted never to fret over every penny that came in and out. Wanted a place to live in that was dry and warm and clean. Wanted to have a full belly every day and to have some money left over. Wanted to be looked up to instead of down on.

And right now, looking at Augusta's face, her amber eyes that managed to summon a spark even though the skin beneath them was smudged dark with weariness, her mouth that could still manage a smile in spite of all she'd seen and done....Right now, God help him, what he wanted most was to stop wanting what he had absolutely no right to want.

"I want—" Liam began. "I wanted—" he corrected himself. "When they were here—Nuala and the lads—I wanted to give them a life that had more to it than working and eating and sleeping. Now it seems I've no right to be wanting anything."

"I know," Augusta said.

"Aye, that you do." Maybe that was what kept him coming to her door: knowing that there was a hole in her heart that matched the one in his own. An impulse seized him, perhaps born of all this talk of wanting. He stepped closer to her, put a fingertip under her chin, tilted her face up, and kissed her lightly on the forehead.

"I'm no better than all this." His shrug took in the tumbledown house around them, the slop-strewn streets outside, the boundaries of his world. "But you are, lass. And don't you be believing any different." And then, because he didn't trust himself not to tell her any more of what he was wanting, he turned and left her there, her amber eyes wide with surprise and her lips trembling with unasked questions.

Chapter Thirty-Two

Monday, September 30, 1839, West Stockbridge, Massachusetts

"Hear that?" Mr. Stocking slammed down the lid on one of the compartments in his wagon. The sound echoed off the walls of the wagon shed. He opened and closed two more bins with the same hollow clatter. "That, my friend, is the sound of success."

"Empty?" Daniel asked.

The peddler nodded. "Almost all of 'em. I got maybe a dozen pieces of tin left. There's mostly notions and elixirs now, and I can sell 'em in the evenings out of my trunk."

"No more selling after the show," Daniel said. Mr. Stocking's smile broadened like that of a smug boy. Daniel grinned back, thinking of all the extra time he and Billy would gain for working with the ponies or practicing their tumbling.

For the peddler, Daniel hoped there might be time for afternoon napping. The added labor of practicing with the band and teaching new songs to Billy, performing with Phizzy, helping Mr. Chamberlain manage the show, and helping Daniel train Ivy and the ponies was wearing on him. Mr. Stocking's vests no longer strained to meet across his belly, and his broadfalls gapped at the waist. His face seemed a bit less round, his eyes a bit more shadowed. Although he had energy enough to fiddle and sing or confer with Mr. Chamberlain long into the evenings, any time he had a quiet moment to sit still, he'd nod off to sleep. Daniel and Billy took turns riding in the peddler's wagon as they traveled from town to town, so he could doze without tumbling off. Aye, a few empty hours in the fellow's day wouldn't come amiss.

"There you are, Jonny!" Mr. Chamberlain crossed from the hotel to the shed in long strides, briskly rubbing his hands together.

"What is it?" Mr. Stocking asked. "You're grinning like a fox who just found the chicken shed door ajar."

"Saddle up, friend," Mr. Chamberlain said. "I got something to show you." He jutted his chin toward Daniel. "You can come along, if you like."

"Shall I fetch Billy?" Daniel asked.

"No need," Mr. Chamberlain said. "Your friend's having a juggling lesson."

"So what's this phenomenon we're going to see?" Mr. Stocking asked.

The conjurer patted the peddler on the back. "The future, my friend. The future."

"There." Mr. Chamberlain made a sweeping arm motion, as if the sight before them were something he'd conjured up rather than something that had likely been there for months.

A scar of broken earth and shattered rock stretched across the landscape, extending east and west as far as Daniel could see. A stream of men gouged the land with pickaxes and shovels, and hauled dirt and stone away from places that were too high or toward those that were too low.

A dozen years ago, Daniel's da had sweated away his days digging alongside scores of dust-caked men just like those down below. They'd laid the foundations for mills in Lowell, Cabotville, Indian Orchard, and Westfield, and dug the canals to hold the water to power them. They'd built row upon row of brick boardinghouses for the Yankee girls who'd worked those mills. But there'd been no brick tenements for the builders, nor any wooden ones either. The Irish had been left to cobble together their own shanties from warped boards and clinker bricks and other construction refuse, and God help them if a Yankee foreman chose not to turn a blind eye to their scavenging.

Daniel had no doubt that the men laboring below were Paddies like himself. There'd be no mills rising from their work, though, but a road of wood and iron. Somewhere there'd be makeshift Paddy camps, far from town to avoid offending decent Yankee folk.

Mr. Stocking whistled. "Didn't know the railroad was building out here in West Stockbridge yet." He and Daniel dismounted and dropped their horses' reins.

"You know who I was raising a glass with while you were hawking your scrap metal?" Mr. Chamberlain asked. "A fella by the name of Alexander Birnie, who's an engineer for the Western Rail Road. He wrote this up for me." He drew a paper from his coat pocket. Flapping it open with a flourish, he laid it on a nearby boulder. The paper was a map showing Massachusetts and part of New York. Someone had written on it with a heavy black pencil: lines and X's and words that were nearly illegible to anyone except the person who'd written them.

"It's a map of our future." Mr. Chamberlain pointed to a thick black line that squiggled from Springfield to Pittsfield, indicating the railroad's future path.

"Well, I'll be damned," Mr. Stocking said. "Be a great way to transport your museum, won't it? You won't get any use out of it this year, though. I heard it's only finished as far as Springfield. They still got the Connecticut River to bridge." He lowered his spectacles with one finger and peered into Mr. Chamberlain's face. "You want to catch a ride on one'a them cars, we'll have to go all the way to Springfield to do it. That's a good fifty, sixty miles from here. Besides, you don't know what sort'a accommodations you'd need for all your peripatetic paraphernalia, never mind how much it'll cost to haul."

"It's not Springfield we're going to. It's here." Mr. Chamberlain pointed to the town of Chester. There was a cluster of X's a fair distance from the center of town. X's were also clustered at several other places along the railroad route. "According to Birnie," Mr. Chamberlain continued, "they've got work crews all the way from here to Springfield." His eyes gleamed with an excitement that Daniel couldn't fathom.

Apparently Mr. Stocking couldn't, either. "You could'a told us that back at the hotel, 'stead of dragging us out to the hinterlands."

Mr. Chamberlain made a tsk-ing noise. "Don't you see the possibilities?" He gestured toward the work site. "Look at 'em. Hundreds of men right here, and Birnie says there's thousands more camped out in Chester and Middlefield." He thumped Daniel on the chest. "Your people, boy. They're hauling 'em in by the boatload."

Mr. Stocking chortled. "You think those fellas have money to spare for your circus?"

"Museum," Mr. Chamberlain corrected indignantly. "Those fellas' wages are burning holes right through their pockets. What else have they got to spend 'em on?"

Mr. Stocking's eyes flickered toward Daniel. It wasn't hard for Daniel to guess what he was thinking. Liquor, that was what they'd spend their money on, had they any to spare. He thought about the rowdies in the pit who heckled Mr. Stocking and made lewd comments at Francesca, who'd called Mr. Sharp "darky" and "nigger," the louts who taunted Mr. Lamb's animals until the teamsters had to throw them out of the menagerie tent. He shuddered at the idea of a pavilion full of such men.

"Birnie says they can't camp near the towns, so they have these shanty villages out in the middle of nowhere," Mr. Chamberlain said. "Those camps ought'a be as good as a mill town for drumming up an audience. Better, 'cause there won't be any preachers railing against us."

"Or any constabulary, should things get out of hand," Mr. Stocking said.

"When has a constable ever been on our side? I'll bet we can fill that tent twice a day for a week if we follow that railroad line."

"We've already got four weeks of shows booked from here to Vermont and back. You want to cancel all those venues and head east instead?" Mr. Stocking shook his head. "Our advance man'll be apoplectic, trying to redo it all."

"No, no. We'll tack some more shows onto the end." Mr. Chamberlain traced the route they were meant to travel for the next month: a loop that ran north into Vermont, then west into New York, then southeasterly back into Massachusetts. "We'll keep on same as we planned until we hit Pittsfield." His finger moved from Pittsfield eastward along the railroad line. "We'll add one more week along the railroad and finish with a coupl'a days in Northampton or Springfield. That'll give us another ten days of showing, and we'll wind up in a good-sized town to boot."

"It'll be mid-November by then," Mr. Stocking said. "Might be a bit cold for folks to sit in a pavilion to watch a show."

Mr. Chamberlain shrugged as he folded his map and returned it to his pocket. "If the weather gets bad, we'll cancel." He gave Mr. Stocking a friendly punch in the shoulder. "Come on, Jonny, where's your sense of adventure?" He slapped Daniel on the back. "You can be your Irish self, boy. Those Paddies hear we got a couple of their own on display, and we won't be able to beat 'em off with a stick." Before Daniel could respond, the conjurer collected his horse's reins and put one shiny black boot in the stirrup. "You think on it, Jonny," he said, swinging up into his saddle. "There's got to be two, three hundred right there in front of us, and hundreds more farther down the line. Not bad at two to four bits a head." He put his heels to his horse and cantered off toward the hotel.

"I don't know, Dan'l," Mr. Stocking said, shaking his head. "You get that many workingmen in one place with no civilizing influence around 'em and a little liquor in their bellies, there's no telling what could happen."

Chapter Thirty-Three

Tuesday, October 1, 1839, Springfield, Massachusetts

"They've all gone mad," Hugh said, watching Ferry Street fill with people shoving against each other like sheep driven into a pen. "What's it about, Eamon?"

"Is it the moon you've been living on, that you don't know?" Eamon said.

"If they was all Irish, I'd think the Pope himself was come to town."

Eamon put an arm around Hugh's shoulders. "'Tis a fool I am, Hugh. How would you be thinking of aught but your own troubles, with your lads laid to rest but a few weeks ago?"

Hugh suppressed a shudder. It had been a mistake, seeking Eamon out. Oh, the man meant kindly, that he did, and Eamon's Katie had been the soul of sweetness and consideration, never mind that they'd only two rooms to fit themselves and their four girls, without adding Hugh to the household. But every sympathetic glance and soft word, every kindness they did him was another stone on his chest, a reminder that he was a coward and a liar and no fit man to be taking advantage of their generosity. It was only the drink that kept him from feeling crushed entirely under the weight of their sympathy and his own guilt.

It seemed hard for Eamon to stay in a somber mood today. The crowds packing the street laughed and joked with a festive air. Eamon found their mood infectious, his eyes sparkling like a boy's on holiday. "It's the railroad, man," he said. "It's opening this very day, and the governor and all here to celebrate."

"Aye," Hugh replied. "I've heard." He'd have needed to be dead himself to have missed the talk. How many of his mates had traded their jobs digging canals and building mills for the promise of better wages laying track? They said even a Paddy had a chance of working his way up to foreman or higher, if he didn't work himself to death first. "But it's naught to do with me, so I never minded the day it was to be done."

"Done?" Eamon said, dragging Hugh with him as he wove through the crowd. "Why, it's hardly begun. It's open but from here to Worcester. It's still building through to Albany. The tracks'll be laid out like spiderwebs across the country before long. Some day it'll be but five days from Boston to Saint Louis. Imagine! 'Tis the future, cousin. The future at our very doorstep." The excitement in Eamon's flushed and grinning face was mirrored in the faces of the men around him, jostling to be the first to the new depot.

The future, Hugh thought, listening to the talk that swirled about him, words light with curiosity, optimism, hope, talking of this new railroad the way folk back to home had talked of America: the opening of a door to a golden future of prosperity and progress. So he'd felt when he and Margaret had first arrived in Boston with Liam still in nappies. He'd not been such a fool as to expect riches, but he had dreamed of a decent wage for a day's work, a proper home for his family, and no landlords to answer to. He'd expected America to give him everything he'd ever dreamed of, but instead it had taken away everything he'd ever loved.

A brass band played over the noise of the crowd as he and Eamon turned the corner from Ferry Street onto Main. The new depot with its sloping walls and square corner towers rose above them, as imposing as a massive ancient shrine. He shoved his way through the crowd, trying to keep sight of Eamon's threadbare jacket.

The ground shuddered and rumbled, and the crowd's motion shifted, some pushing forward harder, some falling back, not sure they wanted to be quite so close after all. In the shift, Eamon and Hugh found an opening and slipped into the forward rank of people.

The track looked like a gleaming ladder of iron and wood

laid on the ground and stretching forever to the east, and west to the river. Folk packed in on either side of it—more than Hugh imagined Springfield could contain. Although the ground trembled beneath Hugh's brogans, the train was still a small, smoking black coal off in the distance.

An Irish child's shout shrilled over the crowd's rumble. "Mam, Mam, when's it coming?"

A woman on the other side of the track tried to manage two squirmy, grimy-cheeked lads. She clutched their jackets to keep them by her, the way his Margaret used to do with Liam, the way she'd have done with Jimmy and Mick, had she lived to see them into trousers. The way the lads jostled and poked each other minded Hugh so much of his own lads that he almost headed across the track to help the woman. Her face was partly hidden by the brown plaid shawl she'd draped over her head, just the way Margaret had worn hers. The wind tugged a spill of yellow curls across her cheeks, and Hugh's heart lurched. The blood pounded in his ears, crashing against the noise of the crowd and the band and the approaching train, a churning roar that battered and dizzied him.

"Margaret? Is it you, love?" he asked. Had she come back to forgive him or to damn him? He shouted her name, and the woman raised her head, looked at him with eyes blue as flax blossoms. "Margaret," he said again, this time a groan. But before he could cross the track to take her in his arms, a metallic screech slashed through the roaring in his head, and his vision was filled with black iron and steam.

"Good God, Hugh, is it altogether mad you are? I feared you aimed to walk out in front of the train." Eamon grasped Hugh by the shoulders, hauling him around to look at him face to face. "You could'a been crushed!"

"It was Margaret. Did you not see her?" Hugh gestured wildly across the track, where the crowd had broken ranks in the wake of the bright yellow coaches clattering behind the engine toward the depot. He tried to pick out the woman's brown plaid shawl, but there was no finding it among the boil of hats and bonnets and coats surging away from him.

"What're you saying, man?" Eamon shouted in Hugh's ear.

"Margaret, by God! She was there, with Jimmy and Mick tugging at her skirts."

Eamon shook his head slowly. "Hugh, no. Don't be doing this to yourself." He clutched Hugh's elbow, dragged him away from the press of the crowd.

Hugh rubbed his eyes and forced a laugh as jagged as broken glass. "Just me mind playing tricks is all. A lass with yellow hair, and she put me in mind of me own Margaret. An idiot, I am."

Eamon draped an arm across Hugh's shoulders. "I know how it is, man. When me own da passed on, didn't I go fancying every bit of wind blowing through the cracks in the walls was himself whistling for me?" He reached in his pocket and drew out his flask. "Still do sometimes, and it's a dozen years gone he is and me across the ocean from his grave."

Hugh nodded his thanks and uncorked the flask. The empty places inside him welcomed the warmth of the rum.

"Come along," Eamon said, his arm still around Hugh's shoulders, their heads together so they could hear each other over the crowd's din. "We'll go down to the square and watch the parade, take your mind from your grieving."

Hugh let Eamon lead him, but he knew that noise and music would not be enough, just as the drink was never enough. Aye, he'd follow Eamon to the parade and festivities, but it'd take more than brass bands and a wondrous new machine to draw his mind from his heart's rue. He needed to leave this place entirely, to start fresh.

That was the railroad's promise, wasn't it?

"It's still building, you say?" he shouted in Eamon's ear and gestured toward the track.

Eamon nodded. "Across the river and west to New York."

"They're still needing hands to work it, then."

"Thousands, they say. It's hard work, I'm told, and dangerous."

That was his answer. He could work hard, and as for danger, well, what did he care, with no one to miss him? He would lose himself in the new work, leave memories and demons behind, make himself into a new man. He squared his shoulders and hugged Eamon in silent thanks for giving him hope. His heart began to warm to the music and festivity of the day.

But his eyes still searched the crowd for a woman in a brown plaid shawl.

Chapter Thirty-Four

Thursday, October 17, 1839, Bernardston, Massachusetts

"We've still not given 'em new names," Billy said.

Daniel gave an absentminded "ummm," paying more attention to the six ponies cantering around the ring. He and Billy stood back to back in the center, each of them holding a longeing whip, Daniel's pointed toward Gray and Billy's toward Teeth. The idea was to keep the other ponies evenly spaced between Gray and Teeth, with all six cantering at a steady pace. Eventually, Daniel hoped to manage them alone, using Gray to set the pace. But Teeth would break ranks and cut across the ring or run up along the pony in front of him or fall back to visit with the one behind, if Billy didn't keep him focused on the end of her whip.

Daniel gauged the distance between the ponies. They were doing much better today, their steps more evenly matched. "Ready?" he warned Billy. "One, two, three—Now!" Daniel and Billy stopped smartly, drawing their whips straight up by their sides.

First Gray, then the rest of the ponies wheeled on their haunches to face the center of the ring. The maneuver was supposed to be crisp and precise, all six of them moving as one, facing Daniel and Billy like spokes on a wagon wheel. Gray and Brown turned with military precision and stood with shoulders and hindquarters squared, heads up, waiting for the next command. Red stopped slantwise so his nose touched Brown's. Socks turned to the right instead of the left, looking over her shoulders at the others as if wondering why they'd all got it wrong.

"Teeth, no!" Billy said. The piebald gelding put his head down to crop the withered grass. Black looked ready to follow suit.

"Bl-a-a-ack," Daniel warned. The pony snapped to attention, though nearly shoulder to shoulder with Teeth instead of centered in his segment of the ring. Daniel shook his head, though he was smiling. "Better than last time," he said. "At least they're all facing in."

"Stand," he commanded, raising his empty hand. The ponies fixed their eyes on him, except for Teeth, who munched away obliviously. Daniel sighed. "C'mon, let's set 'em straight."

"I said, we've not given 'em new names yet. You said we would."

"I thought you'd'a come up with something by now." In truth Daniel had so much on his mind that he'd forgotten entirely about the ponies' names.

"They should be something rare and grand." Billy guided Black into place.

Once Billy's back was turned, Teeth laid his ears back and nipped at Brown. Daniel hissed and flicked the end of the whip in the grass. Startled, Teeth peered at Daniel from under his shaggy forelock with a "Who, me?" expression in his eyes. "Got a good name for the king of mischief?" Daniel asked.

"Kelpie," Billy replied.

Daniel laughed. Although there was nothing in the legends about the mythical water horses being piebald, Teeth did seem the sort who'd drag children underwater and gobble them up. "All right then. Kelpie he is. I s'pose you'll be wanting to call Gray Liath Macha, and Black will be Dub Sainglend." Surely Billy could choose no grander names than those of the horses who'd drawn mighty Cúchulainn's chariot.

Billy fixed her eyes on Gray. "No. That'd be too fierce for her." She went to Gray and rubbed the mare's forehead. "Her name is Pearl." Not *should be* but *is*, as if the pony had sent her a silent message.

"Aye, Pearl it is," Daniel agreed. She was definitely the pearl of the lot: steady and calm and quick to learn, the one who tended most to incombustibility. "And Red, shall he be Ruby, then, if you're naming 'em for jewels?"

Billy wrinkled her nose. "That's too girlish. I have to think on him a bit more. But Black…he's wanting to be named after that black jewel on Mr. C.'s turban. Only I don't remember what it is."

"Glass, most likely," Daniel said.

Billy rolled her eyes and put out her tongue. "I know that. But what's it s'posed to be?"

"Onyx, I fancy."

"Onyx. That's him." She touched his brow as she had with Pearl.

"How are you liking Rinn or Rialta for Red?" Daniel asked as he approached the blood bay gelding. "For this star on his forehead. And isn't he the one for always showing off?"

Billy caressed the white star between the pony's eyes. "Aye, Rinn."

"What about you?" Daniel asked, walking across to Socks. She'd been the hardest pony to clean because of the tangles of matted hair at her fetlocks. Daniel had been tempted to give up and cut it all away. But he'd persisted, and now feathers of long white hair fell in silky waves about Socks's feet. "Silk" he said.

"Oh, that's lovely," Billy agreed, giving the pony a christening touch.

"That leaves you then, lass," Daniel said, turning to Brown, who'd sidled away from Teeth—no, Kelpie, he reminded himself.

Billy crossed her arms and frowned. "She is a puzzle. I'm trying to think of something brown that's precious. At first I thought Mahogany, because Mr. S. once said that's a rare fine wood. But I'm afraid folk'll call her Hog for short."

Daniel laughed. "Were you to ask Silas Lyman for something brown and precious, he'd tell you it was dung."

Billy snorted with laughter. "Is he daft?"

"No. Just a farmer who could tell you enough about manure to fill a book." Thinking on Silas made Daniel remember Lizzie Stearns, who'd been smitten with the young farmer. "Lizzie," Daniel said thoughtfully. "She was the dairymaid to Lyman's, where I was bound out. She'd wear this old gown to do the dairying, and it was just about this sort of brown." He patted the pony's neck. "D'you s'pose she'd be minding having a pony named after her?"

"You might want to choose something else, horse boy," said a feminine voice. Francesca leaned over the low wall with her brothers. "Our mother's name is Elizabeth." The girl arched a stern eyebrow at him.

Daniel took the brown pony's halter and turned her toward Francesca and the Ruggles boys. He clucked softly to make the pony prick up her ears and arch her neck prettily. "Wouldn't your mam be pleased to have such a grand creature named after her?" he asked.

The pony lifted her tail, and a half dozen round clods of manure plopped from her backside onto the grass. Then she broke wind with a whistly sort of puttering noise.

Francesca let loose a gale of laughter that sent tears streaming down her face. Her brothers elbowed each other, snickering. Billy doubled over, hands on her knees, until her giggles turned to hiccups, which made her laugh even more.

Daniel hid his face against the pony's cheek, concealing his own laughter more successfully. "Well," he said, finally turning back toward the acrobats. Maybe not Lizzie, then. Maybe Eau de Cologne would suit her better, eh?"

"Well, horse boy, it seems you've been sharpening your wit," said Harry Ruggles.

Francesca wiped her eyes. "Sharpened by Mr. Sharp, I'll wager," she said.

"Aye, well, him and Mr. Stocking," Daniel confessed. Just as he'd been working with the ponies to make them immune to sudden noises and strange objects, Mr. Sharp and Mr. Stocking had been working with Daniel to make him immune to heckling and insults and to keep his head when a trick didn't go as planned. They'd taught him how to parry words with the hecklers, if he felt in a clever mood, or to to feign ignorance of English and cheerily insult them back—in Irish—if his wits felt a bit dull. He'd learned how to pry humor from a tense situation, to make an audience laugh with sympathy rather than with mockery. The lessons had helped him outside the show ring as well. It had become easier for him to relax with the other members of the company. Strangest and best of all, he could finally talk to Francesca without stammering and blushing, though it was still easier to speak to her when he didn't look at her straight on.

While her brothers fetched the equipment for the morning's practice, Francesca greeted the ponies, learning their new names from Billy. "I swear they're looking better and better every day," Francesca said. "You two have done wonders with them."

Daniel studied the ponies, trying to see them as Francesca did. What he noticed most was what was no longer noticeable—matted hair at Silk's fetlocks or ribs jutting out from Pearl's sides or tangles in Rinn's mane. He didn't notice chipped hooves or wary eyes, ears laid back in suspicion and fear. He felt a singing sensation in his breast.

"We've still not named this lass, though," Billy said when they came to Brown.

"Aye," Daniel said, turning to Francesca. "What do you think?"

Brown lowered her head so Francesca could scratch her ears. The rope dancer smiled at Daniel. "Oh, I think Lizzie would be just fine."

Friday, October 18, 1839, Brattleboro, Vermont

...Imagine, Ethan, me being in a show training six ponies. Mr. Chamberlain says it wasn't a proper circus until we come because there was only the one horse act plus the grand cavalcade at the beginning and that's why he called it a museum but Mr. Stocking says he called it so to dodge the laws against traveling performers in Connecticut. That and so as to make folk think they was being educated by having a bit of fun which also keeps the ministers from preaching against us. Mostly.

Daniel set down his pen to trim the candle and stifle a yawn. Only a few weeks with Mr. Chamberlain's museum and already he appreciated the luxury of staying two nights in one place. Better yet, in a hotel with a private room for himself, Billy, and Mr. Stocking instead of crammed into an attic or hayloft with the other men and boys. Well, all the men but the conjurer, who had his special pavilion in order to maintain the illusion that Fred Chamberlain and Prince Otoo Baswamati were two separate gentlemen. Daniel wondered how long the conjurer would keep up that ruse now that the nights were turning frostier. Even now, with a fire burning merrily beside Daniel's table, the wind rattled the windows, sending tendrils of cold air into the room. In the morning, the frost-crusted grass would crackle under his feet, and he'd be glad for his woolen stockings and stout boots.

Perhaps Mr. Chamberlain was indeed thinking on the emerging season. Each night the conjurer dallied longer indoors to give house shows before retiring to his tent. In his guise as East Indian mystic, he'd read palms or heads or gaze into his crystal for individual customers. As himself, he'd tell stories or perform dramatic pieces with Mr. Stocking and others from the company. Lately, Daniel suspected that the cold did as much as the cash to keep the showman away from his tent of an evening.

Daniel cocked an ear toward the sounds wafting up from the taproom. He'd gone up after supper to write his letter while Mr. Stocking and Billy made music and Mr. Chamberlain did his prognosticating, tonight in East Indian regalia. The fiddle had stopped, and now and again Daniel heard the singsong of the conjurer's incantations. He dipped his pen to begin again.

The door creaked open, making the candle flame flutter. A shadow fell across the page.

"What you doing?" Billy reached for the paper with a sticky hand.

Daniel snatched the letter out of reach. "I'm writing a letter to me friend. And I don't want you soiling it with your grimy paws."

Billy stuffed a butter-and-jam-smeared heel of bread into her mouth. A glob of jam crawled down her chin. One finger captured the escaping jam and guided it back toward her lips. "Anything 'bout me in there?"

"Only the truth. Which is to say, naught that's any good."

Billy held up a second slice of bread. "Pity. I was going to give you t'other piece." She took a bite and grinned, letting jam ooze between her teeth.

"Heathen," Daniel said. "Mr. Stocking's wasting his time, trying to civilize the likes of you." But he laughed while he said it.

"What fun is there in being a boy if you got to be tidy all the while?" She tore the remaining bread in half and put the larger remnant on the table next to Daniel's inkwell.

Daniel set his letter away from the sticky treat. "Hope you washed the dung off your hands before fetching this."

She shrugged. "Adds flavor, don't it?"

He shook his head. It was good bread—all white flour, the butter sweet and deep yellow, and the jam raspberry, his favorite. "You couldn'a brought a bit of tea to wash down the bread, now?" he asked.

"Ingrate. I only got but the two hands." She flopped down on the bed.

"What're they all up to downstairs?" Daniel asked.

"Mr. S. is selling elixirs to the landlord, and Mr. C. is feeling some lady's bumps."

Daniel nearly choked on his bread. "He's *what?*"

"On her *head*, you *ee-jit*." Billy ran her hands over her own scalp and intoned her best impersonation of Prince Otoo Baswamati. "The passions are strong in this one. And secrets." She narrowed her eyes to ominous-looking slits. "Many secrets lie heavy on your soul." She shrugged. "The usual rot." She licked jam, butter, and crumbs from her fingers. "Go on, finish your letter. Don't be minding me."

Daniel picked up his pen to start again, but Billy sitting there staring at him made all the thoughts go out of his head.

"So who is this friend?" Billy asked.

"That lad Ethan that was bound along with me."

"The one helped you get Ivy and get free?"

"Aye. I thought maybe he'd like to hear from me." His throat tightened as he remembered parting from Ethan, how the lad had struggled not to cry. "*I mind what becomes of you,*" Ethan had said. Knowing that had been both a comfort and a burden, for

Daniel had feared Ethan would be the only person who would ever care what happened to him. He'd never expected to become part of an entire community. But the show folk, some of them at least, cared whether he performed well or not. As for who truly cared, well, Mr. Stocking surely, and perhaps even Billy.

"Why don't you ask Mr. Stocking for a bit of paper to write your brothers?" Daniel said. "You've plenty of funny stories to tell 'em."

Billy examined the dirt under her fingernails. "Maybe."

"Mr. Stocking would pay the post for you."

"Da'd probably not even show 'em the letter, just for spite. I'd not be surprised if he told 'em I was dead."

"You think he would?"

"What would you say if you come home without your daughter, eh?"

If even half of what Billy and Mr. Stocking had told Daniel about Hugh Fogarty was true, it would be just like him to do such a thing.

"Anyway, even if he did let 'em see me letter, well, Da can't barely read himself. And Jimmy and Mick, they know their ABCs, but that's about it."

"And Liam?" Daniel pressed.

Billy pushed herself farther away from the light. "He tried to teach me, but he didn't know much, and neither of us had time for school, though I think he would like to'a gone."

"P'raps there's someone you could send to so's Liam could get a letter without your da knowing. Maybe they could read it to him. He'd be glad to know you're alive and well."

The bed squeaked as Billy got up and stood on the far side of it, where she was just a dark shape edged with gold. When she spoke, her voice was a little too loud, too bright, too deliberately careless. "Liam and them've prob'ly all forgot me by now. Anyway, they're prob'ly better without me."

"I shouldn't think—" Daniel began, but Billy kept on talking over him.

"What d'you s'pose Da done with all that money he got from

Mr. S.? Two hundred dollars—that's nigh on a year's pay for him. Maybe enough for Da to mend his ways and make a better home for 'em."

"Maybe," Daniel said. "Still, I fancy they'd be missing you. You said Liam would."

"He'd be having one less mouth to feed, now," she said sharply. She turned and faced the window, a dark shape against the glass. "If he missed me, he'd'a looked for me, wouldn't he?"

"But if he—" Daniel stopped and shook his head. There was no point telling her that if Fogarty had indeed convinced his sons that Billy was dead, Liam would have no reason to look for her. So instead he asked, "How d'you know he's not been searching all this while?"

Chapter Thirty-Five

Sunday, October 20, 1839, Cabotville, Massachusetts

Augusta didn't come to fetch her water at her usual time. Liam waited a few minutes before heading back into his shanty. He left the door ajar so she'd know he was up, so she'd smell the bacon cooking—good bacon, with more meat than fat to it, and no mold to scrape away, and plump new potatoes fried up in the drippings. The lass would be pleased to see what he'd learned from watching her cook. There was no tablecloth, true, but he'd got a couple of bits of calico folded up tidy beside the plates like they were serviettes of fine linen. A chipped mug on the table held a fistful of wild asters he'd gathered on the riverbank, their spidery blossoms like a cluster of snowflakes.

She'd like that. But most of all, he hoped she'd like the notice torn from the newspaper and laid on her plate next to the fancy wee cakes he'd bought at the baker's. It would be worth the expense of the meal, the hours he'd spent in the evening puzzling advertisements out letter by letter from discarded newspapers. It still might be all for naught. The position might be filled already; she might be cross at his meddling. But by God, at least he'd tried.

He squatted by the hearth, turning the potatoes in the bake kettle. They colored up to a fine golden brown, the first time he'd cooked something that hadn't gone from raw to black in an eye blink.

He listened for the sound of Augusta's door, her step in the alley. He glanced up every other minute to see if her door had opened and maybe he'd missed hearing it because of his bad ear or the growing tumult of the neighbors waking and making their own breakfasts, their babies squalling to have their nappies changed and their empty bellies filled.

Still nothing. He couldn't fault her for wanting to sleep in of a Sunday, though he'd not known her to do so before. But what if... He didn't like the *what ifs* running through his head.

He scraped a layer of ashes over the coals and set the bake kettle on top, then he replaced the iron lid and spread another layer of ash and coals on it to keep the meal warm. He paced the alley, hoping she might come out after hearing him moving about outside. He raised his hand to knock and stopped himself three times. Supposing she was, well... working?

He returned to his own shanty. His glance fell on the thin slant of weak sunlight coming through the cracked window. Jimmy's and Mick's toys still lay where Augusta had placed them the day they'd taken the coffins away. The sight decided him, and he turned back to her door. Better to face her anger than to find out too late that she'd stayed abed with a fever and himself too timid to knock. He rapped hard. "Augusta, are you not well?"

Ah, there it was: a rustle of cloth, the scrape of a chair on the floor. A cough on the other side of the door, and Liam found himself studying what sort of cough it might be.

"I've taken a little chill, that's all, Liam," she said, not opening the door.

"I'm that sorry to hear. Hand me out your pitcher and bucket, and I'll fetch you some water. I've breakfast and tea ready. I'll bring it over for you, shall I not?"

"No. No, don't bother. I just want to go back to sleep."

The door stayed closed between them.

"Augusta," he said, his voice lower now. "If you're not—not alone—I'll go. You needn't lie to me. But if you're truly ailing.... I can't be knowing that and not doing something to—"

"Then go for a walk," she said, her words hatchet sharp.

He bit his tongue against the urge to respond in kind. There was someone there, then. And what right had he to care? She'd made no secret of what she did in the evenings, but as long as he didn't see her come and go with her men, he'd been able to pretend it wasn't real. But the idea that one of them was with her now, while the meal he'd made sat cooling on the hearth and his surprise unseen—

"Bloody hell," Liam grumbled as he stomped down the alley. What an idiot he was—his dreams, wishes, ambitions, naught but lies that he'd filled his head and heart with so he'd not have to admit how empty his life was. Just another lie, it was, that he could set Augusta on a different path, that there could be more between them than neighborliness, that there was more than pity in the way she looked at him.

"Tell yourself the bleeding truth, man," he muttered. He was naught but a laborer, a ditch-digger, and Augusta was naught but a whore. Those were the facts, and he might as well face them. And surely a man should do better than be turned witless by a woman's—a *whore's* sharp tongue. Why should he be wandering about the streets, angry and petulant as a scolded child? Might as well go home and eat the breakfast he'd wasted so much money and time preparing.

He saw a figure approaching Augusta's door as he rounded the corner. Damn and bloody hell if it wasn't herself there, bringing in her own water bucket, her shawl draped over her head. She turned away and gathered the edge of the shawl closer about her cheek, but not before Liam noticed the purple mark surrounding her half-closed eye.

"Augusta," he said, and all of his resolve crumbled. He took three broad strides toward her and drew the shawl aside.

She turned so the bruise was in shadow. "There was a disagreement over my . . . fee." She tried to push past him to her door. "It's nothing, Liam."

He blocked her way. "That's it. This—this work of yours. It's over."

She laughed humorlessly. "And who gave you the right to choose my life?"

"I can't be living next to you and pretending that what goes on in there"—he jerked his chin toward her door—"that it doesn't matter."

She drew herself up straight. "Who are you to be looking down on me?" She tried once more to shove him aside and open her door.

He took her by the shoulders and forced her to face him. "It's not me doing the looking down, lass." He cupped a hand under her chin and tried to turn her face up toward his, but her eyes darted away. "It's them." His contemptuous gesture encompassed all the men who'd shared her bed. "They got no more right to be touching you than I do."

She shook her head. "Liam, don't make me out to be something I'm not."

"You're more than this, Augusta. Can you not be seeing the truth of it?"

"The truth is I have to eat. I have to live."

"Oh, aye? And how long is it you'll be living with such as this one for your trade?" He brushed a finger whisper-light to her bruised cheek, and she winced away. "What am I to do should the next one kill you?"

"What are *you* to do? I hardly see that it concerns you." She pulled against his grip.

He held fast and gave her a little shake. "Christ, lass, haven't I just lost everyone that ever mattered to me? I'll not be losing another."

"What do you mean?" she asked.

"You matter to me, Augusta. What you do. Who you're with. What becomes of you."

She finally met his eyes, staring at him as if he'd spoken the words in Irish instead of English. Then she blinked and shook her head. "You don't know what you're saying. It's only gratitude because I helped—"

He cut off her words by putting a finger to her lips. "And p'raps it's naught but pity that has you keeping me company.

What of it? It's more than either of us has had from anyone else in a long time. It's more than most folk have to start on."

"To start what?" she asked.

"Again," he said, almost in a whisper. "To start again." He bent to kiss her unbruised cheek. She turned her head, not away this time, but so that her lips met his.

Chapter Thirty-Six

Wednesday, October 30, 1839, North Adams, Massachusetts

A cymbal crashed, and Pearl leaped through the paper-covered hoop that Francesca and Billy held in front of the entrance to the ring. Close on her heels came Silk, then Lizzie, Kelpie, and Onyx. Rinn jumped through last of all, pausing as he entered the ring to look up toward the box seats, as if the applause were all for him. Daniel directed the ponies in a canter around the ring as the band struck up a jig. But for their plumed bridles and a surcingle around each pony's belly, the ponies were naked, their glossy coats more beautiful than all the blankets and spangles that Professor Romanov had tricked them out with. No bootblack was needed to hide hooves that were no longer cracked and dry. Their well-brushed manes and tails streamed like banners, and silky fringes of hair fluttered gaily around their fetlocks.

As the ponies circled him, Daniel wondered if it was right for anybody to feel this happy. He'd never in his life dreamed anything so grand, not even in that secret green place inside himself.

The jig drawing to an end, he brought the longeing whip smartly to his side. The ponies whirled into position, facing him like spokes on a wagon wheel with Daniel at the hub. Silk still turned to the right instead of to the left, but they spun so handily and spaced themselves so evenly along their circle that Daniel had to forgive her. He held his arms out, and the ponies ranged themselves into two lines, like dancers ready to perform a contra. Mr. Stocking struck up "Flowers of Edinburgh" on his fiddle, and Daniel guided the ponies through a leisurely series of passes and loops and figure eights. They responded as if they were all of one mind—even Kelpie.

"Flowers of Edinburgh" turned into "The White Cockade," and the ponies picked up their pace, weaving more complicated patterns. Daniel felt the audience hold its breath as the ponies seemed on the verge of collision, then safely passed each other, then whirled to turn in the opposite direction, pricking their ears and bobbing their heads in apparent acknowledgment of the applause that broke around them. The intricate maneuvers were not only meant to impress the audience, but to distract them from the acrobats maneuvering into place around the ring.

The ponies settled into a canter on the outside of the ring. Daniel glanced about to make sure that the riders were in their places. *Ready, steady...no, not yet.* Billy still needed a moment to collect herself. Daniel let the ponies make one more circuit of the ring, then he nodded to the acrobats. He turned to face Mr. Chamberlain, who stood at the ready near the band. Daniel gave the whip a tiny flick, then flung his arms into the air and shouted, *"Now!"*

With an explosive crack, Mr. Chamberlain set off a burst of colored smoke over the ring. At the same time, Billy and the Ruggles boys leaped onto the backs of the cantering ponies. To the audience, who'd been momentarily dazzled by the noise and smoke, the riders seemed to have materialized by magic. The acrobats waved and grinned at the cheering crowd, then one by one, they stood on the ponies' backs.

Good, Daniel thought. Not a wobble among them, not even with Billy and Kelpie. He signaled the riders that all was ready for the next stunt. Each struck a new pose, stretching one leg out in front or behind, leaning forward or backward, each pose more difficult than the one before it. Last was Philo, who performed a headstand on Lizzie's back.

Daniel itched to be up there with them, even though he knew his most important job was to stay grounded in the center of the ring. With the tricks still green and raw, someone needed to monitor horses and riders, to slow the pace or stop the performance at any sign of a rider's unsteadiness or a horse's unruliness. Even from the ground, though, his heart synchronized with the thrumming of the hooves in the trampled grass. If a pony stepped amiss, he would feel it before he saw it. If the whip was an extension of his arm, the circling ponies were an extension of his entire being. Never before had he felt such a strong connection, not only with the animals, but with their riders.

Harry Ruggles and Rinn flashed by. Harry tilted his body forward so that it was parallel with Rinn's back, one leg extended straight behind him, his arms spread like wings. The blazing grin on Harry's face was echoed in the proud arch of Rinn's head and the sweep of the bay pony's black tail, held aloft like a flag. Harry waggled the tips of his fingers as if to say, "I'm flying."

Daniel grinned back, then brought his hands together before him. The circle of ponies became two circles, one inside the other, three ponies cantering clockwise and three ponies cantering counterclockwise. The riders leaped, twirled, and changed places as gracefully as dancers, once, twice, three times. The applause crescendoed as the riders began their dismounts one by one, progressing from Billy's simple leap to single, double, and triple pirouettes from Philo, Moze, and Charlie, and concluding with somersaults from Teddy and Harry.

The band struck up a frenetic hornpipe, while Mr. Sharp and Mr. Dale set up a springboard, turning the chore into a crazy dance that included cartwheels and headstands as they pretended to test the board's strength and stability. Then Daniel brought Kelpie and Pearl to the center of the ring. Francesca joined her brothers in a series of vaults from the springboard over the ponies' backs. After each jump, Billy brought forward another pony, making the leaps more challenging until all six stood in a neat row, seemingly oblivious to the acrobats twirling and spinning over and around them.

Daniel monitored the ponies for the slightest sign of uneasiness, holding their attention with soft words and tiny changes in the tilt of his head, the slant of the whip. He'd sandwiched Kelpie, the most mischievous, between Pearl and Lizzie, and he'd placed Rinn, the most energetic, between Silk and Onyx, so that the calmer ponies would hold the more fretful ones steady. Kelpie was usually the first to break ranks. A flick of an ear, a roll of an eye or curl of a lip, a shift of weight, a ripple of the skin along his withers would tell Daniel it was time to end the routine.

The finale was supposed to culminate with the tumblers forming a human pyramid as they vaulted from the springboard and landed one by one on the far side of the ponies, with Francesca at the peak. Then Mr. Sharp would toss a lit torch to Francesca to hold aloft like a beacon. It was a beautiful sight—in practice. But the noise and bustle of a crowd made it hard for the ponies to stay focused on Daniel, and inevitably Kelpie would grow restless long before the final stunt. So Daniel would usually signal the tumblers to break off, and they'd pretend that whatever stunt they'd done last was the true finale.

This afternoon, though, there was a different energy in the air. Billy joined Daniel in front of the ponies. "Now?" she murmured. He answered her with a smile and a soft. "Aye, they'll stand."

And stand they did, as Harry, then Teddy and Charlie leaped and landed to form the pyramid's base. Moze and Philo came next, alighting on their brothers' shoulders as steadily as if on solid ground. Finally, Francesca turned a graceful head-over-heels somersault before becoming the apex of the pyramid.

Kelpie snorted, and Rinn bobbed his head. They would break ranks any second now. Daniel shook his head at Mr. Sharp; adding the torch might be too risky. It was the best they'd ever done before an audience; there was no point chancing their luck any further. Torch or no, the trick had never looked so grand, the ponies never so alert and handsome, the acrobats never so precise and skillful.

Francesca leaped to the ground, landing with a cat's easy grace. Her brothers followed, raising their arms in triumph, then bowing to the cheering crowd. Daniel signaled with the whip, and the ponies reared as one onto their hind legs, came forward two steps, then dropped back to all fours and gracefully bent their right forelegs and bowed along with the gymnasts.

Daniel whipped off his cap and bowed, not to the audience, but to the ponies and the acrobats. As he straightened, he and Billy shared a grin that warmed him down to his toes. And even though he'd never left the ground, he was soaring.

Chapter Thirty-Seven

Thursday, October 31, 1839, Middlefield, Massachusetts

"Good God, Hugh, you attack that rock like it was the very devil himself." O'Neill laughed and clapped Hugh on the shoulder. "Pace yourself, man, or you'll drop before it's yet dinnertime."

Hugh settled his pickax and wiped his sweaty hands on the seat of his trousers. He took a long drink from the bottle of cider that O'Neill offered him, the sweet amber liquid dribbling down his chin. He dragged his forearm across his face, though his grimy sleeve did more to add grit to his cheeks than to dry off the sweat and cider. "I'm fine, Martin. It feels good to be working again."

Since arriving at the railroad camp, he'd assaulted his work with the intensity of a fiend. He rubbed his hands together before lifting his pick again, feeling the tough leathery places where healed blisters were turning to calluses. It was hard work, aye, work that left him limp and drained at the end of the day. And that suited him perfectly—to drop onto his blankets and sleep without dreaming.

It felt good to slash at the mountain with pick and shovel as if he were striking at the very face of God Himself, who'd stolen so much from him. To strike for once with blows that, for all the force he put into them, could do no harm to anyone he loved.

Aye, it felt good to be working out here in the fresh air, even in the damp and the cold. He could breathe again, no matter that the air was dense with stone dust and dirt. It was free air, fresh and cleansing. Perhaps out here he could work his way into healing. Perhaps . . .

If only that young teamster down the way didn't put him so much in mind of Liam.

Chapter Thirty-Eight

Friday, November 1, 1839, Pittsfield Massachusetts

Daniel slipped into the pavilion just in time to watch Francesca begin her *corde volante* performance. It still captivated him to see her float and twirl high up in the pavilion's peak, like a white butterfly blown aloft by the music of Mr. Stocking's fiddling. He held his breath as she let go of the rope, somersaulted, then caught herself and hung by her knees. He was so hypnotized that he almost leaped out of his skin when a long-fingered hand grasped his shoulder.

Daniel clapped a hand over his own mouth to stifle a cry of surprise. Mr. Chamberlain's dark, furious eyes glared at him. "Where is she?" the conjurer asked.

"Uh?" For the moment, the only *she* Daniel could think of was Francesca.

"Billy, you dolt. She's supposed to be on next," Mr. Chamberlain snapped, apparently so angry that he'd forgotten to keep the lass's gender a secret.

"Last I knew, Billy was with Mr. Stocking."

He'd not seen much of the lass all day. She'd left the morning's equestrian drill to Daniel and the Ruggles boys, claiming she had a new song to learn with the peddler. She'd left Daniel with the harnessing of the ponies' wagon for the parade, and she'd not taken her place in the caravan until the very last moment. Daniel had thought she'd been in one of her snits, though he'd not been able to figure out what he'd done to anger her.

Mr. Chamberlain shook his head. "Jonny nearly missed his cue, he was so busy looking for her. Nearly had to have Francesca performing to the slide trombone."

"I—um—"

"Never mind." Mr. C. twirled one end of his false mustache. "I'll read some heads or conjure a ghost. That'll make 'em happy. But she'd better be here for the finale."

Daniel found Billy back at the inn, curled in the straw in Pearl's empty stall, hugging her legs to her chest. He opened the door warily. "Are you ailing?" he asked. She had seemed a bit peakish that morning. He'd never seen her turn away breakfast before.

"I think I'm dying," she said. He couldn't see her face, which she kept pressed against her knees. She held her shoulders tight to her body, as if to hide that she was crying.

"Dying? You've not been at Mr. Stocking's tobacco again, have you?"

She shook her head and rocked herself back and forth. "There's such a griping in me guts. And there's blood. So much blood."

"Blood?" he asked. "Where? What happened?" He put a hand on her shoulder and tried to turn her face toward him. She squirmed away and curled herself tighter. When she finally looked up, her cheeks were wet with tears and flushed bright red. "D-D-Down there. Blood. Just like Mam. There was so much blood down there when she died."

"Down...there." Daniel's stomach somersaulted. He laid her on her side and turned her as much as he could while she curled in on herself like a hedgehog. A dark stain spread across the seat of her trousers. He let her go as quickly as if he'd scalded his hands. *Sweet Jesus, Mary, and Joseph.* Who was he to deal with such a thing? All he know about female troubles was what he'd learned from tending to livestock and an occasional crude joke from one of the farmhands at Lyman's. He looked frantically about the barn, as if he expected a wise old woman to appear and take the burden from him. But there was no one else. "Tell me about your mam, lass. What ailed her when—when she died?"

Billy unrolled a little bit and sat up to face him. "She was having a baby. The baby come and then there was blood everywhere—d-d-down—down there. And then she died, and so did the baby." She hugged herself tighter, as if she could stop the bleeding that way. "I don't want to die, Daniel." She gulped back a sob, released her grip on her knees long enough to wipe her nose on her sleeve, and drew in a long snuffling breath.

Daniel ran a hand across his face. "You're not dying, lass. I can tell you that much." But he wasn't altogether sure she'd be pleased to find out the truth of it.

Mr. Chamberlain's conjuring and Mr. Sharp's Ethiopian fire-juggling took the place of Billy's singing while Mrs. Varley cleaned the girl up and fitted her out with fresh clothes and much *tut-tutt*-ing, and *poor-lamb*-ing, punctuated with cries of "*I knew it all along!*" That Billy meekly tolerated all the fussing was sure proof to Daniel how stunned she was.

After the dust had settled from the show, Daniel stole up to the bed chamber at the inn where the lass had remained hidden all afternoon. "You feeling any better?" he asked the blanket-covered lump that was Billy. Had it been young Ethan back to the Lymans' who was upset, Daniel would have soothed the lad's bruises with cold water and wormwood and listened to him rant about Lyman. Maybe he'd have promised him a ride on Ivy. He knew well enough how to console a lad, for he'd been in the self-same place. But a lass, well, how was he to know what was going on inside her head?

He could leave the consolation to Mr. Stocking or Francesca or Mrs. Varley. No, not Mrs. Varley. She'd smother the lass with her *dear-dear*s and next be measuring her up for a gown and petticoat, and then Billy would be off, and no telling where she'd end up.

An array of remedies littered the table: a cup of gingery-smelling tea, one of Mr. Stocking's elixirs, a tin pan and damp rag smelling sharply of goldenrod—some sort of women's poultice, he supposed.

He took a deep breath and tried the only thing he had to offer. "What're you lying there for?" he said sharply. "Kelpie and

Silk are getting full of themselves and need riding to quiet 'em down. You ought to be outside helping me, 'stead of lying here sulking."

"I'm not sulking," said the lump.

"Then you'd best get your arse out of that bed and onto one of them ponies, 'cause I can't be riding both of 'em by meself. If we wait any longer, it'll be dark."

The blanket moved aside, revealing a wary blue eye and part of a scowling mouth. "Get Francesca or Teddy to do it."

"You know Kelpie likes you best," Daniel said. "And anyway," he added a little less roughly, "Francesca says it'd do you good. She says...she says getting up and doing always helps when she—I mean—you know, to take her mind off—off things." The rope dancer had said no such thing, but Billy wouldn't know that.

The lump stirred, and a rumpled Billy emerged. Part of him expected her to look different, though in what way he wasn't sure. Was he expecting her to all of a sudden look more of a girl? She still had the same boyish manners and graceless stride. But soon there'd be no denying the betrayal of her body that had begun that morning.

Thankfully, she spoke of naught but the ponies and their training as they readied Kelpie and Silk for their ride, speculating about whether Kelpie could ever become incombustible and whether Moze or Philo Ruggles should ride Silk in tomorrow's show.

Soon there was no talking at all as they gave the ponies their heads while there was still enough daylight left to run safely. The sun dipped below the horizon as the ponies finished their race. When Daniel reined Silk in and looked at Billy and Kelpie, the lass seemed, if not happy, then at least distracted.

"Ha!" she said. "We beat you! I knew Kelpie was faster."

Though Daniel had not held Silk back one whit, he'd not been able to nose her ahead of Kelpie. But he'd not tell Billy that. "You never," he said.

"What? Knew Kelpie was faster or beat you?"

"Neither."

"Liar."

"Ingrate."

"Ee-jit."

Ah, there was the old Billy back again. But something different from rivalry or stubbornness lingered in the air between them, like the sulfurous clouds of colored smoke that Mr. Chamberlain conjured in his act. Daniel's fear of disturbing that cloud gave him a vague jangling feeling beneath his skin. Silk picked up the feeling, and she switched her tail testily.

"'Tisn't fair," Billy said, and Daniel felt the cloud drift in his direction.

"All right, so Kelpie *is* faster," Daniel said, trying to push the cloud back.

"That's not what I mean," Billy said. "Francesca said...she told me..." She paused, and Daniel hoped she'd realized this was no fit subject to be speaking of. "It's horrible, Daniel. All me life, every month. It's like—like—It's like being in nappies." She shuddered.

Daniel cast a sideways glance at the lass but could see nothing of her expression, just the shape of her body and Kelpie's, all the color in them washing into grays and blacks. "It'll not be so very bad, once you get used to it. Everyone has to grow up now, don't they?"

"I'm sure you never minded growing up, for wasn't every year that much closer to being free of that Lyman fella? But I'll never be free ever again."

Daniel shook his head. "I never knew a lass that wasn't free." Not that he'd known all that many lasses, but the Lymans' dairymaid Lizzie, Mrs. Lyman herself, the lasses who came and went about town, sure they'd all seemed freer than himself to do as they pleased, at least until he'd got clear of the Lymans.

"Oh, aye?" Billy said with a snort. "How many lasses do you know can do anything they please?"

"Nobody can do everything they please," Daniel said. "That's just the way the world works. There's things women do and things men do and—"

"Aye, you could fill a book with the things men do and have, the places they can go. A castle full of books," Billy said, dropping her reins and spreading her arms wide. "And the things a lass can do?" She held up one finger. "Take care of men. The things she can have?" She held up a second finger. "Babies. I'll not be chained to a cookpot and a sewing basket."

Daniel's mouth flapped like a fish's as he tried to come up with a retort. But outside of Madame Staccato and Francesca, he couldn't think of a single female who'd done aught but run a household. And they hardly counted, for most folk wouldn't consider them decent ladies. He thought on Mrs. Ainesworth and Mrs. Taylor, two ladies who seemed to know their own minds. But he could only imagine them in their kitchens and parlors, making their men's meals and clothes. Surely, though, it was because they wanted to be there, because it was in their nature. He'd never imagined that they'd have chosen something else, if only there'd been something else to choose.

Had it not been dark, perhaps she'd not have told him. But riding back in the deepening blackness, Billy almost felt as though it were Liam alongside her instead of Daniel. She and Liam used to talk about almost everything—their anger at Da, how much they missed Mam, Liam's troubles at work, her struggles to get Jimmy and Mick to mind—everything except where she went, what she did, how she dressed while Liam was at work. Many was the time she'd opened her mouth to tell him, then slammed it closed again, unsure whether he'd take it fair or ill.

So she told Daniel all the things she would have told Liam, had she mustered up the courage. She told him how it had started, when Jimmy and Mick had begun running off on their own, leaving her behind in the dim little shanty with naught but endless chores while they were out having their fun. She told him how she'd decided there was no reason for herself to be trapped inside.

So when Da was away at work or across the river at the tavern, she'd slip out through the Patch's maze of muddy alleys and head for the center of Cabotville. As she walked, she'd listen for music wherever she could find it: a ragged patch of song here, a burst of fiddling there, the artless whistling of some lad strolling down the street. She'd follow each new song and listen until she'd get the tune right in her own head. Then she'd breathe her own life into it and make it come out better, sweeter, gladder, or sadder than she'd heard it. She'd whistle or sing as she walked, both proper songs and songs that she'd invented.

Then one day an old lady with tears in her age-fogged eyes had pressed a penny and a sweet cake into Billy's hand, and she realized that her singing could please someone besides herself and Liam. She'd learned to watch her listeners to see whether they'd be good for a penny or a treat, or whether they'd be so absorbed in her song that they'd not notice her hand in their basket or pocket, not notice the apple or potato slipped from barrel or bin.

She'd quickly learned that it was better to go about in Liam's castoff clothes, her hair hidden under an old cap. Although she'd sometimes get a penny while singing as her girl-self, she'd just as likely get a lecture about how good girls didn't sing in the streets for their suppers. But as a boy, folk would praise her for an enterprising young lad, to be helping his family so.

At first she'd been cautious, afraid she'd run into Da or the lads or someone from the Patch who'd recognize her. But that last day, she'd been careless, walking back toward their shanty along the main path instead of creeping along the shadowy backs of hovels and sheds. Da had caught her strolling along, whistling to herself and jingling the coins in her pocket.

He'd never thrashed her so badly before, trying to make her tell where she'd got the money and where she'd hidden the rest of it, for he was sure there was more somewhere. But he couldn't make her tell; he'd had to tear apart her bed tick to find her hiding place.

Da's mistake was that he'd not burned her boy clothes as he'd threatened, but had only taken them away and flung them in a corner. As soon as Da had gone once more to the tavern, she'd retrieved the shirt and broadfalls. That night, with the boys asleep and Da still gone, she'd hacked off her plaits and her caged-in girl-self along with them.

In the long silence that followed her story, Billy could almost hear Daniel thinking. In among the shuffle of the ponies' hooves in the gravel, the crunch of dried leaves swirling around their feet, the soft huffing of their breath and the swish of their tails, she could feel his disapproving thoughts. Had it been Liam, there'd no doubt have been thoughts of betrayal as well. But when he spoke, all he said was, "And that's when you found Mr. Stocking, then?"

"Aye, and I been free ever since. Until today." She slumped on Kelpie's back and felt his pace slacken in response. "I won't never be free again now." Whyever had she told Daniel all that for? "S'pose you'll be thinking me daft, won't you?" she said brusquely.

Daniel sidled Silk close enough to bump against Kelpie. His knee knocked Billy's, and he poked her with an elbow, the darkness sending his aim a bit off. "Aye," he said, "but you'd'a still been daft had you never decided to change your petticoats for broadfalls."

She took a breath to muster up a retort, then let it out without speaking. It seemed too much effort to put her blustering, sharp-edged Billy-self back on. And yet she couldn't be Nuala again, either. She tried to puzzle out what that left her to be, but could find no answer.

Neither of them spoke again until they came in view of the inn, its windows glowing with candlelight, smells of wood smoke and something warm and savory for supper greeting them. The sound of Mr. Stocking's fiddle, turning "The Minstrel Boy" into a lament with a melancholy sweetness filled the night air. Without a word, Billy and Daniel reined their ponies short of the dooryard, in unspoken agreement that it would be sacrilege to break in on the music.

When the fiddler reached the chorus, the instrument sounded like two fiddlers playing at once, calling and responding to each other, then weaving together in harmony. Whether she would have it or no, the music took hold of her, filled her all the way to her bones. She couldn't help but reply, even if only to hum the song under her breath, so softly she thought no one but Kelpie could hear.

There seemed as much regret in the final notes of the melody as Billy felt to hear it ending. Then a burst of applause and calls for another round of drinks broke the spell. Beside her, Daniel let out a long whoosh of breath. Billy realized that he'd been as spellbound as she.

She slid from her pony's back to lead him into the barn, then turned to see why Daniel wasn't doing the same. He stared at her thoughtfully, almost like he'd stare at one of the ponies, trying to figure out how best to gentle it.

"What?" she said coolly, narrowing her eyes at him.

"Nothing," Daniel said. "Only I'm thinking you might be a bit wrong about being free."

"What would you be knowing about it?"

"Naught, I fancy. Only I can't help wondering what it is that's truly making you free. Is it the clothes, or"—he jutted his chin toward the tavern, where Mr. Stocking had begun in on "Soldier's Joy," bowing the tune so nimbly that a dancer would need to be possessed by the very devil to keep up with it "—or is it the music?"

Chapter Thirty-Nine

Monday, November 4, 1839, Middlefield, Massachusetts

"What d'you think now, Hugh?" O'Neill said as a boy came into the ring to clean up after the camels. "Wouldn't you'a been that sorry to'a missed this?" The soft patter of rain on the canvas blended with the murmur of conversation buzzing through the pavilion as the audience speculated on what the next act might bring.

Hugh nodded. *"Come to the show,"* O'Neill had said. *"Take your mind away from your troubles for a bit."* Reluctantly, Hugh had agreed, though he'd not expected anything of it. He had to admit now that O'Neill was right. He'd been transported into a dream world by the music and the rainbow-colored costumes of the acrobats and jugglers, the exotic animals, the conjurer's tricks. In this world, people could fly or balance on a thread or on the tip of a sword. Wild beasts seemed gentle as housecats and lapdogs. Conjurers made objects disappear and reappear or turn into something completely different. Aye, it was all a lovely dream, a world that he'd never been able to conjure from the depths of bottle or keg.

It was all trickery, of course. If only there were magic and trickery enough to unchain him from his past, to let him start clean and fresh and carefree again, like that rosy-cheeked boy down there tidying the ring, whistling to himself, no more on his mind than—than—

Christ, no, not even here could he escape, for didn't the lad down there put Hugh in mind of his own Liam, back in the days when Margaret was still alive? Hadn't Liam carried himself just so, had that same set to his mouth when he was on a task, and that same bit of a curl that strayed down his forehead over his left eye?

Someone tuned a fiddle, the bow testing the strings tentatively, then sawing across them with a cry like a cat in season, setting the crowd laughing. The boy straightened abruptly, leaning on his shovel, facing away from Hugh toward the other side of the ring, his head cocked at attention.

The squawl of the fiddle ripped across Hugh's heart, for didn't that lad look the very spit of Liam, the way he'd stand alert when his mam would call for him? Bloody hell, he'd never be free of them. Hugh half expected the boy to turn and shout out, "Why did you leave us, Da? Why did you leave us to die?" Would it be forever this way? Would he be forever seeing his lost boys in some other lad's face, his Margaret in any slight, fair-haired woman passing at the edge of his vision?

The hidden fiddler traced his *la sol fa*s like a lament. The boy echoed the notes tentatively at first, glancing furtively about as if he feared being caught slacking at his chores. His voice grew stronger, following the notes as if unaware that hundreds of people listened to him practice. The fiddle moved up an octave, and the boy's voice followed. The crowd stilled, listening for the fatal moment when the boy's voice would stagger and break. But the moment never came, and fiddle and voice met in a note of sweet, bright clarity. The boy swept the audience with a slow, satisfied grin. God, such a grin as Liam would have made, back in the days when Liam still had smiles.

Hugh closed his eyes. He'd give up the drink entirely this very second, he promised, if only the Lord would stop tormenting him with visions of his lost family. But instead, a new torment was added: Margaret's voice singing "*Neaill ghubha Dheirdre*"— "Deirdre's Lament." He opened his eyes, rubbed them hard, and stared at the boy in the ring, face and eyes shining as his voice wove an intricate lacework of song with the fiddle.

"Sweet holy mother of God and all the saints," Hugh said, crossing himself.

O'Neill patted Hugh's arm. "Aye, that lad sings like a very angel," he whispered.

Hugh shook his head. Not an angel, nor a drunken vision. And definitely not a lad.

Nuala.

He cheered himself hoarse when she reached the end of her song. He cheered even louder when he saw how much the others in the crowd loved her. Even though the price of the show was a good portion of a day's wage, some of the Paddies were so enraptured to hear a song in their own tongue that they dug deep into their pockets and tossed pennies at her feet.

Hugh felt the despair lifting from his breast. For surely, if the Lord had seen fit to bring Nuala back to him, there was hope yet that he could redeem himself.

Yes, he'd have her back, and this time it would be different.

"Stolen, by God!" Hugh said. "Me own flesh and blood." He paced in front of the fire, unable to keep still.

The flames of dozens of campfires made the jagged shadows of the railroad men's shantytown loom tall over Hugh and his comrades, as if the collection of ramshackle shacks grew with the darkness the way Hugh's boldness grew with the drink. Clusters of men squatted about each fire, supping on hard biscuit and salt pork, sharing bottles and tobacco, songs and stories. The crowd around Hugh's fire grew, drawn by his intensity.

"I thought you said your children were all dead. Dead of the fever, the lads were, and the lass drownded in the river," O'Neill said.

Hugh spun to face his companion. "Aye, so I thought, when I found her wee frock all torn and bedraggled on the muddy riverbank. But it's clear now what happened." He rubbed his jaw, building a new story in his head, solid and strong enough to push aside the old tale.

"Did you not say the constable showed you her body?" asked McCarthy.

The new story tottered. "You misheard me, Sean, I'm sure," Hugh said. "'Twas her clothes only. The constable said he couldn't show me the body." Aye, that was it. If he told it a few more times, he would believe it himself. A few more after that, and it really would be true.

McCarthy squinted against the smoke. "Aye," he said finally. "That must'a been it. Begging your pardon, Hugh."

"They must'a snatched her," Hugh said. "Snatched her and put a lad's clothes on her and left her own behind."

"Meaning no disrespect, Hugh, but are you that sure?" O'Neill asked. "We were sitting a bit of a ways off and—"

"Do I not know me own daughter?" His throat tightened, the wood smoke blurring his vision. "Do I not know that voice that's the very echo of her mam's?" It was her voice that had convinced him it wasn't yet another of his fancies. When he'd seen her again later in the show, leaping from one pony's back to another as wild and fierce as any boy, he'd barely recognized anything of his old Nuala. He mightn't have known her at all, if he hadn't been looking for her, she made that convincing of a boy.

"It's unnatural," he said. "It's against God, dressing her like a lad and forcing her to play at trick-riding." And yet, hadn't it been a thrill to watch her, fearless and graceful as she was? A lass who could do such things would be a fine comfort and support to her old da. Son and daughter both, she could be. It was a hard thing to say which glowed brighter in his imagination: Nuala's talents or the coins the crowd had tossed at her feet. He'd already framed a picture in his mind of himself and Nuala roaming the country together, putting their troubles behind them with her songs. In time, perhaps, he'd even buy her a pony so she could do her trick-riding, too. Aye, she'd like that, wouldn't she?

"A lass belongs with her da," Hugh said. "Not with a pack of godless show folk."

"Well, there's only one thing for it, then, isn't there?" O'Neill said. "Who's for helping Hugh get her back?"

The chorus of *aye*s that rose around the fire brought Hugh to tears.

Chapter Forty

"Can I ride Lorenzo, Mr. Lamb?" Billy stared longingly up at the camel's droopy face.

"All right. But be careful. He's a fractious beast," the menagerie keeper warned.

"Aye, well, Billy is, too," Daniel said. "So they ought to be getting along famously." He wrapped his scarf tighter around his throat. The afternoon's rain had ended, thank God, but the night air was thick with damp.

Mr. Lamb tapped the camel's front legs with his stick to make Lorenzo kneel so Billy could scramble up into the saddle. "Oh, my. It's not a bit like sitting a horse, is it?" she proclaimed as the camel clambered back to his feet.

"Just don't fall off, eh?" Daniel said. "We'll never be finding you in the dark."

A string of lanterns lit the caravan. Two more bobbed up and down along the length of the wagon train: Mr. Stocking on one side and Mr. Chamberlain on the other, making sure horses were harnessed, cages bolted, and every person and beast accounted for. The peddler patted Daniel's shoulder as he stopped next to the ponies' wagon. "All set, son?" he asked.

"Aye." Daniel stifled a yawn. "It still feels uneasy, this night traveling. Like we're a pack of thieves running off ahead of the sheriff."

Mr. Stocking laughed. "Son, if you knew how many times we've had to do exactly that. I, uh—" He lowered his lantern and peered down the road. "Uh-oh, could be trouble coming." He pointed to a group of lights rapidly approaching the wagon train. "What d'you think, Bert?"

"Looks like more than somebody wanting his money back for a bad show," Mr. Lamb replied. "I'll pass the word along." He disappeared into the darkness, and Daniel heard his voice as he walked along the caravan, alerting teamsters and performers.

"Billy, stay on that camel," Mr. Stocking called. "You can be our lookout." He leaned closer to Daniel. "If there's real trouble, at least she'll be out'a reach," he whispered.

"Aye, if she'll stay put," Daniel replied. He unhitched Ivy from where he'd tethered her to the wagon and swung onto her back. He trotted her to the front of the line, where Mr. Chamberlain stood with a pistol hidden behind his coattails.

Daniel made out the shapes of men holding pickaxes and shovels and digging bars: the railroad workers. Their faces seemed ghoulish in the lanterns' glow, the November air steaming their breath ominously. His stomach did more tumbles than he'd ever performed in the show, and the reins grew slick in his sweaty hands. He leaned down from Ivy's back to ask Mr. Chamberlain, "What d'you s'pose they want?"

"Money. Liquor. Let's hope it's not women." Mr. Chamberlain held up his lantern. "Good evening, gentlemen," his voice boomed cheerfully, as if he were welcoming them for a social call. "What brings you here tonight?"

A handsome, muscular man with a dimpled chin and wavy hair spoke first. "I'm wanting to talk to that peddler fella."

Mr. Stocking joined Daniel and Mr. Chamberlain. "And what can I do for you fine gentlemen?" he said briskly, as though he didn't notice the angry looks on the faces before him.

"We come for what you stole from me."

"Stole?" The little man drew himself up straight and tugged at his jacket. "I may be a peddler, sir, but I'm no thief. If you think I cheated you, I'll be happy to give you satisfaction. Just tell me the particulars."

"Don't be pretending you don't know," the railroad man sneered. "Weren't you the one as stole me little girl?"

The peddler's false smile collapsed.

"Sweet Jesus," Daniel said softly, his insides twisting as he saw the lass's dimpled chin and round cheeks in the man's flushed and angry face. Part of him wanted to flee the caravan, find his secret place, and wrap it around himself until the confrontation was over. But another part of him wanted to be clever and brave and strong enough to keep Mr. Stocking and Billy safe from Fogarty and his angry companions. He tried to kindle that second part and smother the first. He laid his hands against Ivy's warm neck, willing her strength into himself.

Mr. Chamberlain barked out a laugh. "Your little girl? You mean Francesca? Friend, if you think anyone will believe she's your kin, you're mad as a hatter."

Fogarty spat at Mr. Chamberlain's feet. "I mean your 'Irish songbird.' You got her all tricked out like a lad, but I know me own girl. I know her voice."

Now. Speak now, lad. There's no one else who can do it, said the voice in Daniel's head—Da's voice, and Ma's with it. Echoing them were young Ethan, Mr. Stocking and Mr. Sharp, Francesca and her brothers, even Mr. Chamberlain—all those who'd taught him courage and confidence. He was glad that Mr. Stocking had made him practice his Gaelic with Billy. The railroad men wouldn't listen to a Yankee, but they might heed an Irishman like themselves. He drew in a deep breath. "What would be your proof, sir?" he shouted in Gaelic. The Irish words startled them, as he'd hoped they would.

"Proof? You have my word," Fogarty responded, likewise in Irish.

Daniel cast a sideways glance toward Mr. Stocking, who moved his lips as if struggling to translate the conversation. Mr. Chamberlain had disappeared. The peddler nodded to Daniel to keep going. "And what if I gave you my word that I'm Billy's brother?" Daniel asked.

"Then you'd be lying." Fogarty's companions nodded, but not as strongly as they had before. Some of them gave Daniel studious looks, as if trying to find a resemblance between himself and the Irish singer they'd seen earlier in the day.

"Would I?" Daniel took a reckless chance. "Sir," he said,

addressing the man nearest Fogarty, "would you know this gentleman's daughter, were you to see her?"

"Well, no…," the man replied. The others around him shook their heads in agreement. "Only heard Hugh tell about her." He recovered himself quickly, though. "But his word is good enough for me."

"When was the last you saw her?" Daniel asked Fogarty.

"It was six months ago that peddler stole her."

"You saw him do it, then?" Daniel said, hoping he could trick Fogarty into confessing how he'd sold off his child. He nudged Ivy forward to shield Mr. Stocking from the railroad men. But the bloody foolish man stepped forward with him, reaching one hand up to give Daniel's ankle what was probably meant to be a reassuring squeeze. Daniel would have felt more reassured if the little man had retreated to the safety of the wagons and their burly teamsters.

"I saw him take her—" Fogarty began, but he slammed his mouth shut before he could fall into Daniel's trap. "I mean, when I saw her with him, I figured it was him that took her."

Even though Fogarty had caught himself, Daniel saw raised eyebrows and sidelong glances as seeds of doubt planted themselves in the other men's minds. He continued in his most mannerly tones, "Billy maybe looks a bit like your girl, and your fancy's turned them one and the same."

Some of Fogarty's companions backed away from him, nodding sympathetically. Daniel concentrated on the group in front of him, trying to block out the sounds behind him of wagons creaking, animals stirring uneasily, show folk talking together and, he hoped, readying themselves to flee, should he fail to diffuse the railroad men's anger.

"Are you saying I don't know my own flesh and blood?" Fogarty raged. "You're making a pretty little fortune out of my sorrows, with her singing like a trained canary, and me not having a penny of her wages!"

"So there's the truth of it," Daniel said, turning his voice sharp. "You said to yourself, 'I'll pretend to be that child's da, and then I'll have someone to earn my livelihood for me.'" To Daniel's satisfaction, a few of Fogarty's companions began looking narrowly at the man.

"If I'm not her da, how would I know she's a lass?" Fogarty insisted. The narrow looks turned back toward Daniel. "It's simple enough to prove. Give her to me and I'll show you."

"Would you give your very own brother to a pack of rough men to strip the clothes off his back and do God knows what else?" Daniel shouted indignantly.

A coarse bellow broke the night air; Billy had steered Lorenzo to the front of the caravan. Lorenzo bellowed again and opened his mouth wide, exposing huge brown teeth. Some of the railroad men backed up, but Fogarty stepped forward. "Nuala, lass, tell them I'm your da," he said, his voice soft and wheedling.

Billy stared coldly down at him. "Me name's Billy," she said in English. "Billy McBride. I don't know who you are." The camel let out a sound that was part roar, part belch.

"For pity's sake, Nuala, you're all I've left in the world," Fogarty pleaded, with what sounded like true anguish, even to Daniel's skeptical ears. "I swear it'll be different this time. I'll make it all up to you." His voice broke with a wrenching gasp that clutched at Daniel's heart and made him doubt himself for a moment.

Billy shook her head fiercely. "He's not my true da," she said in Irish.

"You've made a mistake, sir," Daniel said, pushing his doubts aside. "Let us be on our way and no harm done, eh?"

A few of Fogarty's companions nodded sympathetically and seemed poised to drift away from the group. A few others remained stolidly by him, their scowling mouths hard and determined. A goodly number, though, seemed caught in a muddle, their brows knotted in confusion as they tried to sort truth from lies.

Fogarty grasped at the sleeves of a couple men who were edging away. "That peddler and that magician have poisoned her mind against me. You've seen how these show folk trick people and muddle their thoughts."

"Hugh's right," said the man who'd stepped out first with Billy's da. "You know how these Yankees turn our children against their families, their homeland, their faith. They've turned her so she doesn't even know her own da. And they've turned this boy's head the same way, so he'll stand against his very own people."

"It's not my head that's been turned," Daniel said.

"If they won't give my girl up, then by God I'll take her!" Fogarty shouted.

The railroad workers roared their consent and surged forward.

Chapter Forty-One

Fogarty rushed toward Billy and Lorenzo. Daniel urged Ivy between Billy's father and the camel, but he had to fall back when Fogarty raised his pickax and swung.

The railroad men shouldered their picks and digging bars and charged at the wagons, but fell back at an unearthly tumult that came from the rear of the caravan. A massive brown beast wreathed in flame hurtled out from behind the menagerie wagons. The creature reared on its hind legs, exposing daggerlike claws. A rail-thin rider shouted curses from atop the demonic animal.

"Sweet Jesus, Mary, and Joseph!" Daniel exclaimed, crossing himself at the sight of Mr. Lamb straddling Griselda's back as though riding a horse. The menagerie keeper looked the very devil himself, wielding a torch in each hand as he urged the giant bear forward. An unholy yowl came from farther down the line, and Mr. Kellogg emerged from the darkness with one of the panthers on a chain. The confused beast dragged him along as it tried to decide whether to fight or flee.

Fogarty stopped midswing, blinded by a shower of rank spittle that Lorenzo spewed over him. Daniel wheeled Ivy to come at Fogarty from behind. Clinging to her mane, he kicked Fogarty between the shoulder blades as Ivy surged past. He whirled Ivy about and charged again, leaning low from her back to grab the fallen pick before Fogarty could recover it. "Run!" Daniel shouted at Billy, using Ivy to drive Lorenzo away from the wagons.

Ivy reared as she came about once more. Daniel clung to her back, trying to keep her steady while he sorted out what to do.

The two remaining camels roared and spat in all directions, hitting railroad workers and show folk alike, while Mr. Lamb rode Griselda back and forth to keep the railroad men at bay.

With a burst of yellow smoke and the sulfury smell of gunpowder, Mr. Chamberlain appeared on top of one of the menagerie wagons. Robed in his Indian conjurer regalia, minus mustache and eyebrows, he spewed bursts of fire from his fingertips, revealing a pair of teamsters on either side of him, armed with muskets. "Back, you sons of Erin!" he shouted. "Or I shall unleash all the serpents your Saint Patrick drove from your cursed island." In front of the wagon Mr. Sharp juggled his torches, the whirling flames making the painted snakes on the wagon seem to writhe, while Mr. Dale fumbled with a ring of keys at the door. Daniel was glad that the railroaders didn't know the threat was empty; Mr. Dale had a positive terror of snakes.

All along the caravan, horses screamed and stamped their feet, and some reared in the traces. Daniel thanked God that Mr. Stocking's incombustibility lessons had caught on so well. Most of the horses were immune to pyrotechnics and theatrics and stood their ground, albeit uneasily, perhaps wondering what new sort of performance this was. A few, however, bolted away into the night, dragging their rigs and struggling drivers behind. The remaining teamsters and performers took refuge on top of the wagons and pelted the railroaders with rocks.

Daniel tried to sort out where his help was most needed, but the melee was already nearly over. Forced back by fear of the bear and panther, the showers of stones, and the threat of firearms and serpents, the railroaders retreated into the night.

"Well, that was fun." Mr. Chamberlain appeared at Daniel's side, dusting off his hands. The smell of sulfur still clung to him. "They thought they were coming to break a few heads. Bet they didn't count on getting eaten, did they?"

"Fun?" Daniel said. "Is it entirely mad you are?"

"No doubt." The conjurer chuckled. "I do find a narrow escape stimulating to the circulation. Others, I suppose, might not agree." He gestured toward Mr. Dale, who leaned limply against the reptile wagon, mopping his brow. The juggler's face constricted with a sudden spasm, and he turned and puked onto the road.

Billy had never hated Da so much. He'd made a right proper mess of the show. Two wagons had broken against the rocks when their horses had bolted, and one of Mr. Lamb's beautiful antelopes had escaped and the other one had been killed when their wagon crashed. Philo Ruggles had twisted his ankle leaping down from a wagon, two of the teamsters were nursing cracked heads, and the panther had dragged Mr. Kellogg a good fifty yards and nearly gotten loose entirely. The worst of it all, though, was that one of Da's friends had hurt Mr. S. And that she could never forgive.

"You're sure you're all right?" Mr. S. kept asking her. But he was the one limping, his face as pale as ever she'd seen it. A tendril of blood oozed down his forehead, and his spectacles were twisted and missing a lens. He insisted that naught was wrong with him, and that he needed to help Mr. C. assess the damage. Daniel grabbed him by the collar and forced him to sit down and let his cut be tended.

"What about your ponies?" Mr. S. asked, as Daniel dabbed the gash on the peddler's forehead with a damp cloth. His face looked strangely naked and vulnerable without his glasses.

"They'll keep," Daniel said. He tipped his head toward the six dark shapes lined up next to them. "I fancy they've been taking a bit of a nap."

"Through all this hullabaloo?" Mr. S. said.

"Barely moved a muscle." Billy heard the pride in Daniel's voice. "Even Kelpie. Absolutely incombustible."

Billy was relieved to see the old spark return to the peddler's eyes. He grabbed Daniel's forearm with one hand and Billy's shoulder with the other. "You fellas done me proud," he said. Billy felt a tremor in the affectionate squeeze that he gave her.

"Hey, Jonny, look what we found!" Mr. C. called out. The conjurer and a half dozen teamsters approached, shoving one of the railroad workers toward them. "This one was still skulking around."

Billy recognized his gait even before the light fell on his face. *Da.* Her stomach churned as though a puke were coming on.

"I want me girl," Da said, trying to shake off the men's grip. "I'll not be leaving without her." The men released him but formed a tight semicircle around him so he couldn't escape.

Da came toward her and fell on his knees. "Nuala, me love," he said, his eyes soft as faded blue flannel. "It'll be different this time, I swear. I've learned me lesson for sure and all."

"I don't know you," she said, steeling herself against his pleas. She crossed her arms and planted her feet solidly, trying to will away the griping in her guts.

"I'd not be lying to you now that you're all I have left in the world," Da pleaded. And Lord help him, were those real tears in his eyes?

Liam had finally done it, she thought. *Someday, Nuala,* he used to say. *Someday, I'll take you and the lads away somewhere he'll not touch us again.* It seemed that someday had come at last. *Good for Liam,* she thought, sorry that she hadn't been there to help.

"Liam and the lads're gone, Nuala," Da said, crossing himself. "Gone to be with your mam. God rest 'em." The tears spilling down his cheeks were real. He sniffled and wiped his nose on his sleeve.

She fought back a new wave of nausea. It was another lie. Liam would never let anything happen to Jimmy and Mick. But fear gripped her stomach tighter, forcing her to step back and steady herself against the wagon. Mr. S. stood closer and put a hand on her shoulder.

"Oh, me darling lass." Da rose to a crouch, his hands on his thighs so that his red-rimmed eyes were on the same level as hers. "Liam and Jimmy and Mick are all gone, love. All three of 'em took by fever and naught I could do about it. Gone just like your blessed mam. It's just you and me left, sweetheart." He reached out for her.

"Liar!" she screamed, lunging past Mr. S. and shoving Da so hard that he staggered into one of the teamsters. "You god-damned lying bastard!" She backed into a round, soft body. Mr.

S.'s arms came around to hold and soothe her. She pushed him aside. If she accepted his comfort, she'd have to accept Da's lies. She huddled against one of the ponies, hugging herself tight, crouching around the storm in her guts.

"Nuala!" Da's voice balanced on that razor-sharp edge between hurt and anger that she knew so well. "Is that any way to talk to your da? Whyever would I be lying?"

"You're lying so's I'll feel sorry and go with you," she said. Da's mouth tightened, his teeth gnawing at his lower lip. "You done the same to Liam, didn't you? Told him I was dead, didn't you? When you come home without me." She filled her voice with the same venom that burned her guts. "Aye, that's what you done. You couldn't tell him you'd sold me away, so you told him I was dead."

"That's enough," Da said, no longer pleading.

"You did! Otherwise he'd'a come looking for me. I know he would." She surged toward him with doubled fists. "And now you're lying to me just the same."

"Shut up! Shut up!" Da shouted. He struck a blow that would have knocked her flat, had Daniel not stepped between them to block it. Billy put her arms over her head and let Mr. S. shelter her as Mr. C. and the teamsters pulled Da away from her.

She heard something that sounded like grunting, and she looked up to see Da with his hands over his face, shuddering with sobs. "Sweet Jesus," he said, catching his breath. He lowered his hands slowly, stared down at them trembling in front of him. "Sweet Jesus, I'm sorry, so sorry, love." He clenched and unclenched his hands, then rubbed them hard against his thighs, tucked them under his arms, put them behind his back, as if trying to disown what they'd done. "I'll never do it again, I swear to God," he said. "It'll be different, I promise. If only you hadn'a made me so angry. You shouldn'a said such things to a grieving man."

"It's true, then. He really is her father," one of the teamsters said.

"He's not!" Billy put her hands over her ears and huddled deeper into Mr. S.'s embrace.

The peddler tucked Billy's head under his chin and held her tightly, rocking her the way Mam used to. "Is that any kind of father you'd want to give a child to?" he said.

"Look, mister, if she doesn't want to go with you, I won't force her," Mr. C. said. "If you want some compensation for your troubles, I'm willing to pay—"

"Oh, no. I'll not be selling her off again so easy. That'd be leaving you with the golden goose, wouldn't it?" Da said.

"It's the money, not the lass you're wanting," Daniel accused. "And for a second I was almost feeling sorry for you." Billy heard him spit in the dirt, then she heard the sound of a scuffle, but she didn't want to look up from the comfort of Mr. S.'s arms.

"Take him away, boys," Mr. C. said. "A long ways away."

"I'll be back," Da shouted. "I'll be back with the law, and I'll have me daughter, that I will." His cries receded beneath the curses of the teamsters dragging him away.

All the while, Mr. S. continued to rock her, rubbing her back and making shushing noises. "It's all right, sweetheart," he finally said. "He's gone. We're not going to let him take you."

"It is a lie, isn't it?" she asked. "All that he said about Liam and Jimmy and Mick."

Mr. S. exchanged a cryptic glance with Daniel. "Of course it is," Mr. S. said. "Of course it's a lie." But Daniel just turned his head away and began tending to the ponies.

Chapter Forty-Two

"You were right, son. This is what comes of all my charades and foolery," Jonathan said as he took a new pair of spectacles from the box that Daniel had fetched from his wagon. They promptly misted over from the chill air, and he had to take them off and wipe them with his handkerchief before trying them again. Daniel's face was no longer a blur, but the new lenses seemed to increase the throbbing in Jonathan's head. He put them aside and tried another pair, careful to rub them warm before putting them on. He glanced at Billy. "If I'd'a made you stay with Sophie, you'd be safe with her now instead of—"

"No, sir," Daniel said. "She'd'a run away from your cousin, and she'd be God-only-knows-where by now."

"Don't fret about it, Jonny," Fred said. He conjured up two glasses and a bottle and poured out a dollop of brandy for himself and Jonathan. "That fella won't be back. Men like that don't turn to the law for help."

"But if he does, we're bound to lose." Jonathan watched Billy, unnaturally silent as she stared morosely into the sputtering fire. "Fred, I think we need to part company."

"Over a little hubbub like this? You know me better than that," Fred said. "I'll stand by you as long as—"

"Not willing to let the golden goose go, either?" Jonathan took a swallow of brandy to warm his insides before he continued. "No, I think some of us had better split up until we see the lay of the land. I have a suspicion that fella'll be dogging our heels until he gets Billy back. I think maybe Dan'l had better take her on down to Sophie's."

Billy roused from her stupor to glare at him, opening her mouth to object.

"Aye, that's wise," Daniel agreed before the girl could speak. "Her da'll not know to look for her there."

"Now wait a minute, Jonny. You're talking about gutting my show," Fred protested.

"You'll still have me and Phizzy and the Learned Horse routine. And Dan'l has taught Francesca and the Ruggles boys to work them ponies well enough that the bunch of us can manage 'em for a while. It'll only be five dancing ponies, since Billy'll need one to ride. If Fogarty comes sniffing around again, we'll tell him she's run away, and the little witch has stolen one of the ponies to boot." He grinned toward Billy and gave her a wink.

"No," Billy said, rising from her seat by the fire. "I can't go to Mrs. Taylor."

"It's the safest place for you," Jonathan said.

She shook her head fiercely. "I got to go back to Cabotville. To find out if it's true, what he said about me brothers."

Damn it all, that was the last thing the child needed to find out. Hadn't she had enough torment for one night without hunting out some more? "Billy, you can stay at Sophie's and write to Liam from there. If—"

"I got to go meself."

"She's right," Daniel said.

Jonathan sighed. "All right, then. Billy, get your things together. You and Dan'l can set out first thing in the morning. Take Pearl. She's the best one of the bunch, and—" He yanked off the new spectacles and ran a hand across his face. "Damn, these ain't right. They're making my eyes water. Oh, hell." He pulled Billy into his arms and held her so tight she let out a surprised squeak. God, he'd hugged the girl more times tonight than in all the six months they'd kept company. She deserved better than that. "Don't worry," he said. "I'll take good care of Phizzy for you." He kissed the top of her head and sent her off to gather her things.

* * *

Hugh pulled his coat tighter and hunched his shoulders against the bitter night air. If only he had a wee dram to warm himself. He checked his pockets, finding purse, pipe, and tobacco, but no flask. Either he'd lost it in the battle or he'd left it behind at the work camp, along with the cowards who'd turned tail as soon as the show people had started to fight back. His mates, indeed! This lot saw a little fireworks and a few beasts showing their teeth, and they'd taken to their heels. When he'd tried to rally them, they'd grumbled that they'd not signed on to do battle with wild animals, poisonous snakes, and armed men. And then McCarthy, damn his eyes, had the bloody nerve to begin doubting Hugh's story, with his wheedly voice and his "Maybe the lad was right. Maybe you are mistaken."

Some of them had begun looking at him slantwise with suspicion and others with pity, as if they believed the grief had addled his brain. They began saying what a good thing it was they'd not carried out their plan, for wouldn't it have been the proper tangle if they'd taken the child by force and discovered that it was the red-haired boy's brother after all? And then they'd begun drifting away into the darkness like smoke, leaving him alone on the boulder-strewn terrain.

So he'd turned back toward the caravan and been driven off, and now he returned again. He groped his way along the road, guided by fences and stone walls. He'd never thought he'd be glad of the Yankee obsession with enclosing even the meanest scrap of land, like dogs marking their territory with fence rails and piles of stone instead of piss. Tonight those markers helped him find his way back to the orange glow of the caravan's campsite. He was glad, too, of the afternoon's rain. The sodden leaves soaked through his brogans and stockings, but they also muffled his footsteps so he could approach in silence. Had the weather been dry, the crackle of shriveled leaves that blanketed the ground would have announced his presence as surely as if he'd shouted his name.

The show people had driven their wagons off the road into a rocky field and had unhitched and tethered their horses. Campfires were kindled, and men began to put right their damaged wagons. The steady *thock-thock* of hammers beat time. Yellow dots of lanterns traversed the field as men searched for missing equipment. The tall, thin form of the conjurer darted from wagon to wagon.

Hugh thought he caught a glimpse of Nuala, then lost her as the figure moved out of the firelight. Finally, he picked out the portly shape of the peddler standing next to that shabby nag of his. He seemed to be readying the beast for travel. The little man clambered into the saddle while another figure mounted a second horse. Someone handed each rider a lantern, and Hugh cursed silently as he saw that the second rider was too tall to be Nuala.

The two riders detached themselves from the caravan and headed toward the road. Toward Hugh. He crept closer, using a stone wall for cover. The horsemen proceeded slowly, moving their lanterns methodically back and forth, as if searching for something. Their upper bodies were mere silhouettes, vaguely human in shape, only slightly blacker than the cloud-shrouded sky. Hugh followed, bent nearly double to keep hidden.

"This is daft. We'll not be finding that antelope by daylight, let alone now," said a voice with the Irish lilt of the red-haired lad.

"Can't argue with you, son," came the reply from the peddler.

"Then whyever did you want to be coming out here?" The boy pulled his horse to a halt.

Hugh held his breath, as still as one of the stones in the wall that concealed him.

"I want to talk to you where Billy can't hear us," said the peddler. He and the lad moved forward again, their lanterns no longer weaving back and forth. They seemed to have given up all pretense of searching for the missing antelope.

Hugh followed as best he could, his feet gingerly probing the ground among the sodden leaves before settling his weight, wary of the snap of a branch that might betray him. The riders seemed more intent on their conversation than on making any progress, so it was no trouble to stay abreast of them. They rode with slack reins, their horses' heads drooping sleepily.

"You're sure I'm the one to be taking her and not yourself?" the lad asked.

"If Fogarty follows and sees that Phizzy and me are still with the show, he'll think Billy's here. We can maybe lead him astray for a while before he figures out she's missing."

Hugh warmed with excitement. He'd have her back then. All he had to do was find out where the lad would be taking her. Then he could waylay them on the road or at their destination. That scrawny stick of a lad would be no match for him.

"Besides," the peddler continued, "you'll be more help to her than I will. Folks in the Paddy camps are more likely to talk to one of their own than to me."

The boy halted again. "What if he wasn't lying about her brothers?" he asked.

"To hear Billy talk, lies are all her father knows how to tell," said the peddler.

Hugh gritted his teeth to hold back his curses. He'd take his vengeance on the peddler later.

"What could'a happened to part 'em, though?" the lad asked. "From what she's said, her da'd not be out here working an honest trade if he had Liam's wages to be feeding on."

Hugh's throat tightened as he struggled not to let the black mood send him charging from his hiding place. He dug his fingers into the leaves until the cold damp gnawed at his joints.

The peddler's horse plodded forward again. "Could be Liam's booted his father out. Or maybe he took the little ones and struck out on his own."

"Aye. She said they talked of doing that many a time," said the boy.

"Still, the way Fogarty carried on..." The riders drew a little ahead of Hugh, and he missed part of the peddler's words. He risked taking a few running steps to catch up.

"You believed him, too, then," the lad said.

"If he was pretending, then he's a better play-actor than Fred. God help her if her pa was being honest for once in his sorry life."

"God help me, too, for I'll not be knowing how to comfort her," said the boy.

Aye, Nuala would need the comfort that only her da could give, not these strangers who'd used her for their own profit, who'd forced her to deny her own flesh and blood, who'd turned her against the one who loved her best in all the world. Surely she'd not have turned her own da aside were she not being held against her will. Who knew what horrors they'd subjected her to, what threats they'd used to keep her from fleeing?

"You'll know what to say, Dan'l," said the peddler. "Didn't you just about talk that mob down all by yourself? You had 'em this close to believing you."

"Not close enough, for didn't they come at us all the same? As for meself, well, I was this close to wetting meself with terror," the boy said. "'Twas Mr. Chamberlain with his tricks and his teamsters and Mr. Lamb with his wild beasts that sent 'em running. But on me own..."

On his own, that scrawny lad would be helpless. Then Hugh would have his vengeance and take Nuala back.

"I wouldn't send you if you couldn't do it," the peddler said. "You've learned enough of playacting and showmanship to get her safe to Springfield. Just act like a coupl'a farmboys and keep your money hid. Once you get to Springfield, stay at Jerry Warriner's tavern. I'll write him a letter to introduce you. Jerry ought to remember Billy, seeing as I bought her in his dooryard. I'll write you there if anything happens."

"What do you think Fogarty'll be doing?" the boy asked.

Hugh knew exactly what he would be doing. He would be going to Springfield. He'd not even have to waste energy following Nuala and the red-haired boy. All he needed was to go back to the place where that fiend of a peddler had stolen her. It mattered not at all if they arrived ahead of him by a day or two or even three. They'd be waiting when he got there.

"I'm pretty sure we haven't seen his backside yet," said the peddler. "If he does bring the law down on us, there's no doubt he'll win. But maybe Fred and I can buy him off before it comes to that. In the meantime, we'll keep traveling like nothing happened. I think maybe I'll write to Sophie. Chester Ainesworth, too. He may not be a lawyer, but the man knows justice."

"And what'll you be telling 'em?"

"The truth," the peddler said. He sighed, his saddle creaking as he shifted his seat. "It's going to be a damn long letter."

Hugh grinned to himself, hardly believing his good fortune. Surely this lucky revelation was a sign from the Lord, a blessing on his plans, forgiveness for his sins. The Lord knew it was only right and proper for a father to have his child back again, and the Lord had put the means of doing it in his way. *Bide a while longer, Nuala, love,* he thought. *I'll be rescuing you soon enough. Soon enough you'll be safe with your da, where you belong.*

Chapter Forty-Three

Thursday, November 7, 1839, Springfield, Massachusetts

The tavern-keeper hemmed and harrumphed over Mr. Stocking's letter, looking from the paper to Daniel and Billy, a slow smile spreading across his face as he read. "Well, well!" he finally said, putting the letter into his vest pocket. "Pleased to meet you, Dan'l." He shook Daniel's hand so vigorously that Daniel felt it all the way to his knees. "Any friend of Jonny Stocking is a friend of mine. Lydia, make sure there's a good room ready for these gents," he shouted over his shoulder. He peered intently at Billy. "So you're that urchin Jonny bought this past spring, hmmm? Looked like a drowned rat, first time I saw you. Jonny's fattened you up pretty fine, hasn't he, boy?" Mr. Warriner clapped Billy so hard on the back that she staggered. "I hope he got his money's worth." With one hand on Daniel's shoulder and one hand on Billy's, Mr. Warriner ushered them into the taproom. "I'm not likely to forget that day. It's not often something like that happens right in your dooryard." He dragged a greasy rag across a table and nudged a bench out with his foot. "Ale, gents?" he asked, motioning them to sit.

"Thank you, sir." Daniel settled stiffly onto the bench, Billy by his side.

"Emily!" Mr. Warriner bellowed, dropping himself onto a bench on the opposite side of the table. "Ale for our guests!"

"So let's see what else old Jonny has to say." Mr. Warriner took the letter out, flapped it open. He hemmed to himself every now and again, pausing occasionally to raise an eyebrow at either Daniel or Billy. Daniel tried to read the back of the letter while Mr. Warriner read the front, but the landlord's beefy hand covered most of the writing. "Well, then," Mr. Warriner finally said, carefully folding the letter before returning it to his pocket. With a chuckle, he shook his head. "That Jonny," he said. "He is a one, isn't he?"

"That he is," Daniel said cautiously. "Uh...how much did he tell you, sir?"

"You know Jonny. He can say a whole book's worth of words without telling you anything at all," Mr. Warriner said, turning to Billy. "Mostly he says you're looking for your brothers. That right, boy?"

She nodded silently.

"And he says your pa's trying to go back on his deal."

"That'd be a fair way of putting it," Billy said.

"That is a pickle. Jonny paid for you fair and square," the tavern-keeper said. "I'm not sure it was strictly legal, but I saw him hand over the money. Still, a father has his rights."

"Even such a one as Fogarty?" Daniel asked.

"The boy was trying to steal Jonny's horse." Mr. Warriner's glance shifted back to Billy. "And you did tear it up like a hellion when Jonny caught you." He wagged a finger at her. "My son acted anything like you, I'd have whipped him good and sound, too. I'd have sworn that you'd steal Jonny's purse and disappear forever. But it looks like he's tamed you pretty well."

Daniel felt Billy tense on the seat beside him. When he glanced down, he saw her fists clenched, fingernails digging into her palms. But she remained silent, and Daniel felt a little flush of pride.

"It seems to me it's not all that complicated," Mr. Warriner continued. "The boy goes back to his pa, his pa gives Jonny his money back, and everybody's happy, hmmm?"

"Happy?" Daniel took a great gulp of his ale before continuing. "I fancy it's not altogether as easy as that."

"Nothing ever is with Jonny. That must be why he wants me to recommend a good lawyer." Mr. Warriner patted the vest pocket in which he'd placed the letter. "Now, Jonny and I go way back. He's a good man, and if there's anything I can do to help,

I'd be happy to do it, so long as I don't get tangled up in any legal trouble myself. I've got my business to consider." He spread his arms to indicate the taproom around them. "So I think you boys'd better tell me exactly what I might be getting myself into."

As briefly as he could, Daniel outlined the events of the past few months, concluding with the skirmish between the railroad men and the show people. Even though Daniel tried to be brief, the three of them had nearly reached the end of the ale by the time the story was finished.

"You say this fella was riding the bear?" Mr. Warriner said in amazement, as Daniel described Mr. Lamb's part in the fight.

Billy and Daniel nodded. "Just like he was on a horse," Billy added.

The landlord blew out a whistly breath. "Now that's something I'd like to have seen!" he said. "So—what part does Jonny expect me to play in all this?" Mr. Warriner asked.

"Only rent us a room while Billy looks for his brothers," Daniel said. "Point Mr. Stocking to a lawyer. We'd not be asking for any favors we couldn't be paying for."

"I wouldn't be too worried about the boy's pa if I was you," Mr. Warriner said. "If the fella's got two pennies to rub together, he'll more likely spend 'em on a bottle than on a lawyer. You Irish might be tight with your families, but you're even tighter with the drink." He drained the last mouthful of ale from his glass and wiped his mouth with his sleeve. "No offense to you boys, of course. It's lucky you fell in with Jonny so you can be brung up proper."

Daniel pushed down the tendril of resentment that uncoiled in his belly. The thing of it was, the tavern-keeper meant no more offense than Daniel might, were he commenting on how much a pig loved living in filth.

"Well, anyway, I'd be happy to give you boys what help I can," Mr. Warriner continued. "So long as it doesn't interfere with business. And maybe you can do a favor or two for me."

"Aye?" Daniel prompted.

"Jonny says you've got a knack for gentling horses," the

landlord continued, tapping the pocket that held his letter. "So happens I just bought a black gelding that could use some calming. He's fine when I'm around, but tries to bite my hired boy every time he turns his back."

"I'll take a look at him, if you like." Daniel suspected it was the lad who needed calming, not the gelding. Folk who got bitten usually deserved it.

"That's fine," Mr. Warriner said. "And one more thing. This show of Jonny's...it'll be coming here?"

"Aye. Once they're clear of Billy's da," Daniel said.

The landlord leaned forward, his eyes glowing like a lad's. "So tell me, boys. How many tickets can you get me?"

Friday, November 8, 1839, Cabotville, Massachusetts

"Gone?" Billy said, her voice quivering. "What d'you mean, gone?"

The woman shrugged, her ragged shawl slipping off one shoulder. "All I know is the house was empty when we come, so we took it. That one across the way was empty, too, that me brother has now." She crossed her arms and braced herself in the doorway, as if daring Daniel to try to run her off.

Daniel suppressed a shudder. Neither the pile of wood and stone that had once been Billy's home, nor any of those crammed cheek-by-jowl along the road could reasonably be called a house. What passed for streets was a maze of muddy footpaths and alleys with pigs and chickens scratching and rooting about among the refuse. Had he really lived in such a place himself once, back when Da worked at building the mills?

"Where did the Fogartys go?" he asked.

"However would I be knowing that, having only just got here meself?" the woman said.

"Surely there must be someone here who knows," Daniel said.

The woman stepped farther out into the street. "Halloo there, Katie O'Donnell!" she yelled. "Mary Carney!"

A head peeked out from the neighboring shanty, then from

the one across the street, and from the one after that. No doubt they'd been watching through their windows, wondering who were these strangers invading the Patch—strangers with horses, no less. The woman's summons gave them permission to satisfy their curiosity openly.

Daniel and Billy were soon surrounded by women and children and old men, all eager to share their knowledge of the Fogartys' whereabouts. The misfortune was that nobody agreed on where they had gone or what had happened to them.

"They're kin to you, aren't they, lad?" Katie O'Donnell asked, peering closely at Billy. "You're the very spit of their Nuala, God rest her soul."

Billy started, and Daniel grabbed her wrist to calm her. "Cousins," he said quickly, to keep Mrs. O'Donnell from interrogating Billy any further.

"That poor wee lass," said Mary Carney. "A fine singing voice, she had. But she's been gone these six months and more." She crossed herself. "Drownded."

"Run off," said another. "Run off and I can't blame her one bit, for the way their da laid into them when he was in his cups."

"Run off *and* drownded," Mrs. Carney said. She gave Billy a sharp look. "Now wait a moment. You lived with them for a time, didn't you? I'm sure I saw you coming out of the house now and again. Always nipping down an alley and running off like you were afraid to be caught at some mischief. Your cousins always had time for a *good day* or *how d'you do,* but never you. Where you been off to all this time, that you don't know what's become of them?"

Billy twisted her cap into a ropy mess, her teeth gnawing her lower lip.

"Working," Daniel said. "Got himself a job as a peddler's assistant, making decent wages, he has. And now he's come back to help the rest of 'em out."

"Well, you're too late, aren't you then, lad?" said Mrs. Carney. "They're all of them dead. Dead of the fever."

Billy hissed in a sharp breath, recoiling as if she'd been struck.

"No," said Mrs. O'Donnell. "Some of them are living yet, I think."

"Which ones?" Billy asked. "Where did they go?"

"I wish I could say for sure," said Mrs. O'Donnell. "But I can barely keep in mind what me own lot are up to, never mind the neighbors."

"Especially neighbors such as Hugh Fogarty," said Mrs. Carney with a sniff. "Give him a bit of the poteen, and he'd get those black moods on him, and you'd best stay out of his way." Several of the others nodded and commenced a string of stories about Hugh Fogarty's drinking and black moods.

"But the lads," Billy said, trying to bring the talk back to the main question. "What happened to Liam and the rest?"

One woman spat into the dirt. "That Liam. Gone down to disgrace just like his da. Took up with a whore, he did, and they run off together."

"He wouldn't!" Billy said, her fists clenched.

The woman jerked her head toward the shanty across the alley. "Why else would a woman be living alone like that, a Yankee among us Paddies? Taking in sewing and laundry, so she said—bah! Taking in men, more like!" She spat again into the mud. "That Liam spent all his time frolicking with her. Lost his job over it, and left the little ones to waste away of the fever."

Daniel seized Billy by the shoulders to keep her from launching herself at the woman. "Hold your temper and your tongue," he said in a harsh undertone.

"'Tis the truth of it," the woman continued. "For didn't I see the coffins coming out of the house me very own self?"

Several of the neighbors nodded, but one of them said. "Oh, no, Biddy, 'tis the Flannerys you're thinking on. Three girls dead and their mam as well, and their da so grief-struck that he couldn't stand to be living here no more, so off to Lowell with him."

"No, 'twas Worcester, I'm sure," said another.

"But Liam, what about Liam?" Billy said, her cheeks red, her voice trembling.

"Didn't he go to work for the railroad along with his da?" Mrs.

O'Donnell said. Then the arguments began again. The more the women talked, the less Daniel knew. Next to him, Billy stared at the ground, her hands gripping her cap with white knuckles as she rocked back and forth on the balls of her feet. "Lies. 'Tis all lies," she muttered.

Clearly, it was time to be gone. Daniel reached into his pocket for some money. "We're much obliged for your help." He dropped a few coins into the hands of Katie O'Donnell and Mary Carney, who seemed to remember Billy's girl-self fondly, and he gave some money to those who'd given the most helpful information. But not a penny to the woman who'd said Liam had taken up with a whore.

Chapter Forty-Four

Sunday, November 10, 1839, Jenksville, Massachusetts

Please let this be the one, Daniel thought. He and Billy had spent two fruitless days searching Paddy camps in Cabotville and Factory Village and Indian Orchard. His knuckles felt raw from knocking on doors. What would he do if he reached the last battered door and still found no sign of her brothers? With a weary heart, he knocked.

A tall young man opened the door. If his shock of yellow curls and twilight blue eyes hadn't betrayed him, his posture would have. Daniel could see in an instant whom Billy had studied in order to walk and stand and carry herself like a lad. Liam was lean, his shoulders and arms hard with muscle under the worn fabric of his shirt.

Before Daniel could apologize for calling so early of a Sunday, Billy shoved past him. "Liam!" she shouted, flinging herself at the young man, nearly knocking him off his feet. "I knew it wasn't true! I knew it!" she said in Gaelic, her arms wrapped tight around him.

A female voice spoke in English from the back corner of the shanty. "What is it, Liam?" Daniel blushed as he caught sight of a woman pulling a wrapper over her shift. She had the same thin, weary look about her as Liam.

Liam extracted himself from Billy's embrace and held her at arm's length.

"Do you not know me, Liam?" Billy said.

Liam rubbed his befuddled eyes. Daniel wondered how much of his confusion was due to Billy's clothes and short hair and how

much was due to the change that six months' of good food, cheerful company, and sunshine had made in Billy's appearance. "It
can't be," Liam said. He cupped the lass's face in his hands as if
holding a bowl made of the rarest bone china. "Nuala?"

"Of course it is, you dunce. Do you not know your own sister?"
she said.

Liam fell to his knees with a thud. "Holy Mother of God and
all the saints." He drew her to him and held her so tightly that she
let out a yelp of protest. Then he began to weep.

Daniel looked away from Liam's twisted face, meeting the
woman's eyes over Liam's head. She was crying, too, and Daniel
suddenly felt that he didn't belong there. He backed away toward
the door.

"No, don't go," the woman said.

"Da told me you were dead. Drownded in the river," Liam
told Billy. He wiped his eyes and nose on his sleeve. "I'd'a gone
looking for you if I'd thought it wasn't true, I swear it."

"He told me that you were dead, too," Billy said. "I knew it
was a lie, didn't I, Daniel?"

"That you did," Daniel said cautiously. There was no sign of
children in the sparsely furnished room: no small dirty shoes by
the door or clothes flung carelessly over a chair, no toys strewn
in a corner.

"He said you and Jimmy and Mick were dead of the fever, but
I knew it wasn't true." She glanced from Liam to Daniel to the
woman and back. "But what's—where's—?" She pulled away from
her brother and looked around the tiny room. "They're out playing so early, are they?" she asked.

"I tried, Nuala, I swear to God I did." Liam held his large
calloused hands out helplessly. "I wish it had been me that died
instead of them."

Nuala shook her head and backed away. "It can't be true. You
wouldn't'a let it happen. I know you wouldn't."

"He did his best," the woman said. "The fever nearly killed
Liam, too."

"It's my fault." Billy's voice broke. "If I'd'a been there, they'd still be alive." Her face crumpled into a sob.

"If you'd'a been there, I'd'a lost you, too," Liam said.

Billy covered her face with her hands. But when she turned to someone for consolation, it was Daniel that she reached for, hiding her face against the scratchy wool of his frock. He held his arms stiffly away from his sides, not sure what to do with them or what to make of the sobbing girl. Then slowly, awkwardly, he folded his arms around her and rocked her, murmuring the Irish words he used to soothe Ivy.

The woman placed a hand on Liam's shoulder. Without looking at her, Liam reached up and covered her hand with his. The touch steadied them both. She wiped her face and stepped back, nudging Liam to stand. "Here," she said to Daniel. "There's a chair here." She waved a hand vaguely about the shanty. The tiny room held a bed, a table, two chairs, and a trunk.

Daniel guided Billy to one of the chairs and took her in his lap, rubbing her back until her sobs receded into hiccuping gasps. He gave her his handkerchief and for once didn't complain about her soiling it. The woman, meanwhile, stirred the fire to life and began to move pots and crockery about.

"All right, love?" Liam asked Billy, reaching out to tousle her hair. She shook her head. "Nor am I," he agreed. "But I'm none so bad as I was before, now that you're back." He met Daniel's eyes. "I'm that grateful to you, sir. Who are you, and how did you come to find her?"

"Me name's Daniel Linnehan. As for how I come to know Billy—"

"Billy?" Liam repeated.

"That's what she's been calling herself. 'Tis a bit of a long story."

"I'll make some breakfast while you talk," the woman said.

"I'm sorry. In the excitement I never—I—well, this is Augusta." Liam gestured toward the woman. "You remember her, don't you?" he asked Billy. "She lived across the way from us."

Billy dried her eyes and nodded. "Aye, but what's she doing here?" she asked.

Liam colored slightly. "She's me wife now. That's a bit of a long story, too."

It was getting dark by the time Daniel and Billy headed back to the tavern. Liam and Billy had spent the morning talking of all that had happened since Billy had left Cabotville. After dinner, Liam had taken them to the burial plot and shown them the rough board he'd cut to mark Jimmy and Mick's grave, there being no money for a proper stone. When the day began to fade, Daniel and Billy took to their horses with promises to return on Monday after Liam's workday was finished.

Billy rode with her cap pulled low over her eyes. Daniel saw her tremble under her baggy woolen frock. "All right, lass?" he asked, although he knew she'd not be all right for a long time.

"I still can't believe it." Billy sniffled and dragged her sleeve across her face.

"Aye." Daniel's own eyes prickled with moisture at the memory of Liam and Augusta, red-eyed, leading Billy and Daniel to the grave.

"It feels like they're out there playing in the streets, only just not come home yet," she continued, with a wave at the muddy road and darkening houses surrounding them, candles and lamps not yet beginning to glow behind their windows. She lifted her face to Daniel, her cheeks shiny with moisture in the fading light. "I should'a been there to take care of 'em."

"Why? So you could'a took sick and died, too?"

"At least I could'a tried."

"Aye, and if you tried as hard as ever you could, and you failed, you'd feel no less wretched for the trying. Liam tried." He ran a thumb along the ridges of scar tissue that twisted around his forearm like tongues of fire. He knew well enough that trying was no comfort. At least Billy'd not have the memory of hearing her brothers cry for her and being unable to save them.

"It's like you're always saying," Billy said. "I'm never thinking of naught but meself. They needed me and I was off singing and playing with horses and not thinking of them at all."

"Mr. Stocking and Phizzy needed you, too. And Pearl and the other ponies, they'd'a missed you, had you not come along." Daniel said. "I'd'a missed you, too."

She smoothed Pearl's mane. "Jimmy and Mick, they'd'a liked to'a seen the ponies dance."

"They'd'a been proud of you. Maybe they are yet, if the priests are to be believed."

The sun had long disappeared by the time they reached Court Square. The meetinghouse steeple and courthouse cupola stood out as gray shadows against an indigo sky, rising above the skeletal branches of the square's elm trees. At Mr. Warriner's tavern, a bright spark moved across the front windows and multiplied as someone began lighting candles or lamps. The tavern sign creaked on its hanger, swinging back and forth in the chilly breeze.

"Here, lass," Daniel said as they tethered Pearl and Ivy to the hitching posts. "You go inside and fetch a lantern. Tell Mr. Warriner we'll bed down our own horses for the night and save his ostler the work." He patted Ivy's neck, told her he'd be only a minute, and went into the barn to get her stall ready.

As his eyes adjusted to the barn's dimness, he let the comforting, musty aromas of straw, hay, leather, and horses push sadness and bad memories to the back of his mind. Something rustled in the haymow overhead—a barn cat pursuing its dinner, perhaps. His eyes widened, drawing in the fragments of daylight still remaining. He made out the openings of the tool bay to his left, and to his right an open bay crammed with a jumble of poles entwined with beans and hops yanked from Mr. Warriner's garden, waiting to be sorted out. Farther down, he picked out the sharp geometric lines marking the half-doors of the stalls, the softer shapes of horses' heads peering curiously out at him.

He fumbled among the tools, grasped a wooden handle, then ran his hand down to find out if it was pitchfork or shovel or rake.

He smiled to himself that he'd gotten a pitchfork on the first try. He carried it to the stalls at the back of the barn that Mr. Warriner had allotted to Ivy and Pearl, pausing along the way to let the other horses sniff at his knuckles, rubbing each one's forehead and murmuring an Irish greeting as he passed.

He spent a few extra moments with Mr. Warriner's black gelding. Not a wicked beast, but fearful and prone to kicking and snapping when startled. Daniel stood out of reach of the gelding's teeth and spoke softly to the horse until the dark head lowered and the animal was ready to let someone touch him. "You're not such a villain, are you, lad?" Daniel spoke in Irish as he rubbed the gelding's forehead. "You just want a bit of a warning before someone comes at you." He stroked the horse's neck, feeling how tense the muscles were. The beast wasn't calm by any means, but he'd not shivered or shied away as he had the previous evening. It was a tiny step forward. "We'll do some work with you in the morning, shall we?" Daniel promised before turning to prepare Ivy's and Pearl's stalls.

He reached up into the haymow with the pitchfork, pulled down generous clumps of hay, filled their mangers, then fluffed their straw bedding. He set the fork aside and collected the two water buckets to bring them out to the trough and fill them.

Something heavy thudded onto the floor behind him, a body jumping down from the haymow. Turning, Daniel saw a man's form standing in the barn's center aisle, his silhouette black against the gray of the back wall and door. There was a scrape and a smell of sulfur as the man struck a lucifer against the sole of his boot and held the match up to light a pipe.

"Are you daft?" Daniel said. What sort of an idiot knew no better than to smoke a pipe in a barn? Then the light revealed a familiar dimpled chin and roguish face: *Fogarty*. Daniel's words clogged in his throat, and he fell back a pace.

"Thought it was you, lad, when I heard the Gaelic," Fogarty said. He shook the lucifer to douse it, let it fall, and stepped on the dead match. "Now where's me girl?"

"Be off with you," Daniel said. He was surprised at how steady his voice sounded while inside every nerve and sinew jangled. "She's wanting naught to do with you."

"A father has a right to his child," Fogarty said. "'Tis the law—God's and man's."

"Then find yourself a lawyer and sue for her, 'cause I'll not be letting you at her," Daniel said, more boldly than he felt. It was one thing to face down Billy's da from the safety of Ivy's back, with Mr. Stocking and Mr. Chamberlain and teamsters and show people behind him. It was quite another to do so alone, close enough that Daniel could smell the drink on the man, close enough that he could see that Fogarty stood strong and steady in spite of it. Close enough that Daniel saw the power in the man's shoulders and fists and knew he'd not be able to match it. He braced himself, ready to fling the water buckets toward the man if he made a threatening motion.

"She belongs to me," Fogarty said. He took a step forward, his stance easy, relaxed, as if sure that Daniel was no threat. "It's unnatural, dressing her up like a lad and turning her into a circus performer."

"What's unnatural is a father selling his daughter to a peddler. What's unnatural is a father leaving his sons to die."

That rattled the man. Fogarty closed his eyes for a long moment before responding, "I was with 'em. I was with 'em to the end." He seemed unsure, as if he had to convince himself it was true.

"Were you, now? That's not the story Liam was telling," Daniel said, feeling a little bolder at Fogarty's discomfort.

"Liam's alive?" Fogarty's voice cracked. The pipe tumbled, then disappeared as Fogarty's hand closed around it, catching it. "Jesus," he said. Daniel wasn't sure if the name was a prayer of thanks because Liam yet lived or a curse because Fogarty had scorched his fingers. "May the Virgin and saints be praised." Fogarty crossed himself. "'Tis a miracle, sure."

"A miracle, aye," Daniel repeated. "That he lived in spite of you."

The hollow clop of a hoof against the barn's floor echoed

like a gunshot. The grays and blacks of the barn turned to mellow browns and umbers in the glow of a lantern. Daniel's shadow stretched before him, like a monster consuming Fogarty in its darkness.

"Daniel?" Billy called out.

Daniel turned to see the lass carrying a tin lantern, Pearl following at her heels. "Get out!" he shouted. His warning was cut off as something hard caught him below the ribs, knocking him onto his arse with the force of a horse's kick and driving the air from his lungs. The water buckets clattered about him as he fell, the sound echoed by the hooves of startled horses rapping the sides of their stalls.

"No!" Billy cried out. "Da, stop it!"

Something caught Daniel a blow against the side of his head and flattened him. Waves of orange, red, and black flowed across his vision. With an effort, he pushed the black aside to find himself lying on his back in the barn's center aisle. Billy's light gleamed along the tines of the pitchfork that Fogarty held pressed to Daniel's chest. There was little need for the threat. His lungs felt as though they'd been squeezed empty. Something wet seeped through his frock beneath his shoulder blades, and for a moment he thought he'd been stabbed. Then he realized that the liquid was cold, and that he lay in the dregs of the spilled water buckets.

"Leave him be, Da!" Billy pleaded. She stood a few paces away, poised on the balls of her feet as if she wanted to plunge into the struggle but feared to make things worse. Behind her stood Pearl, placidly peering over Billy's shoulder as if wondering what was delaying her supper.

"If I'd'a wanted to hurt him, I'd'a hit him with the fork, not the handle, wouldn't I?" said Fogarty. "I've come to take you home, lass. When I heard you in that show, singing like a very angel, I knew it was God giving me another chance to prove meself, to do things right this time."

"It's a fine start you've made, attacking me friends," Billy said.

Daniel tried to get his breath back. He wriggled his fingers along the floor, groping for something to use for a weapon. All he found were floorboards, straw, and dust. Even the buckets had rolled out of his reach.

"What sort of friend steals a child from her home and turns her away from her own father?" Fogarty said.

Daniel's lungs finally opened, and the dimness at the edge of his vision receded. He let out a feeble moan to let Fogarty think he was still helpless.

"It was you turned me away, Da, not Daniel or Mr. S. or anybody else. And they didn't steal me. You sold me, remember?"

"They've poisoned your mind against me so you don't know truth from lies. Well, I'm not having it. You fetch up that other horse of yours and we'll away so's I can be setting you straight. Hurry, now, if you're not wanting to see your friend bloodied." The word *friend* came out of Fogarty's mouth like a curse.

Billy's eyes traveled from her father's face to Daniel's. The set of her shoulders softened in apparent surrender. "All right, Da. I'll go with you, but I can't take the horses. They belong to Daniel."

"We need those horses." The fork pressed harder against Daniel's chest. "Don't make me hurt him, love. It's for your own good I'm doing this."

As Fogarty shifted his weight, Daniel realized that his right hand was only a few inches from Fogarty's feet. Cautiously, he slid his fingers closer to Fogarty's brogans.

Fogarty didn't seem to notice. "Bring me that other horse, lass," he said. "Then we'll go find Liam and be a family again."

With his right hand, Daniel grabbed one of Fogarty's ankles and yanked while he thrust his left hand between the tines of the pitchfork and shoved it away from his chest. Fogarty staggered, one arm windmilling to save his balance, the other trying to hang on to the pitchfork as he fell against a stall door. The door shuddered against Fogarty's weight, the horse within kicking and letting out a furious scream.

Daniel rolled away, trying to shout for Billy to run, but the sound came out more wheeze than warning. He thanked God for the tumblers' training that had him collecting himself almost by instinct. He poised on his haunches and whirled to face Fogarty. The whirling drove his stomach into a somersault and sent his brain reeling.

The horse screamed again. Daniel saw Mr. Warriner's gelding, ears pinned flat against his head, yellow teeth almost glowing as they reached for Fogarty. The next scream was human. The horse sank its teeth into Fogarty's shoulder, lifted him half off his feet, then let him drop. The stall door trembled behind the churning hooves. The gelding lunged again, and Fogarty lurched away from the snapping teeth just in time, staggering backward into the darkness.

Suddenly, Fogarty didn't matter at all to Daniel, for there was something much worse to fear: the smell of burning straw and Ivy's empty stall awash in an orange glow.

Chapter Forty-Five

Daniel couldn't move, suddenly pulled back half a dozen years, hearing Ma's and Michael's cries, unable to find them in the blaze that scorched his lungs, blistered his skin.

"Sweet Jesus," he groaned, shaking his head with a fierceness that set his stomach roiling. *No. Not this.* He had a moment's indecision—to fight the fire or get the horses out? If he chose the horses, the fire would grow even as he turned his back on it, grow enough to kill the horses left behind, and perhaps to set alight the tavern as well. The fire had to come first. He staggered toward the closest stall, threw open the door, and grabbed a water bucket, flung open the next door and snatched another bucket. He discovered Billy by his side, trying to help, but he shoved her away and screamed at her to take Pearl to safety and fetch help.

Then he was conscious of nothing but the fire. He emptied his buckets onto the flames, then flung open the other stall doors, dodging frightened horses' hooves and teeth. Two by two he seized the buckets and emptied them on the fire until there were no more buckets left. He paused with the last one in his hand. The fire was smaller now, but that last pail wouldn't be enough to completely douse it. He tore off his woolen frock and crammed it into the bucket, then used the sodden garment to beat the flames down. Behind him, horses screamed and reared, their hooves banging against walls and floors. There were human shouts, too, but he shut them out, forced himself to see and hear only the fire, fought it as if in the killing of it he could get vengeance for that fire of long ago.

Tears and phlegm ran down his face, clogging his nose and

throat. Smoke blinded him so that he could barely see the flames. He grew lightheaded, his lungs screaming for a breath of clean air. Then someone was beside him with more buckets, more water, and another someone tried to drag him away.

"Got to get 'em...get 'em out..." He sobbed and tried to wrestle free.

"It's all right, boy. The fire's out and the horses are safe." Somebody shook him and pointed out the chain of men and boys passing buckets one to another. "Thank God it got no farther than the one stall," the voice said.

Daniel stared numbly at the man's face. Everything seemed a blur of color and darkness, the firefighters mere ghosts behind a curtain of smoke. His legs crumpled beneath him like hay falling under the scythe. Two men hauled him out between them, and he collapsed in the dirt outside the barn, weeping and puking his throat raw. He wanted to curl into a ball until he stopped shaking, but there was something he had to take care of. Something important, only he couldn't think what it was. Perhaps he would remember if his head didn't feel as though it had been laid open with an ax.

He became aware of people and livestock milling about, filling the street and barnyard. Shouting at the onlookers to give way, a group of men hauled an enormous tawny-colored vehicle into the yard with a clatter and clanging of bells. One of the crew directed some of the bucket brigade to fill two troughs in the wagon, while the rest ranged themselves along long bars on either side of the vehicle. Another pair of men hauled a fat hose from the wagon and dragged it toward the barn to soak down the embers.

"You hurt, boy?" somebody asked.

Daniel squinted up at a large man with soot-stained clothes. He wanted to shake his head, but it felt as though it might wobble off his neck if he did. "I—I—I—" was all he could manage.

"Let's get you in the house. Your cousin's fretting like—"

"C-Cousin?" Daniel babbled in confusion.

A yellow-haired child broke through the crowd, screaming his name. The child flung his arms around Daniel's neck, and—No, *her* arms, Daniel realized, finally able to locate himself in place and time. "You're all right?" Billy shouted, her cry half question, half exclamation.

He winced and shushed her. The shushing felt as though it opened another fissure in his skull. "I har-hardly know," he said.

Gingerly, Daniel shook his head at the glass of rum the landlord's wife offered. "Water," he croaked. He couldn't tolerate anything that would burn his throat any further.

Mrs. Warriner shrugged dubiously. "Water's none too good here," she said. "Ale?"

"Aye, that'll do." He slumped on the settle and closed his eyes. He'd barely had the strength to assure himself that Ivy and Pearl were safe before allowing himself to be led inside. All he wanted to do was shut his eyes and drift away into his safe green place. But not just yet. "Billy?" he said, opening one eye a crack.

"He's fetching your ale," Mrs. Warriner said.

"Alone?" Daniel said, both eyes opening. Who knew where her da might be lurking? He half rose from the settle, then sank back down again.

"He's helping the girls," the landlady said. "You're not the only one who'll be needing a drink. Food, too, I imagine." Her nod toward the front windows took in all the men still out in the barn and the yard, sorting out the horses and making sure the fire was vanquished. "There'll be a lot of—" Her words were cut off by a commotion at the door. "What in the world?" A group of men carried a body into the taproom. "Oh, dear me!" she exclaimed.

"Lay him here," Mr. Warriner said, directing his companions to place their burden on one of the long tables. The burden stirred and groaned feebly.

"What's happened, Jerry?" the landlord's wife asked, her face drawn with concern.

"We found him lying just outside the back door of the barn," said Mr. Warriner.

"Sweet Jesus," Daniel whispered. He clutched the arm of the settle and forced himself to stand. He didn't know whether his stomach curdled from the effort of rising or from the look of the man lying on the table. Fogarty's left arm was bent at an unnatural angle, and one side of his face was dark with blood.

"I've sent Luther for the doctor," the landlord said. "Not sure if it'll do him any good, though. Seems like he's hurt worst right here." His hand fluttered over Fogarty's breast, which moved jerkily with each breath, as if his heart and lungs pained him. "He keeps mumbling something about a horse. He must've tried to help get 'em out and got kicked."

Daniel ground his teeth at the idea of Fogarty trying to help anyone but himself.

"The poor soul!" Mrs. Warriner exclaimed. She disappeared behind the bar and returned with a basin of water and a rag and began to clean Fogarty's face. "Who is he?" she asked.

"Looks familiar, but I can't place him," the landlord replied.

"Found this, too," said one of the men. He laid a scorched clay pipe on the bar. "In the stall where the fire was. I'll wager that's what started it."

Mr. Warriner cast a glance at Daniel. "You see anyone smoking in my barn, boy?" Although there was no accusation in his words, the undercurrent of suspicion in his voice reminded Daniel that, Mr. Stocking's friend or no, he was still Irish and therefore the first suspect when anything went wrong.

"It's not my pipe," Daniel said. "It's his." He pointed toward the man on the table.

Mr. Warriner ran an anxious hand through his hair. "Damn it all if I'm not tempted to throw the worthless mongrel back out into the yard."

Fogarty coughed, a thin ribbon of blood trickling from his mouth. His good arm clutched at his chest, his hand opening and closing with each spasm of breath. "G-God's s-sake, have pity," he gasped. "P-Pity on a dying man."

"He's not dying," said a voice from the back of the taproom. "It's just another one of his lies." Billy stood behind the bar, a pitcher and mug in her hands. Behind her were Mr. Warriner's nieces and hired girls, laden with food and drink. Billy slammed pitcher and mug down on the bar so hard that ale sloshed over the lip of the pitcher, and the handle snapped off the mug.

"P-Pity's sake," Fogarty murmured, his voice barely audible.

"Pity?" Billy snapped. "Aye, the same pity you showed to Jimmy and Mick and Liam, when you left 'em to die." She stormed toward the table where Fogarty lay. "The same pity you showed Daniel when you tried to—" When she saw her father's face, she stopped cold.

"Billy, come away," Daniel said. "Come away from there."

Mr. Warriner peered more closely at Fogarty's face. "Now I know where I've seen him. This fella's your pa, isn't he?" he asked, glancing up at Billy. "That fella that sold you to Jonny. Sold you, set my barn afire…Wonder what else he's done. Wonder why I shouldn't just pitch him out into the road."

"Because he might be dying," Mrs. Warriner said sharply. She waved a hand at the men who'd brought Fogarty into the tavern. "Here, take him into the bedchamber off the kitchen." The landlord's wife bustled away, followed by one of her nieces and the men carrying Fogarty.

"Don't fret, son. I didn't mean that, about pitching him out," Mr. Warriner said, putting a hand on Billy's shoulder to keep her from joining the procession. "The ladies will take good care of him. You get yourself some rest, and we'll call you when you can see him." Billy shrugged him aside and turned toward Daniel.

He closed his eyes, wanting nothing more than to go to bed and leave things be. Leave Fogarty to whatever awaited him. Leave Billy to decide for herself what was to be done with him. He leaned on a chair and bowed his head. Rest, God, he needed to rest. But those voices in his head wouldn't let him—voices that sounded like Mr. Stocking and Ma and Mr. Sharp, saying, *You have to be better than that.* He cursed the voices and told them to let him lie down and sleep. Let Fogarty die and be done with it, for it was all that he deserved. But the voices would not be still. He looked about for Billy, saw her still standing in the middle of the room, her mouth set in a grim line.

"Where's that ale you were fetching?" Daniel asked.

"Oh. Sorry." She returned to the counter and poured out some ale into the damaged mug and brought it to him. Her eyes met his and they winced together as he took the mug in his blistered hand. The cool pottery felt good against his scorched skin.

"You think he really is…you know…," Billy whispered.

Daniel shrugged. "I lived. Liam lived. Go to bed. I'll be up in a bit." He grimaced at his hands. "I need to get something for these." Billy looked toward the kitchen doorway. Daniel nudged her with his elbow. "There's naught you can do. They'll call you if they're wanting you."

Billy had barely left the room when the outer door swung open, and the taproom rapidly filled with men and boys. Mr. Warriner's girls set to work bringing food and drink to the crowd.

Daniel drew the landlord aside. "Sir, I know you've your hands full with this lot, but I need some help from one of your ostlers." He put a hand in his pocket to indicate his willingness to pay, then sucked in a swift, painful breath when brushing against the cloth felt like someone had taken a drawknife to his fingers. "I'm needing me horses readied, and"—He held out the wounded hand—"I don't fancy I can manage it meself."

Mr. Warriner's face softened. "You should go to bed, boy. One of the girls will make a salve for those burns."

"I'd like nothing better, indeed. But Billy's brother—"

"You found them, then?"

"Only one. I'm thinking I should fetch him here."

Mr. Warriner grunted. "I doubt anyone would come out for the sake of a father like that, if he's anything like what Jonny's letter said."

Daniel glanced toward the staircase where Billy had disappeared. "It's not for his da's sake that I'm fetching him."

Chapter Forty-Six

"Billy? Are you awake?" Daniel nudged the lump under the blankets.

Billy rolled over and sat up. "How would I be sleeping? All I can think is how he'll be going to hell, and all on me own account. And he'll be waiting for me there."

Daniel sat on the edge of the bed. "It's naught you done that'd send him to hell, lass. He done it to himself."

She twisted a corner of the sheet. "When I fetched Mr. Warriner and his lads to get the horses out, I never told 'em Da was in there. I never told 'em to look for him."

"Were you even thinking about him being there?" said Daniel.

"There was so much happening all of a sudden," said Billy. "I maybe thought about him once. When things settled, and you and the horses were safe, I wondered where he was. I thought about how he started all this trouble, and how he'd run off just like he always does, and—"

Daniel held up a hand to stop her. "Well, if you thought that he'd run off, whyever would you think to be finding him in the barn?"

"But I—I—oh."

"You are a puzzle, lass. You never felt a drop of guilt over all the thieving and lies you done, and here you are fretting about going to hell over something you didn't do, that you couldn't do naught about."

"What about thinking? Can you go to hell for thinking?"

"Thinking what?"

"Thinking I'm not sure I'd be sorry if he was to die."

Daniel bit his lip. He'd had the self-same thought. "Never you mind that now. Come downstairs. Liam and Augusta are here to see you."

As he led Billy downstairs, Daniel heard Liam and Augusta talking with Mr. Warriner. The taproom was empty of firefighters and gawkers, and only the landlord and two of his hired girls remained to tidy up.

"So that's it, then?" Liam asked the landlord.

"I reckon so," said Mr. Warriner. "He seemed to rally for a little while, but it didn't last. Dr. Swan doesn't have much hope. Set his arm, gave him something for the pain, and said he'd come back in the morning, if there's anything to come back for."

"He's not shamming, then," Billy said.

Liam turned at the sound of his sister's voice. He rushed toward the stairs and drew Billy into his arms. After a long moment, he stepped back and looked down into her face with worried eyes. "Thank God, you're safe. To have come so close to losing you again, and you only just come back." He shook his head and shuddered. "Fetch your things and we'll take you home with us."

"Home?" Daniel repeated, momentarily dumbstruck. He'd not thought about Liam taking Billy away. He'd thought—well, he wasn't sure exactly what he'd thought, other than that Billy would need her brother's comfort. "You're not wanting to see your da?"

"Why?" Liam said.

Daniel opened his mouth, but couldn't think of the words to fill it. Why, indeed? It was what people did, wasn't it? Sitting up with their dying kin, keeping them from facing the next world alone. But really, why? No matter how tightly you held a dying man's hand, how close you watched, he'd still be alone when he crossed that threshold. And what of a man like Fogarty, who deserved to die alone, if anybody in the world did?

Mr. Warriner looked taken aback by Liam's sharpness, but he quickly recovered his hospitable landlord's façade. "No need to go back out into the night. Why don't you folks sit down for a while?" he suggested, indicating a table. "Shall I bring you anything?"

Liam and Augusta shook their heads.

"We've given you a long and wearisome night, sir," Daniel said. "Why don't you go to bed?"

"Won't get much sleep. Not while Lydia is up with that one." He gestured with his thumb toward the door behind the bar. "Anyway, I'd better go check on the barn. Make sure those boys haven't fallen asleep in there. We've been taking turns watching to be sure there's no embers left that might catch again." He took his coat and hat from a hook beside the door and headed out.

Daniel, Liam, and Billy shifted uneasily from one foot to another, avoiding each other's eyes, an uncertain silence hanging in the air. Augusta looked at the floor, one hand entwined in Liam's. Daniel finally cleared his throat and spoke. "Mr. Warriner told me there's no priest in town?"

Liam shook his head. "Father Brady comes up from Hartford but once a month. Anyway, whyever would I bother calling a priest in for him?"

"Should a man be going to his grave with all that on his soul?" Daniel asked.

"Would you be wanting to let him wipe everything clean with a deathbed confession? It'd serve him right and proper to die unshriven."

"Maybe. I don't know. I just think—" Daniel shook his head. Fogarty was a drunk, a liar, a coward. He'd beaten his children beyond the boundaries of discipline. He'd sold his daughter, abandoned his sons. Yet all Daniel could see was Fogarty on his knees, on the brink of weeping, telling Billy she was all he had left.

How would he feel were it Lyman instead of Fogarty in that back bedchamber? Daniel would have every right to relish the man's dying. But even with six years of bitter memories to choose from, what came into his head was his last sight of his former master, defeated and broken.

Aye, maybe you'd pity him, but would you sit by the man were he dying? Answer yourself that, lad, he thought. No answer came.

He turned to Billy. "What about you, lass? Will you be wanting to see him?"

Her face hardened. "It'll do him no good to say he's sorry now for all he's done."

"Maybe," Daniel agreed. "But maybe it'd do you and Liam good to hear it."

"Why shouldn't I leave? It's what he'd do," she said, but she cast an uncertain glance toward the door that led to the kitchen and the bedchamber beyond.

"Aye," Daniel said. "I was only thinking...well, if there was anything you wanted to do...to say...well, if you don't say it now, you might regret—"

Billy cut him off sharply. "I've naught to say to him." She stepped closer to Liam, who put a protective arm around her shoulder.

"Then say naught," Daniel replied. He took up the candlestick that sat on the bar and headed toward the dark kitchen, unsure what he'd do if Billy and Liam didn't follow him. He heard Augusta murmur something to Liam, then the soft cat-like padding of Billy's bare feet across the floor, Liam's hesitant footsteps coming behind her, and the rustle of Augusta's skirts last of all.

The little bedroom stood just off the kitchen, the door slightly ajar. One of Mr. Warriner's nieces sat in a ladder-backed chair next to the bed.

He'd been a handsome man, this Fogarty, with a dimpled chin, full lips, and straight nose. A spill of wavy light brown hair drooped over the bandage around his head. He slept fitfully, his hands twitching on the bedcovers, his incoherent mumblings breaking the silence. Daniel stepped away from the door so that Liam and Billy could come in. He handed Liam his candle and got a stiff nod for thanks.

The landlord's niece glanced up. Before they could stop her, she gently shook Fogarty's shoulder. His blue eyes opened wide, then folded in with pain. "Your sons are here," the girl told him. She gestured for Liam and Billy to come nearer.

Fogarty slowly raised his head to look at his son. The candle cast ghoulish shadows across Liam's face. Fogarty squinted hard, his lips moving as he studied the young man at the foot of the bed. Then his eyebrows rose, and he flopped back onto the pillow with a groan. "Liam," he said, reaching out one hand. "Is it a ghost you are? Have you come to take me, lad?"

Liam's mouth remained clenched in a solid line, the candle trembling in one hand, his other hand balled into a fist at his side.

"I'll leave you, shall I?" the girl asked, then slipped from the room.

Fogarty licked his lips before he spoke again. "Liam? They send—send you to drag me down to Hell?" He blinked blearily, started to shake his head, then moaned and sank deeper into the pillow. "But they'd not'a put you there, surely?"

"No," Liam said finally. "It was you put me in Hell." He stepped close enough to touch.

Fogarty's nose twitched. "I smell...horses? So they'll haunt me to the grave, too, then?"

Liam set his candle down on the bedside table and let out a disgusted sigh. "You smell horses because I rode one to get here. I'm not a ghost, you bloody fool."

"Not?" Fogarty raised his head. "Aye, I remember now. Someone said you lived...lived." His brow furrowed as he tried to recall. "Nuala was there. Where—where's she now?"

"Here, Da," she said, stepping forward.

Fogarty looked from daughter to son several times. "Ah, you're the very...very spit of your mam, both of you." He closed his eyes and took several long breaths, gathering energy before he spoke again. "Come, love, give your old da a kiss." He gestured feebly toward both Billy and Liam. When his hand brushed Liam's trousers, the young man stepped back as if he feared contamination.

Billy moved not an inch.

Fogarty's arm dropped back on the coverlet, and he let out a faltering sigh. "'Tis a sorry...sorry excuse for a da I been, haven't I?" he said.

"Aye, that you have," Billy agreed.

Daniel held his breath, waited for the words of remorse, the plea for forgiveness that surely would come next.

Fogarty nodded carefully, licked his lips, and continued. "I did me best. Everything I've done, all the time...thinking of you."

"Aye," said Liam. "Thinking of how to use us to your advantage."

"That's cold, Liam." He shivered and turned his face away, drawing the blanket to his chin. "So cold." He stared at the wall for a long time, then sniffled noisily and wiped his nose and eyes on the sheet before facing Liam again. "It'll be different now."

"Oh, aye, it'll be different," Liam said.

"Aye, it will," Fogarty said with a tip of his chin, apparently not reading the bitter sarcasm in his son's voice. "Good lad, Liam... knew you'd come 'round." He closed his eyes.

Fogarty would never say it, Daniel realized. He'd never apologize for neglecting and tormenting and abandoning his children. Even as the man lay dying, he tried to put himself in the right. Daniel's compassion ebbed, and he suddenly wanted to shake him, slap him into contrition.

Fogarty's breathing grew ragged, and twice it seemed to cease altogether before beginning again with an exhalation that was part sigh, part groan.

While her father slept, or seemed to sleep, Billy approached the head of the bed. She studied her father's face for a long time. She broke her gaze away and began to fidget, looking from Liam to Daniel as if seeking counsel on what to do. Liam started to turn away from the bed when Fogarty's eyes flew open. He half sat up, his mouth shaping soundless words. Before Billy could move aside, he clutched her sleeve and pulled her to her knees.

"Muh-muh-muh," he said, his panicky eyes fixed on Billy's face. He took a shuddering breath, then finally managed a word—*Margaret*—before dropping back to the pillow. "Su-su-such dreams I've had...ter-terrible dreams." Billy flinched as Fogarty's right hand tightened on her sleeve, his left hand closing and opening in spasms around the sheet. "Margaret, could—could you sing me to sleep, love?"

Billy cast a frightened glance at Liam, who merely shrugged. Daniel stared down at his feet, keeping his own face passive.

He'd expected—what? A deathbed reconciliation, like a scene from one of the treacly moral tales in Mr. Stocking's schoolbooks? He'd been a fool to have imagined such a thing. Fogarty would die as blind as he'd lived, his mouth full of excuses and lies. If Billy turned her back now, who would blame her?

Siúil, siúil, siúil a rúin
Siúil go socair agus siúil go ciúin
Siúil go doras agus éalaigh liom
Is go dté tú mo mhúirnín slán

[Go, go, go, my love
Go quietly and peacefully
Go to the door and flee with me
And may you go safely, my dear].

Billy's singing was thin and quavery at first, a candle struggling against the breeze, but still it made the hair prickle at the back of Daniel's neck. Next to him, Augusta drew in a sharp breath and turned her face away. Although Liam's mouth remained set in a hard, angry line, his eyes still fierce beneath knotted brows, he sat on the bed and took his father's other hand.

Chapter Forty-Seven

Sunday, November 17, 1839, Springfield, Massachusetts

It had been weeks since Daniel had sat down to a dinner as tasty as the one Mrs. Warriner and her nieces and hired girls had laid out in the tavern's private dining room. And yet the ladies might as well have made salt pork and hasty pudding for all that Daniel could appreciate it. At the head of the table, Mr. Chamberlain presided like a squire. On one side sat Liam and Augusta with Billy between them, and on the other sat Mr. Stocking and Constable Ainesworth, with Daniel at the foot.

"All's well that ends well, eh, Daniel?" Mr. Ainesworth said, raising his glass. Expecting to escort Daniel and Billy to safety at the Taylors, the constable had come north to Springfield immediately upon receiving Mr. Stocking's letter. He'd arrived on the heels of Mr. Chamberlain's Peripatetic Museum, only a few days after Liam and Billy had buried their father.

"Aye, that's what they say," Daniel replied, though he wasn't looking forward to this particular ending. Nor, apparently, was Mr. Stocking, who pushed his food around his plate, eating little. Daniel told himself that he should be glad Billy was returning to her rightful home, but instead he felt a terrible gnawing at the pit of his stomach. He should be following Mr. Chamberlain's example. The conjurer had every right to begrudge Billy her happiness, as he'd be losing one of his star performers. Yet he had generously organized this special dinner in her honor. Surely Daniel could muster a bit of joy for the lass.

Dressed in a blue-flowered flannel gown, Billy somehow looked even more un-girlish than ever she had in trousers and vest. The blue ribbon wrapped around her short blond curls was as incongruous as the pink ribbon Phizzy wore in his tail for his Learned Horse routine. She fidgeted with her skirt, as if the fabric scorched her.

"I'd like to propose a toast." Mr. Chamberlain rubbed his hands together and stood. "We're here to celebrate our two young artistes surviving an adventure every bit as perilous as those performed in our hippodramatic pantomimes." He acknowledged Daniel and Billy with a nod and a wink. "Sir, mademoiselle, I salute you." He downed his ale, then set his glass on the table. He placed his palms together as if in prayer and bowed low so that his forehead brushed the tips of his long fingers. "As does Prince Otoo Baswamati," he added in the elegant, cinnamon-flavored tones he used for his East Indian mystic role.

Billy made an odd sputtering noise, and Daniel realized that she was trying to choke down a mouthful of ale rather than spray it across the table.

"Thank you, sir," said Liam. "It's kind of you, indeed, to host this grand dinner for us."

"Not at all. It's the least I could do to ease your parting."

"Aye," Liam agreed. "She tells me she's made some good friends among you." He nodded toward Mr. Stocking and Daniel. "And we're grateful to you for taking care of her. I'll make sure she writes to you as often as she can."

Mr. Chamberlain cleared his throat. "You misunderstand me, young man. It's you she's parting from, not us."

"What?" The word flew from every mouth at the table.

"There's still the small matter of Jonny's two hundred dollars." Mr. Chamberlain told Liam. "When your father took Jonny's money, he bound Billy out as sure as if he'd signed an indenture. Seems to me she belongs to Jonny."

"You've no right," Liam said, rounding on Mr. Stocking. "You've no papers on her. She told me so herself."

"Just the other day I read in the newspaper where a judge declared a lack of papers makes no difference in deciding whether a child is properly bound out. But if you want to spend the money to take it to the courts—" Mr. Chamberlain shrugged as if it were no concern to him. "It could take months. Or you could buy Jonny out, which I am fully prepared to do."

Mr. Stocking pushed his chair away from the table and rose up angrily. "Now, wait a minute, Fred. I'm not holding her to any indenture."

"Not even for a quarter interest in the show?" Mr. Chamberlain raised an eyebrow.

"You trying to bribe me?" Mr. Stocking asked.

"One third, then." Mr. Chamberlain's lips curled into that sly conjurer's smile that he used when he was attempting to probe someone's thoughts. "One third interest"—Fred paused, slowly arching his other eyebrow—"and six dancing ponies."

"This is madness!" Liam slammed a fist down on the table and put his other hand on Billy's shoulder. "You're talking about me sister like you were trading a horse."

Augusta laid a hand over Liam's, encircling Billy between them. "How can you think of taking her away after all she and Liam have been through?" she said.

"I'm not," said Mr. Stocking. "Don't fret about it, Liam. There's not a thing Fred can do to take Billy from you."

Daniel looked to Billy, who was uncharacteristically silent. The tablecloth in front of her was deeply creased, and he realized that she was keeping herself still by clenching the linen as hard as she could. How long would it be before she'd burst?

"That's fine." Mr. Chamberlain shrugged and put his thumbs into his vest pockets. "You and your horse boy can go back to peddling tinware and wooden nutmegs. It's all the same to me." He waved a hand vaguely in Daniel's direction, though the stare that pinned Daniel was anything but vague. "I'm sure I can find another Professor Romanov somewhere."

Daniel felt as if he'd been punched in the chest. To lose the ponies—*his* ponies. To see them in the hands of some stranger who might undo all the good work he and Billy had done with them...

Mr. Stocking flung his hands into the air. "Dammit, Fred, don't use them ponies to threaten us. It'll be your loss, not mine, if you toss Dan'l and me out of your show. Find yourself another songbird. Billy's staying with Liam."

"And who'll be liable for her expenses?" Mr. Chamberlain said.

"What expenses?" Mr. Stocking said. "I'm the one paying her room and board."

"With whose money?" Mr. Chamberlain said.

"You paid me the share we agreed on," said the peddler. "No more."

"Funny, I don't recollect signing any papers on it."

Daniel winced. Since they'd begun traveling with the show, Mr. Stocking had been badgering Mr. Chamberlain to formalize their terms with a written agreement, but Mr. Chamberlain had always put him off, promising to draw up the papers later.

"Then there's the small matter of her education in the gymnastic, equestrian, and thespian arts," the conjurer continued. "That kind of training don't come cheap. Seems I'm owed some compensation if she abandons the show without earning back the cost of her learning. I seriously doubt Mr. Fogarty could afford—"

"You can squeeze me all you want, Fred," said Mr. Stocking, "but you're not blackmailing me into taking her away from Liam."

"Of course," Mr. Chamberlain continued as if Mr. Stocking hadn't spoken, "all that is trivial compared to the question of whether a lad of—how old are you, anyway, Liam?"

The color drained from Liam's and Augusta's faces.

The conjurer smiled slyly and drew a segar from his pocket. He took his time about lighting it and letting out a satisfied puff of smoke. "Now, far's I know, it's not properly legal in this state for a *boy* under the age of twenty-one to have guardianship of a minor. S'pose I was to go poking around in the record books. Wonder what I'd find? S'pose I was to find someone lied on his marriage papers? Wonder what'd happen to his sister then?"

The conjurer put Daniel in mind of a spider trying to weave a web around a fly. Each time one thread broke, he cast out another. It seemed he'd saved his strongest thread for last.

"What difference does it make how old he is?" Mr. Stocking

said. "No court in its right mind would appoint you guardian, Fred."

Mr. Chamberlain squinted at Jonathan over his segar. "Guess they wouldn't. Guess she'd just have to go to the almshouse. Or maybe become a ward of the state. Who knows where she'd end up then? Don't s'pose you got any idea what the law is around here in that regard, do you, Ainesworth?"

"This isn't my jurisdiction," Mr. Ainesworth said. "And I'm no lawyer."

"Then I guess I'd better seek one out tomorrow," said Mr. Chamberlain, settling back into his chair. He nodded toward Liam and Mr. Stocking. "No telling what might happen, should I start asking questions." Laying his segar down in his saucer, he changed his face into what Daniel imagined was meant to be a regretful frown. "Would be a powerful waste, all that talent locked up in the almshouse."

The conjurer had to be bluffing. Daniel looked to Mr. Stocking, who knew Mr. Chamberlain best. The peddler's face was a sickly greenish gray, and his mouth worked as though he couldn't find the words to fill it.

Billy's cheeks were crimson, and her grip on the tablecloth tightened enough to send a shiver through her glass and plate. She looked as though she wanted to upend the table and start shouting at them. Shouting what, though?

"What are you saying, Mr. Chamberlain? If you can't have the girl, then nobody can?" Mr. Ainesworth said. "I may not be a lawyer, but I know what's right, and this isn't it."

"Aye, sir, none of this is right." Daniel stood up slowly, squaring his shoulders. It surprised him how much taller he was than Mr. Stocking. "Seems to me you're all forgetting something." He turned to the peddler. "Aye, even you, sir. I hear a lot of talk about who owes money to who, and where Billy belongs, and what Mr. Chamberlain can give or take if he don't get his way, but there hasn't none of you thought to ask Billy what she wants."

"She wants to stay with her family, is what she wants," Liam said.

"She's told you so herself, then," Daniel said.

"Aye...well...not in so many words, but I know she does." Liam looked down at Billy.

She was still twisting the hem of the tablecloth in her hands. "You never asked me, Liam," she said, without looking up.

"I didn't think I needed to," Liam said. Billy shrugged Liam's and Augusta's arms from her shoulders as if throwing off a cloak. Liam rested his hand on the back of her chair, as if to let her know that he still offered his protection in spite of her rebuff. "All right, Nuala. I'm asking now. Will you come home to live with me and Augusta?"

Mr. Chamberlain folded his arms across his chest. "My offer still stands, Jonny, if you're willing to see reason."

"Damn your offers and your threats, Fred. Well, Billy?" Mr. Stocking said. "You've been steaming away like a teakettle fit to boil."

Billy pushed her chair back. The tablecloth was gray and ridged in tight wrinkles where she'd clutched it. "You're squabbling over me like a pack of chickens cackling over a juicy wee grub." She looked sideways at her brother. "Aye, even you, Liam.

"But all these months Daniel's been on at me to not be always thinking of meself, and Mr. S. has been trying to learn me—*teach* me to keep me temper and mind me manners, so I been trying to hold me tongue."

"Well, now's your chance to speak, lass," Daniel said. "And don't you be letting Mr. Chamberlain's bluster scare you into doing something you don't want to do."

"I don't bloody well know what I want!" Billy shouted. "I want to stay here with Liam and Augusta. I want to ride Phizzy and the ponies, and I don't want Mr. C. to throw you and Mr. S. out of the show." She turned to the peddler, her lower lip trembling. "I want to be singing with you." She tore the bow from her hair and flung it down onto her plate, where it sank in a pool of gravy. "And I don't want folk to be talking about me like I wasn't here," she snapped. "Well, damn you all, and damn me, too, for no matter what I choose, it'll be wrong!" She shoved herself away from the table, knocking over her chair, and bolted out the door.

"No," Daniel said, as Liam rose to chase after her. "Let her go think things out by herself. And when she comes back, we got to abide by her choice. All of us," he added, with a pointed look at Mr. Chamberlain. "You can play all the games you like, sir, but you'll not be keeping Billy long if she doesn't want to stay. Isn't that right, Liam?"

Liam sighed wearily. "Indeed. No one's ever had much luck at making Nuala do what she doesn't want to."

Mr. Chamberlain opened his mouth to retort, but Daniel cut him off with an impatient hand gesture. "As for you, sir, if you do aught against her brother, then you'd best be sleeping with one eye open, for she'll be taking her vengeance on you one way or another. And I'll be right alongside her."

"And so will I," said Mr. Stocking, putting a hand on Daniel's shoulder.

"All right, then," Mr. Chamberlain said. "But she'd better not come running to me when she gets tired of her brother and his vermin-infested little shack."

Augusta had to hold fast to Liam's arm to prevent him from striking the conjurer.

As the diners left the table, Mr. Ainesworth drew Daniel aside. "I've never seen or heard the like. Asking a child to make such a decision? I can't believe they agreed to it."

"I don't know as they have. But they have agreed on one thing," Daniel said, feeling the weight of Liam's and Mr. Chamberlain's angry glares. "They've agreed to leave off hating each other and start hating me instead."

Chapter Forty-Eight

It was hours before Billy returned. Deciding that it would be better to do something other than sit in the tavern or pace the dooryard, Daniel groomed Ivy and polished her tack, while Mr. Stocking went to the wagon shed to inventory his wares, or so he said. Since the peddler had no tin and few notions left, Daniel suspected he would do little more than move things about and write meaningless notes in his ledger while he fretted over Billy's decision. Meanwhile, the Fogartys waited on the settee in Mr. Warriner's sitting room, when Liam wasn't pacing. Mr. Chamberlain headed down to the show lot to supervise preparations for the next day's performance. Mr. Ainesworth had joined him, expressing curiosity about the museum, although Daniel guessed that the constable was more interested in making sure that the conjurer wouldn't follow Billy and try to influence her decision.

It was an unseasonably mild afternoon. Daniel took a stool out to the barnyard to work in the thin November sunlight. He polished and repolished metalwork and buffed saddle and bridle until his arms ached and Ivy's tack looked almost new. He was just shining up the stirrups and buckles for the third time when someone hissed at him from the barn.

Billy lurked in the shadows, gesturing for him to join her. He felt an unexpected surge of delight that she'd sought him out first. The delight quickly faded at her words.

"Where's Liam?" she asked in a hoarse whisper.

So she'd decided. Daniel's stomach clenched as tight as it would if someone had taken Ivy away. "In the sitting room, last I saw him," he replied gruffly. Avoiding her eyes, he gestured with his polishing rag.

Billy trotted toward the hotel, her arms swinging and her shoulders hunched forward like a boy's. Her new gown was already torn, mud and grass staining the pale blue flannel.

Slowly, Daniel hung the saddle in the space Mr. Warriner had allotted him. When he turned, Mr. Stocking was standing in the barn door, a canvas sack in his hand.

"I saw her come back," the peddler said, setting down his sack. "She nipped into the barn when I turned to watch her, like she didn't want to be seen."

Daniel nodded. "It's Liam," was all he needed to say.

Mr. Stocking winced. "That's as it should be." He took his spectacles off and blinked hard a couple of times. "That young man has had sorrow enough." He took a long time wiping his glasses with his handkerchief and putting them back on. "Well, that's it, I guess." He gestured with his chin toward the sack. "Will you see she gets that? It's the rest of her clothes and her books. Not that she'll have much use for 'em. Augusta'll probably trim her out in dresses and ribbons, and she was never much of a one for books."

"Won't you want to be giving 'em to her yourself?"

Mr. Stocking shook his head. "I can't." He moved farther into the barn. "I...um...I need to confer with Phizzy for a while."

Daniel felt aimlessly melancholy. Normally when he felt that way, he would take Ivy for a ride or groom her. But Ivy was in the barn with Phizzy, and Daniel didn't want to intrude on Mr. Stocking's solitude. He finally decided to go up to his room to sort out the things Billy had left behind and to add them to the sack Mr. Stocking had given him. He slipped in the back door and went up the narrow stairway, avoiding the sitting room and Billy and Liam.

When he came back outside, he discovered Billy in the wagon shed, rummaging through the storage bin under the wagon's seat. "Where is it?" she mumbled to herself. "I know he kept it."

When Daniel called her name, she banged her head on the lid of the bin. She turned to him, her face grimy with tears.

He felt a prickling at the back of his eyes and a leaden weight in his chest. What was the good of making friends if you had to be forever leaving them? Surely it was better when he'd not let anyone into his heart. But young Ethan, and now Billy—both of them had made something inside him go soft, and giving them up was more painful than anything Lyman or any bully had ever done to him.

"Here," he said brusquely, thrusting the sack toward her. "Your things."

As she rooted through it, the bag wriggled and jerked as though it held an animal struggling to break free. "Ah!" came her muffled voice, and she emerged with something in her hand. She polished it with a fold of her skirt. "Where's Mr. S.?" she asked, her head down, intent on wiping the object clean.

"With Phizzy," Daniel said.

She dashed into the barn. Daniel followed. Mr. Stocking came out from Phizzy's stall and into the narrow sunbeam that slanted onto the barn's floor. The peddler and the lass stood apart from each other, poised on the balls of their feet like dancers waiting for the music to start.

Then Billy reached out her hand. The object that she held was somewhat the worse for wear; most of its papery brown husk had broken off, and it had lost several kernels, but those that remained glowed like rubies. *"A red ear of corn for the one you love best,"* Mr. Stocking had said, it seemed like years ago.

He couldn't hear what Billy said as she presented her gift, but Daniel had never seen such a smile on Mr. Stocking's face. The peddler took the red ear and gathered Billy into his arms, then kissed the top of her head.

They came out of the barn, Billy's arm around Mr. Stocking's waist, and the peddler's hand on her shoulder. She was still crying, and Mr. Stocking seemed unsteady on his feet, his glasses fogged with tears.

"It's not Liam, then?" Daniel said.

Billy shook her head, then came at Daniel so fast that she nearly knocked him over. She threw her arms around him, and the front of his shirt grew damp. "Here, lass," he said at last. "I can't hardly breathe." But what he really felt was as if he'd been holding his breath all afternoon, and now he finally could breathe.

"You're sure this is what you want, Billy?" Mr. Stocking said.

She nodded as she pulled away from Daniel. "For a while I thought of not coming back here at all, just so's I wouldn't have to choose. After I made up me mind, I still couldn't come back for ages and ages because I didn't know how to tell Liam." She let out a hiccuping sob.

Daniel fished his handkerchief out and handed it to her.

She took a long time wiping her face and blowing her nose. "Bloody hell and damnation! I didn't want to cry. But since I come back and told Liam, I can't stop."

"Is he all right?" Daniel asked.

"He has Augusta," Billy said. "Maybe I'd'a chose different if he was alone." She tried to hand Daniel back his handkerchief, now sodden with tears and phlegm, but he put up a hand to tell her to keep it. "I love him with all me heart, but I couldn't stay there. I know it'd be better, now Da's gone, but it'd still be naught but cooking and sewing and washing up and helping Augusta tend the babies when they start coming, and being trapped in one place all the time. If I stayed, it'd be the death of me. I tried to explain to Liam, but he just couldn't see." She fidgeted with her skirt, making the tear larger. "I think maybe Augusta understood a bit, though. Liam didn't understand, either, when I told him Mr. S. is me proper da, the one I was meant to have."

"'Scuse me." The peddler snatched Daniel's handkerchief away from Billy and wiped his eyes and his spectacles, but only redistributed the damp smears on the glass and his cheeks.

"I'd not have understood, meself, a few months ago," Daniel said. "I'm sorry for your brother, though. He's a good man."

"Aye, he's grand," Billy said. "I'll write to him, and I'll visit every chance I get. Anyway, if I stay, I can't help him, can I? If I go with you, I can send him some of me wages."

"Here." Daniel picked up the sack that held Billy's things. "I s'pose you'll be pleased to have your trousers back."

"Aye, that I will." Billy tugged at her skirt as if she wanted to rip the dress off then and there. Then she stopped herself and smoothed the fabric out. "But maybe I should wear this a while yet. Augusta was up an entire night making it for me—all new cloth, though I told her I'd be fine with someone's made-over cast-offs." She frowned, rubbing at the stains. "And look, I've spoiled it already. It'd be ungrateful, I s'pose, did I put it aside before we take our leave."

Daniel exchanged surprised looks with the peddler.

"That's mighty thoughtful of you," Mr. Stocking said.

"I hardly see the virtue in all this thinking you've been wanting me to do," Billy said, running a hand through her short curls. "All it does is give me a powerful headache."

"I know what you mean," Daniel said with a grin. "Sometimes I've felt me head would burst with all the thinking I've done since I've joined the two of you. But still and all, I been doing a bit of thinking on me own about your trousers."

"Me trousers?" Billy repeated.

"Aye. You know there'll come a time when trousers and short hair and bad manners can't hide that you're a lass, don't you?" He braced himself for her angry denial, but she just nodded grimly. "Don't be looking so sour. It mightn't be as bad as all that," he continued. "I was just thinking that it's grand and all for a lad to be riding like the devil and tumbling and doing tricks and such. But for a lass to be doing it, that's something really out of the ordinary, isn't it? I think folk'd like seeing that even more than what you're doing now."

"You mean I could be like—like Francesca?"

"Better, I'd say," Daniel replied.

A smile flickered across Billy's face, then quickly faded. "So long as Mr. C. doesn't throw us out of his show and take away our ponies. After all, I didn't choose him, now, did I?" She took one of Mr. Stocking's hands. "I chose you." To Daniel's surprise, Billy took his hand, too.

Daniel stood a moment in stunned silence, his ears and face reddening. Then he shook his head and laughed. "You never. The truth is, you were really choosing Phizzy."

"Haven't you learned anything being with me, son?" Mr. Stocking said. "You don't choose a horse like Phizzy, or like your Ivy, neither. A horse like that chooses you."

Author's Note

Readers often wonder how much of a historical novel is fact and how much is fiction. All the characters and events in *Mending Horses* are fictional, except for Jerry Warriner, his tavern, and his household, but the situations are as accurate to the time period as possible.

With the exception of Farmington, Massachusetts, and Chauncey, Connecticut, all the towns and villages mentioned in the book are real places. The names of some villages have changed over time. Cabotville and Factory Village were villages of Springfield, Massachusetts, and are now part of Chicopee. Jenksville was a village of Ludlow, Massachusetts, and Bethel, which in 1839 was a village of Danbury, Connecticut, is now a separate town.

A fortuitous coincidence was my discovery that the opening of the Western Rail Road in Springfield happened on October 1, 1839—perfect timing for my story. I'd known that the railroad was under construction in the late 1830s and early 1840s, but it wasn't until I'd already chosen the date for my story and decided to make Hugh a railroad worker that I learned of the October 1 event, which fit in perfectly.

The "Paddy camps," like "the Patch" where the Fogartys live in Cabotville, were a brutal fact of life for Irish immigrants in the 1830s. No housing was provided for the Irishmen who dug canals, built mills, and constructed boardinghouses for Yankee mill girls to live in. In milltowns and along rail lines, the first homes of the Irish were usually makeshift shanties built with construction rubble scavenged from work sites. Brian C. Mitchell's *The Paddy Camps: The Irish of Lowell, 1821–61* provides an excellent and grim account of the conditions under which Irish workers and their families lived.

While Mr. Chamberlain's traveling show is fictitious, the stunts that his players perform are based on accounts of circuses of the time period. The famous John (a.k.a. James) "Grizzly" Adams (1812–1860) rode one of his trained bears much the same way as Mr. Lamb rides Griselda in the story. Popular equestrian acts included Billy Button, the Drunken Cossack, and the Incombustible Horse, while "learned" animals from pigs to dogs to horses were all the rage. Like Mr. Stocking, circus clown Dan Rice (1823–1900) would ask his learned animal (a pig rather than a horse) to select the biggest fool from the audience. Performers like the Ruggles family and Mr. Sharp and Mr. Dale were often multitalented, with acrobats also doing duty as jugglers, horseback riders, or comedians. Joe Pentland (1816–1873), who is mentioned by one of the performers, was a famous circus comedian of the 19th century. He was also a ventriloquist, a singer, a juggler, and a magician.

The 1830s was a time when circuses were just beginning to evolve into their present form. Circuses of the 18th century were primarily exhibitions of skilled horseback riding, and did not tend to travel. Traveling acrobats, magicians, singers, and jugglers generally performed separately from such shows. Menageries also tended to be distinct entities; at first they were more like traveling zoos than collections of performing animals. By the 1830s, however, show managers had started to bring together menageries, equestrian acts, acrobats, comedians, and singers into large traveling shows. Shows might include things we don't normally associate with circuses today, such as opera singers, displays of artwork, dramatic performances, or panoramas of historic events. Traveling tradesmen, peddlers, teachers, exhibitors, lecturers, and performers—what we might today think of as "sideshows"— often followed a circus in order to take advantage of the potential customers drawn by the larger show.

Like Mr. Chamberlain's Peripatetic Museum, shows that traveled through New England in the 1830s often advertised themselves as museums or educational programs in order to evade laws that either prohibited traveling performers or levied heavy licensing fees. In spite of such laws, newspapers, diaries, and other records show that acrobats, menageries, trick riders, and other traveling entertainers roamed throughout New England. Advertisements emphasized the educational merits of a show and assured readers that performances would be morally uplifting, artistic, and "chaste."

Entertainers usually stayed in local taverns, inns, and hotels, rather than in tents or wagons. (Mr. Chamberlain is an exception because of his desire to maintain his disguise as Prince Otoo Baswamati.) Circus tents, called "pavilions," could accommodate audiences ranging from several hundred to a couple thousand. Some circuses would perform evening shows as well as afternoon shows. If there was no evening performance, members of the company might put on "house shows" at the inn or hotel where they were lodging. A house show might include music, dramatic recitations, or magic tricks.

Going to a show would be expensive: twenty-five or fifty cents in an era when a day's wage for a laborer might be a dollar. While most performers would earn about six or seven dollars a week, a star performer could make a very good living—eleven to twelve dollars a week. Some shows traveled around New England from April to October, and then headed to a large city like New York, Philadelphia, or Baltimore for the winter, where the show (often in a smaller format) might have a semipermanent home in an enclosed venue like a theater or an arena-like building. Others would spend the winter traveling in the South, or they might disband for the winter and reassemble in the spring.

Much of the information on traveling shows came from research at the Museum of the Early American Circus in Somers, New York, which has an amazing collection of posters, account books, and other material from shows of the early 19th century. Another excellent resource was the website of the Circus Historical Society (http://www.circushistory.org) which includes many firsthand accounts of 19th-century circus life. Most important of all were the works of Stuart Thayer (1926–2009), who wrote wonderfully detailed books and articles about pre–Civil War American circuses. His descriptions of circus pavilions and performances helped me create my Peripatetic Museum, and his transcripts of itineraries from early American shows helped me map out my performers' journey.